Dead

Too Long

Also by Ron Handberg

Dead
Too Long

For Susan —

Ron Handberg

40

PRESS

Design: John Toren
Author Photograph: Gregory Handberg

Forty Press, LLC
427 Van Buren Street
Anoka, MN 55303
www.fortypress.com

ISBN 978-1-938473-26-5

For all of my friends and former colleagues who helped make WCCO a great television station

Prologue

MARCH 21, 2014

The dark inside the basement was as deep as the night outside its walls. But the man being led down the stairs, step by step, would never know. The blindfold was snug around his eyes, blinding him to what surrounded him, but not to his future.

The air was moist, stale, and cool, with the pale smell of a disinfectant.

His hands were bound, the grip on his arm as tight and painful as a steel trap. He wanted to cry out but knew he would not be heard. Not here, not now.

Not ever.

"Last step," said the voice on his right, the one gripping his arm. Deep, guttural. A slight accent, but—he knew—not Russian.

He was led ten steps across the basement floor. He counted each one.

"Sit," said the same voice.

One voice, but he knew there were two men. He had seen both, but only in a flash before the blow to the head had left him with his last glimpse of light.

The second voice, no accent, American, breathed in his ear. "One last time, who sent you?"

"*Pozhaluysta, poverte mneh, ya ne znayu!*"

"Speak English!"

"Please, you must believe me, I do not know."

"You know."

"No. I do not see him," he pleaded. "He send me letter. Vot do you say? Instructions. That's all. I beg you. Pleez, you must believe me."

"A letter to kill."

"No, not to kill, not to kill!" There is panic in his voice. "Get their money. Get their money. That's all."

With that, his hands were unbound and he felt the steel tip of the gun barrel press against the side of his head.

"How do you say goodbye, in Russian?"

"No, pleez."

"Say it!"

A sob, locked in his throat. Then, more a moan than a word. "*Poka.*"

Before he could utter another sound or pull away, the basement echoed with the sound of a gunshot muffled by a silencer.

Without pause, one of the men put the gun into the man's now-dead hand and used his now-dead finger to fire a second shot into the ceiling, leaving the gun clutched in his hand, with only his fingerprints on the grip.

The two men looked at one another, then at the body. Even they were sickened by what they saw. "Let's get him out of here," said the one with the accent.

The American instructed, "No, not now. We can't take the chance. The old man next door sees and hears every-thing. Prop him up against the chair. We'll get him later or let him sit here and rot. The place is sealed and no one's going to find him. Even if they do, it's a suicide, right? Trust me."

"I say take him."

"No. You'll do as I say."

Woulda.

       Coulda.

              Shoulda.

One

She stood at Barclay's office door, oblivious to the newsroom hubbub behind her, waiting patiently for Barclay—hunched over his desk—to take notice. Finally, she rapped on the door jam.

He looked up, puzzled. "Yes?"

"Mr. Barclay?"

"That's me, but most people call me George."

"I'm Gabrielle Gooding," she said, smiling, "but most people call me Gabby."

Barclay returned the smile and leaned back, studying her. Young, probably mid-twenties, blond, pretty but not gorgeous. Comfortably dressed in a skirt and sweater, and holding a briefcase. He'd never seen her before.

"Nice to meet you, Gabby. What can I do for you?"

It was her turn to look puzzled. "You don't know?"

"Know what?" he asked, getting up from behind his desk.

She took a step back, wary now, still confused. "Didn't Mr. Ryan tell you?"

Sam Ryan was the new general manager of the television station, Barclay's boss, named only a few months before by the new corporate owners of Channel 7, San Lucas Communications of California.

Barclay sat on the edge of his desk. "Tell me what, exactly?"

"I can't believe it," she said, drawing back still farther. "My God."

He waited.

"This is so weird," she continued, struggling to find the words, to keep her poise. "I can't believe he didn't tell you."

"Sit down, please," he said, pointing to one of the guest chairs. "And tell me what this is all about."

She slumped into the chair but kept her eyes on him. "I'm your new reporter," she said, haltingly, almost in a whisper. "Mr. Ryan hired me, said to report to you today."

Barclay was stunned, disbelieving. "Repeat that," he said.

"I think you heard. I'm sorry. I don't know what to say." But she did. "How could he not tell you? How could you not know?"

At that moment, one of the news producers appeared at the door. "Got a minute, George? We've got a problem."

"Then solve it," Barclay said, quickly shutting the door and returning to his desk. He put his head in his hands, mind racing. *What the hell?* Never in his long career as a news director, here or elsewhere, had anything like this ever happened.

Finally, he looked up. Gabby was fighting her own emotions, mostly panic.

"Take it easy, OK? This is not your fault. I don't know anything about you, or how this all happened, but it's my problem, not yours."

"What do you mean, not my problem? I thought you'd be expecting me. I was sure you'd given your OK. How could he do this to you?"

Good question, Barclay thought. He hardly knew Ryan personally, he'd been at the station so short a time, but his reputation had preceded him: as a hard-nosed, take-no-shit executive who moved from one of the company's new acquisitions to another—to impose the new agenda, the new culture.

Barclay's first instinct was get on the phone to Ryan, or, better yet, to confront him directly, to find out what the hell was going on. Instead, he fought to remain calm—if only for the sake of the young woman, this stranger, who sat across from him.

"OK," he finally said, "tell me about yourself. How did all of this came about?"

Still shaken, it took her another moment to recover. "Not a lot to tell you. I'm twenty-seven, grew up in Portland, Oregon, where my mom and two sisters still live. My dad was a newspaper guy in Portland until he died three years ago. I graduated from USC in journalism and have interned or worked in the business ever since."

"And where did Sam Ryan find you?" he asked.

"I worked at one of his stations in San Jose as a reporter and weekend anchor."

"How long?"

"Three years. I interned at another of his stations in Portland before that."

"You must have impressed him," he said.

She hesitated. "I guess."

"What do you mean, you guess?"

An even longer pause. "He knows me pretty well. I went to USC with one of his daughters. We're best friends."

God Almighty, Barclay thought. What have I got here? A woman I've never met, whose work I've never seen, who's here because she's best buddies with my boss's daughter.

While Barclay was not without sins, nepotism was not one of them.

Where to go from here? What to do with her? What the hell does it mean?

"Just give me a minute," he said. "I need to think about this."

He knew this kind of thing had happened to others, but never to him. It was an ironclad rule: He hired them, he fired them. Period. No exceptions.

Until now.

As SHE SAT WATCHING HIM, Gabby was surprised he was not angrier. Like irate. Who would blame him? This strange woman shows up at his door, uninvited, unexpected. He should be bouncing off the walls. Instead, he simply looks perplexed, she thought. Maybe sad.

Ever since Sam Ryan had told her she had the job, she'd eagerly awaited this day, meeting the great George Barclay, the best news director in the business, she'd been told. Runs a great shop, breaks the big stories. You'll love working for him, learning from him. He can be tough and demanding, and may sometimes break your balls. But he'll never break your heart.

And now this. Damn.

FOR HIS PART, BARCLAY had known the new ownership would bring changes. Of that, there'd been little doubt. And he and others in the newsroom had been girding themselves for the hammer, or hammers, to fall. But this? No way.

Two years before, he and the newsroom staff had helped to block the sale of the station to another media conglom- erate, TriCom Communications, in hopes that if the sta- tion was to be sold, it would go to another local ownership group—with the same sense of public responsibility as the previous owners.

But that was not to be.

In the end, to no one's real surprise, the station went to the highest bidder, San Lucas, whose media reputation was no better than that of TriCom.

In the wake of the sale, Barclay had offered to resign, to move on and give the new owners a chance to bring in their own news director, to pursue their new agenda. It was not an entirely selfless move, since he'd devoted too many years building the reputation and ratings of Channel 7 to watch it all go down the drain.

But the CEO of San Lucas, a fellow by the name of

Jeffrey Barnes, had declined his offer. He'd asked him to stay on and offered him a one-year extension of his contract. "We like what you've done here," Barnes had told him. "You run a hell of a ship, and we'd like to see it continue under our ownership."

Barclay had accepted the offer—after a lot of thought—but *before* Barnes had named Ryan as the new general manager. Now, he realized, the decision to stay may have been too hasty. A mistake. Maybe a big one.

His attention finally returned to Gabby, who had sat quietly, maybe fearfully, while he tried to decide what to do, and what this might mean. "Do you have a video of some of your work, Gabby? Or a resume? I'd like to know what I'm getting into here."

"Mr. Ryan has the video," she said. "I thought he would have passed it on to you."

"He didn't."

"I'm sorry. But I have my resume here," she said, reaching into her briefcase.

Barclay glanced at it. While it didn't tell him much more than she'd already told him, it did include a summary of her academic honors, a long list of references, and details of her TV experience. She was clearly one of the new breed of television journalists, a "backpack" journalist, who'd been trained to shoot and edit video, to write the scripts, and to appear live on the air. An all-in-one package. Cheaper that way.

He put the resume aside. "OK, here's what we'll do. I'm going to introduce you to a couple of people in the newsroom. Tell them that you're here as my guest…that I want them to show you around. That will give me a little time to try and find Ryan and see what happens next."

She started to get up. "OK," she said, "but you should know I already quit my job in San Jose. I even paid my own way out here. I don't have anything to go back to."

"Let's not worry about that now," he told her. "One step at a time."

"OK," she said again, her voice full of doubt.

"Where are you staying?"

"Across the street, at the Hilton. I was going to look for a place this weekend."

"As I said, one step at a time."

Two

While waiting outside of Barclay's door, Gabby had had only enough time to quickly survey the newsroom, but now—as he led her into the middle of it—she realized it had to be almost twice the size of the one she'd left in San Jose. A sea of cubicles housed the reporters and producers, and, to the rear, a foot or so off the floor, was the assignment desk—manned by a couple people with phones in their ears.

"Behold," Barclay said, spreading his arms, "the Channel 7 newsroom."

"I'm impressed," she said, and she truly was.

Behind the assignment desk, there was an array of television screens monitoring the competing stations, and off to one side, a glassed-in enclosure that housed the police and fire scanners, which young dispatchers listened to 24-7.

"How big a staff do you have?" she asked, struggling with what to call him, clearly not yet comfortable enough to call him George.

"About seventy or so," he replied. "A dozen reporters, fifteen photographers, and about ten producers. The rest are assignment people, editors, and assorted other folks. We used to have more, but the recession came along and the old owners cut us back to make the place look more attractive to potential buyers."

"Too bad," she said. "But we took some big cuts in San Jose, too."

"It's happening everywhere," he replied. "No stopping the tide, I guess. Although we tried to slow it down."

Before she decided to take this job—if she actually *had* a job—Gabby did a lot of checking on Channel 7. She talked to people who worked in the market, who told her how people in the newsroom had helped thwart the takeover by TriCom—in part by persuading local minority groups to successfully challenge the bid. But in the end, she learned, the challengers didn't have enough financial backing to actually buy the place.

In stepped San Lucas.

She'd also seen several of the Channel Seven newscasts on tapes provided to her by Sam Ryan. At least one of the shows had been done from a small set she now noticed off to one side of the newsroom, directly in front of a large window that looked out on what she would later learn was Nicollet Mall. She could see bus traffic moving past outside, which she thought odd as a backdrop for a newscast. But what did she know?

"C'mon over here, Gabby. I'll introduce you to some people."

He led her to the assignment desk and waited until Harry Wilson, the assignment editor, was off the phone. "Harry, say hello to Gabrielle Gooding. Or Gabby, as she likes to be called. Harry runs the desk, keeps us in business."

Wilson held out his hand. "My pleasure, Gabby. Welcome to the inner sanctum."

"Gabby's going to be spending some time with us," Barclay said. "And I thought you could find somebody to show her around."

Wilson glanced across the newsroom, searching for an

idle body. He finally settled on Jeff Parkett, Barclay's assistant news director. "How about Jeff?" he said. "He's got his thumb up his ... well, you know."

"Good. Introduce her. I've got to try to find our new boss."

"Is there a problem?" Wilson asked.

"We'll know soon enough," Barclay said as he turned and left, leaving Wilson puzzled and Gabby with fear on her face.

"Do you know what that's about?" Wilson asked.

"Maybe," she said, not wanting to lie. "It's complicated."

He gave her a strange look. "Something to do with you?"

"Maybe."

Apparently not wanting to press further, Wilson got out from behind the assignment desk and led her over to Parkett, who was at his computer, reviewing somebody's audition video. Not hers.

Wilson quickly introduced her and then headed back to the assignment desk, probably happy to have her off his hands.

"You're friends with George?" Parkett asked.

She hesitated. "Not really. We just met today."

"You looking for a job?" He didn't waste time.

"Kind of," she said, trying to keep her composure.

"What does that mean?"

"It's complicated," she said again. "Mr. Barclay will have to explain."

After a long look, he said, "OK. Follow me."

Parkett was big and good-looking, six feet or more and well over two hundred pounds—a real stud who, she'd later learn, once played linebacker for the Gopher football team and who looked as if he could still handle the job. He was maybe five years older than her with a ring on his finger.

He led her through the nooks and crannies of the newsroom, past the cubicles and on to the editing rooms and into the control room, where they were preparing for the noon broadcast. He didn't bother to introduce her to anyone but kept pestering her with questions, few of which she was able or willing to answer. She did tell him much of what she had already told Barclay, except for the crucial fact that she'd been hired by Sam Ryan without Barclay's knowledge. He was clearly not satisfied with her answers, but finally decided not to push it further.

"I wish I could tell you more," she said. "But things are a little up in the air."

As they returned to the assignment desk, Wilson waved them over. To Parkett, he said, "We've got a DOA in northeast Minneapolis. May be a suicide, but one of my friends in the cop shop says it's a little strange."

"We don't cover suicides," Parkett said.

"I know," Wilson replied, "but this may be worth a look."

"Is anybody free?"

"Zach just pulled in up front."

"OK," Parkett said. "Have him hang tight for a minute." Then he turned to Gabby. "Want to take a ride-along?"

"What?"

"Do you want to tag along on this suicide run?"

"Sure, I guess so," she said, wondering if he thought she'd actually enjoy it or was simply trying to get her out of his hair.

"Won't take long. I'll run you up. The photographer's name is Zach Anthony. He'll treat you right."

"OK. Thanks."

BEFORE HE SET OUT in search of Sam Ryan, Barclay retreated to his office, closed the door, picked up his phone and hit the home button.

Rachel answered on the first ring.

"We need to talk," he said, before she got beyond hello.

"George? What's wrong?"

Rachel Armetage was his wife of one year. A widow with two grown children, they had met at a high school reunion the year before that, a meeting which led to their unlikely romance, and which had helped transform him from a single, overweight loner into the man of today. In the process, he had lost more than fifty pounds, firmed his abs, learned to dress better, and become more socially comfortable. No easy feat for a bachelor of some thirty years, all of which he attributed to her.

In that time, however, Rachel had unintentionally become involved in Barclay's investigation of the twenty-year-old murder of one of their high school classmates, an ordeal that had threatened her life and changed both of their lives.

"I think I have a problem," he told her now, quickly repeating the details of his encounter with Gabby Gooding.

"Ryan hired her without telling you?" she exclaimed, as much disbelief in her voice as there had been in his.

"You got it," he said.

"Have you talked to him?"

"I'm going to try and find him now, but I wanted to talk to you first."

"What is there to talk about?" she said. "Find him. Tell him to shove it up his you-know-what. He's a jerk. I didn't like him the first and only time I met him."

Barclay leaned back in his chair, grinning. Leave it to Rachel to cut to the chase. "I can't just up and quit," he said.

"Why not? We don't need the money and you don't need the grief."

Both were true. Barclay had saved enough throughout his solitary, frugal life to build up a tidy nest egg, and Rachel had been left with a substantial trust by her late husband. In addition, she had started her own small decorating firm. Still, he couldn't just up and retire, not without more thought. While he might not *need* another job, he couldn't imagine being without one—not at this point in his life.

"At least I have to see what he has to say. Maybe there was some kind of miscommunication."

"And I'm Venus de Milo," she scoffed.

He laughed out loud.

"I'm serious, George," she said. "Go ahead, talk to him. But don't take any guff. Life's too short."

"I'll talk to you tonight," he said.

Three

The station news cruiser was waiting at the front door when Parkett emerged with Gabby in tow. Once he'd introduced her to the photographer, Zach Anthony, Parkett hurried back into the station, leaving Gabby feeling like a football being handed off from one player to another, and leaving her and Zach alone in the car trying to assess one another.

"Welcome aboard," he finally said, "and fasten your belt." He pulled away from the curb and began navigating city streets new to her—and, who knows?—that she might never see again.

Zach was, she guessed, in his late twenties or early thirties, with short, sandy hair, a two-day growth of beard, and an easy smile. He was dressed as casually, some would say as shabbily, as every other photographer she'd ever known. But unlike the others she'd met today, he did not bombard her with questions. He simply accepted her explanation that she was a visitor from California who'd been offered the chance to ride along.

He did ask if she was in the news business.

"Yeah, I was working in San Jose, at Channel 12 out there."

"Doing?"

"Some reporting and weekend anchoring."

"Isn't that one of our new sister stations?" he asked.

"Yes," she said simply.

"Too bad," he said, and left it at that.

Early May in Minnesota. The last traces of the March and early April snows were gone, but there was still a chill in the air—and in the car—which left Gabby wishing now that she had not left her jacket back at the hotel. Not that she needed another reminder that this was not California.

Zach was clearly not a talker, so to fill the void, she asked how long he'd worked for Channel 7. "Five years," he replied. "I spent a couple of years in Duluth and Cedar Rapids before that."

"So how do you like it here?" she asked, still making conversation.

He gave her a questioning glance. "It's OK, but a lot better before your guys took over. No offense."

"None taken," she replied.

But the hostility in his voice did surprise her. Because San Lucas was the only company she had ever worked for, she had no way to compare it to others. She knew they kept a close eye on the bottom line, cutting resources to the bone, but they had treated her decently, if not generously. Until now, she'd thought that's the way it was in the industry, but clearly it had been a different culture here under the old owners.

As they moved on, while listening to the chatter over the two-way radio, she tried to watch the street signs as they drove down Hennepin Avenue and then up University Avenue into the heart of northeast Minneapolis. Zach clearly knew where he was going, but he was still on his cell trying to reach the assignment desk.

He finally got through. "Is this really a suicide you're sending us on?"

Gabby listened.

"What do you mean, different? A suicide's a suicide, right?"

A few second passed. "OK," he finally said. "It's your call."

She leaned over. "What's happening?"

"I'm not sure," he said. "The desk says we need to talk to the cops at the scene. The guy may have been dead a long time."

"What?" she asked. "A couple days, you mean?"

"Would you believe a *year*?" he said. "Maybe more."

He saw the sudden gleam in her eye and grinned.

As THEY PULLED UP in front of the house, they found two squad cars and a van from the medical examiner's office parked in front. One of the cops was leaning against the fender of the black-and-white taking a final drag on his cigarette. There were no other news cruisers in sight.

"That's Billy DeLong," Zach said, pointing. "I've known him for a couple of years. Nice guy, but a bit of a lech. Best keep your distance."

They climbed out of the cruiser and started to walk toward the officer, Zach leaving his gear in the car.

"No camera?" Gabby asked.

"Not yet. Let's see what we've got first."

As they approached, DeLong flipped his cigarette butt into the street and gave them a quick wave. "Hey, Zach."

"Billy. How goes it?"

"Same as, same as," he replied, not bothering to hide an appreciative glance at Gabby. More of a hard stare, actually.

"So who's your friend?" he asked, holding out his hand.

"Gabby Gooding," Zach said. "She's riding along for a while."

Gabby stood back and took his hand, his grip more of a caress than a handshake. "Nice to meet you, Billy," she said, giving him her sweetest smile.

"The same, I'm sure," he replied with a grin. "Here I thought we had one more blond for the TV screen."

DeLong was in his fifties, she guessed, with a crew-cut, chubby cheeks, and a belly that had begun to sag over his wide black belt. Not exactly a recruiting picture for the city's finest.

"So what brings you here?" DeLong asked. "I didn't know you guys covered suicides."

"We hear it's not exactly typical," Zach said.

"And where did you hear that?"

Zach shrugged. "Got me. The desk told us to check it out."

"You're going to have to talk to the medical examiner. She's still inside and probably will be for a while."

"C'mon, Billy. Give me a break."

Before DeLong could respond, a police forensic van pulled up and parked in front of the lead squad car. Zach looked at the van, then back to DeLong. "Do the forensics guys come to every suicide?"

"Don't ask me. I didn't call 'em. The guys inside must have."

"Wait here," Zach told Gabby. "I'll get the camera."

As he returned to the cruiser for his gear, she studied the house. One story, stucco and stone, set on a narrow lot. From what she could see, it was well kept; the lawn was greening up, the bushes bordering the front were well trimmed, the paint on the shutters and trim showed no signs of aging or wear. To all appearances, it was a typical home in a modest neighborhood. Except that all of the shades and curtains were tightly drawn.

There was no sign of life, literally.

By the time Zach returned with the camera on his shoulder, the front door of the house opened and a woman emerged. She stopped to chat with the forensic cops as they moved up the sidewalk, then headed toward her own car.

"That's Doctor Maxwell," Zach told Gabby, "one of the assistant M.E.'s. I don't remember her first name."

As he spoke, they moved to intercept her, the camera rolling.

They reached her before she could open the door of the car. "Hey, Doctor Maxwell, do you have a minute?" Zach asked.

"Maybe," she said, "if you take that lens out of my face."

She was a woman in her forties, slim as a stick, with fair skin that may never have seen the sun, short, reddish hair, and the most intense green eyes Gabby could ever remember seeing. An imposing figure, Gabby thought, for someone who couldn't weigh more than a hundred pounds.

Zach lowered the camera and quickly introduced Gabby and himself. "Can you tell us what's going on in there?"

"On or off the record?" she asked.

"Better on than off, but we'll take it either way. We just want to know if we've got a story here."

Gabby stood to one side, within hearing distance, but not part of the conversation.

"Off the record, until we know more," Maxwell said. "Dead male, probably in his fifties, although it's hard to know for sure with the condition of the body. Found in the basement with an apparent gunshot wound to the head."

"So a suicide?" Zach said.

"Appears so, but until we do an autopsy we won't know for sure. Maybe not even then. We're listing it as 'undetermined' for now."

Gabby couldn't resist. "Zach...I, mean, we...were told that he may have been there for a while."

"And who are you again?" Maxwell asked, giving her another look.

Gabby hesitated. "Just a reporter from California. Visiting."

"I don't know where you got your information, but you're right. He's been down there for months...maybe a year. Maybe more. Hard to tell right now."

"Jesus," Zach muttered.

"He's what we call a 'DTL', Dead Too Long," the M.E. continued, "And we don't know who he is yet. No ID on the body, or any other personal effects that we could see. That's why the cops got a search warrant and called the forensic people in. For the moment, he's officially a John Doe."

"Can we check with you later? On the record?" Zach asked.

"Feel free," she said. Then, "If we don't learn anything more about him but can find a picture of him without the head wound, we may come to you and the other media for help in identifying him. Maybe somebody out there will know who he is."

"That'd be great," Zach said, "but for now, you're not going to be calling anybody else, are you? Like any of the other stations?"

She smiled and got in the car. "You've got it yourselves for now. For whatever it's worth. The body should be coming out shortly."

As her car pulled away, Zach turned aside with his cell, out of Gabby's hearing. The conversation lasted for several minutes, with Zach doing more listening than talking. When he walked back, he said, "That was one hell of a pissing match. Parkett wants us back now, but Wilson says to stay until they bring out the body. Or what's left of it. I guess he won."

"I'm used to pissing matches," she said. "So we're staying?"

"Those are the orders. Do you have the time?"

She laughed. "Zach, I have all the time in the world."

BARCLAY DIDN'T HAVE all the time in the world, but Sam Ryan was treating him as if he did. He'd been sitting in Ryan's outer office for more than a half-hour, staring at the ceiling and thumbing through an old copy of *Business Week*.

At a desk across from him sat Maria Fallon, Ryan's executive assistant and a friend of Barclay's for many years. She was a survivor, who had managed to keep her job through the sale of the station and the change in general managers. Prim and proper, she was known for years as the power behind the throne, but now, with the change in managers, she was as uncertain as anyone about what the future might hold.

"I'm sorry, George," she said again. "He's still on the phone back to California. I'm not sure when he'll be done."

"That's OK," he said. "I can wait."

"Perhaps you should have made an appointment."

"I didn't have the chance. Something unexpected popped up."

"Nothing serious, I hope."

"We'll have to wait and see," he replied.

Barclay's last general manager was a curmudgeon named Nicholas Hawke, who had lost his job in the midst of the failed sale of the station to TriCom. While he and Barclay had had their share of disputes over the years, in the end Hawke had shown respect for the news department's independence from upper management.

He'd certainly never tried to hire a reporter without Barclay's approval.

After ten more minutes, Ryan's door finally opened. "George," he said, standing in the portal, feigning surprise at seeing him, although Barclay knew Maria had passed at least a couple notes to him as he sat waiting.

He stood up. "Mr. Ryan."

"It's Sam, George. You know that."

"I need some time with you, Sam," Barclay said, glancing at Maria. "Private time."

"I'm afraid I'm kind of on the run, George."

"I don't think this can wait."

Ryan frowned, glanced at his watch and gave a nod toward his office door. "OK," he said. "But we'll have to make it quick."

Barclay followed him through the door and took a chair across from his desk, a piece of furniture Ryan inherited from Nicholas Hawke that was about the size of Barclay's office.

Ryan was in his late forties, and, at about six feet three, as lean today as he must have been when he played point guard for Stanford years before. But he'd lost a lot of his hair in that time and now covered his bald spot with a comb-over that gave him a quirky look, detracting from otherwise attractive facial features. He'd be even better looking, Barclay thought, if he shaved his head and left it at that.

Once they were settled, Ryan asked, "So, what's so urgent, George?"

Barclay leaned across the desk and gave him the hardest look he could muster. "Gabrielle Gooding showed up at my door this morning."

"No shit!" Ryan exclaimed, his face reddening slightly. "Goddamn, I forgot to tell you, didn't I?"

"Yeah."

"I swear, it was on my to-do list. But I thought she was coming next week."

"C'mon, Sam," Barclay said, anger in his voice, remembering Rachel's advice. "Let's not play games. This is no time for bullshit."

Ryan was taken aback, clearly not used to being spoken to that way. "Wait a minute, George … "

"No, *you* wait a minute. In all my years in this business, nobody has ever hired a reporter for me without consulting me first. No, check that. No one has ever hired a reporter for me, period. I consider it a personal and professional insult."

"Jesus, George … "

But Barclay was not finished. "When your boss, Jeff Barnes, kept me on here and gave me that contract extension, he said I'd be running the newsroom, just like always. That there'd be no interference from upstairs. Certainly no hires without my knowledge. That possibility never even came up. Yet, here we are … "

Ryan's facial muscles tightened. "I'm not Jeff Barnes."

"But I assumed you'd keep his word."

He seemed to relax a bit. "Look, George. I apologize. I should have told you. I've been on the road. I've got a thousand things on my mind. I just forgot."

"Forgetting to tell me is one thing, Sam. Hiring her without me is something else."

Ryan got up and walked to his window overlooking the Nicollet Mall and stood quietly for several minutes. Finally he turned back and said, "I didn't realize it was that big a deal. I hire people for our stations all the time. I see somebody at one station who I think will be a better fit at another, I make the move. Nobody's ever challenged me before."

"Then count me as the first," Barclay said. "I don't know anything about Gabby Gooding. I haven't seen her audition video or any of her writing. What makes you think she'll be a good fit here?"

Ryan smiled for the first time. "Because of you, frankly."

"What? What do you mean?"

"Gabby's a good young woman. I know that because she's a family friend. And a good reporter, from what I've been told. Hard working, good on the air..."

"But?"

"But she can be a bit of a handful. Strong-willed, high-strung, and not exactly a team player."

"She didn't strike me that way."

"Give her time," Ryan replied, smiling again.

"So let me get this straight," Barclay said. "You hired her for me so that I could do...what?"

"Make her a better reporter, for one thing. Everyone tells me she has the potential to be something special. Smart, aggressive..."

"And?"

"Maybe teach her some manners. Provide some guidance. All I hear is that you're the best in the business at bringing young people along."

Barclay leaned back in his chair. "So is this a done deal? I've got no choice? She's here to stay?"

"Afraid so."

"What'll I tell my staff?"

"Tell 'em I screwed you over. That I apologized. That it won't happen again."

Barclay got up and walked to the door. "I've got to talk to the staff and to my wife. I'll let you know what I decide."

"Decide what?" Ryan asked.

"Whether to stay," he said.

"Don't make any quick decisions, George. Because, after this, I think we might actually get along."

He may be a prick, Barclay thought as he left, *but possibly bearable as pricks go.*

Four

It wasn't the first time Gabby had seen a body in a bag, nor would it probably be the last. But it never got easier, knowing that she was again witnessing a once-vibrant life stuffed unceremoniously into a piece of heavy vinyl and zipped up like so much garbage. Especially now, when she suspected there was little left of this body but a collection of bones and mummified flesh.

Zach watched her closely as the back doors of the M.E.'s van were finally closed. "How are you doing?" he asked.

"OK," she replied, swallowing hard.

"You could have waited in the car."

"No, I told you, I'm OK. We've got dead ones in San Jose, too."

Zach's camera had captured it all, as the gurney came out of the house and down the sidewalk and, finally, into the van. "I bet I've shot fifty of these baggies," he said, "but this may be my first suicide."

"The worst are the drownings," she said, "especially if they've been in the water for a while."

"Not for me. The crispy critters coming out of a burning building make me barf every time."

As they talked, they began to put the camera gear back into the cruiser. They'd been told not to wait for the forensic people to leave since it could be hours more and they probably wouldn't talk to them anyway.

Gabby looked over her shoulder and saw that Billy DeLong was still standing by his squad car, dragging on yet another cigarette. "Would you mind if I asked Billy one more question? I'm really curious about something."

"Go ahead," he replied. "But I don't think he'll tell you anything."

Billy broke into a broad smile as they walked over, again giving Gabby the X-ray treatment. "Hey, Billy," she said, sidling up next to him. "May I ask you just one question?"

"No. Sorry. You'll have to talk to the guys inside. I'm just a grunt."

"Listen, I'm here today, probably gone tomorrow, so I'm not saying anything to anybody. But I'm puzzled … I'm trying to figure out how you guys happened to find the body … with him dead for so long."

DeLong glanced over his shoulder, clearly undecided. Finally, "Between us, OK? You, too, Zach?"

"Absolutely."

"You probably won't believe it anyway."

"Try us," Gabby said.

"Some guy broke into the house last night … you know … trying to burgle it. Came across the body, got scared, ran like a deer, and called 911."

"The burglar actually called you?"

"Yeah. Doing his civic duty, I guess."

She laughed. "So if it wasn't for him, the dead guy would probably be lying in there for another year."

"Maybe so. Who knows?"

"Thanks, Billy, we appreciate your help."

"Maybe I'll see you again sometime," he said with a wink.

"Never can tell," she replied.

When they were finally in the car, Zach said, "Nice job back there. That question never occurred to me."

She looked across at him, with a small smile. "That's why I'm a reporter and you're a photographer."

"Smartass," he said, beginning to like her more and more. "But I have a question of my own."

"Shoot."

"We've been together for, what? Three hours or so?"

"Yeah, I guess."

"None of my business, but I haven't seen you pick up your phone once. No calls, no texts, no tweets. What gives?"

"I don't have it turned on," she said. "I don't need to talk to anyone."

"Hard to believe. I can't think of any reporter who's gone three hours without a phone pasted to her ear." Then, "No friends, no family?"

"My mom and siblings know only to call me at night. And I don't have any friends I feel like talking to right now. Or who probably feel like talking to me."

He glanced over. "I don't see a ring on your finger."

"And you probably never will," she replied sharply.

Surprised, he drove on, absorbing what she'd just said, content not to probe further.

But she was not finished. "So, if you're wondering about male friends, which I assume you are..."

"Not really..."

"—there are none. The last boyfriend I had decided to beat the crap out of me one day and landed in jail, where I hoped he'd stay for the rest of his friggin' life. It's one of the reasons I've wanted to get the hell out of San Jose."

"Whew," he muttered. "Well, good luck with that."

SHE AND ZACH WERE no sooner back in the newsroom than Parkett was on top of them. He asked no questions about what they'd seen or done but was quick to tell Gabby that Barclay wanted to see her in his office right away.

"Sure," she said, heading in that direction.

"Nice to know you," Zach said to her retreating back.

"Same here," she replied over her shoulder.

As she wound her way through the cubicles, Gabby could feel eyes following her. They already know, she thought. Or if they don't know, they suspect that something strange is going on. Well, let them wonder.

She found Barclay sitting at his desk, as she had hours before, but this time he apparently was watching for her. "Hey, Gabby," he said as she stood at the door. "C'mon in, and shut the door, if you would."

She did as she was told, although closing the door was no guarantee of privacy. His office had one large window that overlooked the newsroom, with no blinds, allowing him to look out and everyone else to look in, as she was sure they were now doing.

"Grab a chair, please," he said. Then, "So how did it go? The ride-along?"

"Good," she replied, and quickly gave him the details of the long-dead suicide.

"Sounds weird," he said, "but we can get back to that later."

She sat quietly, heart in her mouth. Watching, waiting.

"I finally talked to Ryan," he said. "He says he simply forgot to tell me about you. That he thought it was next week that you were coming. He apologized."

"And you believed him?"

"That he forgot to tell me? Maybe. But, as you know, that wasn't the issue. Hiring you without telling me was."

"And what did he say about that?"

"That he's done it before. That it's not that unusual at San Lucas."

She shrugged. "Maybe so, but I've never heard of it."

Barclay got up and sat on another guest chair next to her. "While you were gone, I've talked to some of the key members of the staff. Parkett, Wilson, and some others. I told 'em the situation. They're as pissed as I was, but also feel some sympathy for you. They realize none of this is your fault."

She shifted uneasily in her chair.

"So it comes down to this," he continued. "Do I quit and leave you sitting here with a new job in a hostile newsroom, or do I believe Ryan when he says it will never happen again?"

She said nothing, waiting.

"I've decided we both should stay. Give it a try."

Letting out her breath. "Thank you. You won't regret it."

"I hope not. Ryan sent down your audition video. I liked what I saw. You seem to do well." He went back to his desk. "I'll issue a memo to the larger staff in a few minutes. The situation may be uncomfortable for you for a while, but things will eventually settle down."

"I hope so," she said as she started to get up.

"Hold on," he said. "There's something more."

The other shoe, she thought.

"Ryan tells me you may have left some baggage behind in San Jose."

She tensed up. "Like what?"

"Like you wouldn't have won the Miss Congeniality contest. That you were 'a handful,' as he put it. Is that true?"

"Probably," she replied. "I know I made enemies. A few people thought I was too aggressive, not as compliant, not as ladylike, as they would have liked."

"Does that include the news director? I haven't spoken to him yet."

"It's not him, it's her. And, no, she wasn't a big fan of mine."

"OK. That's history. You've got a clean slate now. I like aggressive reporters, but I don't want the newsroom to become a battleground. Clear?

"Clear."

Barclay then said, "I heard something else."

"What's that?"

"That you got badly hurt a while back. Assaulted by some guy. That you ended up in the hospital."

Where could he have heard that? she wondered. Sam Ryan? The only one she'd told was Zach, and that was just minutes ago.

"I don't know what you heard," she finally said, "but I'd rather not talk about it."

"You're sure?"

"I'm sure."

"OK. I understand. But I'm here if you ever change your mind."

"Thanks. It's a bad part of my life that I want to forget about."

Then, as she was at the door, Barclay added, "I only have one absolute rule."

She stopped. "What's that?"

"Never lie to me. If you make a mistake, admit it. Do not lie about it. Because if you can lie to me, you can lie to the public. And I won't tolerate that. Understood?"

"Understood."

"Good. Then welcome aboard. Let's make it a fun ride."

BARCLAY'S NEWSROOM MEMO was brief and to the point.

> I'd like to welcome a new reporter to Channel 7 News. She is Gabrielle (Gabby) Gooding, who joins us from one of our new sister stations, Channel 12 in San Jose, California, where she has worked as a reporter and weekend anchor for the past five years. She is a journalism graduate from USC, with honors, and will be serving here as a general assignment reporter. For the time being, she will be sitting with Harry Wilson on the assignment desk until she gets the lay of the land (and until we can find her a desk) and has a chance to meet all of you. I hope and trust you will join me in welcoming her to our staff and making her feel at home.

The memo, when it made its rounds, not unexpectedly caused a considerable stir. By then, word of the Barclay/Ryan confrontation had spread not only within the Channel 7 newsroom, but to virtually every other newsroom in the Twin Cities. As the whispered conversations moved from cubicle to cubicle, there was surprise—and disappointment—that Barclay apparently had surrendered so easily to Ryan's perceived edict. And despite Barclay's request to the contrary, there quickly developed a simmering resentment to Gabby's hiring.

No surprise, it took less than a half-hour for a couple of reporters to be on the phone to friends in San Jose, including a couple at Channel 12. And it took even less time for word to leak about the reputation Gabby had left behind. Indeed, the newsroom became so preoccupied with the flap that Parkett had to angrily prod people to get back to work.

"It's kind of ugly out there," he later told Barclay. "People are both pissed at you and sorry for you at the same time. They think you got screwed over."

"Does that surprise you?"

"A little, I guess."

"Not me. But it, too, will pass. Give it some time."

"Fine, but we've still got to get the newscasts on the air."

"Then why the hell are you standing here talking to me?" Barclay said.

GABBY, FOR HER PART, was not unaware of the commotion she had caused. As she retreated to the assignment desk, she could feel the long looks and sense the rumblings. But, she decided, since there was nothing she could do about it, she'd spend her time studying the assignment board and listening in on conversations Harry Wilson had with various reporters and producers.

Several staffers, heeding Barclay's memo, did make it a point to introduce themselves and welcome her to the newsroom. But even those conversations seemed guarded. And for every person who took the trouble to say hello, there were probably five or ten who did not.

Sitting next to her, Wilson sensed her discomfort. "Listen, Gabby, relax, OK? You're innocent in all of this, OK? Give people a chance and they'll come around."

"Thanks. I'm fine."

Barclay had actually urged her to take the rest of the day off, to go back to the hotel and start the search for a place to live. But she'd said no, deciding she didn't want to look like she was retreating in the face of what she knew would be some hostility.

Later that afternoon, Zach stopped by the desk. "Wanna get a bite to eat?"

She thought for a moment. "Sure, but I'd like to see the early shows first."

"No problem."

"And I'd like to give the M.E. a call. See if we're on the record yet."

He smiled. "You don't waste any time, do you?"

Five

Even if Dr. Maxwell had been inclined to take Gabby's call, she was in no position to do so. She was hunkered over the John Doe, still encased in the body bag lying on a blue plastic table in the autopsy room at the Hennepin County morgue.

The room was a stark, antiseptic white, lighted by large fluorescent bulbs, with a terrazzo floor easily cleaned of any human spillage.

On the other side of the table was her assistant, Sean Davis, and standing off to one side was Detective John Philips, one of the two Minneapolis homicide cops who had been at the house earlier in the day. As they stood over the open bag, both Maxwell and Davis wore protective gowns and plastic face shields, along with activated charcoal masks to ward off the smell of a decaying body.

"OK," Maxwell said, "let's get him out of the bag and undressed and see what we've got. Want to give us a hand, Detective?"

"No thanks," Philips said, covering his nose and taking a step back. "I don't even know why I'm here. It's a fuckin' suicide."

Giving him a look, she carefully took the man's feet,

Davis his shoulders, and gently lifted the body onto an adjoining table. Maxwell had no idea what the man may have
weighed before his year-long repose in the basement, but
she knew he would be considerably lighter now. Much of
the moisture in the body had long since disappeared, and
most of his organs would have shriveled and shrunk, leaving him but a shadow of his former self. His precise weight
would be calculated later.

Once he was out of the bag, Davis took a series of photos from every angle before they began to remove the man's
clothing. Maxwell had long since learned how difficult it is to
undress a corpse, especially one whose limbs were as brittle
as this one, so she simply took a scissors and cut away the
clothes, piece by piece, carefully bagging them for a later,
more precise examination, both by her and possibly by the
crime lab.

But even at first glance, the clothes seemed quite ordinary:
Wrangler jeans, size 38, an Izod T-shirt, boxer shorts, black
socks, and a pair of loafers, brand unknown. None of it had
identifying marks of any kind.

Nor was he wearing any jewelry: no rings, no watch, no
bracelets.

As they leaned over, they could now see clearly what the
clothes had concealed. He was more of a mummy than the
kind of corpse they normally saw. Most of the flesh was still
attached to the bones, but with a leathery, yellowish look—almost transparent. The veins were dark and hardened.

Maxwell knew that if the body had been found outside—
after a year with the elements and animals—there probably
would have been virtually nothing left but skull and bones
and a few pieces of flesh.

A skeleton, at best. And the cause of death more difficult
to determine.

But with the year or more inside, in the basement, decom-
position had been much slower. And the cause of death was

clearly apparent, as it was when she first saw him in the house.

Half of the man's head had been blown away.

The bullet had entered the right side of the head, slightly behind the ear, and exited on the left side, near the top of the skull, following an upward trajectory. Maxwell closely examined the wound, but did not touch it for fear of disturbing what might be there: gunshot residue.

She thought the angle was a bit peculiar since most gunshot suicides to the head she had seen typically went through the mouth and out the top of the skull. Still ...

"Let's do X-rays first," she said, "Top to bottom."

As Davis went about setting up the X-rays, she walked over to the detective. "Have you found an ID yet?" she asked.

"Not that I know of. The forensic guys were still at the house when I left. They'll come up with something, I'm sure. You can't lie around dead for as long as he did without somebody missing you."

"Let's hope so," she said. Then, "When I arrived, the gun was still in his hand."

"That's right. Nobody touched anything before you got there."

"Do you find that a little strange?"

"What?"

"The gun."

"No, why?"

"Well, in my experience, the shock of the shot can cause the hand to immediately relax, releasing the grip on the gun. Not always, but usually."

He shrugged. "You'd know more about that than me. I've seen it both ways."

"It was an automatic, right?"

"Yeah, a .45 auto."

"Find the bullet?"

"Still looking."

With the X-rays finished, Maxwell returned to the body

and scanned it from head to toe, looking closely at every inch of skin. "Whoa," she suddenly said, putting her gloved finger into a small hole in the chest that was partially hidden by the chest hair that remained. Turning, she shouted at Davis, "Quick, look in the bag!"

Her assistant gave her a puzzled look. "For what?"

"A mouse!"

"What?"

"You heard me," she said, as she widened the hole and pulled out small pieces of what looked like hair and matted fur and bits of string. "I think a mouse found a home in our John Doe's chest. Just gnawed himself a hole and climbed right in."

"You gotta' be shitting me," Davis said, tentatively spreading the cover of the bag and reaching inside, searching every corner. "No mouse," he finally said. "Thank God."

"Must still be in the basement then, because he's definitely been camping out here."

The detective tried to stifle a laugh. "Wait 'til I tell my partner. He'll love it!"

Maxwell continued her examination of the body, looking for scars, incisions, tattoos, anything that might help in the future identification of the man. She found only one small tattoo of what looked like a flag on his right ankle.

"Anything obvious on the X-rays?" she asked Davis.

"Nothing," he said. "No sign of any old injuries or surgeries."

"This could be tough," she muttered, standing back. Then, "OK, Davis, let's open him up. See what we can see."

"I think I'm leaving," the detective said. "Give me a call or send me a report when you can."

"Will do."

"Be sure to include the part about the mouse," he said, laughing over his shoulder. "And give him a name, will you? Like Mickey."

Despite herself, she had to laugh, too.

WHEN BARCLAY ARRIVED HOME, Rachel was waiting at the door—an Amstel Light in one hand, a glass of red wine in the other. "Still employed?" she asked.

"Last I heard," he said, taking the beer and planting a kiss on her cheek.

She followed him into the condo. "And your manhood's still intact?"

He laughed. "Last time I checked, yes." Then, turning, "Do *you* want to check?"

She grinned. "Later, maybe. First, tell me what happened."

By now, they had passed through the living room and into the kitchen, followed by Rachel's two salt-and-pepper cats winding between their legs, vying for attention. Barclay's cat, Seuss, kept his distance, glowering, as usual.

After their wedding, Barclay had sold his sterile, nondescript man cave on one side of downtown (at a significant loss) and moved in with Rachel at her much more comfortable condo on the other side. It was a significant improvement in his lifestyle, but he was obliged to bring along Seuss the Siamese.

They each grabbed a stool at the kitchen counter.

"So?" she said. "Give."

He sipped his beer, watching her, wondering where to begin.

Rachel had changed little since he'd seen her two years before at their twenty-fifth high school reunion— freckles on her forehead and the tip of her nose, reddish hair cut short with the first hints of gray, wearing only a hint of makeup and a smile that lit up the room.

He hadn't gone to the reunion expecting to see her; in fact, he barely remembered her. He'd gone in hopes of seeing another girl for whom he'd had a long-distance high school crush—only to be shocked to learn that she'd been raped and murdered several years before. Rachel had come to his aid that night, beginning a friendship that ended here, together.

Now, as he looked across at her, he quickly recounted his meeting with Ryan, reciting the give-and-take of their conversation and the reasons he decided to stay on the job. "He made it clear that even if I left, Gabby would stay. I couldn't leave her in that position. The newsroom would crucify her."

"Do you believe him?" she asked. "That he won't do it again?"

"Don't know. But if he does, I'm gone."

Rachel took a sip of her wine, staring at him over the rim of the glass. "I hope so," she finally said. "Or you're not the man I married."

One of Rachel's cats, Sophie, the white one, jumped into his lap and pawed at his chest, looking to be scratched. Seuss looked on, in obvious disapproval.

"So what about this Gabby?" she asked. "What's she like?"

"Seems OK, but I don't really know. She looks good on her audition video, writes pretty well, but comes with something of a reputation."

"What does that mean?"

He shrugged. "Word is that she can be hard to handle. I finally talked to her news director in San Jose, who pretty much confirmed what others have said, including Ryan. Not that she's a bad reporter; the opposite, in fact. But she apparently suffers no fools and says what she thinks. Which can piss people off."

"You think you can handle her?"

"Time will tell, but we seem to have reached an understanding for now."

As they sat discussing her, Gabby was twelve blocks away—asking questions of her own about Barclay. She and Zach were at a table in one of the Hilton's restaurants, each sipping a beer as they awaited their dinners.

"So are the stories about Barclay true?" Gabby asked.

"What stories are those?"

"That he's as good as they get," she said. "A legend, according to some of the people I've talked to."

"I don't know about that," he replied. "But he's pretty damn good. Hires good people, is a hell of a journalist himself, and keeps upper management off our backs. At least until now."

He went on to tell her about some of the stories the station had broken over the years under Barclay: exposing a pedophile judge, breaking up a child porn ring, and, a year before, helping the cops track down the killer of one of his high school classmates—almost twenty years after the case went cold.

"He didn't do all of it himself, of course," he said. "But none of them would have happened without him, in my opinion."

And he went on, "He's not like a lot of news directors you hear about. Guys who sit behind closed doors, worrying about ratings and budgets and waiting for their first chance to move on to the network, or a bigger market, or to become a general manager some place. Barclay's different. His office door is always open. He sits in on the daily meetings, critiques the newscasts, and prods all of us to do a better job. I know that sounds like a big kiss, but that's the way it is. And that's why people were so upset when they thought you caused him to get screwed over by Ryan."

She sat back. "Wow."

"But don't cross him. Don't lie to him … "

"I know. He warned me."

"He gives us a lot of freedom, but we're never out of his sight for long. And don't get him angry. I've seen him drop-kick a waste basket halfway across the newsroom."

It was only as their food arrived that Gabby realized just how hungry she was. She'd missed lunch and had been operating on fumes all afternoon. As Zach watched, picking at his pasta, she wolfed down a burger and fries, barely coming up for air.

"Jesus … " he muttered, looking at her nearly-empty plate. "Amazing. You must have really good metabolism."

"Sorry. I was famished."

As she dabbed the last of her fries in the ketchup, he asked, "So, tell me, where did you get this bad-girl reputation that everybody's talking about?"

She leaned back, smiling. "It's mainly a myth."

"Oh, yeah. That's not what I hear."

"Listen, I grew up in a family with two older sisters. Who, I thought, were smarter, prettier, and more talented than I was. We were in constant competition, mainly for my dad's attention, when I think about it now. That toughened me up, I guess."

"Your dad?"

She looked away, her chin trembling slightly. "He died a few years ago. Way too young. Broke all of our hearts, especially mine. He's really responsible for getting me into the news business."

"How so?"

"Because he was a terrific journalist. For years, he was a reporter and editor for the Portland *Oregonian*. As tough a news guy as you'd ever meet. Took no crap from anybody, including his bosses and the people he was covering. But he won more awards than I'll ever see in my lifetime. He taught me to respect the business, to work harder than anybody else, especially the men in the newsroom."

Zach glanced at her, quizzically.

"Look," she said. "I try to be nice. And usually I am. But sometimes I get impatient with things … and with some people. I want to be out there, sticking my nose in places it probably doesn't belong." She paused. "People say I can be too aggressive, too rough around the edges, but that's who I am. I've tried to tone it down a little, but every time I do, I feel my dad sitting on shoulder, whispering in my ear, *'Don't take any shit.'*

"Well," he said, smiling, "I'd take it easy here for a while till people get used to your style. What did Barclay tell you? That you're starting with a 'clean slate?' I'd remember that if I were you. You're in Minnesota-Nice country."

"Trust me, I will. But I can't change who I am, either."

"Might want to give it a try," he said.

After they'd paid their bill and were standing in the hotel lobby, he asked where she was planning to look for a place to live.

"I have no clue," she replied. "Everything I own or care about is packed in my SUV, so I don't have to worry about moving anything out here. I'll take a few days to look around, see what I can find."

"Rentals are tough right now," he told her. "More expensive by the day."

"Really? Any suggestions?"

"Well," he said, hesitantly. "I've got a spare bedroom in my apartment, if you want to land there for a while. No strings attached, no ulterior motives. Might give you a chance to find something you like, and it'd be cheaper than the hotel."

"No strings?" she repeated.

"No strings."

"Thanks. I'll think about it and get back to you."

"I'll be around," he said.

Back in her hotel room, Gabby paced the floor, occasionally stopping in front of the bathroom mirror, studying the reflection. *Could she have aged in a single day?* The stress clearly had taken a toll; the skin around her eyes and cheeks seemed to sag, her shoulders slumping like an old lady's. Her hair was a tangle, and her sweater bore the final drop of ketchup from dinner. What a mess.

She had never thought of herself as particularly pretty, although others would disagree. A slim, nicely muscled body, with small, "pert" breasts, as one of her early boyfriends called them. He must have read that somewhere.

In her view, her sisters had inherited more of their mother's beauty than she had, leaving her, she thought, with some of her dad's more hardened features. Still, she'd never had trouble attracting men, although finding the right kind of man had always eluded her. She'd made some bad choices in her young life and had finally decided to stop worrying about it and concentrate on the job. Especially now.

As she started to strip and get ready to jump into the shower, the phone buzzed. Her mother, she knew immediately. Or maybe one of her sisters.

She was right the first time. "Hey, Mom."

"Where have you been?" her mother asked. "I've tried to get you for the last hour or so. I left a message. I was getting worried."

"I was eating dinner," Gabby replied. "And I forgot to turn on my cell phone."

"So how did it go?"

"Not too well," she said, reporting—as briefly as she could—the turmoil that had transpired during the day. "But it turned out OK," she finally said. "I have the job, but I'm not too popular in the newsroom."

"Why, for heaven's sake?" her mother demanded.

"Because they think I snuck in through the back door. That I'm only here because Sam Ryan's a family friend."

"But that's not true," her mother insisted.

"Don't be so sure, Mom."

"Have you seen him yet? Sam?"

"Not yet. Maybe tomorrow. But I'd just as soon keep my distance for now."

The conversation continued for another ten minutes before Gabby finally begged off. "I'm exhausted," she said. "And I don't know what's going to happen tomorrow."

But she actually did have an idea.

Six

She was waiting outside Barclay's door when he arrived in the morning.

"Hey, Gabby," he said, clearly taken aback to find her there. "You're an early bird."

"I hoped to catch you before you got busy," she said.

He unlocked the office door and invited her in. "So what's up?"

She stood at the door. "I wanted to tell you that I think there may be a story in that suicide Zach and I went to yesterday."

"Really?"

"I know I just started, and I know nobody knows me, and I'll obviously do anything you want me to do, but I think somebody ought to follow up on it. Maybe me, if you'd like."

She said all of that without taking a breath.

He smiled. She was living up to her billing. "You know, we don't normally cover suicides…"

"I know, but this is different. I've just got a feeling. Ask Zach. He feels the same way. Harry Wilson, too."

"OK," he said, settling in behind his desk. "We've got our morning meeting in about ten minutes. Why don't you sit in on it and pitch your idea—your suspicions—to the group. That'll give them all a chance to get to know you… and you, them."

"You're sure?"

"Why not? But you may find it a tough audience."

THE GROUP GATHERED around Barclay at a small conference table set off to one side of the newsroom, and included Jeff Parkett; Harry Wilson; a woman named Robin Shuster, who was the executive producer; the five and six o'clock newscast producers, Trent Masters and Sylvia Thurgard; and the photo chief, Adam Springer.

Once Gabby was introduced to those she hadn't yet met, she sat back and watched and listened to the give-and-take over the list of the day's assignments and possible future story ideas—a discussion that took the better part of an hour. It was only then that Barclay finally turned to her. "As some of you know, Gabby and Zach got sent out on a suicide yesterday, which Harry here thought might be a story. Well, Gabby agrees with him, and she's here to pitch it. Gabby?"

"Thanks, I appreciate the chance," she said, and quickly reviewed what she and Zach had found at the house in northeast Minneapolis. "I admit we don't know much yet, but I do know the guy had been in that house, dead, for a long time ... and would still be there if some burglar hadn't busted in. What's more, the guy apparently carried no ID ... "

"So that's the story?" Parkett asked, skeptically. "A suicide dead for a long time?"

"Think about it," she said. "From what I could see, the house didn't look abandoned. The yard was in good shape. No mail piled up. No old newspapers on the stoop. It looked like it was lived in, except for the drawn drapes. If somebody's been living there, they've been roommates with a rotting corpse for a year or more."

"So," Wilson said, joining in, supporting her, "if nobody's living there, except the dead guy, who's collecting the mail, who's paying the bills, who's keeping up the yard? And everything else?"

"And," Gabby said, "why hasn't anyone declared him missing? Whoever he is."

"Maybe he *is* on a missing persons list," Parkett argued. "He just doesn't happen to live at that particular address, so no one thought to look for him there."

"If he didn't live there, then who does?" she asked.

"Wait a minute," Barclay said, holding up his hands, "before we get too excited. We haven't talked to the cops, we haven't talked to the M.E., except at the scene. There may be explanations for some or all of that."

"Like what?" Gabby challenged.

He shrugged. "I don't know, but we best find out before we go much further."

"I agree," she said, "but I don't think we can forget one other possibility, unlikely as it may be. That he wasn't a suicide...that someone killed him."

"C'mon, Gabby," Parkett protested. "This isn't some mystery novel."

"C'mon, yourself, Jeff," Robin Shuster, the exec producer, said, breaking in. "Don't shush her up." Heavy-set, with dark brown hair, and piercing blue eyes, she had a commanding presence. "What if she's right? What if it turns out this guy was not a suicide but a murder victim? A long shot, maybe, but a hell of a story if it turns out to be true. And we might have it alone."

Parkett persisted. "So if somebody killed him, why would they leave the body there and hide the fact that he's there for all this time? Why not dispose of the body right away, bury it somewhere...and be done with it?"

There was silence around the table.

"I can think of a couple of things," Gabby finally said. "Maybe the killer couldn't manage the disposal at the time...and never found another opportunity..."

"Unlikely," Parkett said.

"And maybe he knew," she went on, "that if the body was

found, he would somehow be tied to the killing. So he kept up the pretense of someone living there…paying the bills and so forth." She paused. "Or, maybe, the guy who killed him got himself killed later, leaving nobody knowing that the body was there."

"So who's been paying the bills since then?" Parkett asked.

She smiled. "You got me there, Jeff."

There was more animated give-and-take before Barclay once again broke in. "OK, I've heard enough. Seems to me the story is worth pursuing, for a while at least. But there's a lot of work to do. I'm going to have Gabby sit down with John Knowles and drain his brain before we go much further."

Knowles was head of the station's investigative unit.

Barclay went on, "Since Gabby is an unexpected addition to our staff, I think we can spare her for a few days or so. See where this may lead, if anywhere."

An hour later, he came in search of her and led her across the newsroom to a small office tucked away to one side. They waited at the door until the man sitting inside looked up. "Hey, John," Barclay said, ushering Gabby in. "This is Gabby Gooding. Gabby, John Knowles."

Knowles got up from behind the cluttered desk and shook her hand. "Hi, Gabby. Welcome. I've heard about you."

"Almost everyone has, I guess," she replied with a smile.

"Grab a chair, and ignore the mess."

Knowles was in his late forties, slender, with a narrow face to match, his half-glasses hanging from his nose. A former network news guy in DC who found himself with a drinking problem, he'd come to Minnesota to get sober at the Hazelden rehab center. Staying on, he'd landed a job at Channel 7 as head of the station's I-Team. Now, years later, he was still sober and a consummate investigative reporter.

Barclay stood in the doorway and gave Knowles a shortened version of the staff debate over the suicide story. "Gabby feels strongly that there may be something there, and I thought the two of you could chat about it. See what you think ... and what we should do next, if anything. You've got the time?"

"Sure."

"Then I'll leave you two alone."

Knowles had been a point man, along with a retired St. Paul cop and cold case detective, in Barclay's investigation of the rape and murder of his old classmate. Knowles had more sources in his back pocket than most other reporters had in their iPhones.

"So," he said, leaning back in his chair, "tell me all about it."

Gabby filled in what Barclay had left out, reciting every detail she could recall from the scene, and the reasons for her suspicions. Along with the doubts others had raised. Knowles listened carefully, never interrupting until she was finished.

He asked, "You haven't spoken to the M.E. since yesterday?"

"No. I left a message, but she hasn't called back."

"So you don't know if they've done an autopsy yet, or, if they have, what they found?"

"No, but I hope to get a copy of the autopsy report."

"Not in Minnesota, you won't," he said. "They're not public records here."

"Really? They are in California."

"I know, and in Wisconsin, too. But not here. And that makes things more difficult."

She stared at him across the desk, thinking.

"And I'm guessing you haven't talked to the cops or the forensic people," he said. "You don't know what they may have found in the house ... or if they know who the dead guy is yet."

"That's right."

"So you've got a long way to go, and it's not going to be easy going, if there's a story there at all."

"I understand," she said.

Knowles leaned in. "I'm not sure you do. To get what you need, you're going to have to get inside the cop shop, and the M.E.'s office. And neither of those is going to be easy."

"I didn't think it would be. Especially being new in town."

He smiled. "I do have some of those contacts," he said. "And if you'd like me to work with you on this, I'd be happy to."

"You have the time?"

"If George asks me to, I'll make the time."

"I'd appreciate that," she said, "as long as it remains my story. OK?"

He grinned. "No problem. I'm not looking for glory. Let me make some calls. Stop by later this afternoon and we'll see where we are. Meantime, you should keep trying to get hold of this Maxwell, the M.E."

"Will do," she said, and got up, leaving Knowles watching her walk away.

Yup, he thought, *she is what they said she was.*

PARKETT CAUGHT UP with Barclay halfway across the newsroom. "You sure you know what you're doing, boss?"

"What do you mean?"

"You know what I mean. Gabby. It's her first day, for Christ's sake. She doesn't even know where the damn bathroom is."

"Everybody has a first day," Barclay said. "You remember yours?"

"No."

"Neither do I."

"Well, shit … "

"Give her a break, Jeff. A little room. She's not a kid."

"How much room?"

"Enough to see what she can do. A day, maybe two or three. Who knows? She could surprise you."

"Maybe so," he said, but there was not a lot of conviction in his voice.

IT WAS SHORTLY BEFORE noon that Gabby finally got a return call from Dr. Maxwell, who obviously remembered her. "I thought you were just visiting from California."

"That was yesterday," Gabby said. "I'm officially working here today."

"That was fast."

"I know."

"So what can I do for you?"

"I'd like to meet with you, if possible. To talk about the suicide. And the autopsy, if you've done it."

"I can't tell you much," Maxwell said.

"Even if we stay off the record?"

"I'll talk to my chief, but don't count on it."

"Can we at least meet? Get to know each other?"

There was a pause at the other end of the line. "Tomorrow morning at nine," she said. "There's a Caribou coffee shop just down the Mall from your station. I'll see you then, unless I'm called out on another case."

Seven

By afternoon, the morning clouds had given way to bright sunshine, warming the air and giving the day a clean, fresh feel. The windows in the news cruiser were down, the wind whipping Gabby's hair, as Zach navigated the same streets they had taken the day before.

Now, as they pulled up in front of the abandoned house, there was no sign of squad cars or any other activity. The street was quiet, save for the spring chirping and singing of the birds vying for territory and mates.

"Everybody must be working," Zach said as they sat in the car. "Or sitting inside, watching TV."

There were no other cars on the block, except for a black Chrysler 300 with tinted windows parked on the opposite side of the street, a few houses down.

Gabby climbed out of the cr uiser. "Let's see what we can see and talk to some of the neighbors, if they're home."

She had talked Wilson into loaning Zach to her for a couple of hours, promising to free him up if he was needed. "It won't take long," she'd said.

As they stood on the sidewalk, nothing seemed to have changed. The drapes were still drawn, with no sign of life. And while she knew it probably would be futile, she climbed the three steps to the stoop and rang the doorbell. She could hear the chimes inside, but no sound of footsteps or voices. After waiting for several minutes, she retreated to the sidewalk and began to follow the narrow walk around the corner of the house, with Zach trailing behind her. As in the front, the side windows were all covered with blinds or drapes, giving them no glimpse of the inside.

By the time they turned the corner of the house, the Chrysler 300 had moved up a couple of spaces on the street and was now within about fifty yards of the news cruiser, easily dentified by the Channel 7 logo displayed on the front door.

"What the fuck are they doin' here?" said one of the two men hunkered down in front seat.

"What do you think?" said the other. "Pokin' around."

"How do they know about this?" said the first.

"The cops were here for most of the day. You think people don't talk?"

"Why would they give a shit about a suicide?"

"They must know he'd been there for a while. People aren't stupid."

"I told you we should have gotten him out."

"It wasn't our decision, Harry. My friend didn't want to take the chance."

"So what do we do now?"

"Wait for instructions."

They hadn't seen Gabby and Zach the day before. In fact, they hadn't arrived until the last black-and-white was pulling away. They had not gotten a call until late in the day.

The first man quickly snapped some photos with his long-lens camera, trying to focus on both Gabby and Zach before they disappeared around the house.

"Just got the back of their heads," he said.

"We'll wait," said the other.

"WE REALLY SHOULDN'T be here," Zach said. "This is some-body's private property."

"Who's going to complain?"

"I know, but still ... "

The backyard grass was as neatly-trimmed as the front. The yard was small, part of it taken up by a single-car garage fronting on the alley that ran behind all of the homes. A small window in the back door of the house was uncovered, allow-ing them to see a small portion of the kitchen. But that was all.

As they were about to walk back to the front, an old man stepped out of the back door of a neighboring house, staring at them. He was tall but bent over, walking with a cane, still in his bathrobe, his gray hair tied in a ponytail. "Who are you?" he asked, hobbling toward them. "And what are you doing here?"

Gabby stepped up to meet him at a fence that separated the two yards. "I'm Gabby," she said, "from Channel 7 News. And this is Zach."

"You're here because the police were here?"

"That's right."

"You news people!" Said with disgust. "Can't you let the poor man rest in peace?"

"We'd like to," she said, "but we don't know who he is. Do you?"

That gave him pause. "Not really. I'd never met him. Never seen him, actually, never seen anybody, for that matter. But if he died there, he must have lived there, don't you think?"

"That's what we'd like to know," Zach said.

"What's *your* name, and how long have you lived here?" Gabby asked.

The man leaned against the fence. "Name's Clarence Ped-ersen, that's with a *d* and an *e*. Been here twenty years. My wife's folks owned it before us, but the wife died a couple of years ago. Cancer."

"Sorry to hear that," she said. "So you haven't seen anybody living there for ... what?"

"Two years at least. Before my wife passed."

"Didn't you find that strange?" she persisted.

He shook his head. "None of my business. Whoever owns it, kept it up. Didn't let it go to pot. Can't say that for some people around here."

"How about before that?" Gabby asked.

"Hard to remember. Memory's not so good these days, you know."

"Try."

"Some guy, I think. Never saw much of him, either. Kind of a loner. Came and went. Then the place went vacant. He must have sold it."

"Did you know his name?"

"Never asked. Never told me. Can't remember actually meeting him, now that you mention it.

"Did the police talk to you?" Zach asked.

"Sure. Asked the same questions you're asking."

"How about the other neighbors?"

"Don't know about that. Suppose so."

Zach took out one of his business cards and handed it to Clarence. "If you see or hear anything next door, please give me a call. Anytime, day or night."

"OK," he replied, taking the card, "but I probably won't be here much longer. My daughter's trying to put me in a nursing home, I think."

"Well, good luck," Gabby said, as they retreated to the front of the house.

When they turned the corner, they found an intense sun cutting through the trees, momentarily blinding them. "Damn," Zach said, as they both turned aside, trying to shield their eyes. "I forgot my shades in the car."

"Forget it," Gabby said, trying to blink away the glare. "This won't take long."

At the end of the sidewalk, as they turned toward the next neighboring house, Gabby paused and looked across the street toward the parked Chrysler 300. "Was that car there before?" she asked, staring, trying to penetrate its darkened windows.

"I think so," Zach replied, "but maybe farther down the block."

"Can you make out anybody inside?"

"No."

As they started to walk slowly down the sidewalk, keeping an eye on the car, it suddenly came alive, lurching forward, tires screeching, rubber burning. It careened toward them, swerving away at the last moment, its rear-end fish-tailing as it jumped the curb and sped away, leaving a spray of gravel in its wake.

"Jesus!" Zach shouted, pulling Gabby back.

She pulled out of his grasp and quickly turned, watching the car careen around the next corner and disappear. "I guess that answers that question," she said.

"What the hell?" Zach said. "They could've killed us, if they'd wanted."

Gabby stood, hands on hips, trying to ignore the small tremors lingering in her own body. "They were obviously watching us, huh?"

"I would say so."

"But who?"

"Not somebody who wanted to stop and say hello."

"This is freaky," she said.

"Freaky?" Zach replied, with a sharp look. "Fucking scary, I'd call it."

"So what do we do now?" Gabby said.

"Get the hell out of here."

"Let's check a couple more houses down the street first."

"No way. Later, maybe."

"I'll come back tonight in my own car."

"Not alone, you won't," Zach said. "Not after this."

THE CHRYSLER PULLED INTO the parking lot of a Cub grocery store a couple of miles away, the driver tucking the car between two food delivery trucks. The other man was on his cell phone, waiting for four rings before it was finally picked up.

"What?" came the voice on the other end.

"Bad news," said the man in the Chrysler.

"What?" the voice repeated.

"TV people were at the house, poking around. Talking to one of the neighbors, we think. The old guy next door."

His words were met with silence.

"We've got pictures of them. A guy and a woman. Said Channel 7 on their car."

"Did they see you?"

"The car, but not us. We took off before they could get our plates or anything."

"Find out who they are."

"Then what?"

The phone went dead before he got an answer.

AS GABBY AND ZACH pulled into the station parking ramp, she asked, "Is your offer still good? About staying at your place?"

"Sure."

"I wouldn't stay for long... just till I can find something of my own."

"Stay as long as you'd like," he said. "There's plenty of room."

"I'll pay, you know."

"Whatever. I'm not worried about it."

"What'll your friends think?"

He laughed. "All kinds of dirty thoughts, but who cares?"

After more discussion, they agreed to make the move that night, after revisiting the neighborhood they'd just left.

WHEN THEY'D TOLD BARCLAY what had happened at the house, he asked John Knowles to join them in his office. "I don't like the sound of this," he said. "We may be in over our heads already."

"It was weird, that's for sure," Zach said. "They were obviously watching the house, and then us... when we got there."

"Why watch the house now, when everything's over?" Barclay asked.

No one had any answers.

"You couldn't see who was inside the car?" Knowles asked.

Gabby said, "Just a couple of shapes, that's all."

"And nothing on the plates?"

"Are you kidding?" Zach said. "It happened too quick. The car was there, then gone."

They all sat quietly for a moment. Then Knowles said, "I've got some calls in to friends at the cop shop, but no one's gotten back to me yet."

"And I'm meeting with the M.E. in the morning," Gabby said. "But she seemed hesitant on the phone, so I'm not sure I'll get much more out of her."

When Barclay heard they planned to return to the neighborhood that night, he objected. "Let's just hang tight for now," he said. "No sense in pushing things until we know more."

"Like what?" Gabby asked.

His answers were rapid-fire. "Like who the dead guy is? Like was it actually a suicide or something else? Like who may have been in that car? We need some answers before we do more nosing around. It's too chancy, right now."

She disagreed and was tempted to argue, but held her tongue. *The new me*, she thought.

"I'll keep working my sources," Knowles said, "but I have a feeling this may take a while."

ZACH'S APARTMENT WAS LOCATED on the third floor of a large complex in the Uptown area of south Minneapolis, not far from the chain of lakes that were the beautiful signature of the city. It was an oasis for the young, urban population, featuring a wealth of bars and restaurants, parks, and housing that included everything from single-family homes, to duplexes, to buildings like Zach's. If you were young single, and looking for a little life in your life, this was the place to be.

Assuming you could afford it.

The apartment was not the bachelor pad Gabby had expected. Far from it. The living room was large, with a small den off to one side, a spacious, well-equipped kitchen, a bathroom with two sinks, and two bedrooms, each with a double-bed and walk-in closet.

What's more, the place was immaculate. Nothing seemed out of place, with no sign of even a speck of dust, as far as she could see. "Sure you aren't married?" she said. "Like to a housekeeper?"

"Afraid not," he laughed.

"They must pay photographers better here than in San Jose," she said as she wandered through the rooms. "This is beautiful."

He followed along. "No college loans. No expensive hobbies. No needy girlfriends. It's just me and the dog I hope to get."

"A dog? When?"

"Soon, I hope. They've started to allow them, as long as they're small."

"I'll probably be long gone by then," she said.

"You don't like dogs?"

"I'm more of a cat person. We had three of them back home in Portland."

They stopped at one of the bedrooms. "This is your digs," he said. "Should be plenty of closet and drawer space. There's a lock on the inside of the door, if you feel the need. We'll have to share the bathroom, but that shouldn't be a problem. I'm not in there much."

"This is great," she said.

"Help yourself to anything in the kitchen. It's pretty well stocked. And I'll get another entry card from the manager, so you can come and go as you'd like. There's only one thing I'd ask."

"What's that?"

"If you find the love of your life while you're here, please do your lovin' somewhere else."

She grinned. "That's not likely."

"You never know," he said.

"What about you?" she asked. "No love of your life?"

"Not at the moment. But that's another story."

"I'd love to hear it."

"Really? Well, maybe we can trade stories some day."

IT TOOK THEM NO MORE than a half-hour to carry all of her suitcases and other belongings from her Explorer up the elevator and into her new bedroom. It took another hour to get her settled in, and another twenty minutes to eat the soup and sandwiches they'd fixed for dinner. By then it was early evening, and dusk had fallen into darkness.

As they sat in the kitchen, wondering what to do next, Zach's cell phone sounded. He looked at the incoming number, frowned, and answered. "This is Zach."

There was a pause at the other end, then a halting voice. "This is Clarence. You left your card with me, told me to call."

Zach glanced at Gabby. "Yes," he said. "Clarence. Nice to hear from you."

"I think someone's in the house next door. A light's on in the kitchen."

"Really?" Zach said, working to keep the excitement from his voice. "Did you see anyone?"

"No, just the light."

"No cars, no people?"

"No, just the light," he repeated.

"OK, Clarence, thank you so much. Don't go outside, but

if you see anything else, give me another call. OK?"

"Not to worry, I'm going to bed soon, anyway."

Zach put the phone down and repeated for Gabby what Clarence had said.

She got up from her chair. "Let's go. We can take my car."

"Hold on. You're forgetting something."

"What?"

"Barclay. Told us to stay away."

"But he didn't know about this."

"All the more reason."

"C'mon. We'll just drive by. Stay in the car. See what we can see."

Zach remained in his chair, staring at her, debating. "OK," he finally said. "But remember, no chances, no heroics. Or it'll be our ass. Or asses."

"Relax, will you?" Gabby said. "What the hell can happen?"

SHE WAS BEHIND the wheel of her Explorer as they slowly drove along the darkened street past the house, seeing no sign of light from the front. There were several cars parked on the street, but the Chrysler 300 was not among them. Two doors down, three people were sitting on their front porch, their figures visible from the light of the front window and by the bright tips of the cigarettes two of them were smoking.

She pulled to the curb.

"No, you don't," Zach said. "We're staying in the car, re-member?"

"We'll just stop for a second," she said. "Quick conversa-tion."

"No way! You don't screw with Barclay's orders."

"C'mon. Don't be a wuss."

"I'm serious. Keep driving."

Reluctantly, she pulled away. "Now what?" she said.

"Let's try the alley."

She drove to the end of the street, around the corner, and

into the alley. "Douse the headlights," he said. "Just use the parking lights."

They moved even more slowly down the alley, past garages and garbage cans, basketball hoops and swing-sets in back-yards, but no sign of people. The car crept along and finally pulled to a stop behind the house. "I don't see any light," she whispered, shifting into Park. "Whoever was there must be gone."

"Yeah," he replied, quietly, staring into the dark. "Let's move on."

Before she could touch the shift or the accelerator, they were frozen by a blinding light from the middle of the back-yard. A spotlight, more intense than the afternoon sun, bore directly into their eyes. "Holy shit!" Zach shouted.

The light did not waver, its beam as penetrating as a laser, forcing their eyes aside, making whoever held it invisible.

Zach turned and shouted, "Drive!"

"I can't see!"

She frantically tried to shift out of Park, her foot fumbling for the accelerator, as the spotlight bore in on them.

Zach again: "C'mon, move!"

She yelled angrily: "You don't think I'm trying!"

She finally found the accelerator and pressed it to the floor, tearing away, hoping there was nothing, or no one, in her sightless path.

By the time they were back at the apartment nursing a beer, their nerves had quieted but their minds were as unsettled as ever.

"What was he doing back there, anyway?" she asked, more of herself than Zach. "Standing in the dark, waiting. For what?"

He shrugged. "He might have been looking out the front window when we passed by and got curious when he saw us pull over to the curb. Figured maybe we'd come through the alley."

"That sounds a little far-fetched," she said. "We barely stopped out in front."

"I know, but somebody was in the place. At least Clarence says there was."

"Maybe he was waiting for someone else and was surprised when he saw us stop."

"Anything's possible, I guess, but one thing's certain: he got a good look at us."

"And that's a little scary. Especially if it was the same guy who saw us this afternoon."

He drained the last of his beer. "We don't say anything about this to Barclay, OK? Nothing. And from now on, we play it cool. *You* play it cool. Or we could be in deep, deep shit. And that's the last thing you want right now."

"You're right about that," she agreed. "I'll behave, I promise."

Eight

G abby was waiting at the coffee shop, thumbing through the *Star Tribune,* when Dr. Maxwell walked in, glanced around, and finally spotted her. Gabby got up quickly, thanked her for coming and asked what she'd like to drink. "Just a small dark-roast with a little cream," she said. "It's only nine o'clock and I've already had more than my quota for the day."

When she returned with the drinks, Maxwell was glancing at the paper Gabby had left behind. "More madness and mayhem," she said, pointing to one headline on the latest Middle East conflict and another on a high school shooting in Utah. "I wonder if it will ever stop?"

"Probably not in our lifetimes," Gabby replied.

They sat quietly for a moment before Gabby said, "You know, I don't even know your first name. Just Dr. Maxwell."

She smiled. "It's Cindy. Cynthia, actually. And you're Gabby."

"Gabrielle, actually."

"Good. That's out of the way."

Maxwell wore a deep red blouse and lipstick to match, which, along with her reddish hair, tended to give her pale skin some color. Her green eyes were as vivid now as the first time Gabby had seen them, and her sparkling teeth were a dentist's delight. She seemed to have made the most of what she'd been given.

They spent the first few minutes getting acquainted. Gabby briefly described her own personal and professional background before learning that while Maxwell had grown up in a small town in Iowa, she had done all of her medical training in Minnesota, both at the University and at the Hennepin County Medical Center. "I know many physicians don't want to do what I do," she said, "but I found out long ago that I could learn more about the living by examining the dead. I can't tell you how many medical advances have come from pathologists doing what I do. It's our little secret. I realize some people think of it as gruesome, but I find it very satisfying and rewarding."

"Are you married?" Gabby asked.

"Once. Never again."

"Really? You sound bitter."

"So would you, if you knew the guy. He was like living with one of my corpses. And I see enough of them."

Gabby wanted to laugh, but didn't. "No kids?"

"No, blessedly. They'd probably be like him."

Gabby wisely decided to move on, switching subjects, briefly describing everything that had happened since they'd first met outside the mystery house, including the encounter with the Chrysler 300, but excluding the scare of the night before. "It's pretty clear that someone was watching the house when we got there that afternoon. But who they were and why they were there remains the mystery."

The medical examiner listened without interruption. Finally, she said, "Have you told any of this to the cops?"

"No. I'm still waiting to make contact. And I'm not sure how much I should tell them, once I do."

Maxwell took a sip of her coffee. "Are we still off the record?"

"If we need to be, yes," Gabby replied.

"Then I wouldn't count on the cops being much help. From what I hear and see, they're convinced it was a suicide, plain and simple."

"And you're not?"

"I'm not sure. Officially, we're still calling it 'undetermined,' and that won't change until we find out who the guy is. Or was."

"No progress there?"

"Not from my end. We have most of his teeth and some partial prints off his mummified fingers, but as far as I know he's still a man without a name."

"DNA?"

"Sure, skin and hair, fingernails, but that will take some time to identify. Then you have to find a match. Same with the fingerprints. The crime lab may be working on all of that now, but I suspect it's not a high priority with them."

Gabby got up to get more coffee, but Maxwell declined. When she returned, she asked, "So what more can you tell me about the autopsy?"

"Not that much," reciting what little they'd found in the external exam. "We're still guessing at his age, maybe fifty or so. Dark brown hair, maybe five feet ten, 180 pounds, when he was alive. Small tattoo, like a flag, on his right ankle. Gunshot wound to the head. Gunshot residue on his hand, in his hair, and on his cheek."

"Anything else?"

"Well, one really strange thing was the mouse nest we found in his chest."

"*What?*"

She laughed. "That's what I said. Never seen it before. The mouse chewed a neat little hole and made a home for himself and his family inside the cadaver."

Gabby stared at her, aghast. "Was he still in there?"

"No, thank goodness. But probably still in the house,

somewhere." Then, after a pause, "Most of the man's internal organs were all shriveled, and not of much help. And since there was no urine left in the body, it's impossible to do a tox screen."

"So why the doubts about the suicide?" Gabby asked.

Maxwell leaned back in her chair. "For some of the same reasons you have, I suppose. The fact that he lay there for so long, undiscovered. That we've not been able to identify him yet. That he's not on any missing persons list, as far as we know. It just seems very strange, that's all. Certainly not your normal suicide."

"Anything else?"

The M.E. repeated her thoughts about the gun, still in the grasp of the man after his death and the strange angle of the bullet's path. She demonstrated, using her finger as a gun, holding it against her head as she thought the dead man must have done. "It seems like an awkward way to hold a gun if you're going to kill yourself, but I'm no expert in that area. The cops may have a different view."

She glanced at her watch. "I have to get going. I've got two more clients waiting in the morgue."

"Can we talk again?" Gabby asked, writing her various phone numbers on a paper napkin and handing it to her.

"Sure, as long as we stay off the record, for now. I don't want to find myself on the television screen."

"No problem. But one more thing."

Maxwell was at the door. "What's that?"

"Has anyone else … in the media, I mean … been talking to you about this?"

"Not so far."

"Good. Will you call me if anything changes?"

"I'll try," she said. "And thanks for the coffee."

WHEN GABBY WALKED into the station, the first person she saw was the last person she wanted to see. Sam Ryan was standing by the lobby reception desk, looking as though he'd been waiting for her—although she knew that couldn't be. No one knew where she'd been or when she'd be back.

"Gabby!" he said in a booming voice. "Where've you been? I've been hoping to see you."

She stood back, fearing he might rush up and give her a bear hug. Family friend or not, that would be awkward. Not here, not now. He was still the GM. Sensing her hesitation, he instead grabbed her hand and shook it like a pump handle. "I thought you'd stop up to see me before now," he said. "It's been a couple of days."

"Sorry, but I've been really busy," she said, working up a smile. "I was going to drop by your office today."

"Well, that's good . . . that they've got you busy. I knew it wouldn't take you long to get into the swing of things."

He put an arm around her shoulder. "How's your mom? How's the family?"

Gabby glanced at the receptionist, who was watching with interest. "Good, I think. I talked to Mom my first night here."

"And how are they treating you in the newsroom? Is old George on your case?"

"They've been great," she said. "He's been great."

"And you've found a place to live?"

"Yes. Temporarily, I mean."

"Good for you," he said, releasing her. "I've gotta run, but let's get together for lunch or dinner sometime. OK?"

"Sure."

"And if anyone gives you any grief, you just let me know."

"I'll be fine, but thanks."

As he left, Gabby glanced again at the receptionist, knowing every word of this encounter would soon be passed on in every corner of the station.

That's all I need, she thought.

HARRY WILSON WAS WAITING when she arrived at the assignment desk. "Where've you been?" he asked, not looking all that happy.

"Meeting with Cindy Maxwell, the M.E. Why?"

"Because I need to know where you are when you're not here. That's the way it works."

"Sorry, but nobody told me that. I thought I was kinda on my own."

"I know Barclay gave you a long leash," he said, "but it's still a leash."

"I'll remember."

"Two other things. We finally found a spot for you," pointing to one of the cubicles just a few feet away, "so make yourself at home."

"Good. I appreciate that."

"Second, John Knowles would like to see you as soon as possible. He's in his office."

Knowles was, as usual, hunkered over his desk, half-glasses drooping from his nose, slowly turning the pages of some kind of report in front of him. Gabby rapped softly on the doorjam.

"Hey, Gabby," he said, looking up. "C'mon in. Grab a chair."

She slid into a chair across from him. "Harry Wilson said you wanted to see me."

"I do, but the grapevine tells me you've been doing some private-eye work of your own."

"The grapevine being Zach," she said.

"I did run into him, yes."

She smiled. "Then he told you most of what I can tell you. Except that I just left a meeting with the assistant M.E., Cindy Maxwell."

"You work pretty fast."

"I'm not sure how helpful it was," she replied, quickly re-capping their conversation, "except that she shares some of the same doubts about the suicide that I do. But she's got nothing very concrete. Just a lot of conjecture."

"Which is why I wanted to see you," he said. "I called in a favor and arranged a meeting tomorrow with the head of the Homicide division, a Lieutenant Eric Winslow, who's agreed to talk to you—to us—off the record."

"That's great."

"Maybe, maybe not. He's a nice guy whom I've gotten to know over the years, but he's not personally involved in the investigation. He's willing to listen to what we have to say, and he'll try to have one of the detectives assigned to the case sit in, too."

"My guess is they won't tell us much," she said. "It's probably too early, and from what the M.E. says, they're eager to get it off their books."

"But it's a start, and you'll at least get to meet the guys."

The meeting was arranged for the next morning at City Hall.

As she got up to leave, Knowles said, "This may sound sexist, and probably is, but you may want to dress ... uhh ... "

"What are you trying to say, John?"

"I think you know. You'll want them to remember you, and not just your name. Cops love pretty women who are ... you know ... proud of ... "

"I get the drift," she said. "I'll do my best."

BARCLAY RAN INTO ZACH outside his office. "Hey, Zach. I hear you've got a new roommate."

"Word travels fast," he replied with a grin.

"So how's it going?"

"Fine so far. She just moved in last night. And she probably won't be there for long. Just until she can find a place of her own."

"Well, thanks for doing that," Barclay said. "It's good of you."

"No problem. She seems nice enough. A little headstrong maybe, but nice."

"I trust you'll keep an eye on her."

"If she'll let me, but I wouldn't count on it."

FOR HER PART, Gabby spent the rest of her day getting settled into her new cubicle, which she shared—back to back—with another reporter, Sarah Andrews, whom she'd met only briefly before then.

Sarah, Gabby learned, had been at the station for a couple of years, arriving from the same Duluth station where Zach had once worked. A year or two younger than Gabby, and an inch or two shorter, she carried herself with a confident, self-assured air that belied her age. What's more, she seemed to be the only non-blond female reporter on the staff.

To Gabby, she seemed pleasant enough, although visibly miffed that she had to share her cubicle space. "Like, I can't figure out why they have to stuff two of us into one of these things," she said, irritably. "It's hard enough to concentrate in this place without having to work, like, shoulder to shoulder."

Gabby started to apologize, but Sarah cut her off. "It's not your fault. I'm not blaming you. We just ought to have more space."

Gabby let it go at that, but once again felt like an intruder.

As she sat at her computer, thinking about the suicide, she tried to list all of obvious but unanswered questions: (1) Who was the guy? (2) Why didn't someone, somewhere, miss him? (3) Who paid the electric, heating, and other bills? (4) Who collected the mail, and from where? (5) Who took care of the yard and the house? And, finally, of course, the big remaining question: *If he didn't kill himself, then who did?*

Her thoughts were interrupted when Sarah turned abruptly and asked, "So what are you working on?"

She was startled. "Just something that Zach and I ran across. It's probably nothing."

"The suicide I've heard about?"

"Yeah."

"Is it true he'd been lying there dead for a year or so?"

Gabby nodded.

"Yuck!" Sarah said, turning back to her desk.

Gabby was relieved she didn't ask more, but found her apparent disinterest a little strange. Had their positions been reversed, she would have wanted to know more.

Nine

Back at the apartment after work, she found Zach already there sitting at the kitchen table, holding in his lap what—at first glance—Gabby thought was a small stuffed animal until it gave a tiny, almost inaudible, growl.

She stopped in her tracks. "What the heck is that?"

Zach laughed. "It's our new roommate."

She came closer and leaned over. "Is that really a dog?"

"Of course," he said, holding him up, balancing him in the palms of his two hands. "A teacup poodle. A rescue dog. I just got him at the pound."

She slid into a chair across from them and heard another low growl. "He's so small," she said. "A baby, for God's sake. He can't weigh more than a couple pounds."

"A little more than four, actually. And this is about as big as he'll get. But you're right, I could barely see him, tucked away in the back of the cage."

She was amazed and amused. "I knew you were looking for a small dog, but this is ridiculous."

"They tell me he was only six ounces or so when he was born ... so he's come a long way in two years."

Gabby walked around the table. "May I hold him?"

"If he'll let you. He's a little skittish from being caged up."

She gently took him from Zach's hand and held him up at eye level, feeling a small shiver pass through his body. "It's OK," she whispered, fondling his drooping ears. "Don't be scared."

It was like holding a squirrel or a kitten, she thought.

He finally nuzzled against her cheek and seemed to relax. The shivers passed. "He *is* cute, I'll give you that," she said, "but it's going to be like walking on egg shells around here. I'm afraid I'll step on him and kill him."

"We'll just have to keep our eyes open, I guess."

By the time she sat down and cradled him in her arms, his eyes were closed and he was dead asleep.

"He's had a long day," Zach said, smiling across the table.

"So have you named him?" she asked.

"Yup."

"What?"

"Guess."

"C'mon! How can I guess?"

"Try."

"OK. Runt."

"He's not a runt. He's full-grown."

"OK. Tiny Tim."

"Demeaning."

"I give up. What is it?"

"Barclay."

Gabby hooted. "Are you serious?"

"Why not? Barclay's been good to me, as a friend as well as a boss. I thought it was appropriate. But don't you tell him, the real Barclay, I mean."

"That's weird. I'll never know who you're talking about, the boss or the dog."

He laughed. "You'll just have to figure it out."

Once Barclay was settled into a makeshift bed, an old laundry basket, they returned to the kitchen, where Gabby filled Zach in on everything that had happened—from her meeting with Cindy Maxwell to her encounter with Sam Ryan to her meeting with John Knowles.

"You've had quite a day," he said.

"I know. I'm beat. And I don't have a lot to show for it."

"What do you mean?"

"Like I've been spinning my wheels..."

"Nice wheels, though."

She shot him a look. "It doesn't feel like I'm getting anywhere. I'm meeting with the cops tomorrow, but I doubt they'll tell me much."

"Maybe there's not much to tell."

"We'll see."

"But at least you've got a place to sit now."

"Yeah. Back to back with Sarah Andrews. And she's not too happy about it."

"Don't worry about her," he said. "She's a short-timer. She'll be out of there as soon as a bigger market comes calling. She has Chicago and New York in her sights."

"Really?" Gabby said, relating how little interest or curiosity she had shown in the suicide story. "It kind of surprised me. I think most reporters would have wanted to know more."

"Doesn't surprise me. I heard about her from my friends at the station in Duluth. She's got about as much substance as a stick of gum."

"I thought Barclay hired only good people."

"Everyone, even Barclay, makes a mistake now and then."

FRESH FROM THE SHOWER, clad in PJs, a robe and slippers, Gabby returned to the living room to find Zach stretched out on the couch, Barclay huddled against his chest.

"He's still sleeping?" she said, moving closer. "Is he ever awake?"

"Give him a break. He woke up for a bite to eat, then dozed off again. He needs his *zzzzs*."

She leaned over them, listening. "He's snoring," she said. "The damn dog's snoring."

"What?" Bending over. "You can hardly hear him."

She slipped into a chair across from them, watching, smiling. "You are cute, the two of you. You look like a proud new papa with a babe in your arms."

"He just needs a little loving," Zach said. "Like all of us."

"Aha," she said, "which reminds me. Remember? You said you'd tell me about your lost love ... or loves."

"I remember, but why would you care?"

"Because I'm a reporter. I'm curious by nature."

"Or nosy."

"Maybe."

"Forget it."

Despite Zach's reluctance to talk about himself, she had managed to learn a fair amount about him in their brief time together: that he'd grown up in northern Minnesota in the Iron Range town of Virginia; that his parents and one brother still lived there; that he'd graduated at the top of his high school class but passed on college to pursue his passion for photography. "I wanted to be a storyteller," he'd told her, "only with pictures, not words. Like a lot of kids, I wanted to go to Hollywood to get into the movie business, but I had no money and decided I'd get my feet wet first in television. And here I am, ten or eleven years later, shooting suicides."

He'd said it with a laugh, but there'd been bitterness in his voice.

She'd tried to argue with him, knowing by now that he was one of the most respected photographers on the staff. But she also knew that newsroom cutbacks had given him fewer and fewer chances to pursue the kind of stories that lit his creative fires, relegating him more and more to spot news—murders, traffic accidents, house fires, and assorted scandals that seemed to be the increasing staple of local television news.

While he said he'd long since given up any thought of going to Hollywood, she knew he had not abandoned his dream of making movies. In fact, he'd paid a few hundred dollars for an option on the movie rights to a small, largely unknown novel involving an unsolved murder in northern Minnesota. But he hadn't told her any more about that than he had about his love life.

"C'mon," she said.

He shook his head, feigning irritation. "So what do you want to know?"

"Everything you're willing to tell me."

He took a deep breath. "OK. Her name is Carolyn. I met her six months or so ago, covering a news conference at the state capitol. She was doing PR for the state transportation department, talking, you know, about road projects, highway budgets, that kind of stuff. Boring, but she was pretty good at it for someone in her twenties. We hit it off right away, at least I thought we did. Dated for a few weeks, but then it ended almost as quickly as it began."

"Ended by whom?" she asked.

"Not by me."

"So what did she say?"

"That I'm too quiet."

"You *are* too quiet," she said.

He grinned. "Maybe so, but you'd think she would have discovered that on our first date, not weeks later. There must have been more to it, but she never explained. There one day, gone the next."

"And broke your heart?"

"Not my heart, just my self-esteem."

"And you haven't dated since?"

"A couple of blind dates, but they went nowhere."

"So?"

"So why do you think I got a dog..."

She laughed. "Seriously..."

By then, Barclay had raised his tiny head off Zach's shoulder, yawned, and closed his eyes again.

"So do you miss it?" she asked.

"What?"

"The ... uhh ... companionship?"

"You mean the sex?"

"Well, that, too, I suppose ... "

"You *are* nosy. Listen, I've had my fill of romances for the moment. I'm just going to concentrate on the job and work on the screenplay for the novel I bought."

"Maybe I could help," she said. "With the screenplay, I mean. I can help write."

"Maybe. We'll see."

Before either could say anything more, the ring-tone on her cell phone sounded. She glanced at the screen, then headed into the kitchen. "Hey, Mom. What's up?"

"I was getting worried about you," her mother said. "Nobody's heard from you. Your sisters are wondering if you're OK."

"I'm fine, Mom. Just busy. Sorry I haven't called."

"Have you found a place? An apartment or something?"

"Not yet. I'm staying with a friend temporarily. A photographer from work. He's offered to let me stay until I can find something of my own."

"He?"

Gabby could hear the surprise in her voice. "Yes, his name's Zach. Nice guy."

Zach, overhearing Gabby's end of the conversation, smiled. He could picture her mom, frowning, wondering if her daughter was safe, or already in the clutches of another bad boyfriend.

When the conversation was over, Gabby returned to the living room. "I think I'll head for bed," she said. "I'm exhausted and I have to meet with the cops in the morning."

"Not yet," he said. "Tit-for-tat, remember? I told you my story; now it's your turn."

"C'mon. It can wait."

"No way. Fair's fair."

Reluctantly, she slumped into a chair, folding her legs beneath her. "OK, but can we please keep it short?"

"Whatever," Zach said, waiting.

"His name's Craig ... " she began.

"Is this the guy who beat on you? Who ended up in jail?"

"Yeah, that's him. Craig Jessup."

"How'd you end up with *him*?"

"Gimme a minute, OK? Like you and your friend Carolyn, I met him covering a story. A year or so ago. One of those demonstrations. You know the scene, a couple hundred protestors trying to block the street, tie up traffic, cause a little chaos. Facing a bunch of cops, with lots of pushing and shoving and shouting, mainly for the benefit of the television cameras. Including mine. Happened damn near every other day for a while, until we all got tired of covering them. Then they stopped."

"So he was one of the protestors?" Zach asked. "Or one of the cops?"

"Neither. He worked for the mayor, one of his deputies, and was there to observe and report back to City Hall. I knew who he was but had never spoken to him until he came on to me after the third or fourth protest. Good-looking guy, smooth as silk, a few years older than me, it turned out, who claimed to be single and fancy-free."

"Not true?"

"Technically, true. But it was only later—after we'd been dating for a few weeks—that I learned from others that he'd been divorced a couple of years before, from an old high school sweetheart. The fact that he hadn't told me should have been my first clue that something was amiss, but by then I thought I was in love. Head over heels, actually."

"Then?"

"Then we moved in together, despite my family's objections

and the advice of some of my friends, who—it turns out—knew more about him that I did, but had always been hesitant to interfere, to get in the way. Love conquers all, you know. I blissfully ignored them, along with some of the other early warning signs."

His eyes narrowed. "What signs?"

She moved over to the couch next to him, taking Barclay from his arms into her own. "Increased possessiveness, for one thing. Always wanting to know where I was and what I was doing when I wasn't with him. At first, I thought it was kind of sweet, you know, loving, but then it started to get on my nerves. He didn't like any of my friends, the few that I had, and was always there to take me to work and pick me up. Stuck to me like a leech on a log. It was like I had no life of my own, that I was just one of his possessions, like his motorcycle or his DVD collection. There was also some verbal abuse—angry words, then apologies, then more angry words.

"I finally woke up one morning, and said, 'Screw this!' I'd become something I knew I wasn't... some kind of love slave to this guy. I told him I wanted out... and got ready to pack up. That's when it got ugly. And that's when I called his ex-wife."

Zach leaned forward. "You did? His ex-wife?"

"Damn right. She was surprised I hadn't called before. Told me she was going to call *me*, to warn me, but was afraid of what might happen if she did."

"To you or to her?"

"She didn't say, but when I told her what was going on with me, there was this silence on the other end of the line. Then, out of the blue, she said, and I quote, 'Get the fuck out of there! Now!'

"I'll spare you the sordid details, but she said by the time their marriage ended she was afraid for her life and fled back to her parents' house. The divorce, she said, was as messy as it could get, but, luckily, there were no kids ... so she came out of it OK."

"Damn," he muttered.

"But that's not the worst of it. Somehow—I still don't know how—he found out about the call and went crazy. Accused me off all kinds of crap and ended up ... well, beating the hell out of me. Most of it in places you couldn't see: two broken ribs, cuts and bruises from my chest to my thighs. I broke my nose and got a black eye when I fell after one of the punches. A neighbor heard the racket and my screams, I guess, and called the cops. The next thing I knew I was in the hospital."

Zach got up and paced the room, cracking his knuckles as he walked. Finally, he stopped and sat back down. "So did they arrest the prick?"

"Of course. And off to jail, charged with third-degree assault. But he was out on bail a couple of hours later, I'm told."

Zach could only shake his head.

"Can I go to bed now?" she asked.

"Are you kidding? Finish. Please."

She leaned her head back on the couch. "Long story short, he managed a plea bargain, thanks to some help from the mayor. He got thirty days in jail, a fine, and a couple of years of probation. I got a restraining order that ordered him to stay away from me, but that didn't stop him from making some disguised threats. Said I hadn't seen the last of him ... that he'd find me wherever I was. That's when I went to Sam Ryan and asked him to get me the hell out of San Jose."

"Have you heard from him since? Does he know you're here?"

"No, I haven't heard from him, and, no, I don't know if he knows where I am. Wouldn't be hard for him to find out, I guess. I did get a new cell phone, changed my e-mail address, got off Facebook and Twitter, traded in my old car for the Explorer, and do try to stay on guard. But who knows? Last I heard, he'd lost his job ... and could be anywhere, I suppose."

"Here?"

"Maybe, but I doubt it. He's a California guy, and like all of us out there, we think of Minnesota as in the middle of nowhere, and cold. That's one of the reasons I asked to come here, because I thought it would be one of the last places he'd follow me to."

"So what kind of loony tune is this guy?"

"Your guess is as good as mine, but while I was in the hospital they had me meet with a domestic abuse counselor—a psychologist—who asked me to describe what had happened. After hearing me out, he said that while he hadn't yet met or talked to Craig, it sounded to him like he might be a classic case of a psychopathic deviate...somebody with an anti-social personality disorder. Sort of the ultimate narcissist...who thinks only of himself, who likes to control relationships, often with violence or threats of violence. That was certainly true of me."

"Does Barclay know about this?"

"None of the details, and I don't want him to know. It's my problem, not his or yours."

"Have you got a picture of this dude?"

"Of course."

"I'd like to have it."

"Why?"

"Because four eyes are better than two."

"I told you, I don't want you involved."

"You're living here. I am involved."

He reached over and took Barclay back. "Now go to bed, OK? Try to get some sleep."

"Gladly," she said.

Easier said than done, she thought.

As she lay with her head buried in the pillow, surrounded by the silence of the apartment outside her closed door and the muted sounds of traffic beyond her window, Gabby could think only of what she had *not* told Zach:

Of the malevolent grin on Craig's face before he struck the first blow; of the crunching, penetrating pain of that blow to her mid-section; of the first scream that somehow lay throttled in her throat.

Of her utter disbelief that this could be happening to her.

In her time as a reporter she had covered more than her share of stories of domestic violence, of women who had been tormented verbally and emotionally, then tortured physically.

Stories of love for a man that was turned inside-out, upside-down, in an instant of irrational anger and violence.

But she'd thought it could never, ever, happen to her. She was too strong, too independent, too proud.

Yet it had, in one blistering moment.

A moment that would forever change who she was ... and who she is. That whatever her life was before, it would never be the same again. No matter what. No matter where.

Ten

Despite sleeping little and fitfully with those images of Craig Jessup floating in the darkness, Gabby was on time the next morning to meet John Knowles outside the Homicide office at City Hall. As she approached him down the long hallway toward Room 108, the first thing she heard from his lips was a low wolf whistle.

"Don't be an old geezer," she said, managing a grin.

"Perfect," he said, looking her up and down.

True to her word, she had dressed for the occasion: a low-cut blouse, the only push-up bra she owned, and a pair of tight-fitting jeans. "I feel like I ought to be out walking the streets," she said.

"You'll knock 'em dead," he replied, approvingly, but before opening the door to the office, he quickly briefed her. "As I told you, you'll be meeting Lieutenant Winslow, the head of Homicide, a guy Barclay and I worked with in the cold-case investigation of Barclay's old high school classmate. He's a good man, but I don't know how much he knows about this mystery suicide of ours."

"OK," she said.

"He told me he'd have a Detective John Philips with him. He's one of the cops assigned to the case, so he may have filled him in by now. We'll see."

"So how much do we tell them about our own investigation?" she asked.

"As little as possible. Let them do most of the talking."

Once inside the waiting room, they cooled their heels for about twenty minutes before they were ushered into Winslow's office—which was more spacious and less austere than Gabby had expected. There were even a couple of paintings on the walls and two tasteful pieces of pottery on the credenza. Winslow was standing by his desk, waiting, and quickly introduced himself and Detective Philips—who, living up to Knowles's prediction, gave Gabby an appreciative once-over, including, she noticed, a quick glance down her blouse.

The two cops were a study in contrasts. Winslow was squat with a graying crew-cut, broad shoulders, a disappearing neck, and biceps that strained the fabric of his shirt. His hands were huge, but his grip soft, like his eyes, which Gabby found surprising. Philips was a third again as tall, as lanky as Winslow was stubby, with a lean face, a nose that was a trifle too long, a quizzical smile, and brownish-blond hair that was cut to fall where it wanted. He was, Gabby decided, a few centimeters short of handsome, but yards away from ugly.

"Good to see you again, John," Winslow said. "How's our friend Barclay doing?"

"Doing well," Knowles replied, smiling. "Married, since the last time you saw him, but hasn't lost a step. Still runs a hell of a newsroom."

After spending a moment recalling a few details of the old case, Winslow said, "So I hear you're interested in this John Doe suicide."

"If it is a suicide," Knowles said. "We'd like to hear your take on it."

"What do you mean 'if'?" Philips said. "We think it's pretty clear-cut."

"Really?" Gabby said, quickly. "And why's that?"

Philips looked at Winslow, then back at Knowles and Gabby. "Are we on or off the record here?"

"Better on than off," Knowles replied. "But you tell us."

"Off," Philips said. Then, "To answer your question, there's no real evidence that points to anything but a suicide. And I don't quite get why you're pursuing this."

Not wanting to challenge him, Gabby simply asked, "Have you identified him yet?"

Philips again glanced at Winslow. "No, not yet."

"Don't you find that a little strange?" she pressed. "What, almost a week after you found the body?"

"You're new in town, aren't you?"

She nodded.

"Then you wouldn't know that the medical examiner handles about four thousand deaths a year in this county alone. Ten or twelve percent of them—four to five hundred—are suicides. Got that? Four to five hundred a year."

"But how many of those go unidentified?" she pressed.

That gave him pause. "I'm not sure, but we'll ID him eventually. Just takes time."

She was not done, despite a warning look from Knowles. "And how many of those suicides lie undiscovered for a year or more? With no one coming forward to claim the body? To report him missing?"

"It happens," Philips said.

"How often?"

"You'd have to ask the M.E., but probably not that often," he admitted.

At this point, Winslow decided to intervene. "So what have we got here? Sounds to me like you're playing cop. That you've got reasons of your own to believe it's not a suicide. That this guy, this John Doe, was what? Murdered? Spare me."

Before Gabby could respond, Knowles held up his hand. "We don't know what to think, frankly. That's why we're here. Seems to us, Gabby, Barclay, and others at the station, that there are too many unanswered questions. And that you—no offense—have pretty much pushed it to the bottom of the pile."

"Listen," Winslow said, his voice sharper now, showing anger, "we've had a dozen homicides already this year, and we're not even into the heat of summer. Who knows how many more we'll get? It wasn't that many years ago the press was calling this 'Murderapolis,' and it's my job to see that it doesn't happen again. So I've got to use the people I've got in the best way I know how. And that doesn't mean chasing phantom suicides. Get it?"

He'd said all of that while barely taking a breath.

"Hold on, Eric," Knowles said. "We're not here to piss you off. We just think there may be a story here. You have to admit it's a strange case, with more questions than answers. We'd like to cooperate, if we could. But we'd need your help."

"Like what?" Philips demanded.

"With some of those answers," Gabby said. "Like I assume you've found no fingerprint or DNA match. No personal belongings. No match on any missing person reports. If you've checked all of that, there's no sense in us trying. You've got all the tools."

Philips and Winslow listened, but did not dispute her assumptions.

To strengthen her case, she was tempted to tell them about the mysterious Chrysler 300 and the spotlight in the backyard. But she decided against it for now. Instead, she said, "We've already checked county records and discovered the house is owned by a corporation, Zimbronics, Inc. But their offices are located in Delaware, with no local address. And the phone number in Delaware is out of service. That's as far as we've been able to get so far ..."

With a glance at his boss, Philips said, "Well, you're ahead of us. We haven't had the time to do even that much."

Gabby pressed on. "So you don't know who's keeping the

house up, who's mowing the grass, paying the bills ... "

"No, none of that," he said, growing irritation in his voice. "It hasn't been a priority."

"Then you don't mind if we keep going," Knowles said, "without getting in your face."

"OK, OK," Winslow said, finally. "Here's the deal. Detective Philips will try to keep you in the loop, assuming we come up with something. And assuming you will return the favor. But I don't want to see anything on the ten o'clock news accusing the cops of not doing our jobs, of screwing up an investigation, of you guys solving a mystery that we couldn't solve. Understood?"

"Understood," Knowles said. "But we'll have to talk to Barclay first."

"Do that," Winslow said. "And give him my regards."

As they left the office and were closing the door behind them, Gabby paused long enough to hear a whispered, "Nice ass," coming from back inside.

She smiled, but gave Knowles a sharp elbow to the ribs.

EMERGING FROM CITY HALL to begin the ten-block walk back to the station, they found the morning had turned blustery and cool, with a hint of rain in the air. Glancing at the gathering clouds, Knowles asked, "Want to take the skyways? Or my jacket?"

"No, let's stick to the sidewalks," she replied, wrapping her arms around her body against the chill. "The fresh air feels good."

They'd said nothing for the first block until Gabby suddenly stopped and said, "So what do we tell Barclay?"

"About what?"

"About the idea of working handin glove with the cops on this."

"He won't like it, but he'll understand, if there's no other way. He did it himself in that old case we were talking about."

"Tell me more about that," she said. "I've only heard bits and pieces."

"That's because it's a long story."

"We've got time," she said, resuming her pace.

"OK, I'll make it as short as possible. As you may have heard, it began when he went to his twenty-fifth high school reunion in hopes of seeing a girl that he'd had a long-distance crush on back then, only to find—to his shock and chagrin— that she'd been raped and murdered almost twenty years before, a case that was still unsolved. In time, he was persuaded by some of the dead girl's friends to take up where the police had left off. He got me involved, along with a retired St. Paul cop and a young Ramsey County detective who was handling the cold case.

"In the end, using his own intuition and pursuing leads the police had never followed, he was able to track down the killer. But in the process, he was damn near beaten to death, and another woman—who is now his wife—was taken hostage by the bad guy and threatened with death herself. It was all pretty scary, trust me."

"Wow," was all she could think to say.

"We aired the story the night it all ended. I've got it in the archives back at the station if you'd like to see it."

"I'd like that," she said, absorbing yet another piece of the George Barclay legend.

AT THAT MOMENT, Zach stood nervously just inside Barclay's office. "Have you got a minute, George?"

"Sure. What's up?"

"I probably shouldn't be here," Zach said. "And Gabby would be pissed if she knew I was."

"Sit down, Zach. And speak."

He sat on the edge of the guest chair. "Did you know that Gabby got beat up a few months ago? Ended up in the hospital?"

"Just that," Barclay said. "Nothing more. She didn't want to talk about it."

"Well, I got her to tell me about it, and it isn't pretty," repeating much of what Gabby had told him the night before. "Reason I'm here is that she doesn't know where this guy is. He could be here, for all she knows."

"And you're worried?" Barclay said.

"A little. He sounds like a mean bastard. Made some threats. I just wanted you to be aware. Maybe alert some of the other folks in the newsroom without getting her pissed off."

Barclay leaned back and looked out into the newsroom. It was no secret that TV reporters and anchors, usually women, were sometimes the target of stalkers thanks to their visibility and, often, to their good looks. He knew that years before he'd arrived at Channel 7, a stalker of a female anchor had committed suicide in the lobby when confronted by police and that years earlier a young anchorwoman in Iowa had been abducted—and probably murdered—in a case that was still unsolved.

So the dangers could be real and were not to be ignored. Still, he didn't want to overreact, to cause an unnecessary stir that might do more harm than good. "I need to think about this," he finally said. "But you were right in coming to me, and I'll do what you say. Get the word out without causing a commotion. You have a picture of this guy?"

"Yeah. She gave me one."

"Good. Make some copies. And thanks for coming in."

"No problem," Zach said. "I hope it amounts to nothing."

"Me, too," Barclay said, while trying to ignore the sudden queasiness in the pit of his stomach.

Eleven

Gabby could sense the eyes of the newsroom follow her as she headed for her cubicle, staring at her strange morning attire, making her feel more than ever like a street-walker strutting her stuff. The only thing missing was a pair of spiked heels.

She knew now that she should have gone home to change clothes or brought a change with her.

Damn you, Knowles, she thought.

When she got to her desk, Sarah Andrews looked up. "Jesus," she exclaimed. "Did you come straight from the club?"

"What club?" Gabby said, already irritated.

"Whichever. Just looks like you were out all night and never went home."

Gabby settled into her chair. "May be hard to believe, but Knowles asked me to dress like this. To impress some cops."

"I'll bet you had them panting," Andrews laughed.

"I don't know about that, but I did hear one of them say I had a nice ass. So that's something."

"Did it help?"

"You never know," Gabby replied, turning to her own desk to quickly check her messages. There were only two: one from the assistant M.E., Cindy Maxwell, asking her to call, and the second from John Philips, the detective she'd left only a half-hour before, asking if she'd like to meet for a drink, to discuss their "new cooperation."

Turning back to Andrews, she said, with a grin, "What d'ya know? It may have worked."

CINDY MAXWELL PICKED up on the first ring. After an exchange of greetings, Cindy tol d her, "I'm thinking of hiring an artist to try and depict what our John Doe might have looked like before the bullet took half his head off."

"Really?"

"Yeah. And if we do, would you consider broadcasting the picture in hope that somebody might recognize him?"

That gave Gabby pause. "I suppose you'd also ask the other stations?"

"Probably so, yes," Maxwell replied. "To get the widest exposure."

Which Gabby knew would mean every other station in town would know about the story, if there was one. Goodbye to any hopes of having it alone. "I'm sure we would," she finally said, "but could you hold off a few days?"

"I guess so, but why?"

"Because we're now working with the cops in hopes of using some other means to identify him. But it may take some time."

Maxwell wasn't fooled. "You want to keep the story for yourself."

"That, too," Gabby admitted.

"I respect that, but I don't want to wait too long. We can't keep him in the freezer forever. This guy may have a family somewhere out there, and it'd be nice for them to know sooner rather than later that dear old dad is dead and gone."

Gabby muffled a laugh. "I hear you. I'll be back in touch in a few days."

"Good. I'll be waiting here among my clients."

Before she could hang up, Gabby said, "One more thing. Do you have a picture of that tattoo on the guy's ankle that you told me about?"

"Of course."

"It's a flag or something, right?"

"That's what it looks like," she replied. "But I haven't pursued it."

"Could you e-mail me a copy?"

"Sure. I guess so."

"Thanks. I'll talk to you soon."

As she hung up the phone, Barclay was once again waiting outside of Sam Ryan's office, biding his time and holding his temper until Ryan finally emerged. "You always catch me on the run, George," Ryan said, irritably. "What is it now?"

"It'll just take a minute," Barclay said, following him back into his office. "Seems like you forgot to tell me something else about Gabby."

Ryan looked puzzled. "What's that?"

"That she asked you to get her the hell out of San Jose. That she'd been beat up and threatened by some goofball of a boyfriend. And that's why you brought her here."

Ryan looked surprised. "How did you find out about that? She made me promise not to say anything … to anybody, including you. She wanted a fresh start."

Barclay leaned over the desk. "How I found out isn't important, but this is: she has no idea of where this dude is. That he's threatened to find her, that he could be here now, for all we know."

Ryan sat back in his chair. "I knew none of that. I do know the guy served some time in jail … and got probation. But that's all. She never told me about the threats. Just that she wanted out of San Jose."

"OK, but here's what I want you to do," Barclay said. "You must know everybody who's anybody in San Jose, including the mayor, who this Jessup guy worked for. Use your contacts, find out what you can about where he is now ... what he's doing ... if he's living up to his probation ... "

"I don't have time for that," Ryan protested. "Shit, I've got a station to run, a boss to keep happy."

"Make the time," Barclay pleaded. "Or I'll send one of our reporters to San Jose to do it for you." He paused for a breath. "Now that we know of a possible threat, however remote it might be, we can't ignore it. If something were to happen ... "

"All right. Relax. I think you're way ahead of yourself on this, but I've got to go back for a management meeting next week and I'll check around. But I make no promises. I think it could be a wild goose chase."

"Maybe so, but thanks," Barclay said.

BEFORE SHE RETURNED the detective's call, Gabby tried to remember if he'd been wearing a ring. The fact that she *hadn't* noticed probably said something about where her head was right now. All work, no play. And what the hell? Married or single, makes no difference. This isn't a date, just a drink with a cop who might be helpful in the future.

After three tries, she finally reached him, and they agreed to meet after work at Brit's, an English-style pub that was a favorite station hangout just down the Mall. "But not before 6:30," she told him. "I've gotta watch the news."

"Fine with me," he said. "I'll see you then unless I get called out on something."

AN HOUR LATER she was in her Explorer, headed for the mystery house in northeast Minneapolis to try, once again, to find any of John Doe's neighbors who might know something more about him. The chances were slim, she knew, but she felt she had to make the effort one more time.

To escape the newsroom, she'd convinced Harry Wilson to let her go home to change from her slut clothes into something decent. Once there, she'd not only done that, but also took time to give Barclay (the poodle) some fresh water and a short walk.

She'd simply neglected to tell Wilson about this other side trip.

Now, as she pulled up in front of the house, the first thing she saw was a small moving van parked next door at old Clarence Pedersen's place. Walking up the sidewalk, she was met at the front door by Clarence and a younger woman, whom she immediately guessed was the daughter he had mentioned on their first visit.

Clarence, still with his ponytail, was dressed in a shabby gray suit, a wrinkled white shirt, and a blue tie that hung loosely under his chin. He struggled down the steps, one hand on his cane, the other on the arm of the woman.

"Hello, Clarence," Gabby said, "you remember me? Gabby Gooding, from Channel 7?"

Clarence's body might be frail, but his memory was strong. "Of course," he replied, "you were with that nice young fella, Zach."

Gabby held out her hand to the woman. "And I bet you're Clarence's daughter. He mentioned you the first time we met."

The woman looked puzzled, but returned the handshake. "Nice to meet you, and you're right, I am one of his daughters, Margaret Eldridge. But I'm afraid we don't have a lot of time."

The old man pointed at the moving van. "See. Didn't I tell you? They're selling the house and moving me to a nursing home. That's where we're headin' now."

"That was quick."

"He finally took one fall too many," the daughter said, a slight irritation in her voice. "Two days ago, he lay on the floor, helpless, for six hours before one of us finally found him. He could have broken a hip, or worse. It was time to get him out of the house and into someplace safe. And," with a turn of the head, "away from that spooky place next door."

"I understand," Gabby said, stepping aside to let them pass.

But Clarence was not ready to leave. "Almost forgot. A cop stopped by to ask about you and your friend."

"A cop?" she said.

"Yup. Said his name was Sergeant Preston. I remember because, you know…"

She shook her head.

"Sergeant Preston, the Canadian Mounties…his horse, Rex…his dog, Yukon King…"

Gabby had no clue.

"You're too young, I guess. Kind of a pudgy guy, curly hair, with a nose flat as a skipping stone. Even flashed his badge for me."

"When?" she asked.

"A day or so after you were here. One morning."

"Did you see his car?"

"Yeah. A big black one. Don't know the make, but it was long and black. Looked too fancy for a cop car, you ask me. And another cop was inside, I think."

"So what did he want to know?"

"Your names. Knew you were from television."

"Did you tell him? Our names?"

"Sure. Showed him Zach's card. But I could only remember your first name. Hell, he was a cop."

His daughter was growing impatient. "C'mon, Dad, we have to go."

"Please. Another minute," Gabby said. Then, "What else did he ask?"

"What you talked to me about. About the dead guy next door. I just told him what I had told you and the others cops, earlier. That was it."

Gabby walked down the sidewalk with them, watching as his daughter helped him into her car.

"May I ask where you're going?"

"To a place called Comfort Care in south Minneapolis," the daughter replied. "He'll be safe there."

Gabby leaned into the car window. "Good luck to you, Clarence, and thanks for everything."

He gave her a smile and a wave, but then looked away, his smile crumbling as they started down his street for the last time.

As she stood at the curb and watched the car turn the corner, Gabby noticed a woman across the street, kneeling next to a flower bed, almost hidden in the shade of an over-hanging maple tree. She crossed over, shuffling her feet on the pavement in hopes the woman, whose back was turned to her, would hear her approach and not be startled.

When that didn't work, she paused on the sidewalk and half-shouted, "Hello, there. Excuse me."

The woman turned and looked up. She was wearing jeans, a broad straw hat, work gloves—and a smile. "Yes," she said, getting up off her knees.

Gabby walked closer and introduced herself.

"From Channel 7?" the woman said. "Really? That's my favorite station." Then, looking more closely at Gabby, "But I haven't seen you on the news."

"I'm new in town. I haven't been on the air yet."

The woman took off her gloves and shook Gabby's hand. "I'm Angela Metlove," she said. "I saw you talking to old Clarence and his daughter. It's so sad that he's leaving. And so sudden."

"I know," Gabby replied.

Angela appeared to be in her fifties, slightly pudgy but well-tanned and healthy-looking, with a cheerfulness that seemed to wrap its arms around you. "So what can I do for you?" she asked, still smiling.

"Have you lived here long?" Gabby asked, glancing at the small bungalow.

"Only a couple of years. Moved here after our kids went

off to college. We needed to downsize and," looking over her shoulder, "we found this little house."

"I'm interested in the man across the street," Gabby said. "The one they found dead a few days ago ... "

"That's what I figured," Angela replied. "I saw your news car here the other day."

"Did you know him?"

"No, never met him. Never saw him. We thought the place was vacant. Owned by a bank or something."

"Did any of your neighbors know him?"

"Not that I know of, but we don't know many of the neighbors. Except for Clarence. As I said, we haven't been here that long, and there's been a lot of turnover in the neighborhood. People coming and going. We tend to keep to ourselves."

"So," Gabby said, glancing across the street, "did you ever see any activity over there?"

"Only the lawn service. They'd come once a week. Mow the lawn, water the grass, trim the bushes when needed. Kept the place looking good."

"Do you remember the name?"

"Sure. Green & Grow Lawn Care. Green and black truck."

"No other deliveries or other things like that?"

"Not that I can think of. But, like I said, we thought the place was vacant."

Gabby thanked her and gave her one of her cards. "Call me if you see anything unusual, OK?"

The woman took the card and studied it. "So why are you so interested?" she asked. "We heard it was a simple suicide."

"Probably was," Gabby replied. "But we thought it deserved another look."

By the time she pulled away from the curb, her iPhone had told her the Green & Grow lawn service was located in the northeast suburb of Columbia Heights along Central Avenue, according to her GPS. She briefly debated going there, but decided against it—knowing she was already behind schedule. Later, she thought.

More important than the location of the lawn service was the information Clarence had provided that the phony cops now knew Zach's name and phone numbers. Learning where he (they) lived, she thought, would be an easy next step, if they cared to take it.

Even more reason to be on the alert.

She tried to reach Zach on his cell but got no answer. She left a message, briefly describing her conversation with Clarence, telling him to take care.

Even then she had an odd sense of foreboding, confirmed only later when she would learn that the message had come too late.

BARCLAY WIGGLED IN Zach's arms, licking his face, eager for his walk, as they rode the elevator down from his apartment. Zach had to struggle to hook up his leash before they stepped outside into the bright, sunny, afternoon.

He had no more than put Barclay down on the sidewalk and taken a step when he was suddenly and roughly slammed against the wall of the building, his breath coming out in a gush, instant pain penetrating his shoulder like the tip of an arrow. "What the…?"

The attack was so sudden, so unexpected, so out of nowhere, that he thought for a moment he'd been hit by a car. He fell to his knees, trying to suck back his breath, momentarily paralyzed by the shock.

But there was no car. Standing above him, legs spread, was a guy the size of a fullback, a small smile playing across his lips. In one violent spasm, he grabbed Zach's hair, yanked him to his feet and shot his knee into his groin. As Zach screamed and fell back in agony, the man grabbed the leash and—with a grunt—viciously kicked Barclay across the sidewalk and into the wall. The dog landed with a tortuous yelp at Zach's feet.

All of this happened in less than thirty seconds.

Zach fought to ignore the pain and to focus, but when he did, he found the man's face inches from his own, his breath hot like the fumes from an exhaust pipe. "Mind your own business, asshole. Or next time, I'll stuff that little dog up your ass."

By now a small crowd had formed, standing back, not sure of what they had just seen. But the man paid no heed, slowly strolling off, as if without a care, leaving Zach and his moaning dog in a heap on the sidewalk.

WHEN SHE GOT BACK to the newsroom, Gabby again found Harry Wilson waiting, again looking upset. He led her into a small conference room off the assignment desk. "Took quite a while to change your clothes," he said.

"I didn't know I was being timed," she replied, testily.

"Don't be smart. Where've you been?"

"I decided to make another stop at the suicide house. Met another neighbor."

"You should have called. I need to know where you are."

She sank into a chair, trying to stay calm. "Jesus, Harry! What is the deal? Do you babysit every reporter like this?"

"No, just you. Barclay's orders."

"What?" She bolted out of her chair, ready to head for Barclay's office.

"Sit down, Gabby. And listen."

She sat back. "I'm listening."

Wilson moved in closer. "Barclay briefed a few of us on your troubles in San Jose. The old boyfriend on the loose ... "

"Oh, my God," she whispered, searching the newsroom. "Where is Zach? I'll kill him."

"Relax. Zach was worried. So is Barclay. All of us are. Shit happens, and we don't want it happening to you."

"I should never have said anything. I can take care of myself."

"Really?" Wilson said. "That's not what I heard."

"That was a one-time thing. I learned my lesson. It won't happen again."

"You sure?"

She didn't have a ready answer.

Wilson went on. "Until we know where this guy is and what he may be up to, Barclay wants to err on the side of caution. Wants someone with you whenever possible or, shy of that, to know where you are while you're on the job."

She could only shake her head, fighting off her anger. "I thought I left all of that behind in San Jose."

"Only a few of us know," Wilson said. "And that's how it will stay. Trust me."

"I just want to do my job. That's all I've ever wanted to do."

"This won't keep you from doing that. But we'd like you to keep staying with Zach, if you would, until we sort this all out."

"That's fine, if I don't murder him first."

Wilson laughed.

She got up and looked out into the newsroom. "Where is he, by the way?"

"Don't know," Wilson said. "We didn't have anything for him, so he took off early."

"Strange. I left a message for him."

Twelve

By the time Gabby got to Brit's, the place was packed—
virtually every table was occupied, with standing room
only at the bar. She stood just inside the door, allowing her
eyes to adjust from the bright sunlight outside to the dim-
mer light inside, hoping to spot Philips in the crowd. While
she saw a couple of familiar faces from the station, there was
no sign of the detective. After a minute or two, as she was
about to thread her way through the maze in search of him,
she heard the door behind her open and felt a hand on her
shoulder.

"Hey," he said, as she turned, "Glad you could make it. A
table just opened up outside. Is that OK?"

"Great," she replied, looking back into the din of the bar.
"It's crazy in there."

Philips led her to a table on the sidewalk patio, protected
by an umbrella from the late afternoon sun. He held the chair
for her, then took a seat across the table. Despite herself, the
first thing she did was glance at his left hand.

No ring.

After sitting quietly for a few moments, he said, "Before
we talk business, tell me a little about yourself."

Not again, she thought. Then, sighing, "Only after you."

He smiled. "OK. But it may put you to sleep."

"Try me."

At that moment, the waitress arrived to take their orders. A Bud Light for her, an Alaskan Pale Ale for him. And an order of rings.

"Typical Minnesota story," he said, when she'd left. "Grew up on a farm down south. Graduated from Mankato State with a degree in law enforcement. Worked for a couple of years with one of the suburban police departments, then here in Minneapolis for the past six years, the last two of them in Homicide."

Makes him in his early thirties, she thought.

As he'd talked, she noticed for the first time a slim, almost invisible, scar running from the tip of one ear to the base of his neck. *Surgery or injury?* she wondered. And his eyes, she saw now, were a deeper, more penetrating blue than she had first realized, rarely blinking, giving him an intensity that she imagined would be intimidating for a perp sitting across from him.

"You always wanted to be a cop?"

"Not always. But if you pick enough rocks out of the fields, and ride the beans often enough, you'll want to be anything but a farmer."

She grinned. "But your family's still on the farm?"

"Yup. They love it as much as I hated it."

Once the beers and rings arrived, he asked, "So how about you?"

With another sigh, she quickly repeated the same story she'd told so often since arriving, concentrating on her journalistic experience, deleting most personal details, getting through it as quickly as she could. Then, hoping to move on, she said, "I have to tell you, I was surprised to get your call so soon after our meeting. You didn't strike me as all that interested in any cooperation."

He took a moment. "You're right, but to be honest, you

were correct about one thing. We *had* pushed John Doe to the bottom of the pile. My partner and I are up to our asses ... our necks ... in work: two unsolved homicides on the north side, along with a cold case going back ten years that we're trying to solve. So we thought we could take our time on this."

"What changed your mind?"

"You did," he admitted. "The questions you raised. The points you made. Pissed me off at the time, but you were right. We should have been asking the same questions and trying harder to get the answers. My boss agreed. Gave me crap after you left."

Before she could respond, he went on. "But it was more than that. I couldn't escape the feeling that you knew more than you were telling us. Whatever it is, it's convinced you and your partners that something's screwy here. Am I right?"

She sat quietly, debating. To tell or not to tell? How far to trust him?

"You're pretty perceptive," she finally said.

"So tell me."

"OK," she said, quickly recalling for him their encounters with the Chrysler 300 outside the house, the strange light from the back yard, and the counterfeit cop who met with Clarence. "Seems clear that somebody wants this to go away, who doesn't like us poking around ... "

"My God," he said, "why didn't you tell us this before?"

"Because we're reporters and you're cops. We're not supposed to mix. Until now, I guess."

"But this changes everything."

"We agree. That's why we came to you. There's only so much we can do ourselves."

"What did he look like? This cop?"

She gave him the description that Clarence had given her. "He also said he saw a light on inside the house the night we got the spotlight in our eyes."

"So?"

"So somebody got inside. He must have had a key."

"So?"

"So what was he doing in there? What was he looking for? Or trying to retrieve? Maybe your forensic guys missed something."

"Jesus..."

"C'mon, you're the cop. Isn't there a chance that whoever was in there may have left fingerprints? On the door handle? The light switch? Who knows where."

Philips could only shake his head. "So you'd like me to bring the forensic team out there again?"

"Up to you, of course. May be too late, but it might be worth a try."

"I've got to think about this," he said. "Talk to my partner. To the boss."

"That's fine, but remember, this is our story...if it turns out to be a story. We don't want every other station or newspaper in town jumping on it. No leaks, OK?"

"You've got my word."

"One other thing," she said, and told him about her visit with the neighbor across the street. "I thought about going to the lawn service myself, but knew they'd probably flip me off. Why wouldn't they? But with a cop along, they might be more cooperative."

He thought for a moment. "Unless something comes up, I could meet you there in the morning."

"Good. How about ten o'clock?"

They quickly finished their beers and rings, and after a quick shake of hands, they parted ways, each heading in their own direction.

He, she noticed, never bothered to look back at her allegedly nice ass.

By the time she got back to the apartment it had turned dark outside.

Once inside, she was surprised to find it also dark, the only light coming from a small lamp over the stove in the kitchen. Before she could turn on an overhead light, she saw Zach lying on the couch, half hidden by the shadows.

"Zach?"

No answer.

She hit the switch, the light erasing the shadows, causing Zach to quickly turn his face away.

Still in the doorway, she said, "Zach, what's going on?"

From the couch, "Kill the light, OK?"

"What?"

"Kill the light."

She did as she was told, then walked slowly toward the couch, settling down next to his legs, leaning over him. "Are you sick or something?"

"No," he said.

Only then, as he turned toward her, could she see his reddened eyes, one tear still clinging to his cheek. "What the hell's happened?" she demanded. Then, looking around, "Where's Barclay?"

He raised himself up. "At the vet."

"*What? Why?*"

"Because he got kicked half-way across the sidewalk. Like a fucking football."

"What are you talking about? Tell me!"

He swallowed hard. "I came home to give him some food and a walk. We were no more than out of the front door when some guy came up behind us, threw me against the building, and sent Barclay flying."

She stared at him, disbelieving.

"It happened so fast ... so goddamned fast ... that I was, like, what the hell? Barclay was moaning, lying there against the wall, curled up. I looked up. The guy was still there, a big smirk on his face. Before I could do anything, he pulled me up by my hair, kneed me in the balls, and said, 'Mind your own business, asshole.' Then he walked away, like nothing had happened."

"My God! Are you OK? How is Barclay?"

"He's alive, for now at least. Some lady stopped, knew where a vet was, and helped me get him there as quick as we could. He's got a ruptured spleen, internal bleeding, a bruised liver. No broken ribs. Thank God, they got him into surgery right away and got the bleeding stopped. He's resting now. They're supposed to call me when they know more."

She held back her anger. "It's my fault. I tried to call you, left a message, to warn you. I should have tried again."

"What message? Warn me about what?"

She quickly told him about Clarence's encounter with the make-believe cop a couple of days before. "Clarence gave him your card. He must have figured out where you lived from that."

"Jesus, Gabby, what have we got ourselves into here? That guy could have put a knife into me instead of his knee!"

She got up and wandered the room. "*We* haven't gotten ourselves into anything," she finally said. "*I've* gotten us into this. It's my fault, all of it."

"Bullshit! I've been pushing it as much as you."

"What did the guy look like?"

His description matched the one Clarence had given her, the same as she had passed on to Philips. "I've got to call him," she said. "I'm supposed to see him in the morning, but this can't wait. And Barclay's going to kill us when he hears about it."

"We won't tell him," Zach said. "Not yet. Let's see what your cop says first."

She sat back down again, noticing for the first time the bag of ice between his legs. "So how bad are *you* hurting?"

He gave her an exaggerated grimace. "Lemme put it this way. I wouldn't try getting romantic with me."

"No chance of that," she replied with a grin.

They were interrupted by Zach's phone. "Yes," he said, listening. Finally, "OK, I'll be there in the morning."

"The vet?" she asked.

"Yeah. He's doing OK. They've got him sedated. They took out his spleen, but he apparently can get along without that, I guess. They'll know more tomorrow."

"Poor thing," she said. "I'm so sorry."

"Not your fault. Not anybody's fault. Except for the prick who kicked him."

Later, after she'd called Detective Philips and was getting ready for bed, she stopped by the open bathroom door—as Zach stood at the sink, brushing his teeth. "I've got a confession to make," she said.

"What's that?" he said, slurring, his mouth still full of toothpaste.

"When I came home, before I spotted you on the couch, I was ready to be really pissed off at you."

"About?"

"About you going to Barclay, telling him about my problems in San Jose."

He rinsed his mouth and leaned back against the sink. "Sorry you were pissed, but I don't think I had much choice. "

She stood against the doorjamb, listening.

"If something would happen to you," he said, "and I hadn't said anything to anybody, I'd have trouble living with myself. Barclay and a few others in the newsroom had to know about it. You're part of the family now. We watch out for each other."

"But … "

"No buts," he said. "It's a done deal. Get over it."

Thirteen

The Green & Grow Lawn Care was not difficult to spot. Two of its green and black trucks were parked in front of a low-slung building in a strip mall along Central Avenue. The building was flanked on one side by a self-service laundromat, on the other by a Chinese take-out restaurant.

Gabby pulled up in front and quickly spotted Detective Philips across the parking lot, standing next to a police cruiser with Columbia Heights Police stenciled on its door. He waved her over and introduced her to a uniformed officer by the name of Jeff Maloney who looked like he was about twelve years old. "This is out of my jurisdiction," Philips said, "so I thought we ought to have a little local support."

"Good idea," Gabby said, shaking Maloney's hand.

"So how is your friend's dog?" Philips asked before going further.

"I don't know any more than I told you last night," she said. "The vet hadn't called when I left this morning. We're hoping for the best."

"Good," he said. "I've already explained things to Officer Maloney, so let's get started."

The lawn care office was housed in one large room divided by a counter with a desk and several file cabinets behind it. At the desk was a heavy-set man with about a three-day growth of a graying beard. He seemed more curious than startled when they came through the door, Officer Maloney leading the way.

"What's this about?" he said as he got up and walked to the counter.

Maloney quickly introduced Philips and Gabby, not mentioning that she was a reporter.

The man's name, he told them, was Jerry Neville, the owner of the place.

Philips took over. "We're interested in one of the homes you service in northeast Minneapolis on St. Agnes Avenue. Know the one I'm talking about?"

"Sure," Neville said. "Where they found the dead guy."

"So you heard about that," Philips said.

"Sure. A neighbor told one of my men when he came to do the lawn, day before yesterday."

"Which neighbor?"

"I don't know. You'd have to ask Jesse, but he's out on a job now."

"Did you know the owner of the house?" Philips asked.

"No, never met him."

"Did any of your men?"

"Not that I know of." He leaned across the counter. "But why all the questions? Isn't the dead guy the owner?"

"We're not sure. That's why we're here."

"I don't think I can help you. We made the deal over the phone. Cash in advance for a year of lawn care and snow removal."

"He mailed you the money?"

"Yup. A cashier's check for a thousand bucks. Said he's out of town a lot and didn't want to worry about the lawn in the summer and the snow in the winter. Which was fine with me. A bird in the hand, you know."

Philips thought for a moment. "Did he say how you could reach him? A phone number, an e-mail, or something?"

"Nope. Just said if there were any problems, he'd get in touch with me. Haven't heard from him since."

"And when do the thousand bucks run out?"

"In September. The fifteenth. So I guess we'll just keep mowing and watering until then."

Gabby leaned across the counter. "Didn't that seem strange to you? Making a deal like that?"

"A little, I suppose. But who's to argue? Like I said, a bird in the hand."

"Did you ask him to sign a contract or something?"

"Why would I? I had his money."

She gave a frustrated glance at Philips. Then, "Do you remember the phone call? When you made the deal?"

"Not really."

"Nothing distinctive about his voice?" she pressed.

The question seemed to take him aback. "Now that you mention it, he did sound a little rough. Gruff, I mean. And in a hurry. Like the kind of guy you might not want to meet in an alley."

Philips gave him his card. "Talk to your guys. If you can think of anything more, give me a call. We're still trying to identify the guy, and anything you can tell us could be important."

Once outside, they thanked Officer Maloney for his help and asked that he forget what he'd seen and heard inside. "We don't know where all of this is leading," Philips told him, "and we'd like to keep it to ourselves for now."

"You got it," Maloney said as he got back into his squad car. "And good luck."

As he pulled away, Gabby said, "One thing we do know, if our John Doe was dead for a year or more, he couldn't have been the one to send him the thousand dollar check last September. Eight months ago."

"True," Philips replied.

"And why," she asked, looking back at office, "did our

mystery man pick this particular lawn service?"

"Probably out of the Yellow Pages. Or off the Internet."

"Maybe. Or maybe he lives around here and has seen it passing by."

"So how would that help?"

"My friend Zach tells me this is not exactly the wealthiest part of town. Blue collar, working class type community ... "

"OK."

"So I wonder how many Chrysler 300s are running around town? Dozens, maybe, but not hundreds, I'd guess."

Philips smiled. "You are a reporter, aren't you?"

She returned the smile. "I try to be."

"You'd like me to ask Officer Maloney and his buddies on the force to keep an eye out for any Chrysler 300s driving about?"

"Along with a description of our phony cop, the one who kneed Zach. Maybe we can get a composite drawing. There must be an artist at the station I could ask."

"Damn ... "

"I know it's a long shot, but the cops spend their days patrolling the streets, so why not ask them to keep their eyes open?"

"Let me think about it," Philips said. "I'll get back to you."

This time he did look back, shaking his head as he walked.

Before she left the parking lot, she put in a call to Zach, who answered immediately. "Where are you?" she asked.

"At the vet."

"How is he?"

"Sleepy," he replied. "They've got him sedated and want to keep him that way for another day or so."

"Did he recognize you?"

"Yeah. He even licked my hand. The little guy's a fighter, I'll tell you that."

"Good."

"You're at the lawn service?"

"Yes," she said, then quickly recounted the meeting with the owner and repeated the idea she had floated to Philips.

"Sounds like a stretch to me," he said. "But there is a guy in the promotion department who's a pretty good artist. Maybe he could do that composite."

"Great," she replied, "but if we ask him, we'd have to tell Barclay what's been going on."

"I think we should anyway. He deserves to know."

"OK. When we're both back at the station, I'll try to set up a meeting."

"I'm heading back now," he said.

AT THAT MOMENT, Barclay was in another meeting, discussing the newsroom budget with the station's controller, a guy named Chet Maguire. Barclay hated talking budgets, especially in the face of ever-increasing cutbacks, so he was not disappointed when his assistant, Parkett, rapped on the door.

Barclay waved him in.

"You've got a phone call," Parkett said.

"Better take a message."

"I don't think so. It's Sam Ryan, calling from California."

Maguire got up. "I'll get back to you later."

Barclay picked up the phone. "Hey, Sam."

"I've only got a minute," Ryan said, "so I'll make this quick."

Barclay waited.

"When I talked to the mayor and the police chief here in San Jose, they admitted they didn't know where Gabby's old boyfriend, this Jessup kid, is. They hadn't even thought of him until I mentioned it ... and the chief did some checking. No one has seen him for weeks, and he's skipped his last two meetings with his probation officer."

"Jesus ... " Barclay muttered.

"There's an arrest warrant out for him, and the chief says he'll put some of his people on it. Try to find the guy.

Claims he didn't know about the threats. Says he'll keep me informed."

"Do you believe him?" Barclay asked. "That he'll really try to find him?"

"I think so. The mayor is putting pressure on him, too."

"What else did the mayor say? The guy worked for him, for Christ's sake."

"That he may be a schizo. Turned into a different guy after this business with Gabby. Missed work, always angry, lashed out at coworkers for no apparent reason. They tried to get him into counseling, but he'd have none of it. The mayor said he finally had no choice but to can the guy. End of story."

As Ryan talked, Barclay studied the picture of Jessup that Zach had left on his desk. Blond, blue-eyed, fair-skinned, with a high forehead and a slightly receding hairline. Looked like a Minnesota import from Sweden.

Ryan, again. "You there, George?"

"I'm here. Just thinking. And looking at a picture of the guy."

"What do you think?"

"I think we need to know more. The faster, the better."

"I wouldn't get all uptight," Ryan said. "He's probably down on the beach surfing."

"Or he could be outside our front door," Barclay said, with heat. "Keep the pressure on, Sam. Please. We need to know where this guy is."

"I'll do my best, George."

A HALF-HOUR LATER, Gabby had no more than walked into the newsroom than she and Zach were immediately ushered into Barclay's office. Without a word, he shut the door behind them and took a seat behind his desk. "Grab a chair, please," he finally said.

They quickly exchanged glances and did as they were told.

"I have some troubling news," he said, and quickly related

the essence of his conversation with Sam Ryan. "In short, Jessup is in the wind, may have skipped town. Nobody seems to know, although they're trying to find out as we speak."

Gabby bowed her head and closed her eyes. The beat goes on.

"As Ryan says, he may just be down at the beach, surfing..."

"He doesn't surf," she said, raising her head.

"...Or he may simply be hiding out somewhere in San Jose," Barclay went on. "But until we know something for sure, I want you to take even more precautions."

"Like what?" Zach asked.

"Like the two of you sticking together like glue. Where one of you goes, the other goes. No exceptions, until we know what's happening. I'll alert Wilson on the assignment desk. "

"What good will that do?" Zach said. "How can I protect Gabby? I can't even protect my little dog."

Barclay gave him a quizzical look. "What are you talking about?"

Gabby put a hand on Zach's arm. "Let me tell him."

"Tell me what?"

"We were going to come to talk to you," she said. "Today, actually."

Then, quickly and without hesitation, she told him everything they had neglected to tell him until now: the strange light in the backyard, the counterfeit cop, and, finally, the attack on Zach and his dog.

Barclay appeared dumb struck. And pissed. "I can't believe what I'm hearing," he finally said, a tremor in his voice. "I thought I told you to back off the story! How in the hell could you not tell me all this?"

"I didn't get attacked until yesterday," Zach protested, "and I was more concerned about my dog than telling you or anybody else."

Barclay seemed to ease up. "I didn't know you had a dog. How is he? How are you?"

"He's at the vet and looks like he may make it. And I'm OK, except for a few aches and pains."

Gabby grinned. "Tell him where you're hurting."

"Forget it," he replied.

Barclay leaned back in his chair, shaking his head, his anger still smoldering. "So now we've not only got some wacky kid who may be after Gabby, but a couple of thugs who may be after both of you. What kind of mess are we in?"

"But there *is* some good news," she countered. "We're now working with the cops and seem to be making some progress," telling him of her visit to the lawn care service and the possibility of identifying one of the thugs. "At least we know what he looks like."

"Nice try, but I'm not exactly a fan of my people getting knocked around. Or worse. We have to back off. And I mean that. Let the cops do their jobs."

"And give up what could be a good story?" she protested. "These guys wouldn't be doing what they're doing if they weren't afraid of something. We just have to find out what. And we won't do that by sitting on our behinds."

"No story's worth risking your life ... or lives."

"Funny you should say that," she said, knowing she'd probably cross a line. "After what I've heard about you and your last story."

"That was different."

"How so?"

"That was me, not one of you guys. Besides, I was stupid. And careless."

Zach finally spoke up. And stood up. "We're not stupid. And we won't be careless anymore. Gabby's right. The risks are worth it. The story's worth it. And I don't think the cops will solve it without us. Even now, they don't care as much as we do. They've got more on their minds than some dead guy that no one knows or gives a shit about."

"Sit down, Zach. Relax," Barclay said. "Let's talk this through."

They waited.

"Understand," he finally said, "that I can't risk either or both of you getting hurt again. Or worse. That's a given. So, the question is, how do I prevent that and still let you pursue the story?"

"You can't," Gabby said. "It's impossible. We can minimize the risk by being even more vigilant, but we're never going to get the story sitting in the newsroom or holed-up in the apartment. For one thing, we'd both go crazy. We'll stick together, like you say, and keep our eyes wide open, watch each other's back. Maybe, after what they did to Zach, they'll figure we'll back off. And so will they."

Barclay stared at them across the desk. "And if they don't? What then?"

"Then we'll give it up," she replied. "Leave it to the cops."

"I have your word?"

They both nodded and crossed their hearts.

"OK. In the meantime, we'll monitor your phone calls, Gabby. No one will give any information about you. For your part, don't give your number to anybody you don't trust."

"That's fine," she said.

"Then what's next?" he asked.

First thing, they said, was to get a composite drawing of the bad guy—while his face was still in fresh in Zach's memory.

"I'll arrange it with the promotion department," he said.

"Good. And we need to talk to Knowles, to see what he may have come up with."

"Anything else?"

"Maybe. Do you have any idea of how many tattoo parlors there may be in the Cities?"

He looked puzzled. "Dozens, at least. Probably many more. Why?"

She told him about the tattoo on John Doe's ankle. "The M.E. is supposed to send me a copy of it. I thought we could check around, see if any of the tattoo artists recognize it. It might give us a clue as to who the guy is."

"That could take days. Weeks."

"Not if we could get all of their e-mail addresses, send them the photo, and ask for their help. Do we have any interns who could help with some of the legwork?"

"I'll talk with Parkett and see who he can round up."

They got up to leave.

"Remember," he said, as they stood at the door. "I have your word."

Fourteen

Sitting astride his new Harley Road King parked in a free-way rest stop, Craig Jessup wasn't sure where the hell he was. Somewhere in North Fuckin' Dakota, but that was about it. He hadn't looked at a map since he'd crossed the Montana border a couple of hours before, and the last road sign he'd seen pointed toward some town called Dickinson.

He had passed through mile upon mile of prairie land and rocky badland canyons as far as the eye could see, with grazing cattle dotting the uneven terrain in every direction. The state's booming oil industry was to the north, he'd been told, confirmed by the unending stream of heavy trucks and semis along the way and by the nonstop line of trains that rolled along the tracks on one side of the freeway.

To Jessup, the country had the forbidding look of the Moon or Mars, and he wondered how people could live in a place like this. Not that he really gave a shit; he was only passing through, moving now as quickly as his Harley could carry him.

Before he could slide off his 'cycle and head for the toilet, another Harley—older and less pristine—pulled up next to him. "Hey," the other rider said as he dismounted, casting an appreciative eye on Jessup's Harley, "Nice bike. Just get it?"

"A while back," Jessup replied, turning away, in no mood for conversation.

Trouble was, Harley guys like to talk to other Harley guys, and this fellow was no exception.

Clad in a black leather jacket and chaps like Jessup, he had a tan, weathered face sporting a waxed handlebar mustache. Beneath his helmet, a red bandanna clung to his head, and silver rings hung from his ears. "Name's Lester," he said, holding out his hand. "Where you headin'?"

Jessup returned the handshake. "East," he replied vaguely.

"I can see that," Lester laughed. "But where east?"

"Not sure. Minnesota, maybe. Or Wisconsin. Have to see."

Lester followed him inside the rest stop, continuing his steady chatter, receiving mainly grunts in reply. But he was not about to give up. "Saw you've got California plates. Must have been on the road for a while."

"You got that right."

Jessup had left San Jose more than a week before, easing into the first half of the journey by sticking to less-traveled highways, holding to the speed limits, staying at small, out-of-the-way motels—or, when the weather was decent, pitching his tent in a corner of a campground.

He knew that once his probation officer notified the cops and court that he was missing, there was a remote possibility that they might be on the lookout for him. While unlikely, it was enough of a risk that he'd decided to keep a low profile until he was well beyond the California border.

So far, so good.

He'd even sold his old Harley for this new one, asking his father to register it in his name, explaining the request was for insurance purposes. His father, who was on the slow road to dementia, had not objected. So, for now, no one knew where he was, what he was driving, or where he was going.

Which is exactly what he wanted.

He'd made the decision to pack up and leave shortly after

learning that Gabby was headed to Minnesota. Despite her efforts to keep those plans secret, they were not difficult to discover. He still had friends of friends at the San Jose TV station who had been more than happy to reveal where she was bound.

It was testimony to the enemies she had left in her wake.

What he would do when he found her was still unclear in his own troubled mind. One thing *was* clear: she had ruined his life by pressing the assault charges, having him thrown in jail, and taking out the restraining order. She had destroyed his reputation, costing him all but his most loyal friends and, eventually, his job. This left him with a seething anger that had lingered and grown by the day, tormenting him, turning him from a Dr. Jekyll into a Mr. Hyde.

All because of his one bad, angry moment.

He was convinced that it was he, not she, who was the victim here. Yet he was the one who had paid the price.

In his deluded dreams, once he did find her, he could picture her begging for forgiveness, pleading for another chance, standing before him, contrite and helpless in his spell. *No way*, he thought.

Too late, too bad.

"So," Lester said, as they stood side by side at the urinals, "any chance that you'd like to move on together for a while? Gets kinda' lonely out there on the road. Might save a buck or two at the motels. Grab some weed along the way."

That was the last thing he wanted. "Thanks," he said as zipped up, "but I'm kind of a loner, know what I mean? That's what I like about the bike. It's just me and wind and the road. No offense, understand."

"None taken," Lester replied, turning to leave with a friendly wave. "You take care, now, and keep that shiny new bike shiny side up, right?"

Jessup watched him walk away. "Will do," he replied. "You, too."

Jerk didn't even wash his fuckin' hands.

Jessup lingered inside the rest stop, waiting until Lester had roared his way out of the parking lot. Then he unfolded a map he carried in his backpack, tracing his finger east along the line of Interstate 94. He guessed it was another five to six hundred miles to Minneapolis, and since it was already late afternoon, it would be another day or so before he'd reach his destination. No problem, he thought. He was no longer in any particular hurry.

She would still be there.

Unaware. Unsuspecting.

Fifteen

Gabby and Zach had no sooner left Barclay's office then his assistant news director, Jeff Parkett, stood at the door. "We need to talk," he said, stepping inside and closing the door behind him.

"About what?" Barclay said, wearily. "I'm tired of talking."

Parkett grabbed a chair. "About what the hell's going on."

"What do you mean?" he asked, knowing full well.

"C'mon, boss. You can't shit a shitter. If you want privacy, you should put shades on your windows. The whole newsroom knows something's happening with Gabby and Zach, and I think I deserve to know."

Barclay leaned across the desk, a touch of anger now in his voice. "You're right, but until twenty minutes ago, when they walked into my office, you knew damn near as much as I did."

"So?"

"So things change," he said, leaning back, reluctantly repeating in detail everything he had just been told by Gabby and Zach.

Parkett was stunned. "I had no idea," he said. "Is Zach OK?"

"A little gimpy, but better than his dog, I guess."

Parkett waited a moment, as if gathering courage, then said, "You know, George, with all due respect, this woman has spelled trouble from the day she walked in the door. Think about it: She's hired behind your back, forgets to mention why the hell she wanted out of San Jose, and then brings a whole suitcase full of problems with her."

Barclay started to protest, but Parkett cut him off. "Let me finish. First day here, she gets this suicide bug up her ass and she's off and running—defying your orders, by the way, to back off when things got dicey. She's a loose cannon, George. A loner. Besides Zach, Knowles, and Wilson, I don't think she's made a friend in the newsroom. None of us know where she is half the time and when we try to tighten the reins, she gets pissed off. And now this: getting the shit beat out of Zach and his damned dog."

"Enough, OK!" Barclay said. "You've made your point."

"Have I?"

"To be fair," Barclay said, "you haven't liked her from day one. You've made that clear more than once."

"With good reason, I'd say."

"Maybe. But you know what you're missing? Or refusing to admit? That she may be on to one hell of a story. And isn't that why we're in this business? To tell stories, to get at the truth? She may be a handful, but I'll tell you, I think she's got better instincts and more guts than most of the people sitting out there in judgment of her."

Parkett could only shake his head. "I think you've got blinders on, George."

"Maybe so, but I'm not going to rein her in. Not yet. She and Zach gave me their word to play it cool, to take precautions, and I want to let them see this through."

Parkett got out of his chair. "You're the boss. I hope you're right. And I won't give you any more grief. But I'm telling you, you're playing with fire. *We're* playing with fire ... and I just hope you're not blinded by the smoke."

"So do I," Barclay said. "It'll be up to all of us to keep our eyes open."

As THAT SMALL DRAMA unfolded, Gabby was at her desk, retrieving an e-mail from Dr. Maxwell, who had sent along a photo of the John Doe ankle tattoo. She printed it and took it to a window where the light was better, holding it up, studying the image. It could be a flag, as Maxwell had suggested, but it was difficult to tell. It had the look of a wrinkled photograph, the wrinkles apparently the result of the shriveled skin on the man's ankle. Square, like a flag, it had a red border with a blue circle in the middle and two blurred, indistinguishable words beneath the circle.

Back at her computer, she Googled flags and carefully scrolled through page after page of flags from virtually every country in the world, both current and historical. None bore a close resemblance to the image on the photograph.

If it was not a flag, then what was it? It was another clue as mysterious as the dead man himself.

She switched off the computer and leaned back in her chair, closing her eyes, swallowing yet another disappointment, another dead end.

"Can I ask you a question?"

Startled, her eyes snapped open to find her cubicle neighbor, Sarah Andrews, facing her.

"Sure. What is it?"

"Do you have some kind of exclusive rights to Zach?"

"What do you mean?" Gabby said.

"That's the buzz in the newsroom. I've asked for him to shoot a couple of my stories and was told he's off-limits, that he's assigned to you, like, exclusively."

Gabby wasn't sure how to reply. Finally, mimicking Sarah, "Like, I don't know about that, but we are working together on this suicide story, that's true."

"And I hear you're living together."

"Only temporarily. Until I can find something of my own."

"Convenient," Sarah replied, a snarky tone in her voice.

Gabby couldn't let it pass. "Listen, don't get the wrong idea. There's nothing going on. Zach had a spare bedroom and I needed a place to land. Period."

"Right," she said with a smirk, turning back to her own desk.

ZACH WAS IN the promotion department, watching as Keith Dunnel, one of the station's graphic artists, sketched a likeness of the man who had attacked Zach on the street. While that encounter had been brief and violent, the man's visage was firmly embedded in Zach's memory: deeply set, dark eyes beneath heavy eyebrows that needed a trim, dark curly hair, sunken cheeks, and, most prominently, a flattened nose that seemed to meld into those cheeks.

"How about the chin?" Dunnel asked.

"Not square, not pointed," Zach replied. "Normal, I'd say."

"Ears?"

"Normal, too. Not elephant ears or anything like that."

It took another twenty minutes to finish, but by the time it was done, Zach thought the composite was about as good as it was going to get.

"Not exactly a movie star, is he?" the artist laughed, studying the sketch.

"You should smell his breath," Zack replied. "It's still stuck in my nose."

"One good thing. He shouldn't be hard to spot in a crowd. That nose makes him look like a fighter who took too many punches."

Zach grinned and took a copy of the sketch. "I owe you one."

"No problem. Just keep him away from me."

By the time he got back to the newsroom with copies of the sketch, the first of the early evening newscasts was over and the daytime staff had begun to scatter. "Let's get out of here," he told Gabby. "The vet says we can come get Barclay."

"In a minute," she said, first studying his sketch, then holding up the photo of the tattoo. "Any idea what this could be? And don't say flag, because it isn't—as far as I can tell."

He studied the image. "I don't know. Some kind of sports insignia? Maybe a military emblem of some kind? Could be anything, I suppose."

"That's the problem," she replied. "It could be anything."

As they packed up their things and prepared to leave, Wilson waved them over to the assignment desk. "Here," he said, handing each of them a small canister of Mace. "The boss says you should have these. And don't go anywhere without them."

"Are you serious?" Zach said.

"*He* is. And he hires and fires."

"What the hell's next?" Zach asked. "A bodyguard?"

By then, Wilson had turned and walked away.

A HALF HOUR LATER, Gabby was waiting in the car, doors locked, watching as Zach emerged from the vet's clinic, cradling a blanket-wrapped Barclay in his arms. "How is he?" she asked, once they were in the car and settled.

"Tired but alert, and happy to see me."

She leaned across the seat and lifted the edge of the blanket covering the dog's head. He looked up at her with sad eyes, but almost purred when she scratched him behind his ears. "Poor thing," she whispered. "Let's get you home."

As they drove, Zach reported on what the vet had told him: the prognosis was good, and with rest and loving care, the recovery should be complete. The stitches in his belly should dissolve on their own, and he'd be fine without his missing spleen.

Ever cautious, Gabby continued to check the rear view mirror, feeling silly but unwilling to take even the slightest chance. Still, she wondered, how careful could they be? Their eyes couldn't be everywhere, all the time. It was inevitable that they would be exposed and vulnerable from time to time, in places and from persons unknown.

At least we know what one of them looks like, she thought. *But what about the other? And are there more?*

She tried to shake off the willies, remembering the bravado she had shown in Barclay's office. *"We're never going to get the story sitting in the newsroom or holed-up in the apartment."* Brave words at the time, but as she glanced across at the bundle in Zach's arms, she wasn't so sure.

Is the story worth the risks? And what is the story? She still had no clear idea of what they were dealing with: a long-dead guy, still unidentified, whom others had taken great pains to hide both his identity and his death. And they were still as determined, if not more so, to keep others—like them—at bay.

Zach peered over at her. "What's going on in that head of yours?"

"Some self-doubts," she admitted, repeating what she'd been thinking.

"Forget it," he said. "We can take care of ourselves. And the story *is* worth it, whatever it turns out to be."

She gave him a grateful glance, reassured, but not convinced.

IT WASN'T ESP, but Barclay was having some of those same thoughts as he sat in the living room of his condo, sipping an Amstel Light. His wife, Rachel, sat beside him, holding a glass of cabernet, convinced he was in some distant land. "George? Hello? Moon to Earth, come in, please."

"Sorry," he said with a grin. "I was just thinking."

"I could tell. What's going on?"

In the year they'd been married, they had promised one another to share everything—the good and the bad, the important and the inconsequential. No secrets, no hidden thoughts. And, so far, it had worked. But sometimes George had to be coaxed. "Parkett was on my ass today," he finally said, repeating the conversation with his assistant news director. "He thinks I've got blinders on with Gabby. That she's a loose cannon who's a risk not only to herself and Zach, but to all of us."

"Is she?"

"Maybe, but," recapping his defense of her, "sometimes you have to take a chance for what could be a good story."

"You always were a sucker for a good story," she said, grinning. "And for taking chances. I should know."

She didn't need to remind him. In his pursuit of the killer of that old high school classmate, Rachel had become a pawn in a game that could have cost her her life.

"But it's more than that," he said. "It wasn't so long ago that the newsroom was full of people like Gabby, reporters who weren't content to simply cover the stories that hit them in the face—the floods and fires and tornadoes—but who actually wanted to do some *reporting,* pursuing leads, investigating, digging, uncovering stuff that nobody else had. Pushing the envelope, if you will.

"Today, for the most part, we've left that kind of reporting to the newspapers and to the alternative press, like *City Pages.* It's been a long time since we've broken a story that nobody else had."

This was not unique to Channel 7. All across the country, weather, sports, and traffic had become the staple of local television news, absorbing much of a newscast's limited time, often elbowing out stories on government, politics, and the economy. It was little wonder considering the staff and budget cutbacks in the industry and the increasing reliance by the public on digital news—making the Internet almost as important as television as a source of news. Even more important to younger people.

Podcasts were often getting more attention than newscasts.

And it wasn't limited to television. More newspapers were cutting back to three days a week in print, while others were being sold to billionaires whose objectives and influence on the news were yet to be fully known or felt.

This growing frustration had led Barclay to seriously consider his own future. The television news business had been his life and, until recently, a fulfilling profession. He had seen dozens of young people come through his newsroom, many of them moving on to great careers in larger markets or the network news divisions, thanks in part to the firm but gentle mentoring he had provided.

Indeed, he had had his own share of new opportunities over the years, from stations in Chicago and LA, and from the network itself. But he'd deliberately chosen to stay on at Channel 7, even under the new ownership, because of his pride in what the station had accomplished and his love for Minnesota and its Midwestern values.

Now, he wasn't so sure. Sadly, and with a heavy heart, he had watched the changes happen—the increasing emphasis on the glitzy and the glamorous to the exclusion of the significant. The deterioration may have been slow, but it was as inexorable as the retreating Arctic ice pack, leaving him without the same sense of satisfaction in coming to work each day.

And he had little hope of doing much about it, not if he wanted the station to remain competitive in the ever more competitive ratings wars.

But what else could he do? What else was he capable of doing? He hated suits and ties and the guys who wore them, and he could never see himself sitting in endless meetings discussing how to promote a new widget, or how to turn bad news into good news for some uncaring corporation.

"So what are you going to do?" she asked. "About Gabby?"

"Have another beer, I think."

She laughed. "That's a good solution."

"Seriously, I think I have to let it play out for a while. See where it goes. It would be hard to retreat now."

"And what about her old boyfriend?" she asked. "The one from San Jose. Anything new on him?"

"No, but Ryan gets back tomorrow. And he may know more."

She slid closer to him on the couch and put her arm around him. "Is it OK if we forget all of this for a while and have dinner?"

"Perfect," he replied. "After another beer."

She whispered in his ear, "Lush."

ACROSS TOWN, GABBY and Zach were sprawled on the couch, Barclay dozing between them, as they sipped their third beer of the night and began to feel the effects. Neither had spoken for the past ten minutes, content to let a Norah Jones CD fill the silence.

When the last note sounded, Gabby turned to him and said, her words slightly slurred, "Sarah Andrews was on my case today..."

"About what?"

"About dominating your time. She said she wanted you to shoot some stories with her, but was told you were unavailable."

"Forget her. She's a zero on a scale of one to ten."

"Still," she said, touching his hand with hers, "I truly am sorry about all of this. That you're stuck with me. At work, and here. I thought I'd be moving on by now."

He made no move to remove her hand. "No need to be sorry. I've told you that a dozen times. It's nobody's fault. Besides, it's nice having you here."

"Right."

"I mean it. You can stay as long as you'd like. Even when this is all done and you're free to leave. I've appreciated the company..."

Before he could go on, his cell sounded. He glanced at the number and gave Gabby a curious look. Then, "Carolyn?"

His former girlfriend.

Gabby started to get up, but he waved her back.

He listened for a moment, then said, "It *has* been a long time. How've you been?" Another minute passed, and Gabby was feeling increasingly uncomfortable. "No, I don't think that would work," he finally said. "Not now, anyway. Hard to explain, but a situation at work has got me pretty much tied down." Another pause. "Yeah, I am surprised. The way you left it, I thought things were pretty much over and done ... "

Feeling like an interloper, Gabby finally got up and walked to the kitchen, grabbing the final piece of leftover pizza from dinner, attributing the twinge she felt to the last beer or maybe the pizza.

When Zach joined her, he said, "Well, that was strange."

"She wants to get back together?"

He sat across from her. "Yeah. Said she's been thinking things over. That she may have acted too quickly. Wanted to know if I might be feeling the same."

"Are you?"

"Hell, I don't know. I've gotta think about it. Not often that you get dumped and the dumper wants to get back together."

She said nothing.

"Besides, it's academic since Barclay says you and I can't be apart, and since I'm guessing you wouldn't want to go along on a date with Carolyn."

Gabby flashed a grin. "Amen to that."

LATER, AS SHE LAY in bed, she tried to understand that twinge she'd felt in the kitchen. Jealousy? How could that be? To this point, Zach had shown no visible signs of romantic interest in her ... nor she in him. Sure, there'd been some fun flirtations, some innocent give-and-take, but that was all. They were just buddies, right? Friends and temporary roommates. Colleagues pushed together by circumstances, sharing some intrigue and a touch of danger, but nothing more.

Yet he hadn't moved her hand.

No doubt the enforced time together and the shared purpose, had brought them closer. But did that explain his protectiveness and his staunch defense of her and of the story they were pursuing? Maybe so, but that was business, nothing more. He believed, as strongly as she did, in the story, and was as dedicated as she was in solving the puzzle.

That was as far as it went.

Still . . . he hadn't moved her hand.

She turned over and hugged her pillow. It had been so long since she had felt anything but anger toward any man that she knew her emotions could not be trusted. Any attention, any sign of affection, could be misconstrued. She couldn't remember the last gentle touch or endearing whisper of a man. Only the pain. So she had to be careful.

The last thing she heard before sleep came was the sound of Zach quietly shutting his bedroom door.

Sixteen

Sam Ryan was waiting impatiently at Barclay's door when he walked into the newsroom the next morning. "Hey, Sam," he said, taking small satisfaction in having kept him waiting, not vice versa. "Been here long?"

"Long enough," he said curtly, following Barclay into the office.

"Grab a seat," Barclay said. "How's California?"

He ignored the question and stayed on his feet. "I've only got a minute. I'll make it quick."

Surprise, surprise.

"OK."

"I did more checking before I left San Jose. As you feared, this guy Jessup is apparently on the run. The cops have tried to track him down, but he's nowhere to be found. Bank accounts closed, apartment locked up, mail stopped, motorcycle missing. Probation officer doesn't know where he is, and even his father, who apparently has Alzheimers, says he can't remember the last time he saw him."

"Shit," Barclay said under his breath.

"One of his friends said Jessup talked to a couple of the people at the television station that he got to know when he was living with Gabby. And it's possible one or more of them told him something, but they're not talking—at least not to me."

Barclay leaned back in his chair and closed his eyes. Ryan waited. "So what do you suggest?"

Barclay quickly briefed him on what he had already done: ordering Gabby and Zach to stick together and to take even greater precautions, not only because of Jessup but also from the threats in the suicide case. He had forgotten that Ryan had not yet heard about the attack on Zach and his dog.

"Goddamn, George. I don't like the sound of any of this."

"Neither do I, but I'm not sure what more to do. We could add a couple of more security guards here at the station, but you probably don't have the budget for that. And it probably wouldn't do much good anyway. I don't think either Jessup or these other goons are going to invade the station. The danger, if and when it happens, is likely to be on the outside."

Ryan jabbed a finger at him. "I gotta tell you, George, this scares the hell out of me. If something happens, we're screwed. The owners will be down on me like shit on a flat rock. And you'll be right there with me."

"That's the least of my worries," Barclay said.

"Not mine. I didn't get into this business for this kind of crap. I don't like ripples in the water, let alone these kind of waves. Bad publicity is bad business, and I don't want to see this station dragged into the headlines because of something like this…"

"Listen," Barclay said, smarting. "Don't you lay this one on me. You're the one who brought Gabby here. You knew what she'd gone through in San Jose. You must have known that this guy was some kind of lunatic to do what he did to her. I'm just trying to protect her, to see that she's safe and that we don't make the headlines."

If Ryan was upset by Barclay's outburst, he didn't show it. Calmly, he said, "I want to be kept absolutely in the loop on this. And I want to see Gabby and this Zach kid as soon as possible. I need to talk to them face to face."

With that, he turned and walked away.

HAD BARCLAY FOLLOWED him out of the office and walked a hundred feet across the newsroom to a window overlooking the Nicollet Mall, he just might have caught a glimpse of the man they'd been discussing.

Craig Jessup was sitting at one of the outside tables at the same Caribou coffee shop where Gabby had met the assistant M.E. several days before. Sipping an iced coffee, ostensibly reading that day's *Star Tribune,* his eyes instead were focused on the doors of the television station just down the Mall.

In the ten days since he'd left California, he had managed to grow a half-inch blond beard with mustache and had covered his receding hairline with a Twins baseball cap. Together with a pair of dark glasses, and a pierced gold ring in his lip, he bore little resemblance to the man Gabby had last seen, or the man portrayed in the photo that had been distributed to key personnel in the newsroom.

He'd left his motorcycle and gear at one of the suburban motels near the airport, taking a bus into downtown. Dressed now in a pair of khakis and a long-sleeved Harley T-shirt, he could be anybody enjoying a morning coffee, except for the nervous drumming of his fingers on the tabletop, which drew curious glances from a couple sitting nearby.

It was the first time he had actually seen the Channel 7 station, which was constructed with massive hunks of Minnesota stone and had the look of a fortress. He'd taken the time to circle it twice, seeing the employee entrance and the sloping driveway into the underground garage in the back, as well as the front entrance he was studying now. In the time he'd been sitting here, there'd been little traffic in and out of that entrance—so he assumed most people came and went through the back. That was unfortunate, since there was no comfortable place like this coffee shop to observe that end of the building.

He wondered how much, if at all, Gabby had changed since he'd last seen her. Because of the court's restraining order, he had not been close to her since the day he went to jail, but he'd often watched her from a distance thanks to a pair of binoculars and night goggles. She seldom was alone, and when she was—it was clear—she was on guard.

But, somehow, she had eluded his surveillance long enough to make it out of town and on to Minnesota without his knowing. For a time, at least.

He had no clue as to where she was living, and so far today, he had seen no sign of her. But that didn't surprise him. Too soon, he knew. He'd called the newsroom twice, asking for her, but each time was told she was unavailable, and his requests for her personal extension or cell phone number were politely refused. Strange, he thought, but perhaps that was station policy. Or, maybe they were protecting her. From whom? *Him?* Unlikely, but who knows what she may have revealed about her past. Or about him.

Nah, he thought. She's too proud, too private, to reveal those kinds of details. After all, she apparently came here to begin a new life, and would be reluctant, or ashamed, to share the tawdry stories of her past life.

Little did *he* know.

GABBY AND ZACH WERE nowhere near the television station. They were across town, parked in front of the Comfort Care nursing home in south Minneapolis, waiting for Detective Philips to meet them. They had just been inside, visiting with the old John Doe neighbor, Clarence Pedersen.

They'd come to show Clarence the sketch of the man who had attacked Zach, the man they believed was the same one who had visited Clarence, posing as a cop. They found him in his pajamas and a scruffy robe, slumped in a chair, half asleep, surrounded by several others who looked in no better shape. When they'd roused him, he seemed genuinely pleased to see them. "I don't get many visitors," he'd said, nodding to those around him, "and they don't talk much."

After a few minutes of conversation, they'd shown him the sketch, which he'd studied for a long time before finally agreeing that the image did closely resemble his memory of "Sergeant Preston."

"His nose may have been a little flatter," he'd said, "but it's pretty close."

When told the man in the sketch was not the cop he had pretended to be, he wasn't surprised. "I thought there was something funny about him. Too gruff, too rough around the edges to be a cop. But then he showed me his badge and I figured, what the hell?"

They'd spent a few more minutes visiting before wishing him well and promising to keep in touch. "Poor guy," Gabby said, once in the car. "He looked a lot happier when he was back home."

"Can you blame him?" Zach said. "Who could be happy in a place like that? Looked to me like a lot of old people sitting around waiting to die. Maybe *hoping* to die. Pretty depressing, I'd say."

As they talked, Philips pulled up behind them in an unmarked squad car. They all got out and spent a few minutes catching up. Turns out, Philips didn't have much to report. He told them he had run into roadblocks trying to locate where the mail for John Doe's house had been sent. "Both the post office and the utility companies are very protective of customer privacy. We're trying to set up a meeting with the postal inspectors and may have to get a subpoena to pry the information out of the utility companies. It's a pain in the ass, but we're working on it."

"There has to be a post office box somewhere," Gabby said.

"Sure, but whether it's at some post office branch or at

one of those commercial letter boxes, we just don't know. It's going to take some more time."

"The box must be rented by the same company that owns the house," she said.

"You'd think so," Philips replied. "But it's a Delaware company and we're still trying to figure out who those guys are."

Zach pulled the sketch out of their car and said Clarence had agreed on the likeness. Philips examined the drawing and said he'd make copies and—as Gabby had suggested—pass them out to the cops who patrolled the streets in Columbia Heights, where the lawn service was located. "I don't think there's much of a chance that they'll spot this guy," he said. "Probably not one in a thousand, but it can't hurt to try."

He also said he'd get someone to compare the sketch to the scores of mug shots stored in the police computers. "Just so you know," he said, tiredly, "I've got other stuff I'm supposed to be working on. My partner's already pissed that I'm spending as much time as I am on this."

With that, they parted ways, leaving Gabby and Zach even less hopeful and more frustrated than when they'd arrived.

RETURNING TO THE NEWSROOM, they were met immediately by Barclay, who took them in tow and said Sam Ryan was expecting them, like now.

Zach, who had never met the man, asked, "What does he want with us?"

Barclay quickly recapped his conversation with Ryan, including his report that Craig Jessup apparently had disappeared from San Jose, leaving no trace behind. "I had to give him all the details of the attack on you, Zach, and the continuing threats. He's my boss, and like all of us, he's worried about you. He demanded to meet with you and express his concerns. So here we are."

"Jesus," Gabby muttered. "Watch. He's going to try to send me back to Portland to live with my mother."

"Just cool it," Barclay said. "Hear what he has to say."

Actually, Gabby was feeling some guilt, knowing she should have stopped to see Ryan by now, as a courtesy, before it came to this.

He was waiting for them, and after a quick introduction to Zach and a warm greeting for Gabby, he wasted no time in getting to the point. "George has told me everything," he said, "and I gotta' tell you, I'm not liking what I'm hearing."

Gabby and Zach sat attentively, hands folded in their laps. Zach was amazed by the size of Ryan's office and couldn't take his eyes off the man's comb-over, stifling a grin.

"I'm not only worried about you," Ryan said, "which I surely am, but also about the station and its reputation if something bad were to come out of this."

And about his own ass, Barclay thought.

Gabby tried to say something, but Ryan waved her off. "You wanted to get out of San Jose to avoid trouble, Gabby, and now here you are in double trouble. I don't know what the hell to do."

He took a breath, allowing Zach to break in. "You don't have to do anything! We've told George that we can take care of ourselves, and we will. We're not kids."

"You're not running the station, either, young man. I am, and this is the desk where the buck stops. I'm also a friend of Gabby's family and feel some personal responsibility there, too. Her mother would be on my case if she thought I looked the other way in a situation like this."

"Leave my mother out of this, Sam, please," Gabby said.

"I can't. Not entirely. I brought you here, for Christ's sake."

Barclay had remained silent until now. "Sam, you're right. The buck *does* stop with you. You *are* ultimately responsible for the safety of the staff and the reputation of the station. But you also have to understand that these two are not a couple of your salesmen or engineers. They're journalists, and journalists take risks each and every day, somewhere. We don't know, but this story could be important to the station and to the community. There *is* danger involved, but we can control some of that. I worry more about this Jessup character. If he's on the loose, as we think he is, he would be a danger to Gabby wherever she is, here, or back in San Jose. Or even in Portland.

"It's too bad we're facing both of these possible threats at the same time, but I don't think we can back away from either."

Ryan leaned back in his chair, clearly perplexed. You could almost see his mind churning, balancing the risks, which were considerable, versus the rewards, which—to his mind—were negligible. Yet he knew this was a television station with a storied history of investigative reporting, and he had no desire to be seen as the man stepping in to stop this one.

Jessup was something else. There was little they could do about him, he decided, except to watch, wait, and be on guard. "I've got to think about this," he finally said. "Talk to the folks at corporate."

As Barclay and the others started to get up, he said, "Hold on. Just so you know, I've hired more security for the building, and I'm counting on you two to live up to the promise you've made to George. No unnecessary risks, OK?"

"OK," they replied, almost in unison.

Harry Wilson intercepted the three of them as they returned to the newsroom. "I thought you should know," he said, "that some guy has called twice for Gabby. Wanted to know her extension or cell phone number . . . "

"Shit," Barclay said, shaking his head.

" . . . and wouldn't leave his name or a message."

Gabby sank into a chair. "You think it's him?"

Barclay said, "Can you think of anyone else it might be?"

"The only people who know I'm here, besides the staff, are

Philips and Cindy, the M.E., and they both have my numbers. And old Clarence Pedersen, of course, but we just saw him and I can't see him calling. Or if he did, he'd leave a message."

She looked at Zach. "Am I missing anyone?"

"Only ones I can think of are the Homicide chief and Philips's partner, but why would they call? And if they did, they'd leave a message, too."

"Maybe it was somebody from your old station," Wilson suggested. "Someone who knows you're here."

"Maybe," she said, "but I can't imagine who that might be."

Barclay took a deep breath. "We might be getting ahead of ourselves. Seeing shadows. But we can't ignore it, either. Keep your eyes wide open, including those in the back of your heads."

AN HOUR LATER, Barclay called a meeting of his key staff people, the same group which had met to discuss the mystery suicide when Gabby first arrived. He wanted to discuss the latest on the Craig Jessup threat and to bring them up-to-date on the suicide investigation. For some, it was first they had heard of the attack on Zach and his dog, and about the search for the attacker, including the sketch that had been made.

Gabby and Zach were also there, sitting quietly, listening.

"We don't know where this may lead," Barclay said, "and we're doing everything we can to protect Gabby and Zach, as they are themselves. It seems clear this suicide story has some meat to it or these dudes wouldn't be doing what they're doing to stop it. Having said that, the question remains: is it worth the risks? So far, we've decided it is. But it's a moving target, and we're prepared to give it up if things get much worse."

One of the producers said, "And we still don't know what the story is?"

"No, not really."

"And we're working with the cops on this?" asked another.
"Yes."

"I thought that was a no-no."

"It is, unless there's no choice. And there doesn't seem to be much of a choice in this case."

Further questions got more pointed: *Are the resources we're spending on this, all of Gabby's and Zach's time, worth it? How much more time are you willing to give it? How long can we keep the story to ourselves? What do we do if we run into this Jessup character?*

He responded to each as honestly as he could, but had to admit there were no answers to some. Then, the questions were aimed at Gabby and Zach: *How do you feel about all of this? What are you doing to protect yourselves? Why are you so convinced that the story is worth the effort and the risk when so little is known?*

Like Barclay, they tried to answer with as much candor as they could, but sensed that skepticism remained. "Look," Gabby said, "we didn't go looking for this story. It kind of dropped into our laps, and we're doing what I think most of you would want us to do: following it. That's all we can tell you."

Barclay closed the meeting with this warning: "It's crucial that we keep all of this in-house until we know more about the goons and about Jessup. No leaks, no idle gossip with your buddies at the bar. Understood? I hope so."

Not everyone, it turned out, would get the message.

Seventeen

The weekend was coming and going more quickly than Gabby would have expected, considering they'd done nothing special, sticking close to the apartment, and when they did go out for groceries or to walk the dog, they'd gone together, as promised. Ever vigilant of those around them, they'd studied the passing cars, and kept a safe separation from those who approached or passed them on the sidewalk.

They were feeling foolish in the process. But their word was their word.

Zach spent the bulk of his time working on his screenplay, laboring at the computer, resisting—for now—Gabby's help. "I need to try to do this myself," he told her, "but if I get hung up, I may come get you."

The screenplay was based on a mystery novel that was—in turn—based on the real story of a man who was accused of murdering his wife and dumping her body while kayaking on Lake Superior. Having worked in Duluth, Zach was aware of the actual case and got to know the author of the fictionalized version, *Murder on the Big Lake*.

He'd bought the movie rights for a pittance, and now had eighteen months to come up with a finished screenplay and to find an angel or two who might be willing to finance at least a trailer of the film in hopes of persuading a studio or someone with deeper pockets to produce the entire picture. He knew the chances were slim to none, with more screenplays floating around than maple leaves in the fall winds.

But he was determined to try—to fulfill his boyhood dreams.

Gabby had read the novel and found the writing amateurish, at best. But she could also see its potential as a film—two people alone on the roiling waters of Superior, one intent on murder, surrounded by its towering cliffs and enshrouded by the lifting and falling fog. She saw it as another *Life of Pi,* with a wife killer instead of a tiger on board.

But, like Zach, she knew there were huge obstacles to face.

For her part, she had spent her time reading and viewing DVDs of a number of newscasts and investigative reports the station had done in the past year. It was her first chance to seriously study the station's style of reporting and the storytelling capabilities of the reporters she had seldom seen on-air since her arrival.

She had talked to her mother twice, trading small talk, reassuring her that she was doing fine, that she was continuing to look for a place of her own to live.

She also had lots of time to think about the mess she found herself in, and how it had come to be. She had arrived full of hope, firmly committed to building a new life, both personally and professionally, leaving the past where it belonged: in the past. She had taken to heart the hard lessons learned in San Jose, and was determined now to present herself as less strident, less self-assured, and more cooperative, to be the "team player" that was the mantra these days.

But how was she to know that it would be a disaster from the get-go? How an unknowing and disbelieving George Barclay would await her. How, as a result, she would earn—through no fault of her own—the suspicions of virtually the entire staff. And, then, to be rid of her, being sent on a non-story ride-along, a suicide that had spiraled into a life-threatening event.

It had been like walking into a minefield, blindfolded and barefoot.

True, she had so far made little effort to make friends in the newsroom. While she knew that wasn't her strong suit, there'd also been too little time and opportunity to become part of the "team." At least that's what she'd told herself. Besides, she thought, she wasn't alone. Few others had gone out of their way to get to know her better, or to make her feel more welcome. And many still harbored their resentments.

As her mind churned, she couldn't help but wonder what her father would have done if he were in her shoes. He certainly wouldn't have backed away from the dangers, of that she was sure. He was the bravest, smartest man she'd ever known. She could almost feel him, again perched on her shoulder, again whispering in her ear, *"Stick with it, Gabs. Take care of yourself, but don't let 'em buffalo you."*

She'd been in San Jose working when he died. So suddenly. So young. Dead of a massive heart attack, collapsing in the street in the midst of his investigation of corruption in Portland's housing inspections department. She'd never forget her mother's voice on the phone, the words almost indistinguishable among the sobs. "He's gone, Gabby, he's gone."

How could that be?

She had seen him only a few weeks before on a rare visit home. As energized as ever, full of vim and vigor, doing what he loved to do best—going after the bad guys, exposing those who had the balls to violate the public trust. She'd inherited his passion if not all of his skills, and was—to this day—determined to try and live up to his legacy.

He had died before her affair with Craig Jessup. Before the romance faded. Before the beating. Had he lived, she was convinced, Jessup would no longer be a threat to her. Which brought her back to the moment.

How could she have known that Jessup would follow her across the country? She thought she'd had left him behind along with the rest of her former life—a violent slice of her past that could have no impact on her future.

Could he really be here? Could those phone calls truly have come from him?

And why would he come? With vengeance in his heart? With some deluded hope of reconciliation? Surely not that, not after what he had done to her, and she to him.

Which left retribution as the only plausible reason.

She could never reverse the past or erase her mistakes, but now, with painful hindsight, she failed to fathom how she'd ever allowed herself to become involved with him. Perhaps it was because so few other men, at least anyone as attractive or attentive, had had the patience and the will to crack the self-absorbed shell into which she'd crawled. He'd been relentless in his pursuit, his undivided devotion disguising the flaws that would appear later.

She had been swept away on the wings of what she believed was true love, not realizing until far too late that she'd been ensnared like a rabbit in a trap, that to him devotion was possession and that love was measured by her willingness to be everything he wanted her to be.

As she'd told Zach, by the time she'd come to her senses, he had assumed almost total control of her life, from the friends she was allowed to keep, the time she could have to herself, what food she could to eat, how much and when she could drink, how often they would have sex, and who would decide.

There'd been no sign of his violent side until the rabbit was already halfway out of the trap, until he knew that she wanted to escape. It began with a few harsh words, unprovoked arguments, then a push, a shove, an apology, another push, more harsh words. Another shove.

Then, finally, the battering. Sudden. Paralyzing. Terrifying. Her last glimpse of him was through a hazy cloud of pain.

What would she do if she were to meet him now, face to face? Call 911? Mace him? Hide behind Zach? Sic his poodle on him? No, she told herself, she'd call him a sick son of a bitch and spit in his face.

Eighteen

The Monday morning rush was over and Officer Billy Hernandez, "Taco," to his less sensitive Columbia Heights police buddies, was relaxing in his squad car, a cup of Starbucks coffee to keep him company. So far, it had been an uneventful shift with two small fender benders and a shoplifting call at a local convenience store. In the latter, the young thief had gotten away on his bike with two Milky Way bars and a Pepsi before Billy could get there. Still, he had to fill out a report.

Now, with four hours left before he could call it a day, he pulled out on to Central Avenue to continue his routine patrol, in hopes of spotting a kid on a bike with chocolate on his lips.

The Heights was not exactly a crime-ridden suburb, and Officer Hernandez often wished for a little more excitement. Not too much, mind you, but enough to make use of some of the expensive police training he'd received in his two years on the force. So far, he'd never fired his gun in the line of duty, and had used his Taser and his pepper spray only a few times—to break up fights and to subdue a couple of burglary suspects he'd caught in the act.

Billy was in his late twenties, married for three years, with twins, a boy and a girl, who were the lights of his life.

As he pulled up at a stoplight on Central and Forty-Sixth Street he glanced at the car in the next lane, also waiting for the light to change. Although the black Chrysler 300 had tinted windows, the driver-side window was halfway down, allowing Billy to get a glimpse of the man behind the wheel. He looked once, then again, not missing the driver's flattened nose before he turned his head away. The light changed and the Chrysler took off—but not until Billy had glanced at the sketch on the seat next to him

"Damn," he said, pulling into the other lane, now two cars behind the Chrysler. He got on the radio. "This is Hernandez in Three. I think I have the Chrysler 300 the Minneapolis PD is looking for. The driver looks like the sketch I was given. What d'ya want me to do?"

There was a pause at the other end. Then, the dispatcher, "Do you have a plate number?"

"Not yet," Billy said. "He's a couple of cars ahead."

"Better pull him over. See what you've got. Be careful."

"Roger."

"Where are you?"

"Coming up on 42nd and Central."

"We'll get you some backup."

Billy gunned it, pulled around the two cars ahead of him, and hit the flashers. No siren, not yet. See what the Chrysler would do. He could now see the plates: California, 5482A.

He gave the guy ten seconds to see lights and pull over. When he didn't, he hit the siren. Then the car finally did slow down and moved to the curb, the squad car about fifteen feet directly behind him. He called in the plate number, debated waiting for backup, but then got out and walked slowly, cautiously, toward the driver's side door, his right hand held loosely over his unsnapped, holstered pistol.

Before he reached the back fender, the car's backup lights flashed on and—in an instant—the car flew backwards, careening into the front end of the squad car, missing Billy by mere inches. The sudden, violent shock of the crash sent him reeling, stumbling and falling backwards, landing on the street. By the time he recovered and reached for his gun, the Chrysler—with a crushed trunk and its back bumper lying on the street—was speeding off, careening off Central onto Fortieth and out of sight.

"What the hell?"

He reached for his shoulder mike, shouting into it. "This is Hernandez. The guy just rammed the front end of the squad and took off!"

The dispatcher asked, "Are you OK?"

Breathing hard, "Flat on my butt, but, yeah, I'm OK."

"Can you pursue?"

Billy looked at the battered grill and twisted hood of his car, the radiator leaking fluid onto the pavement. "Don't think so. The front end looks like an accordion."

Another radio cut in. "This is Maloney. I'm about eight blocks away. Which way did he go?"

By now, Hernandez was on his feet. "West on Fo rtieth, moving fast."

Maloney replied, "I'm on it."

Billy could hear the siren wailing behind him and watched as Maloney's squad sped by, skidding around the corner, almost taking out a light post. Another siren was coming from the south, and then a third from the east. The cavalry was riding to the rescue.

All Hernandez could do was stand and watch, still shaking, angry at himself for not waiting for backup. He knew he would face a chewing out, maybe worse, for that lapse of judgment. He should have known; the guy in the sketch was wanted on an assault warrant, not for some stupid traffic violation.

Shit!

On the other hand, he knew he was damned lucky. Had he walked directly behind the Chrysler instead of off to one side, as he'd been taught, he was convinced the guy with the flat nose would have sent him flying without a second thought, turning him into a human hood ornament.

Instead, he was alive and upright, thinking now only of his twins, who could have been minus a father. Maybe this cop thing wasn't such a great idea, after all.

A small crowd of gawkers had gathered around the squished squad car, but Billy paid them no heed. He climbed back into the car, and listened to the radio traffic. Three Heights cars were in the hunt, along with two from Minneapolis—crossing the border to provide assistance.

They ought to have him by now, Billy thought. Although he'd taken off like a shot, he couldn't have gotten that far, not with just three or four minutes of lead time. But he also knew there was a maze of residential streets and alleys that he could have disappeared into, maybe into his own garage, if he lived nearby.

Billy waited. And waited.

A half hour later they found the car abandoned on a dead-end street in northeast Minneapolis, probably four miles away. They brought in a canine unit and canvassed the neighborhood, but there was no sign of the suspect or any indication of where or how he may have fled. There was a bus stop a block away, or he may have been picked up by one of his buddies or simply walked away. Few in the neighborhood were home at the time, and none who were at home had seen him come or go.

Billy got that word as his chief arrived to talk to him and to inspect the damaged squad car. He was clearly upset, but was also concerned about Billy's shaken condition. He could see that it had been a close call and held his anger, simply telling Billy to wait until the tow truck arrived, then go home. They'd talk more the next morning.

That was fine with Billy. He just wanted to kiss his wife, hug his kids, and have himself a beer and a bump.

IT WAS EARLY AFTERNOON when Gabby got the call from Detective Philips reporting on what had happened in Columbia Heights. "Unfortunately, the driver got away," he told her. "The car was turned over to the sheriff in Anoka County, which has jurisdiction, but they've promised to let me know what, if anything, their forensic people find."

"Jeez," she said. "Is the cop OK?"

"Yeah, he was lucky. He could've been killed. The guy in the car sure didn't give a damn."

"What else?" she asked.

"The plates were stolen in California a couple of months ago and somehow found their way here. And the car itself was registered to a suburban Chrysler dealer, which reported it stolen off their used car lot several weeks ago."

"And?"

"If the guy had time," Philips said, "he probably wiped the car clean and took anything that could lead us to him. On first look, we found nothing significant, but we'll have to wait for the forensics."

Gabby said nothing, her mind racing. Finally, she said, "It does seem to prove what we first suspected, that the guy, maybe both of them, could live around there."

"That's true. You deserve the credit. You had a good hunch."

"But you can't canvas the whole damn city."

"True again. That's why we'd like to ask you guys and the rest of the media to publish the sketch. See if that helps us find the guy."

"*What?*"

Philips laughed. "I knew that'd get a rise. But relax. We'll only connect him to this incident, not to the dead guy in the house or the mystery suicide. We're simply saying that he's wanted in an assault, and in the attempted murder of the Columbia Heights cop. Certainly nothing about the attack on Zach and his dog."

"But seeing his sketch on TV or in the newspaper is going to make him go for even deeper cover," Gabby argued.

"Maybe. But that won't make any difference now. He knows that we're on to him, that we're out looking for him."

What Gabby thought, but didn't say, is that it could also make him and his partner or partners more desperate.

He seemed to read her mind. "I know what you must be thinking. Once he sees the sketch he'll know it's probably your buddy Zach who provided the description ... "

"That's right. Until now they may have thought they'd scared us off. Not anymore. They'll know we're still in the chase."

"But it's not just you anymore," Philips said. "They'll know that you now have the cops on your side."

"But you've got guns and we don't."

He laughed.

"Not funny," she said. "But I'll talk to our producers and see if I can get the sketch on the early newscasts."

"Good. We'll send over an official release to go along with the sketch. And I'll give you another call if we turn anything else up."

"One more thing," she said. "Did you ever find out where John Doe's mail was being delivered?"

"Sorry, I forgot to tell you. A rental box at a FedEx store in Roseville. But it was closed out the day after the body was found."

"No surprise. Who was renting it?"

"Guess."

"Zimtronics."

"Right on. With a phony signature on the rental agreement. So now we have to start the whole process over again, to try and figure out where the mail is going now. It'll take some time."

"OK. Keep in touch."

When she turned in her chair she found her cube mate, Sarah Andrews, staring at her. "I didn't mean to eavesdrop," she said, "but what have you gotten yourself into? I mean, what I heard, 'You've got guns, we don't...running for cover...still in the chase.' It sounded like a TV movie."

Gabby smiled, but was slightly pissed that she'd been overheard. "Not as dramatic as it sounded, I'm afraid. That was a cop on the other end, maybe involving this suicide investigation we're into."

"Really? Tell me more."

It was the first time she had shown any real interest, but Gabby was hesitant to reveal too much. "One of the guys we're interested in may have tried to run down a cop in Columbia Heights today, and this detective I know has asked us and the other stations to run a sketch of him on the air."

"No kidding."

"It's still very tentative, so please don't say anything to anyone, OK?"

She pursed her lips. "It's like my lips are sealed."

GABBY FOUND ROBIN SHUSTER, the executive producer, at her desk reviewing some of the scripts for the early newscasts. "You got a minute?" Gabby asked.

Shuster looked up. "Sure. What's up?"

Gabby quickly briefed her on the situation and the police request to show the sketch on the air. "They're going to e-mail me an official release, and I'd be happy to write the piece, if you'd like."

"OK," she said, "I'll tell the five and six o'clock producers to leave a little room."

"Thanks."

"The other stations will have it, too?"

"Just that he's wanted for trying to kill the cop, nothing about our suicide story."

"This is the same guy who attacked Zach?"

"We think so, yes."

"This is getting goddamned weird," she said.

Next Gabby went in search of Zach, who—because he couldn't go out on stories—had been relegated to the editing booth, helping to assemble stories other photographers had shot for the evening news. It wasn't an assignment he savored but had accepted under the circumstances.

He was as surprised as everyone when told of the close encounter between the Columbia Heights cop and the bad guy. "Sounds like I was lucky to only get a knee in the groin," he said. "This is one nasty man."

"Did it give you any second thoughts?" she asked. "About what we're doing?"

"No," he replied without hesitation. "You?"

"Not really. But I'd feel a lot better if they'd caught him."

Zach leaned back, hands cupped around the back of his neck. "Even then, there'd still be at least one more that we know about. And I think Philips may be right. Now that these guys know the cops are involved, they may care less about us."

"Maybe," she said, "but they still know we may have started the whole thing."

He shrugged. "Nothing we can do about that now."

GABBY'S BRIEF STORY appeared in the middle of the five o'clock newscast, read by one of the anchors just before they broke for the weather.

Minneapolis and Columbia Heights police have asked for the public's help in identifying the man whose likeness appears in this sketch. He is wanted for an assault in Minneapolis several days ago, and, today, for the attempted murder of a Columbia Heights police officer, who narrowly escaped death or serious injury when the suspect rammed the front of his squad car. He is described as six feet tall, 250 pounds, with curly black hair and a quite prominent nose. If you know the identity of this man, please call the Minneapolis police Tip-Line.

AMONG THOSE WHO WERE watching and saw the item was Barclay, at home after spending the day, out of touch, at an all-day management retreat. Caught unaware, he quickly put in a call to Gabby, who brought him up to date.

"Was that your idea," he asked, "to give the sketch to the cops in Columbia Heights?"

She admitted that it was.

"Good thinking," he said, "but where does this leave us?"

She repeated what she and Zach had discussed. "We just don't know. If the cops find the guy, it could help, I guess. If they don't, and he's still out there, then nothing changes."

"I think you're right. Let's see what the public appeal brings, but in the meantime, keep your guard up."

"We will," she promised, again.

Nineteen

Craig Jessup was running out of options and before too long, he feared, out of money.

By now, he had spent several days moving from spot to spot around the television station, varying the time of day, never staying too long in one place, never doing anything that would draw unwanted attention. He wore different clothes and went go out of his way to avoid eye contact, speaking to no one unless spoken to—and then only in a perfunctory way.

Hia aim was to become as invisible as a six feet, good-looking guy with a ring in his lip could be.

Despite this persistent and solitary surveillance, he had yet to catch a glimpse of Gabby. *Did she never go outside? To lunch? For a drink after work?* The only exception came late one day when he may have seen her in the passenger seat of a station car leaving the underground garage. But the car had passed by so quickly, bathed in the glare of the late afternoon sun, that he couldn't be sure. And even if it was her, he'd had no way to follow.

Now, more than ever, he was convinced they must be protecting her.

But that wasn't his only frustration.

He'd called a friend of his at Gabby's old television station, who was no particular friend of hers, in hopes of getting

Gabby's new cell phone number. But he was told that no one had spoken to her since she'd left the station, and that she'd left no new number that anyone was aware of. Further, he learned, Sam Ryan had been poking around the newsroom, asking whether anyone had seen or heard about *him*.

Alone, that bit of news was scary enough to dictate a change of tactics. But there were other factors.

Knowing there might be an attempt to trace his movements, he had emptied his bank account in San Jose and opened another in Santa Cruz, some thirty miles away. He'd also cancelled all but one of his credit cards, using the remaining one as sparingly as possible—mainly for identification. As often as he could, he paid for things in cash, but with the cost of his motorcycle journey, the motel, and other expenses, the cash was now running low. And there was precious little left in the new bank account.

It had taken most of his savings to pay the defense lawyer in his criminal assault case and the two-thousand-dollar fine the court had imposed. With his mother dead and no siblings, he was the sole heir to his father's estate, but that money was in a trust and wouldn't be available until his father's death. And who knew when that might be?

Also, when it did happen, he'd have to return to California to collect, facing whatever consequences his flight from probation would bring.

In short, he literally could not afford to hang around much longer.

So, for the past three days he had paid careful attention to people leaving the station at the end of the day, especially those who would move on to one of the nearby bars. It quickly became clear that a favorite hangout was Brit's, the pub just down the Mall. Virtually every day at least two, three, or more employees—often the same people—would walk out of the station and head for Brit's.

He decided, reluctantly, to join the crowd, to become

visible. He began to hang around Brit's in the late afternoons, sometimes sitting at the bar or at a table off to one side, sipping a draft beer, watching who would come and go, no longer hesitant to strike up a conversation or become part of the crowd.

Say what you will about Craig Jessup, he was—as Gabby once described him to Zach—"smooth as silk." On cue, he could be clever and funny, with a bright smile and an engaging laugh. He made friends easily, remembering names, quick with a story or joke, and—with the women—was a bit of a flirt, always careful not to cross any boundaries and become a tiresome jerk.

Those traits were what led the mayor of San Jose to hire him years before. He could work a crowd, a consummate glad-hander, uniquely able to recruit supporters and placate opponents, always with a cheerful smile and a friendly arm around the shoulder.

And that's what had surprised the mayor when the other, darker side of Craig Jessup had so suddenly, so inexplicably, emerged, like a fierce thunderstorm that broke from a blue, cloudless sky. The transformation remained a psychological mystery, and it simply baffled him.

The bar was crowded enough that Jessup could move around without attracting special attention. But he mostly stood at the bar, nursing his beer, exchanging pleasantries with anyone who seemed in the mood to talk, always managing to keep an eye on where the Channel 7 employees happened to be sitting or standing.

Twice he was able to grab a chair at a table next to that group, glancing at his watch now and then, as if he expected someone to join him. Despite the din in the bar, he could overhear some of their conversation, which varied from news stories of the day to sports to station gossip.

The second time, there were two men and a woman, a brunette with a nice tan and a tight sweater, who seemed bored with her companions and would give him a not-too-coy glance now and then. Jessup took that as an opening and finally worked up enough courage to interrupt. "Sorry," he said, leaning over, "but I couldn't help but overhear a little of your conversation. Are you folks from Channel 7?"

One of the guys, pointing to his cap with Channel 7 logo, said, "How'd you guess?"

Jessup laughed, putting on his brightest smile. "Sorry. I didn't even notice."

Looking slightly irritated, the guy asked, "What can we do for you?"

"Didn't mean to butt in," Jessup said. "Name's Michael Craft, from Boston. Here visiting a buddy, who must have gotten hung up in traffic."

"You don't sound like you're from Boston," the woman said. "No funny accent."

Jessup leaned a little closer. "I was only there for a couple of years. Working at WBZ until I got laid off a month ago. That's why I perked up when I heard you were from Channel 7."

"You looking for a job?" she asked.

"Not really. I got an OK severance. But I'll have to land someplace before too long, so I always try to keep my eyes and ears open."

"What did you do at 'BZ?"

"Producing on the overnight shift. Writing for the early morning news shows."

"The Graveyard."

"You got that right."

The woman moved her chair, making room, stretching her pair of lithe legs in the process. "Want to join us?"

"Sure, if you don't mind. Until my buddy shows up."

To his immense relief, no one at the table apparently knew anyone at WBZ, or much about Boston—since he'd never been there in his life.

The men, who never bothered to introduce themselves, ignored him, involved in their own spirited conversation about the latest pitching woes of the Twins. Leaving him to her.

"So," Jessup said, "what do you do at the station?"

"Reporter."

"Really? How long?"

"A couple of years. But I hope to be moving on before long."

"To?"

"Somewhere south. Atlanta, maybe. Or Phoenix. I'm tired of the snow and cold."

"I get ya," he said. "I got enough of that in Boston."

As the conversation continued, Jessup was at his convivial best: amusing, mildly flirtatious, inventing his personal history as he went. Grew up in Missouri, one of three kids, a journalism degree from the University of Missouri, a series of jobs that took him from the West Coast to the East Coast, never staying long at any one place. Something of a news vagabond, he admitted with a laugh, always looking for new adventures.

All lies, of course, but delivered with his self-deprecating, convincing sincerity.

And he listened as well as he spoke, patiently exploring the woman's past, gently but not intrusively questioning where she'd grown up, went to school, and worked. "Golly," he finally said, "here we've been doing all of this talking, and I don't even know your name."

She smiled. "I wondered when you'd ask."

"So?"

"Sarah," she said. "Sarah Andrews."

"Nice to know you, Sarah."

"And you," she replied, shifting slightly in her chair, showing a little more leg.

By now, almost forty-five minutes and two beers later, her two male colleagues had left, but only after she'd declined to leave with them. "You're sure you're OK?" one had asked, giving Jessup another hard look.

"No problem," she'd said. "I'll just wait till his friend gets here."

The fact that his "friend" hadn't yet arrived didn't seem to trouble her.

"So tell me, Sarah, are they doing any hiring over at your place?"

"Not really," she said. "Only one recently, and that was kind of freaky."

"What do you mean?"

"A reporter. She just showed up. The boss didn't even know she was coming."

"That *is* freaky."

She shrugged. "I know. The new GM brought her in without telling anyone."

"Strange. Never heard of that before. Where's she from?"

"San Jose. It's funny, but I sit next to her and still don't know squat about her. She's not around much, and doesn't talk much when she is there."

"I worked in San Francisco before going to Boston," he said. "Maybe I know her."

"You do get around, don't you?"

He flashed a grin. "That's me."

"Her name's Gabby Gooding. A blond. Mid to late twenties, I'd say."

He feigned surprise. "Really? Small world. I didn't really know her, but I recognize the name. We used to monitor the San Jose stations from time to time, and I remember that she did some weekend anchoring. I didn't know she had moved...but I haven't been back there in a while."

"She's hasn't been here that long."

"You don't happen to know how I could get ahold of her, do you? I'm thinking of heading back to the Bay area, and she may know of some contacts I could call."

For the first time, a look of suspicion crossed her face. "You sure you're not just looking for another hookup?"

Surprised, he spread his hands in mock innocence. "The idea!"

She giggled. "She's camped out with one of our photographers, Zach Anthony. He lives in Uptown somewhere."

He leaned in. "So she's living with this guy?"

"Just rooming with him. At least that's what she says."

"I see."

"Give me your cell number and I'll have her give you a call."

"Some jerk on the street grabbed my cell and took off and I don't have my buddy's phone number. But once he gets here, I'll get it for you."

"Well, I'm afraid I can't wait," she said. "I gotta finish up a script for tomorrow. Are you going to be around here tomorrow night?"

"If you're going to be here, I'll be here," he said, with one of his patented grins. "But why don't you give me your card in case something comes up. I can give you a call."

She eased out of her chair and gave him her card. "I hope you do. You seem like a nice guy. Stick around town, OK."

"You can bet on it," he said as he watched her go.

He would never see her again.

Twenty

Gabby was at her desk the next morning when the young woman approached. She was slender, brown-haired, and freckle-faced, looking like the teenager she probably was, wearing a University of Minnesota sweatshirt with Goldie the Gopher splashed across the front.

"Ms. Gooding?" she said.

Gabby looked up. "It's Gabby, actually."

"Jeff Parkett asked me to speak to you."

"And you are?"

"Linda. Linda Wilkins. I'm an intern here."

"Nice to meet you Linda. What's up?"

She stood nervously. "He asked me to check on tattoo parlors for you."

"Oh, right," Gabby said, suddenly remembering the request she'd made. "Sit down, please."

She slipped into Sarah Andrews's empty chair. "This will only take a minute."

Gabby waited.

"I don't know if you know, but tattoo parlors and body artists have to be licensed, either by the state, cities, or counties."

"I guess I'd never really thought about it," Gabby said.

"I hadn't either, until I was asked to look. What I found are literally dozens, if not scores, of those places in the Twin Cities. And hundreds of individual body artists, all of them licensed."

"No kidding."

"I stopped in and talked to a couple of them. They said it would be almost impossible to trace a tattoo like the one Jeff said you had. Especially if it's as old as you think it may be."

Gabby leaned back and closed her eyes. Another possible lead shot to shit.

"I'm sorry," Linda said. "I could keep looking, if you'd like. But it could take a long time."

"No, no, but thanks for trying. Maybe I can find another way."

"Is there anything else I can do for you?"

"I don't think so, not now."

The young woman started to get up. "Jeff told me that you started out as an intern, is that right?"

"That's right. In Portland, like a lifetime ago."

"Would you do it again, do you think? Knowing how the business has changed? Is changing?"

The question caught Gabby off guard. "I'd have to think about that," she replied. "But, yeah, I think I would. It's kind of in my blood. Like you say, the business has changed, even since I started. But from everything I can see and hear, it still needs people who are curious, ambitious, and like to write. You might end up working somewhere on the Internet instead of a station like this, or at some newspaper or magazine, but you'd still be covering the news. And I guess that's what's important."

"Thanks," she said, without much conviction.

"So what do you want to be?" Gabby asked.

"Like you. A reporter. But who knows what 'reporting' will actually mean by the time I finally get out of school?"

Gabby smiled. "I suspect there will still be opportunities. But you may have to search harder than I did to find them.

I'd be happy to talk more with you at some point, maybe over coffee or a Coke."

"I'd appreciate that. Just tell me when."

"I'll come find you one day when I get a break."

As she walked away, Gabby's cell phone sounded. She checked the caller. Detective Philips.

"Hey," she said. "Give me some good news, OK."

"Sorry," he said. "We checked the Chrysler. As we suspected, the obvious places like the steering wheel and gear shift were wiped clean."

"Surprise."

"There *were* plenty of prints all over the car, too many to count, really. Which isn't surprising, considering it's a used car that got stolen. Who knows how many people have been in it over the past couple of years? Our print people tell me it would take weeks, if not months, to try and match all the prints. And they're not eager to try."

"I understand," she said, trying to hide her disappointment.

"Buck up. There *is* some good news."

"Tell me."

"We got dozens of responses to the broadcast of the sketch, and we've started to check those out with the help of the Columbia Heights cops. It'll take awhile, but we've begun with the tips from that part of town. Which brings me to the other good news. My boss has freed me up to pursue this thing pretty much full time. The Heights hit-and-run has convinced him that this could be bigger than he first thought. My partner will keep working on our other stuff with another detective while I concentrate on this."

"That's great," she said.

"One more thing. You remember asking if we were going to go back to the house to check things out again? After the neighbor saw lights in the window?

"I remember."

"Well, we're finally going to get there later this afternoon, if you'd like to stop by."

"I'd like that," she said.

"Good. About three o'clock. I'll see you then."

"OK."

There was a pause, then, "Now that I'm on this full time, we'll probably be seeing more of each other. Maybe grab another drink sometime?"

"That's fine, but it will have to be a threesome. Barclay doesn't want Zach and me apart."

"Even with a cop?"

"That would leave Zach alone, and Barclay wants us together."

Another pause, disappointment in his voice. "OK, a threesome it will be."

Two hours later, as she and Zach were sitting in the lunchroom munching on sandwiches they'd brought from the apartment, John Knowles appeared at the door, looked in, and wandered over to their table.

"Hey, John," Gabby said. "I thought you'd fallen off the end of the earth."

"Sorry about that," he replied. "I've been kind of busy."

"Sit," she said, offering some of the potato chips they'd brought with them.

He took a handful, carefully putting one after another into his mouth.

"So what have you been so busy with?" she asked.

"Your story. Talking to a bunch of people, following a lot of bad leads. Getting nowhere, very fast. I've been hesitant to come talk to you until I had something to say."

"You're here now," Zach said, hopefully.

Knowles leaned back. "Like you, there are things I still can't get my head around, like, what is this corporation called Zimtronics? And why would it want to own a house in northeast Minneapolis, a house hiding a dead guy? I've tried my damndest to find out, but I've run into a brick wall. Because the company's registered in Delaware, our Secretary of State's office knows virtually nothing about it—just a post office box, and a phone number that's been disconnected. I ran it through LexisNexis and other places for the names of the officers, and came up with nothing."

Gabby and Zach could see his frustration. "So I figured it must be a straw company," he went on, "set up to protect the identity of whoever actually owns the house."

"But why?" Gabby said.

Knowles shrugged his shoulders. "That's what I kept asking myself. So I decided to try one place we haven't tried until now."

"What?"

"The Feds," Knowles replied. "I've got a couple of contacts in the US Attorney's office and one of them agreed to see me. Guy by the name of Hank Shields, one of the army of prosecutors over there. We go back a long way, but that doesn't seem to count. They're all as tight-assed as you can get, but I did learn a couple of things..."

"Like?"

"Like he didn't know—or says he didn't know—anything about our suicide John Doe. To his knowledge, nobody from the Minneapolis PD had talked to anyone in their office about the case, but he said that doesn't surprise him. If they were talking to anyone, it would probably be the FBI."

"So," Gabby said, "another dead end?"

"Maybe not. He seemed to perk up when I mentioned the name Zimtronics and how it was tied to the suicide. But that's a bit of an exaggeration. When he heard the name he kind of sat back in his chair and gave me a strange look. It seemed clear to me that he recognized it."

"What then?" Zach asked.

"Nothing, really. At his urging, I told him everything I could about the case, but he just sat there and listened. In the end, he wanted to know Detective Philips's name and the name of the medical examiner handling the John Doe. He promised to get back to me, but didn't say when. And that was it. He got up and hurried away to what he said was another meeting and left me sitting there until his assistant came in and ushered me out. I found the whole thing a bit strange."

Gabby and Zach sat quietly, absorbing what they'd been told. Finally, she said, "That's good work, John. But does he know that it's *our* story? Whatever it is?"

"He knows," Knowles said. "I said it often enough. But I don't really trust any of them. The media's not exactly their best buddies. We'll just have to wait and see."

"But it seems like you rang some kind of bell with him," Zach offered. "That's a plus. If the Feds show some interest, there may be something there."

"We can hope," Knowles replied.

As THEY TALKED, Sarah Andrews was at her desk, searching the Internet for any information on her newly-found bar buddy, Michael Craft. Facebook offered pictures of a number of users by that name, none of whom bore the slightest resemblance to the man she'd met. She also tried several other social media search sites, again to no avail.

This struck her as very strange. Unbelievable, actually. She didn't know of anyone in the news business who was not on one or more of the sites. It was a professional necessity, a tool of the trade, to say nothing of a personal choice to keep in contact with friends and family.

Finally, with a growing uneasiness, she put in a call to WBZ-TV in Boston and asked for the news department. "I'm trying to reach one of your former employees," she said to the voice on the assignment desk. "Michael Craft, one of your overnight producers. Said he got laid off recently ... "

"Who?" came the response.

"Michael Craft."

"Are you sure he was at WBZ?"

"That's what he said."

"Well, I've been here five years and I've never heard of him. He must have been at one of the other stations."

"Thanks," Sarah said, with a pause. "I must have mis-understood."

As she clicked off, she realized that Craft had never spoken in detail about his experience at 'BZ or anyone he knew there. He simply said that he had worked the graveyard shift and had gotten the boot. Nor, she had to admit, had she asked him much about it. Maybe it was the several beers or his be-guiling line of chatter, but she'd obviously been had, which left her angry and a tad ashamed.

But why would he lie about who he was or what he did, especially if he wanted to get a thing going with her, or was actually interested in a possible job at Channel 7? The an-swer, clearly, was that he was interested in neither, or, that he figured she was too dumb or awestruck to check up on him, which pissed her off even more.

Simmering, she could hardly wait to confront him that night at the bar, if he showed up.

It was at that moment that Gabby returned to the cubicle.

"Hey, Gabby," she said, casually, "you ever hear of a guy named Michael Craft?"

"No, I don't think so," she replied, sitting. "Why?"

Sarah debated, finally saying, "No reason, really. I ran into him last night at Brit's, and he said he used to work in the Bay area. Remembered seeing you anchor in San Jose."

Gabby's antenna was suddenly at full height. "Tell me more. What did he look like?"

"Tall, good-looking blond with a beard. Funny guy, with a line of bullshit a mile long."

Gabby's face turned ashen. "What did you tell him? About me?"

"Nothing, nothing," she said, realizing now that she may

have made a big mistake. She would say no more, and certainly make no mention of the lies she'd apparently been told, that he probably was not who he said he was. "He was just hoping to make some contacts back in your old stomping grounds, and that you might have some ideas."

"That's all? You're sure?"

"I'm sure," she lied, remembering now that she'd also told him Gabby was living with Zach. "But what's the big deal? Do you think you know him?"

"No, probably not," she said. "I just like my privacy."

IN THE CAR, as they drove to meet Philips at the suicide house, Gabby told Zach what Sarah had said to her.

"Did you show her Jessup's picture?" he asked.

"I didn't have it with me. I should have, I know."

Zach kept his eyes on the road. "What else did she say?"

"Nothing. But I had the feeling she was holding something back."

"Why?"

"I don't know. Just the look on her face, I guess. A little guilty, maybe, but I could be wrong."

As they pulled up in front of the house, the crime scene van was just leaving. Philips stood in the doorway and waved them in.

As eager as she had been to see the house, to get a look inside, she now had second thoughts. "This is going to be spooky," she told Zach. "It's like his ghost may still be hanging around."

He laughed. "If it is, maybe he'll tell us who the hell he is and what happened to him. Keep your eyes and ears open and tell me if you hear any voices."

She gave him an elbow in the ribs. "I'm serious. Not about the ghost, but about it being spooky."

"Want me to hold your hand?"

Before she could respond, they were at the front door.

"C'mon in," Philips said, leading them through the entryway and into the living room. "This is probably a waste of time. There's not much to see."

They stood for a moment as Gabby tried to escape the feeling that she had invaded a forbidden place. The living room was fairly large—larger than you'd expect by looking at the house from the outside—with an archway connecting it to the dining room. All of the furniture in both rooms was covered by sheets that could have been there for years. The air was musty and filled with tiny dust particles pirouetting in the sunlight from the windows that Philips or someone must have undraped.

She breathed in, but if she expected to smell death in the air she was disappointed.

"The crime scene guys were only here for an hour," Philips told them as they moved on into the kitchen. "They were kinda pissed, since a couple of them had spent most of the day here when the body was discovered. But they did as you suggested, Gabby, and redusted some of the obvious places that the guy who was here that night might have touched. We'll have to wait and see if anything comes of it."

Zach, wearing the latex gloves Philips had given each of them, opened the kitchen cupboards and found them all empty. It was the same with the drawers. No dishes, no silverware. No pots or pans. Aside from the refrigerator, which was also empty, there were no appliances. No toaster or coffee pot or microwave. "The burglar who got in here and found the body must have been disappointed," Gabby said. "Doesn't look like there was anything in this whole house to steal."

The stairway to the basement was located at one end of the kitchen. "Now to the scene of the crime," Philips said as he opened the door and hit the light switch, leading them down the steps. Gabby hesitated, but only for a moment, taking a deep breath.

The basement was unfinished: bare concrete floor and cement block walls. A partition closed off one area from the rest of the basement, where the furnace and hot water heater were apparently located. The air was much cooler here than the upstairs. And moist.

As she stood at the foot of the stairs, her eyes immediately fastened on a small spot on the floor, reddened by what she knew must have been dried blood from the John Doe's bullet wound. Clearly, no one had been here to clean it all up.

Philips walked to the blood spot. "He was sitting here on the floor with his back against a chair. We eventually found the bullet inside the furnace room. It had passed through the guy's skull, through the wall, and was lodged in one of the furnace ducts. Not much left of it by then."

Gabby stood next to him. "Dr. Maxwell said he was still holding the gun … "

"True."

"And that it's unusual to find it that way."

"Like I told her, I've seen it both ways. But now that we know it probably wasn't a suicide, whoever shot him probably wiped the gun clean and put it back in his hand."

"But she also said there was gunshot residue on his hand. How could that be if someone else held the gun to his head and shot him?"

Philips stared at her. "You're starting to piss me off, you know that?"

Zach stood back and listened as Gabby persisted. "Could the bad guy have forced our John Doe to fire a first shot before he got shot himself?"

"We didn't find a second bullet," Philips said.

"Did you look for one?"

"Not that I know of. We only followed the trajectory of the head shot. Which led us to the furnace room. And only one bullet was missing from the .45."

She shrugged her shoulders. "The killer could have replaced it. Maybe that's what that guy was looking for the other night. The second bullet."

Philips held her eyes. "OK. You guys take off. I'll stick around and see what I can find. But I'm sure as hell not calling the forensic people back again."

"Don't get pissed," she said. "You thought it was a suicide. You had no reason to look for another bullet back then."

He waved them away.

As they walked up the steps, she looked back, watching him watching her. She couldn't really tell if there was amusement, admiration, or anger in his eyes. Maybe a little of all three. But he sure as hell wasn't watching her rear end.

Twenty-One

When Sarah Andrews walked into Brit's that evening, she was accompanied by the same two men who'd been with her the night before—Eric Samples, a technician, and Roger Ostby, a photographer. Together, they scanned the crowded bar for a glimpse of Michael Craft, but—no real surprise to her—found no sign of him.

All she had told the two in advance was that Craft apparently was not the man he'd said he was, and that she wanted to confront him.

"I knew he was a phony the first time I saw him," Samples said. "Coming on like that, all smiles with that bogus gift of gab. I wanted to warn you, but I thought you could take care of yourself, that you'd figure it out sooner or later."

"Well, I didn't," she admitted, still surveying the crowd, "and that's my fault."

Ostby, who was about six feet two and 230 pounds, said, "I hope he does show up, so we can have a nice long talk with him."

"I don't want you to do anything," Sarah said. "Just leave him to me."

They took the same table as the night before and ordered a round of beers and a basket of fries, waiting. Twenty minutes later, as she watched the entrance, she saw Harry Wilson walk

182 | Ron Handberg

in and grab a seat at the bar. "I'll be back in a minute," she said, leaving the table to join Wilson.

"Hey, Sarah," he said as she took a stool next to his. "I didn't see you over there."

"You have a minute?" she asked.

"I guess so, but I hope it's not about work. I just left that behind."

"I'm worried," she said. "And I need to talk to somebody."

Wilson was a no bigger fan of Sarah than was Zach or almost anyone else in the newsroom. He considered her a lightweight who was all show and little tell. But it was clear from her expression now that something significant was troubling her. "Are you sure I'm the right guy to talk to? If something's really bugging you, maybe you should stop by Barclay's office tomorrow."

"Please," she said. "It could be important."

Sighing, he took a sip of his beer. "OK. Shoot."

She quickly repeated the details of her encounter with Craft the night before. "He was a cute, nice guy and I didn't think much more about it until I started checking up on him today … and found out that everything he said was probably a lie."

Wilson looked confused. "So?"

"So he said he might be looking for a job and wondered if we were doing any hiring? I said there was only one hire recently … a woman named Gabby Gooding."

Wilson groaned and put his head in his hands.

She went on. "He said he knew of her … that he'd worked in the Bay area and had seen her do some anchoring in San Jose."

He looked up, fear in his eyes. "What else?"

"When I found out today that he wasn't who he said he was … I remembered the rumors in the newsroom about one of her old boyfriends … who … "

He reached into his jacket pocket and pulled out the

picture of Craig Jessup. "Is this the guy?"

Shaken, she took the picture and studied it. Finally, she said, "I think so. But he has a beard now and was wearing a Twins cap."

"Holy shit," he muttered.

"What?"

He grabbed her forearm. "What else did you tell him?"

She pulled her arm free. "Hey! That hurt!"

"Sorry. What else?"

"You gotta understand. At the time, there was no reason to be suspicious. I thought he was who he said he was."

Wilson had lost his patience. "Sarah, what else?"

Reluctantly, "He wanted to get in touch with her to check on some possible contacts in the Bay area. I told him I didn't know her cell number, but that she was staying with Zach somewhere in Uptown. I said I'd have her call him, but he claimed he'd lost his phone. That's all, I swear."

Wilson finished his beer with one big gulp. "I have to make some calls," he said. "Please don't mention any of this to anyone else."

She pointed to Samples and Ostby across the way. "They saw him, too."

"That's OK. Just don't say anything more to them."

"Is he the guy? The old boyfriend? Am I in big trouble?"

"No. You had no way of knowing. I just wish you weren't so trusting."

"So do I, now."

As WILSON WATCHED HER walk away, he picked up his phone and—with some trepidation—put in a call to Barclay at home. He answered on the first ring.

"George? Wilson here. Sorry to bother you…"

"No bother," Barclay replied. "What's up?"

He quickly explained where he was and what he'd just been told.

"You think it was Jessup?"

"I showed her his picture. He's got a beard now, but she's pretty sure it was him."

An almost inaudible "Son of a bitch," came from the other end of the line. Then, "I guess it's no big surprise."

Wilson waited. "What do you want me to do?" he finally asked.

"Call Gabby and Zach. Play it as calm and cool as you can, but they have to know that Jessup may know where they're living. At least the area of town."

"You're sure you shouldn't make the call?"

"No, you're the one who talked to Sarah. You've got more of the details."

"OK, if you say so."

"Do you know if Zach's phone number and address are listed anywhere?"

"I doubt it," Wilson said. "I know he doesn't have a land line at home."

"Good. That may help. While you call them, I'll call the desk and tell them not to give out Zach's number or address to anybody. And to pass the word."

"It may be too late. She talked to the guy late yesterday."

"Nothing we can do about that," Barclay said. "Just make the calls."

"Gotcha."

"We'll talk in the morning."

ZACH WAS DRYING OFF the poodle after a bath in the bathroom sink when he heard his phone sound in the other room. "Will you get that, Gabby?"

She found the phone in his bedroom. "Yes?"

"Gabby? Harry Wilson here."

"Hey, Harry. Zach's kinda tied up."

"You'll do fine," he said. "But brace yourself."

"What do you mean?"

By now, Zach had joined her, carrying Barclay, wrapped in a bath towel. "What's happening?"

"It's Harry Wilson," she said.

Before she could click the speaker, Wilson told her to listen carefully, repeating what Sarah Andrews had told him, and what he had told Barclay.

She closed her eyes and fell back onto Zach's bed. "I knew it! I knew she was hiding something. The bitch."

"Hold on," Wilson said. "I'm no fan of hers, either, but give her a break. She didn't know any better. Not everyone in the newsroom was given the word about this guy. She didn't get suspicious until she found out he wasn't who he said he was."

"So she's sure it was him?"

"Looks that way. And he may know where you're living by now."

"Hold on," she said, and quickly repeated everything for Zach. Then she took Barclay out of his arms and handed him the phone.

Wilson asked, "Your phone's not listed, is it?"

"No," Zach said, "but if he's got a computer, it won't take him long to find out the building I'm in, if not the apartment. You know that."

"Probably."

"So what do we do now?" Zach asked.

"Be even more cautious. Keep the Mace handy. And we'll meet with Barclay in the morning. That's all I can tell you."

"OK. Thanks for the heads-up."

Across town, Barclay was back on the phone, calling a number he hadn't called for months. It took four rings, but once the voice came on there was no mistaking it. Gruff, husky, hoarse. A whiskey voice born of too many shots of Wild Turkey.

"J.J. How're you doing?"

"Like shit. Who wants to know?"

Barclay laughed. "It's George Barclay, J.J."

"I'll be damned."

John Jacobs, J.J., was a retired St. Paul detective who had worked with Barclay in his pursuit of the cold case killer of Barclay's old high school classmate. Not only had he helped him solve the case, but had become his personal bodyguard after Barclay had been attacked and seriously injured by the killer.

In short, they had a history.

Barclay regretted that he hadn't talked to Jacobs more than once or twice in the many months since all of that had occurred, and was pleased to find he was still up and about, apparently as feisty as ever. He would be in his late seventies by now, a tough ex-Marine, who was long since divorced with a couple of grown kids living in other states.

"Sorry I haven't kept in closer touch," Barclay said.

"Why should you? You're a married man now. Don't have time for old bachelors like me. How's that going, by the way?"

Jacobs had been one of the ushers in their wedding

"Just fine. Rachel sends her regards."

"Good. She's a nice lady."

"So how are you doing?"

"Still upright, when I'm not drinking. And no replacement parts yet."

"I'd like to talk to you about another job," Barclay said.

"What kind of job?"

"Surveillance, mainly. No need for that gun of yours."

"I'm pretty much retired, you know."

"You said that last time."

There was a pause, which gave Barclay time to quickly explain the situation with Craig Jessup. "We think this guy's in town and may know where this reporter, Gabby, is living. He could be a threat to her, and I'd like to know where he is ... and what he's doing."

"OK. So what would you want me to do?"

"Hang around Uptown, where she's living. We'll give you a picture of the guy and a more recent description of him. All you'd have to do is keep your eyes open…hang around the streets, the coffee shops, the bars…whatever. And if you spot him, let me know. That's it."

"You'd pay me?"

"Of course. Expenses, too. Except for the Wild Turkey."

"Can I think about it?"

"Sure. Until tomorrow morning. If you decide it's OK, stop by the station and we'll set you up. I can't wait much longer than that."

"All right. I'll let you know."

Twenty-Two

For Gabby, not surprisingly, it was yet another restless night as she struggled for sleep that would not come. Her mind was adrift, a thousand dreamless thoughts dancing behind closed eyelids. Jessup, Sarah, her dad, the blood-stained basement floor. The images would appear, then disappear. In and out. Out and in.

Elusive. Maddening.

She clung to her pillow, burying her head in the softness, hearing nothing but the silence of the night. Unlike her, the city, outside her window, was fast asleep.

She had been up twice, tiptoeing to the kitchen for a glass of milk, stopping the last time to pick up Barclay from the couch, holding him tight, drawing momentary comfort from his small, warm body, hearing his contented growl that was more like a cat's purr.

She paused once outside Zach's open door, reassured by his soft, measured breathing, tempted to slide in next to him simply to feel the closeness of another human body.

Bad idea, she knew.

Back in bed, staring at the ceiling shadows and willing sleep to come, she was startled by the sudden ring of her cell phone. The light on the bedside clock said 2:15.

She rolled over and reached for the phone. "Yes?"

"Gabby?"

"Yes. Who's this?"

"Philips. Sorry to wake you."

"I was awake."

"Thought you'd want to know. They may have found our guy with the nose."

"What?" She sat up and threw aside the covers.

"Not him, yet, but where he may be living. I just got the call and am on my way."

For a moment, she was lost for words. Then, "Where?"

"In Fridley, just across the border from Columbia Heights in Anoka County. Thanks to one of the tips, they've got the place surrounded and under surveillance, but don't know yet if anyone's inside."

"You're sure?"

"Yeah. The call came from the Columbia Heights chief."

Gabby looked up and found Zach, groggy-eyed, in shorts and a T-shirt, standing at the bedroom door. "I heard the phone."

She quickly repeated what she'd been told. Then she said to to Philips, "Zach and I will be there as soon as we can. What's the address?"

"It's just off Fifty-Third Avenue NE. Take 694 to the University Avenue exit and take a right. It's only a block or so from there. I'll be watching for you."

"OK," she said.

"One more thing. You were right. Again. I did find a second bullet in the basement. It was lodged in one of the ceiling studs. The forensic guys missed it and so did my partner and I. Good call on your part."

"It was just a guess."

"I know, but still ... "

"Forget it," she said. "We gotta go."

Z<small>ACH</small> <small>WAS</small> <small>ALREADY</small> <small>IN</small> <small>A</small> sweatshirt and jeans, holding his camera gear, by the time she'd climbed into her own clothes, run a comb through her hair, and brushed her teeth. She felt like crap, fighting off her fatigue and a raging headache that had suddenly engulfed her.

They didn't speak until they were in the car, virtually alone on the road at that hour. "We're at least twenty minutes away," Zach said, glancing at his GPS. "Maybe a little more."

"It sounds like they're taking their time, so we may be OK," she said, her head against the car window, eyes closed, listening to the hum of the tires on the pavement.

"Are you all right?" he asked.

"No. It's like I've got a fire in my head."

"Where did that come from?"

"From no sleep, I think. It just hit me."

"There's aspirin in the glove compartment."

"Good." She reached in and took two, washing them down with a bottle of water she'd grabbed on the way out of the apartment.

Zach was on his cell phone to the station's overnight dispatcher. "Nate, this is Zach … are you awake?"

"Of course," came the response. "Sleepy, but awake."

"Good," Zach said. "Have you heard any radio traffic out of Fridley or Columbia Heights in the last half hour or so?"

"No. Nothing. What's going on … and where are you?"

"In my car, on our way to a possible story. You've got my cell number, right?"

"Sure."

"OK, if you hear anything on the police or the Anoka sheriff's frequencies from that part of town, call or text me right away."

"Will do."

"Call Wilson at home. Tell him he should head for the station. And don't say anything over the two-way. No telling who might be listening in."

"Want me to call anyone else?"

"Not now," Zach replied. "Just keep an ear on the radios."

Several minutes passed before Zach asked, "Is the headache any better?"

"No, not yet."

"So what's keeping you awake all night?"

"Guess."

"Jessup."

"Among other things."

"Like?"

"I don't know. My mind's a jumble. It's like I'm a juggler without hands. Everything seems to be coming down around me. Craig. The dead guy. Now this. I feel like I've hardly had time to breathe. It's all happening too fast. So I wind up spending the night staring at the ceiling and sipping milk."

"And worrying."

"Of course. But not just about me. Who knows what Craig may be up to? He didn't follow me out here to say hello. He must have something else in mind ... and here you are, stuck with me, smack in the middle of whatever that might be. And if something does happen, I know you're going to play the hero ... and get yourself hurt again. And I could never forgive myself for that."

"Listen," Zach said, glancing from the road to her, "if worrying about me is keeping you awake all night ... well, that's bullshit. Trust me, we can deal with Jessup if and when he ever shows up. And there's sure as hell no sense in losing sleep over it before then."

"Yeah, but he didn't beat the crap out of you. I've seen and felt what he can do. I know what he's capable of ... "

"That's when you were by yourself. You're not alone anymore, and you won't be until all of this is settled."

It wasn't until they were on I-694, heading east, that Gabby got another call from Philips. "Remember, take the

University exit and head south," he told her. "You'll see the barricade on Fifty-Third."

"So what's happening?" she asked.

"Nothing at the moment. I'll fill you in when you get here."

In another ten minutes they were there, and, as promised, Philips was standing next to a Fridley patrol car, waiting. Aside from the barricade and that squad car, there was no other sign of police activity within their view.

"Where is everybody?" Gabby asked as she got out of the car and Zach retrieved his camera gear.

"Laying low, right now. The house is two blocks over and they're still not sure if he, or anybody else, is inside. They've got the place surrounded and are trying to quietly evacuate the nearby homes without drawing any attention."

"Who's here?" she asked.

"Everybody. Fridley, Columbia Heights, and the Anoka County sheriff's people, who are in charge of the scene. Their swat team is a few blocks away, waiting for a call."

By now, Zach was standing with them. "Are they sure it's him?"

"The owner of the house recognized the guy in the sketch as the guy renting the place. Said he also knew he drove a Chrysler 300."

"Have they tried to contact him?"

"Haven't had a chance. The owner says there's no phone in the house."

"So what's the plan?" Gabby asked.

"I'm not running things," Philips replied. "I was called as a courtesy. But they tell me once they have the area secure, they'll call in the SWAT team and try to make contract with whoever's inside. They're hoping they can surprise him ... or them."

Zach said, "Our dispatcher back at the station says he's heard nothing over the police or sheriff's frequencies."

"I know. They must be using a special channel reserved for situations like this. They're afraid the guys inside might be monitoring scanners just like your dispatcher. They don't want to take a chance."

"Can we get closer?" Gabby asked.

"Maybe. I told the lead detective, a guy named Meyers, that you have a stake in this whole thing...that it was your sketch that led them here. But you gotta understand, he doesn't want this to turn into a media circus. That's why they're keeping it so quiet until they know what they're dealing with."

"So what do we do?"

"Wait," Philips said. "I'm going back in there now, and if and when it's OK, I'll come back and get you."

An hour passed. With little traffic to control and an early morning chill in the air, the Fridley patrolman retreated to his squad car, leaving Gabby and Zach standing alone, shivering as they waited. It reminded her, fleetingly, of the warmth she had left behind in California.

"How's the headache?" Zach asked.

"Better, thanks. The aspirin helped. But I can barely keep my eyes open."

The sky had lightened slightly, which left only another hour or so until actual daybreak. Something had to happen soon.

Ten minutes later, Philips approached through the shadows. "The houses on both sides and across the street have been evacuated," he told them, "and still no sign of movement in the house itself. So the party's about to begin."

"What about us?" Gabby asked.

"It took some persuasion, but I finally got permission to bring you along, with conditions. You've got to stay close to me, and when we get there, take cover behind one of the squads. There are a couple of helmets and flak jackets waiting. Keep your camera out of sight, and no lights, no noise until we see what happens. Agreed?"

"Agreed," they both replied.

"Remember, my ass is on the line on this," he said. "So don't screw me."

They followed him along the darkened street quietly, and so close behind they were almost tripping over one another. Gabby held Zach's arm loosely to avoid stumbling on cracks in the sidewalk. An ambulance stood on one side of the street, lights and motor off. They saw or heard nothing until they rounded a corner at the end of the block when—suddenly— they faced a line of squad cars, all parked diagonally, their now-darkened headlights and spotlights aimed at an older, two-story home in the middle of the block.

Philips took them behind the squad car parked farthest from the home and handed each a flak jacket and military-style helmet. "Put these on and stay put," he whispered. "Don't make a sound and keep your heads down."

"So what's going to happen?" she whispered back.

"Don't know. We'll just have to wait. It shouldn't be long."

Whatever chill she may have felt was gone now, along with the headache. She knew she was about to witness something she'd never seen before in her young reporter's life, and she was filled with a mixture of apprehension and excitement.

Zach had his camera on his shoulder, checking and re-checking his equipment.

Fifteen minutes passed when—on some unheard cue—all of the squad car lights flashed on, lighting the house as brilliantly as if the scorching sun had abruptly emerged above the trees. Zach fell to his knees and crawled around the front of the squad, taking cover behind the front tire. He aimed his camera in the direction of the house and began to shoot.

Gabby raised her head slightly above the squad car window just as a voice on a loudspeaker shattered the neighborhood silence. "THIS IS THE POLICE. YOU IN THE HOUSE, SHOW YOURSELF. HANDS HIGH, BEHIND YOUR HEAD. DO IT! DO IT NOW!"

She could hear a helicopter approach ... and then it was there, low overhead, hovering, its blazing spotlight fixed on the house. The bullhorn voice repeated its demands, but the house remained dark, with no sign of movement. She was on the ground, next to Zach, and whispered in his ear, "Are you getting all of this?"

He gave her a look, like, what the fuck do you think?

She saw lights come on in homes at either end of the street, and then the darkened figures of people as they emerged—held at bay by officers stationed next to the temporary barricades.

What seemed like an hour to her, but was really only fifteen minutes, went by with more shouted orders and more silence from the house. There was no parted curtain or shade, no sign of an inside light, or the opening of a door. Finally, with police patience exhausted, two armor-clad officers wearing gas masks approached the house behind shields, momentarily taking cover behind a large oak tree that dominated the front yard.

Then came an explosive sound and the shattering of glass.

And almost immediately, the smell of tear gas filled the morning air.

Then another shell went into another window, this one on the upper story, then another from the rear of the house.

The gas filled the air even at their distant outpost, and Gabby quickly covered her nose and mouth, the stinging tears falling on her cheeks.

Suddenly, Philips was there, wearing a mask and handing one to both her and Zach. "Sorry," he said, momentarily removing his mask, "I didn't know they were going to do that."

Choking, but before donning her mask, she asked, "What now?"

"Not sure. If anybody's in there, the gas should force them out. I suspect the cops will probably wait a few more minutes and then send the SWAT team in. But I don't know. I'm just an observer like you."

By now, dawn had broken and the sun was visible peeking over the roofs of the houses on the eastern side of the street. And, true to Philips's prediction, the masked SWAT team had gathered around the shelter of the house and—in one unified movement—stormed through the front and rear doors, using steel battering rams, shouting "POLICE! POLICE!" as they entered.

Then, nothing. No shots. No cries. Just a muffled series of "CLEAR."

Philips left, and by the time he returned twenty minutes later the tear gas had dissipated, allowing them to remove their masks—although both Gabby and Zach still had trouble ridding their throats and eyes of the lingering effects.

Philips's expression was hard to read, but he wasted no words. "The guy with the flat nose is inside, but he's dead. Has been for a while, apparently. Bullet wound to the back of the head, I'm told, like an execution."

Gabby was stunned.

"But that's not all. All of his fingers are gone. Cut off."

She felt the bile rise in the back of her throat.

"That last part is off the record. The medical examiner is on the way, as are the Anoka County forensic people. You won't hear anything official for a couple of hours, at least. Meyers, the lead detective, says he may hold a news briefing later this morning."

"So we still don't know who he is ... or was?"

"Not so far. But they may find something more when they search the house."

"And no sign of his buddy?" Zach asked.

"Not inside, no."

"So," Gabby speculated, "once the other bad guys knew this guy was being hunted, they decided to get rid of him—and any trace of who he is."

"That's a good guess," Philips replied.

"So, if you believe that, then by circulating the sketch, we got him killed."

"He tried to kill a cop, Gabby, and may have killed the guy in the basement. I wouldn't waste any tears."

As he walked away, a photographer and reporter from both Channel 6 and Channel 10 walked up, cleared finally by the cops at the barricade. They exchanged greetings as Zach quickly introduced Gabby to the three men and a woman.

"We've heard about you," said Tyler Wilkins, the Channel 6 reporter.

"Really?" Gabby replied with a friendly smile. "Well, it's nice to meet you all."

As the photographers set about recording what was left to see, Tyler asked Zach, "You been here long?"

"Long enough," Zach said with a small grin.

"What does that mean?"

"You'll have to wait and see."

The other reporter, Amy Wiggins, said, "So what have we got here?"

"A police raid with one dead guy inside," Zach said. "The cops are supposed to hold a briefing in a couple of hours, I guess."

Tyler was not to be fooled. "You've been here all along, haven't you? You're screwing with us."

"Would I do that?" Zach said as he pulled Gabby aside, far enough away not to be overheard. "Call Wilson. He should be in by now. Tell him what we've got … and to let Barclay know. Ask him what he wants us to do now."

Twenty-Three

Barclay was up early, as usual, when the call came. He was sitting at the kitchen counter, sipping his coffee, skimming editions of the *Star Tribune,* the *St. Paul Pioneer Press,* and the *New York Times,* at the same time switching television channels to catch some of the local and national morning news shows, taking notes on stories that might deserve a follow-up by his staff.

This early morning news gluttony drove Rachel crazy, so she often chose to stay in bed—as she did this morning—until he was finally out of the kitchen and in the shower.

Barclay checked the face of his iPhone. "Hey, Harry, you're up with the birds."

Wilson quickly told him what Gabby had just reported from the scene.

"No, shit? You mean we've got the whole damned thing to ourselves?"

"That's what she said. They were alone until it was all over, thanks to that cop friend of theirs."

"I'll be damned."

"So what d'ya want me to tell them?"

He thought for a moment. "OK. Have Gabby do an opening stand-up out there now and then relieve them with another crew and a live truck, whoever's available. They can wait for the briefing, whenever that comes. And talk to some of the neighbors. Get Zach's video back into the shop and start the editing. Gabby can do a short voice-over for the noon show and finish her piece later—when we get the official word."

"Got ya," Wilson said.

"And tell them congratulations. That's a nice little coup to have."

"Amen to that."

GABBY AND ZACH were way ahead of him. By the time they heard from Wilson, they'd already interviewed two of the neighbors from down the street, and one who had been evacuated from an adjacent home. Gabby was now sitting on the bumper of a squad car, writing the brief opening to her piece.

"Are you set?" Zach asked.

"In a minute," she replied.

By then, the Anoka County medical examiner had arrived, along with the forensic mobile lab. There was also a van from the BCA, the state Bureau of Criminal Apprehension. Yellow police tape surrounded the house and the neighboring homes.

"OK," she said as she took a quick glance at herself in her mirror and ran her fingers through her hair. "I look like hell, but let's do it."

Zach stationed her as close to the house as they were allowed to be with the police moving in and out. He gave the cue, and she began.

The early-morning quiet of this Fridley neighborhood was shattered when a police SWAT team fired tear gas into this home behind me—attempting to flush out a fugitive they believed was responsible for the attempted murder of a Columbia Heights police officer. When the man failed to respond, and when police finally entered the home, they discovered

that he was indeed inside but dead, the victim of an appar-
ent gunshot wound.

She did the standup twice, the second time glancing over
her shoulder as she mentioned the house behind her. It had
been so long since she'd appeared on camera that she had to
ask Zach if it had looked OK.

"Sure," he replied. "Like a pro. Now let's get back to the
station."

As BARCLAY EMERGED from the shower encased in a towel,
Rachel stepped out of the bedroom, sleep still in her eyes.
"Hey," he said, "I was just ready to take a shower. Want to
join me?"

She laughed. "Nice try. I heard the water running."

"Ah, shucks."

She wore a filmy nightdress he'd given her for her birthday,
and he found it hard to take his eyes off of her.

"Down, boy," she said, heading for the kitchen. "I need
my coffee."

He followed along, the view from the rear as enticing as
the one from the front. Despite a year of marriage, he still
couldn't get over the wonder of her. and the fact that she had
actually allowed a guy like him to come into her life.

She poured her coffee and settled onto a stool at the counter. "I also heard you on the phone a while ago," she said.
"What's going on?"

He leaned against the counter and repeated what Wilson
had told him. "We've got video of the whole thing from start
to finish. By ourselves."

"That's great," she replied. "But did they really cut off all
of his fingers?"

"Thumbs, too, I guess."

"How gross is that? Who are these people, anyway?"

"I wish we knew. That's what we're trying to figure out."

"Be careful, OK?"

WILSON AND PARKETT were waiting as Gabby and Zach walked into the newsroom dragging their feet, exhaustion clearly written on their faces. "Nice job, you guys," Parkett offered with a grin, grabbing each of them around the shoulders.

It was the first time, Gabby realized, that he had ever said a kind word to her.

"Thanks," she muttered, settling into the nearest chair.

"We already wrote a short piece for the morning show," Wilson said, "and we'd like to send you back out to the scene for a live shot at noon, if that's OK."

"That's fine, if I can just keep my eyes open."

"We've already thought of that. We set up a cot in the Green Room so you can rest for an hour or two before you go back out again."

"What about Zach?" she asked.

"I'm OK," he said. "Unlike you, I did get some sleep before all of this."

Once in the editing room, Zach found the video on the full-screen monitors even more compelling than he had seen through the camera. The lights from the squad cars and the police helicopter had turned near-darkness into near-daylight, enabling him to capture all of the sounds and sights of the drama unfolding in front of them.

"Jesus, that is spectacular stuff," Parkett said, staring at the screen.

"All I did was point and shoot," Zach said. "The cops did the rest."

Parkett sat down next to him. "Now we've got to figure out how to edit this stuff for all of the shows. We'll use just enough at noon for a tease, promising more later, then promote the hell out of it all afternoon."

"That's fine with me. Just tell me what you want and I'll start cutting."

Minutes later, Barclay was at the edit room door, silently

watching as the two men worked on the video. Finally, he grabbed a chair next to them. "Nice work, Zach. That's pretty dramatic stuff."

Zach turned. "Thanks, but it's nothing like being there. It was like we were in the middle of an action movie set. Cops on bullhorns, cops in armor, a helicopter overhead, tear gas grenades exploding. It was unreal."

"And where were *you* when all of this was happening?"

"Underneath a squad car."

"And Gabby?"

"Behind the squad."

"And where is she now?"

"In the Green Room," Parkett replied. "Trying to get a little rest. Zach said she didn't sleep all night."

Barclay thought for a moment. "If she's still awake, I'll talk to her and see if she'd like one of the interns to get her some fresh clothes. And maybe she can even get a shower in before the noon show."

Zach handed him a key to the apartment. "Good. I think she'd like that."

WHEN BARCLAY GOT BACK to his office, he found John Jacobs waiting for him, his six feet five frame stretched out on one of the office chairs. "Hey, J.J.," he said, "Nice to see you. Thanks for coming in."

"No sweat," Jacobs replied, rising to shake hands. "It's not like I've got anything better to do."

Barclay laughed. "You're looking good. Haven't changed a bit."

And he hadn't. Aside from his pure white crew cut, you'd never figure him for almost eighty years old. Broad-shouldered with a trim waist, he looked as if he could still fit in the Marine uniform he had worn some sixty years before.

"And you haven't, either," J.J. said. "I'm glad to see you haven't gained all of that weight back."

"Rachel would probably pick up and leave if I had," Barclay replied.

After they caught up on each other's lives, and after Barclay had once again apologized for not keeping in closer touch, he got to the point. He pulled out a picture of Craig Jessup. "This is the guy we'd like you to watch out for," he said, quickly explaining his background, his physical description, and the potential threat he posed to Gabby. "I'm told he has a beard now, at least the last time he was seen, and that he may be wearing a Twins' cap. And that he may know where Gabby and Zach live."

"You just want me to hang around Uptown watching for him?"

"That's it. Text me if you spot him, day or night. I'll take it from there."

"I don't text."

"Then call me. You've got a smart phone, right?"

"Just a cell."

"That'll do."

"You don't want me to follow him?"

Barclay thought for a moment. "Sure, if you can do it without being spotted. But we don't know what this guy may be capable of, so you'll have to be careful."

Once they'd agreed on their financial arrangements, Jacobs took the picture and walked to the office door. "I'll be in touch," he said.

THE REST OF THE DAY was little more than a blur for Gabby. After a couple hours of rest, she returned to the scene of the standoff for the live report at noon and then spent the rest of the day and evening reporting on the latest developments for each of the day's other newscasts, showcasing their dramatic, exclusive footage of the raid and continually writing updates for the station's website, all to the continuing chagrin of their competitors.

By the time she walked off the set after the late news, she felt like she might collapse in a heap.

To no one's surprise, the Anoka County sheriff's office remained tight-lipped about what they had found—or failed to find—inside the house. They acknowledged that a male victim had been discovered inside, dead of an apparent gunshot wound, but that he had not yet been identified. He was, however, believed to be the same man who had attempted to run down the Columbia Heights police officer.

While Gabby was aware of other details that had not been revealed, like the man's missing appendages, she agreed to Philips's request not to report them—at least for now.

One detail known to Philips but not revealed to her or anyone else was the unexpected presence of two FBI agents at the scene. Not even the local law enforcement knew exactly why they were there, or what their interest could be in a clearly local case.

And the Feds weren't saying.

The entire episode had transformed the newsroom's opinion of Gabby and its respect for her—not only for her reporting coup, but for the stamina and resiliency she'd shown in working from early morning till late night, without complaint. For that day, at least, she and Zach were the heroes of the newsroom. People who had not spoken more than a few words to her would now not leave her alone.

Throughout the long day, Barclay had been by her side or not far away, offering advice and encouragement, reviewing her scripts, giving her breaks when he could, and keeping the glad-handers at bay.

Even Sam Ryan, the GM, had made a rare visit to the newsroom to offer his congratulations. "Damn fine job," he told Gabby and Zach. "I even got a call from a buddy over at Channel 10," he laughed, "wondering how the hell we got the tip … whether we had a cop on the payroll."

By the time the late news was over, all Gabby wanted was

to get back to the apartment, have a couple of brews, give Barclay a cuddle, and head for bed—having little doubt that, for this night, at least, she would sleep soundly.

ON THE OTHER SIDE of town, in the upscale suburb of Orono, the phone was answered on the first tone.

"They raided the house," said the voice on the other end.

"I know. I've been watching it on television."

"They won't find anything, except ... "

"They'd better not."

"I was going to move him tomorrow ... "

"A little late. What else are they going to find?"

"It's clean. Nothing's left. Not a spot. I saw to that."

"The problem is, they found it. You left a trail. I'm not paying you to leave a trail."

"I didn't leave the trail. He did."

"I hope you're right. *You* should hope you're right."

End of conversation.

Twenty-Four

While Gabby had spent the day scurrying around the newsroom, John Jacobs, J.J., had been walking, apparently aimlessly, on the streets of Uptown. He would stop occasionally in a coffee shop or grab a seat on a bus bench, looking like a lonely old man with nothing better to do than while away the day. But on closer inspection, you'd see that his eyes never stopped moving, restlessly scanning the streets and sidewalks for any sign of a young man he'd never met or seen.

His only clues were an outdated photo and an updated description, which by now could have again changed.

J.J. had done his share of surveillance in his many years on the St. Paul police force, but typically that had involved watching the movements of someone he knew, waiting for a drug deal or a burglary to go down, or babysitting a house or a bar or a parked car, watching for a wanted felon to appear.

Those jobs had involved a lot of sitting, usually in an unmarked squad car, drinking coffee by the gallon and smoking heaters by the pack, sometimes for hours on end. Now, at least, he could move around, stretch his legs, get a little exercise.

Grumpy as he was at times, he'd been pleased to get the call from Barclay. Life had been largely lifeless since he'd left the force years before. His ex-wife was long gone and his two grown kids lived in opposite ends of the country and had no particular fondness for him. Not that he could blame them; like a lot of cops, he had not been a terrific father, spending too much time away from home, either at work or at some cop bar, hanging out with his buddies to the exclusion of wife and kids. He had four grandchildren, but rarely heard from them or about them, seeing them only at Christmas or Easter, feeling more and more like a stranger and sensing that they were feeling the same.

Except for a couple of hours each day at the fitness club, and coffee twice a week with a few of his old cop colleagues, who were even grumpier than he was, he mostly stayed at home—watching senseless reality shows, listening to talk radio, and feeling increasingly isolated and useless.

More than anything, he missed being a cop ... so he was happy to be back on the street, however briefly it might be.

Because he had spent most of his life in St. Paul, he hadn't realized just how big an area was included in the so-called Uptown neighborhood. So, knowing he couldn't come close to covering it all, he decided to concentrate on the several-block section that surrounded the apartment building where he'd been told Gabby and Zach lived, only to discover that even this smaller area was populated by a lot of young men who came close to the description of Craig Jessup.

After about five hours of walking the streets, he decided this could take more than a little while.

And, he thought, more than a little luck.

Turns out, he got a little of that luck and sooner than he could have hoped.

Shortly after five that afternoon, he wandered into a bar called Ziggy's and spotted what he thought might be his man. Sitting between two others at the bar, a beer in front of him, his eyes were fastened on a TV set above the bar. On the screen was the young woman J.J. knew to be Gabby Gooding, reporting on the early-morning police raid.

"... *the neighborhood is now returning to normal. The police barricades are gone, but the house remains surrounded by yellow police tape, and two squad cars are still at the scene ...*"

J.J. took a spot on the other side of the circular bar where he could get a better look at his prey. Everything seemed to fit: He was about the right height, blond with a beard, wearing a Twins cap. He seemed to take no notice of J.J. or anyone else around him until Gabby had finished her report and a commercial flashed onto the screen. Then he suddenly finished his beer with a gulp and slid off the bar stool.

The movement was so abrupt that J.J. had had no time to think. Flustered, he waited a beat until Jessup had his back to him, heading for the door, before he got up himself and followed along at a safe distance.

As far as he could tell, Jessup had not even given a glance in his direction.

Wrong.

Once outside, he gave a quick look to his right and left—then spotted Jessup a quarter of the way down the block, moving swiftly. The after-work crowd had begun to fill the sidewalks—so J.J. quickly became one of them, moving along in their midst, while placing a call to Barclay on his cell.

"I think I found him," he said once Barclay picked up.

"Where?"

"At a bar called Ziggy's, just off Hennepin. But he's on the move now."

"Did he spot you?"

"Don't think so. He was too busy watching Gabby on the news."

"Where's he heading?" Barclay asked.

"I can't tell. He's just walking down the street, but in a hurry."

"Can you stay with him?"

"I'll try."

"Don't take any chances. And keep in touch."

"Will do."

Jessup continued his quick stride. He looked back only once, showing no apparent fear of being followed. J.J. kept pace, but paused now and then to glance into a store window, allowing other pedestrians to move ahead of him, but never losing sight of his quarry.

After three blocks, Jessup came to a halt at a bus stop and joined a group of about seven others waiting for an approaching Metro Transit bus, which left J.J. with a quick decision: join him and risk exposing himself, or lose him, perhaps never to find him again.

He got in the back of the line.

Once on the bus, already crowded with homeward-bound commuters, Jessup took one of the few remaining seats in the front. J.J. passed him by, choosing to stand near the rear door, where he could see but not be seen, unless Jessup had eyes in the back of his head.

Despite being jostled by those pressing around him, he got back on the phone with Barclay and told him quickly—and quietly—where he was. "Heading where?" Barclay asked.

"You've got me. Down Lake Street, that's all I know."

There was a pause at the other end. "I guess you'd better stay with him," Barclay finally said. "But be careful."

"Not to worry."

"You're sure he hasn't spotted you?"

"Pretty sure."

But at that precise moment, as if he might have overheard their conversation, Jessup abruptly turned in his seat and seemed to look back directly at J.J., a small smile on his lips.

"Uh, oh."

"What?" Barclay said.

"Gotta go," he replied as he put the phone back in his pocket and quickly turned his head, looking out the bus window.

Maybe, he thought, *the asshole* does *have eyes in the back of his head.*

He moved farther back in the bus and took a seat just abandoned by another passenger, but still within view of Jessup. *What now?* Had Jessup actually seen him? *How could that be?* Was he imagining things? Or was it nothing more than a casual glance on Jessup's part? Perhaps, but he didn't think so. The look had been too focused, the small smile too knowing.

Which left him with another decision: what was he going to do when Jessup eventually got off the bus? Did he dare to follow him? And what if, at the end of the line, wherever that was, they were the only two left on board? Unlikely, but...

He noticed the younger woman sitting next to him was holding a bus schedule, and he leaned over. "Excuse me," he said, "but I think I got on the wrong bus. Would you mind if I looked at your schedule."

"Of course not," she said, handing it to him.

His finger traced the columns on the schedule and quickly discovered the final destination of this bus was at a park-and-ride in suburban Bloomington, not far from the Mall of America. There would be a number of stops before then, any one of which could be the one where Jessup might disembark.

He gave the schedule back to the woman. "Thanks, so much," he said.

She gave him a sympathetic look. "Where is it you're trying to go?"

"I'm not really sure," he replied, hiding behind his age. "I get a little confused."

"Can I be of help?" she asked.

"No, no. If I can't figure it out, I can call my son. He knows I get lost sometimes."

"You're sure?"

"I'm sure, but thank you. You're very kind."

As he spoke, the bus pulled up to yet another stop. And suddenly, Jessup was at the front door, then out onto the street. All in less than thirty seconds. He watched as the bus pulled away, with a larger smile—more of a smirk, really—playing across his face.

"Shit," J.J. muttered, as his eyes searched frantically for any street sign.

"What was that?" the lady said.

"Nothing. Sorry. That may have been my stop."

"Really? You can pull the cord," she said, "and get off at the next stop. It's only a few blocks away."

"Good idea," he said, following her instructions.

"And good luck," she said as he headed for the door. "I hope you find your way."

By then Jessup had crossed the street and he began to walk in the opposite direction to wait for another bus that would take him back to the Uptown area.

He couldn't be sure, but after seeing how the old man had reacted to his look back—the sudden turn away, the flash of panic in his eyes—he was fairly convinced that he'd been following him.

But that wasn't the only thing.

He'd first spotted him as he came into the bar, but had thought little of it at the time. Just another old guy. However, when, out of the corner of his eye, he'd seen the old man watching him and not the TV, he'd felt the first twinge of suspicion. Then, after he'd left the bar and saw the gray crew-cut above the crowd on the street, he'd become more convinced. And, finally, when he'd followed him onto the bus, little doubt remained.

If his gut was right, then they knew he was here and were out looking for him. The bitch, Sarah, in the bar must have checked up on him and talked. That was the only way. That meant he had to be even more cautious and to act even sooner.

But how and when?

Aside from her image on the television screen, he still had not seen Gabby. Not in person. Once he'd learned of Zach's name, he'd had no trouble finding the apartment building. But since then, while spending hours watching, usually at a distance, usually at night or early morning, he still had caught no glimpse of her. Cars by the dozen went in and out of the underground garage, but from his vantage points, he was never able to spot her or the guy she was with.

He'd have to get inside. Some way. Somehow.

Twenty-Five

Gabby and Zach were eating breakfast when the call came from Barclay. Once on the speaker, he quickly relayed what had happened with J.J. the day before. "I didn't want to bother you last night," he said, "to let you get some sleep, but it's clear now that Jessup is in the area. Jacobs first spotted him in a bar just a couple of blocks from your place."

"What bar?" Zach asked.

"Ziggy's. You been there?"

"Sure. It's one of my favorites."

Gabby said, "So if he spotted J.J., then he knows we're looking for him."

"Probably."

"So what happens now?" she persisted.

There was a pause. "I guess it's time we let the cops know that you're being stalked," Barclay said. "When I get a chance, I'll make some calls."

"But we have no proof," she said. "I haven't even seen him, let alone been accosted or bothered by him."

"I know, but don't forget there's a warrant out for him in California for skipping out on his probation. That should be enough to keep him at bay for a while."

"I don't know . . ." Gabby said.

"I'm also going to keep J.J. in the area. If he spots him again, he can let the cops know. That's the best we can do for now. Aside from the two of you being even more cautious. If that's possible."

"OK," Zach said. "We'll keep our eyes open even wider."

"Good. I'll see you when you get into the shop."

As they were about to leave the apartment, Gabby picked up the poodle and held him close. "You know who's getting the worst of this deal?" she said. "This little guy."

Which was true.

Because they didn't dare walk the dog nearby, they were forced to take him to one of the nearby parks or lakes for his outings, and then only after they were certain they weren't being followed. The result was that he got fewer and shorter walks, and he was beginning to display what she thought was a listlessness that was sad to see.

"He's a dog, Gabby. He's fine."

"No, he isn't. He looks sad. And bored."

"You want to get him a treadmill?"

"Not funny. But he does need more exercise. More attention."

"A nanny?"

"Less funny. I think we should see if we can take him to work."

Zach could only smile. "Great. I'd love to see you introduce one Barclay to the other. It'd be a hoot."

"It's your fault for naming him Barclay in the first place."

"I never planned for the two of them to meet. And he is *my* dog, remember."

"Then you should take better care of him."

"And you should stop spoiling him."

When they got to the station, they found John Knowles waiting outside of Gabby's cubicle. "Hey, guys," he said. "I heard you were on your way in. You have a minute?"

"Of course," she replied, but seeing Sarah Andrews on the other side of the cubicle, motioned to a vacant nearby editing room.

"So what's up?" Zach asked.

Knowles closed the door behind them. "I just got off the phone with Hank Shields, the assistant US Attorney I told you about a few days ago ... the guy I met with. He wouldn't tell me much, but he said the FBI would be interested in talking to you ... to us ... and wondered if we'd be willing to do that."

Gabby said, "Have you talked to Barclay about it?"

"He wasn't happy with the idea, but he knows we're in a bind and finally said OK. As long as we get as much or more than we give."

"He's the boss," she said. "But what do they want?"

"To know what we know, I guess. They've already talked to your friend, the assistant M.E., and to Detective Philips, and now they want to sit down with us."

"Are they going to tell us what *they* know?" she asked.

"I wouldn't count on it."

"Still, what can it hurt?" Zach said. "We're going nowhere as it is."

"Good," Knowles said, getting up to leave. "I'll make the arrangements." Then, "By the way, the M.E. is apparently pissed that you haven't gotten back to her about running John Doe's picture on the air. She still wants to do it ... as one last attempt to identify the guy."

HE WAS RIGHT. Cindy Maxwell was visibly upset when Gabby and Zach stopped by her office later that day to pick up the picture. "We can't keep this guy a Popsicle forever," she said, heat in her voice. "We need to know who he is, or who he belongs to. If we don't, we'll have to get one of our friendly funeral chapels to do a pro bono burial."

Gabby quickly apologized, blaming the fast-moving events

of the past several days for her forgetfulness.

"I've been following it all on the news," Maxwell said. "And the Anoka County M.E. called me to compare notes on the body they got from the house in Fridley. Pretty messy deal, from what he said."

"You mean the missing fingers," Gabby said.

"Not only that. They blew most of his head away. He's going to be even tougher to identify than our own guy. But they did find the bullet that killed him, buried in one of the walls. From a .45 automatic, just like our guy in the basement. Apparently the shooter couldn't find it, or didn't have time to dig it out."

Gabby took a deep breath. Then, "I understand the FBI was here to talk to you."

"A couple of days ago. They wanted a copy of the autopsy…and everything else we had. Pictures. Fingerprints. Blood samples. You name it, they wanted it."

Zach asked, "Did they say why they're so interested?"

"Are you kidding? They're about as tight-lipped as you can get. Not unfriendly, mind you, but all business."

Gabby said, "So let's see the picture."

Maxwell took the photo from a folder on her desk and laid it in front of them. "This is the best we could do," she said. "Thanks to Photoshop."

The picture was a frontal view of John Doe's face, but had been expertly doctored to hide the bullet wound on the side of his head and to show him with eyes open, his sagging facial skin tightened, as though he were alive.

It was the first time Gabby and Zach had actually seen a likeness of the man. "That's pretty good," Zach said, studying the photo closely. "If somebody actually knows this guy, they should be able to recognize him from this."

Maxwell took out another sheet of paper. "And this is what we'd like you to say about the picture, but the exact wording is up to you, of course."

Gabby took the sheet.

The Hennepin County Medical Examiner's office is asking the public's help in identifying this man, whose body was found recently in a northeast Minneapolis home, an apparent suicide victim. He is believed to be in his fifties about 180 pounds, with only one identifiable mark on his body—a small tattoo on his ankle. If you have any information about this man, please call the medical examiner's office.

Gabby said, "So you're sending the picture and this out to all of the stations?"

"This afternoon. But I'm not sure how many will use it."

"And I see you're listing it as an 'apparent suicide,' even though you know it isn't?"

"That's what Detective Philips and the FBI guys asked me to do...so I did it."

Gabby was pleased. That should lessen any possible interest by their competitors.

As they got up to leave, Maxwell said, "I'll let you know if we get any response, but I wouldn't count on it."

"Trust me, we won't," Gabby replied.

LATER, ACROSS TOWN, Craig Jessup was back on the streets.

He had always prided himself in his uncanny ability to remember names and faces. It was a gift. After he'd met someone and spent a few minutes chatting, he could recall—even weeks or months later—not only who he or she was but small details of their lives: their families, their employment, their politics, even some of their secrets. It was another trait that had made him an invaluable political asset to the mayor of San Jose, whose memory of names and faces was as weak as Jessup's was strong.

So it was surprising that Jessup did not recognize Roger Ostby, who, by chance, found himself sitting about ten feet from him at an outdoor table at a Starbucks a few blocks from Zach's apartment.

Instead, it was Ostby who remembered him.

True, Jessup had met Ostby only once, only briefly, at Brit's bar the night he was hitting on Sarah Andrews. And, true, they'd had only a brief conversation that night. But, at six feet two and over 230 pounds, Ostby cut the kind of figure that Jessup should have recognized and remembered.

And now, minutes later, he was about to regret that he hadn't.

It was a gorgeous, sunlit afternoon, softened by a cool breeze. Jessup was staring at the passersby on the sidewalk, more vigilant now after his encounter with J.J. the day before. As he sipped his coffee, he heard movement behind him and turned to find Ostby in a chair across the table from him. Staring, head cocked, with a small grin.

Jessup returned the stare, his mind and memory churning. Finally, "Hey, buddy, can I help you with something?"

Ostby's grin widened.

Then it dawned. The guy at Brit's. Only now without the Channel 7 cap.

Jessup quickly finished his coffee, pushed back his chair and started to rise. But not before a vise-like grip clamped on his bicep. "Sit down, sport. Don't rush off. Lemme buy you another coffee."

Jessup tried to pull away, but the grip tightened even more, sending a spasm of pain shooting up into his shoulder. "What the fuck!" he said, grimacing, looking around for help. But no one was watching.

Ostby leaned across the table. "Sarah Andrews sends her regards, sport. She even went looking for you to pay her respects. But, what d'ya know, asshole, you were nowhere to be found. Turns out, you weren't even who you said you were."

"Let go my arm, or ... "

"Or *what*, sport?"

Jessup made another unsuccessful effort to get free.

"So who are you, sport? Really? Not the guy you said you were, that's for sure."

"Why do you give a shit?" Jessup snorted.

"Because we don't like our reporters screwed with. Lied to. Hustled by a fraud. We're kind of particular that way."

Jessup, of no meager strength himself, again tried to get up and twist free, but Ostby held firm, the smile never leaving his face. "Stay away from her, sport. Stay away from the station. Be on your..."

Before he could finish the sentence, he saw Jessup's other arm come up from under the table, a flash, so fast it was a blur.

And then—the tip of a switchblade beneath his chin.

He immediately released his grip and jerked his head backwards. But not before he felt the sting of a small cut.

Jessup stood up, still holding the knife, smirking. "Tell your friend Sarah that she's a pig, and I wouldn't screw her if she were the last bitch on earth. And, yeah, one more thing, you and your buddies stay the hell away from me. You got that, *sport*."

Then he walked away, in no particular hurry, never looking back.

WITHIN THE HOUR, Ostby was in Barclay's office, a small bandage beneath his chin, excitedly explaining what had just happened at the coffee shop. "I've never seen anybody move so fast," he said. "It was like it came out of nowhere. He could have had that switchblade sticking out of my Adam's apple if he'd wanted to."

Barclay was stunned, and immediately summoned Gabby and Zach to this office, and asked Ostby to repeat the story for them. As he finished, Gabby sank back into her chair. "I've been trying to tell Zach that he's no one to fool with," she said, glancing at him. "If we needed any more proof, this is it."

"It's my fault," Ostby said. "I obviously provoked the guy. Pissed him off. Wanted to scare him. I kind of thought he might take a swing at me, and I was ready for that. But the knife was a whole 'nother deal."

Barclay could only shake his head. "This pretty much settles it. We have to get the cops involved, sooner than later. I've been putting it off, but no longer." He turned to Ostby. "Please keep this all to yourself for now. We'll get Gabby's cop friend, Philips, over here and you can file a formal complaint. That together with his problems in California should be enough to get the cops looking for him."

"I already said something to Sarah Andrews," Ostby said. "I ran into her on my way in here."

Gabby said, "If I see her, I'll ask her to keep quiet. But George, Philips doesn't know anything about Jessup. And I'd rather that he didn't."

"Why?" Barclay asked.

"Because it's personal. He already thinks I'm a magnet for trouble. And he's got enough on his plate already."

"That doesn't wash," he said. "He should know that you're facing a couple of threats, not just the one. I'm surprised you haven't told him by now."

"I didn't think he needed to know. Jessup has nothing to do with our John Doe. Before long, the whole world is going to know, and I don't like that. I don't like being seen as a victim."

Until now, Zach had remained quiet. "George is right, Gabby. The more people we've got looking for Jessup, the better off we are. *You* are. Until we find him and deal with him, we'll have to constantly look over our shoulders. We don't need that. We need to forget Jessup and concentrate on John Doe. That's our job."

Gabby held up her hands in mock surrender. "OK, OK. But cops or no cops, I wouldn't count on getting him. He's not only dangerous, but smart. Trust me on that."

"Speaking of John Doe," Barclay said, "Knowles tells me that the FBI guys are going to be here in the morning, to talk to you."

"Are you going to be there?" she asked.

"I don't think so. This is your gig. But be tough!"

PREDICTABLY, MINUTES LATER, as Gabby walked back to her cubicle, she was confronted by Sarah Andrews. "Jesus, Gabby, I ran into Roger Ostby ... "

"I know. He said he saw you."

"Jesus! Sticking him with a switchblade! What kind of guy is this, anyway?"

Gabby guided her into their cubicle. "Take it easy, Sarah. The whole newsroom doesn't need to know."

"So tell me," Sarah persisted.

"He's a bad dude," she replied, deciding then that she had to tell her more or the questions would never end. "He beat the hell out of me and sent me to the hospital back in San Jose. Got sent to jail but walked out on his probation and followed me here, I guess. Looking to make more trouble. We're not sure what. George is alerting the cops here in hopes we can find him and get him sent back to California."

Sarah settled back in her chair. "He sure as hell fooled me. A real con man. But I have to tell you, he didn't strike me as dangerous. Live and learn, I guess."

"As I did," she replied. "The hard way. I had some broken ribs and a lot of bruises to show for it."

"I'm so sorry that I got involved ... saying what I did to him."

"You had no way of knowing," Gabby said. "But I'd appreciate it if you keep all of this to yourself. The fewer people who know about this, the better. Until it finally gets resolved."

"No problem. And if I happen to see him again, I'll call you or George right away."

"Good. In the meantime, we should just keep trying to do our jobs."

Twenty-Six

By the time Gabby and Zach got to the conference room the next morning, Knowles was already there with two buttoned-up guys seated by his side, one lanky with close-clipped light brown hair, dark shaded eyes, and ears that seemed a trifle too large for his head, the other shorter, but with a taut body, a straight, somber face, and lips that seemed perpetually pursed. Both were relatively young, in their thirties, Gabby guessed, and neither—at first glance—seemed capable of launching a smile.

Both rose as Knowles introduced them: "Lanky" was Roger Dimitri, "Pursed lips," Nathan Upchurch. They shook hands and offered a brief thanks for agreeing to meet, politely, but still without a smile. These are two serious dudes, Gabby decided, wondering if all FBI agents were as tightly wound. Aside from attending a few FBI news conferences over the years, she had never actually met an agent before, at least not up close and personal like this.

After a pregnant, somewhat awkward pause, Knowles took the lead. "Maybe we should set some ground rules," he said. "We're here to listen and to offer what we can, but as I mentioned to you on the phone, while we seem to have a mutual interest in this case, we don't want to jeopardize our story by getting into bed with you guys."

"We don't 'get into bed' with the media," Dimitri said, with a trace of a what-do-you-know smile on his lips. "And just so we're straight from the get-go, we're not here by choice. We're here because our boss told us to be here." Glancing at his partner, "To be frank, we've not had the best experiences with the media…"

Gabby shot them a look. "Fine, but then why are you here? You asked for the meeting."

"For two reasons: one, to see if we might be able to help one another, and, two, frankly, to make sure you don't screw up an important federal investigation by the reckless pursuit of your story. It's that simple."

"We don't pursue stories recklessly," Gabby replied, an edge to her voice.

"I didn't say you did. We just want to make sure that you don't."

"So what *is* your interest?" she asked. "All *we* know is that we've got a long-dead guy in a Minneapolis basement and another guy, apparently connected to him, who attacked Zach here along with a Columbia Heights cop, who was then found dead in a Fridley house. Both of them were killed execution-style, from what we've been told. That would seem to be a local case, not a federal case."

The agents exchanged glances. "You're right," Dimitri said, "we knew nothing about the first killing and had no interest in it until…"

"Until what?" she interjected.

Irritated, Dimitri shot her a look. "Until Mr. Knowles here talked to one of the U.S. attorneys and mentioned the name Zimtronics, telling him the John Doe was found in a house apparently owned by Zimtronics. That got our attention."

"Why?" Zach said. "From the little we've been able to learn, the company doesn't really exist. No office, no phone number, no officers that we can identify. A phantom company, if you will. Of course we don't have your resources ... "

Neither agent said anything for a moment. Then Upchurch spoke for the first time. "This is where things get a little dicey. Where we have to be careful in what we say. We need your assurance that nothing we say will go beyond this room."

"Wait a minute," Knowles said. "How can we give you an assurance like that before we know what you're going to tell us?"

"And," Gabby quickly added, "what is your point in telling us anything at all?"

"Just this," Dimitri replied quickly. "We know that you've been doing a lot of poking around in this case. That's your job. And we know that you'll probably continue. That's also your job. What our boss is worried about is that—in the process—you're going to unknowingly stumble on to some things that could jeopardize *our* investigation."

"OK," she said. "That's what's in it for you. But what's in it for us? Aside from doing our civic duty by cooperating with the FBI."

Dimitri smiled for the second time, albeit grudgingly. "Just this. We'll tell you as much as we can, and cooperate with you, and with Detective Philips, as our investigations continue. And we'll guarantee that we won't work with anyone else ... any of the other media ... if all of this does develop into a story for you and into an eventual prosecution for us."

The room fell quiet.

"I don't know," Gabby finally said. "We're not used to working with law enforcement, and yet we now find ourselves holding hands with both the local cops and with you guys ... whom we've never met before. Please, don't take offense. It's not that I don't trust you, but I don't."

Upchurch rose out of his chair, his face flushed. "Are you kidding me?" he said angrily. "You want to talk about trust? Give me a break! I've been screwed over by the media more times than I want to count."

Dimitri pulled him back down. "Settle down, Nate. Relax. Let's see if we can work this out."

Unfazed by the outburst, Gabby said, "Maybe we can, but I don't want to check in with you guys every time we get a lead or find somebody who's willing to talk with us."

Knowles cut in. "I agree, but let's face it, Gabby, we have no leads right now, nobody to talk to. Let's at least hear what they have to say."

"He's right," Zach said with a glance at her.

She shrugged, still unconvinced.

"So we have your word?" Dimitri said. "What we say now goes no further?"

"Only to our boss," Gabby replied, as Upchurch—still upset—flipped open a folder and shuffled some official-looking papers, finally pulling one aside. "Here's the deal," he said, ignoring Gabby, glancing at Zach, "You're right, Zimtronics no longer really exists. It's still registered as a corporation in Delaware, but even with our 'resources,' as you put it, we've never found a trace of one of the key figures connected to it. And that's not for lack of trying. The Bureau has been looking for years . . . for so long and so unsuccessfully that the search finally was allowed to slide to the back burner.

"So when we learned what you learned, that the house in Minneapolis is owned by Zimtronics, it became our first clue in years. When I say 'our,' I mean the Bureau's. I haven't been involved in the search until now. Nor has my colleague here. The investigation predates us by years."

"What kind of company is it . . . or was it?" Gabby asked.

Dimitri took over. "Zimtronic is, or was, a privately held corporation, which, it turned out, is owned by a principal owner of another company called Diabetrics. It was not a subsidiary of Diabetrics, per se, but a secret, sister company." He paused. "Diabetrics itself was formed in the mid-90s to raise money . . . investor dollars . . . to research and develop a new 'wonder drug' to treat diabetes. At least that's what they said they were doing..."

"And?" she interjected.

"And, to make a long story as short as possible, they apparently never had a serious intention of developing that drug. It was a Ponzi scheme, pure and simple."

"How long did that go on?" Knowles asked.

"For several years. Like most Ponzi schemes, they raised millions and millions of dollars, repaying some of the early investors with proceeds from the new investors, while continuing to send out optimistic but false reports on the progress of their laboratory tests and phony clinical trials. Until, like most of these scams, it was eventually exposed and came crashing down around them. They ran out of new investors as some of the old investors panicked and demanded their money back. Money Diabetrics didn't have."

"And when was that?" Zach said.

"In 2001."

"And why haven't we heard about it?" he persisted.

"Because it was long before your time, I'd guess," Dimitri replied. "And because it was basically an East Coast story, overshadowed a few years later by the frenzy over the Ponzi King, Bernie Madoff, and by our own Tom Petters. If you Google Ponzi schemes, you'll see just how many of them there have been over the years, most of which you've never heard of.

"The FTC finally caught up with Diabetrics, and put it out of business, arresting and charging four of the firm's principals. Before the trial could begin, three of them pleaded guilty and got sent away for five to seven years each."

"So?" Gabby's question hung in the air.

"So," Dimitri went on, "a fourth executive, the CEO and owner of Diabetrics, a guy by the name of Harlan Overton, disappeared while out on bail, escaping what could have been fifteen to twenty years behind bars. That was early in 2002. He hasn't been seen since."

"And with him went a whole bunch of money, I bet," Knowles said.

"You got that right. Anywhere from five to ten million, according to our best estimates. Maybe more."

"One more guess," Knowles said. "He was also the owner of our Zimtronics."

"Right again."

"Wait a minute," Gabby said. "We've already researched Zimtronics, and I don't remember seeing the name of Harlan Overton or a company called Diabetics. I could be wrong, but..."

"No, you're right. Because we—the Feds—have made it that way."

"Explain," she said.

"At the time Diabetrics imploded, we didn't know about Zimtronics or its connection to Overton or Diabetrics. It was only after he vanished that we learned that it existed, and that Overton owned it, apparently to launder and conceal some of the gains from Diabetrics. So we kept that knowledge to ourselves in hopes that Overton would not know what we knew and that it would eventually lead us to him."

"Like here," Knowles said.

"Like here. Maybe."

Knowles again. "But what about the names of the people listed as officers of Zimtronics?"

"All of them are fictitious, invented by Overton to hide his ownership."

There was a pause in the conversation, as they absorbed what they'd been told. Finally, Gabby said, "Do you really think he might be here?"

"We have no real idea. He could be anywhere. He had to surrender his passport at the time of his arrest, but with his money he could have arranged for another fake passport and could be who-knows-where in the world, enjoying his money. We suspect that wherever he is, he has a new identity, and he's probably had some kind of plastic surgery or facial reconstruction because his pictures are in every FBI office in the country. The pictures are probably faded by now after so many years."

"Can we see copies of those pictures?" Zach asked.

"Don't know why not," Dimitri said. "But I wouldn't want to see them on TV. Not yet, anyway."

"That's no problem," Knowles said.

"Maybe I'm dense," Gabby said, "but if he is—or was—around here with a new identity and all of that money, why would he need to own an ordinary house like that? And who was the dead guy inside?"

"We can't answer the last part," Upchurch said, "not yet, anyway. And we can only guess at the first part. He might actually have lived there at one time with his new identity, hiding in a modest neighborhood in a flyover part of the country where we'd be unlikely to look. All of his ties, family and otherwise, are on the East Coast. He has no connections that we know of to Minnesota or Minneapolis. So it might be … or might have been … a perfect place to become all but invisible."

"Then what?" she said. "Once enough time had passed, he decides it's safe to move on to bigger and better digs and was afraid to sell the place because there happened to be a dead body occupying the basement?"

Upchurch met her gaze. "Maybe. Or maybe he took a flyer and is long gone from Minnesota."

"I don't think so," Knowles said. "If he was long gone, why were these thugs trying to keep Gabby and Zach from poking around? Why are two guys dead? Two guys who may have known too much about who Overton really is and where he is."

"Now you know why we're here," Dimitri said. "Those thoughts are our thoughts. And why we think it might be beneficial to work together."

"Explain that again," Gabby said.

"If Overton *is* around here," Upchurch said, "he may

think the only threat to him is coming from you guys and the local cops … because of the body in the basement. He may not know that the FBI has gotten involved and has made the connection to Zimtronics … and ultimately to him. If that's true, we'd like to keep it that way."

"To keep him from running again," Knowles said.

"Hopefully."

"How old is this guy?" Zach asked.

"He was thirty-seven when he took off in 2002," Dimitri said. "Which would make him in his late forties now."

"Married?"

"No, not then. All business. Kind of a wonder boy of finance, they said."

They sat quietly for a moment before Gabby spoke up. "We need to talk to Clarence Pedersen again."

"Who is he?" Dimitri asked.

"A former neighbor of the death house. An old guy who's now in a nursing home. Zach and I talked to him weeks ago … and, remember Zach? … he had a vague memory of a man who once lived in the house. Years ago, before it went vacant. He never met him or spoke to him, but he may have seen him. And if we have those pictures of Overton, it might jar his memory."

"But what if he'd already had plastic surgery or whatever by then?" Zach said.

"It might still ring a bell. It's worth a try."

"Good," Upchurch said, "We have pictures of him here with us, including several from the time of his arrest and from the Diabetrics' brochures."

As she took the pictures from them, Gabby felt—for the first time in a long time—a twinge of hope and a whisper from her dad, sitting on her shoulder. *"Now you're getting somewhere, Gabs."*

Twenty-Seven

As Gabby and the group left the conference room, Craig Jessup stood outside Zach's apartment building... more precisely, to one side of the garage doors that led to and from the underground parking area. Holding his cell phone to his ear, as if in deep conversation, he watched the occasional car pass through the doors and on to the one-way street... the drivers' eyes always looking in the direction of the oncoming traffic... away from where he stood.

He was waiting for the first driver to emerge who might happen to be talking on a cell phone, further diverting attention away from him. He knew it was a long shot and that he couldn't stand there much longer, that the gray-haired guy was probably still on the lookout for him, and who knows? After the knifing incident at Starbucks, maybe the cops, as well.

To lessen the chances, he had shaved his beard and head, put the gold ring back on his lip, belted his pants below his hips, and wore an oversized pair of shades.

Six cars had passed by before a hurried-looking young blond on her phone came through the doors, impatiently awaiting her chance to dart into the passing traffic, oblivious to everything else. With one eye on her, Jessup took the chance and moved quickly, slipping behind her and into the garage before the doors could fully close.

To his relief, there was no sign of movement inside the garage, no other cars on their way out, no other people that he could see. Unfortunately, the interior was well lit, but at this time of day, midmorning, there were relatively few cars still parked there. Most of the residents would have left by now, at work or shopping, or still be sleeping.

He had no idea if Gabby and her friend Zach would be home, but he guessed not. He had not dared to stand and watch for them, but decided they were most likely at work. Regardless, he had to take the chance. If he could not see her, he had to *feel* her, to sense her presence even in her absence. To perhaps get a whiff of her lingering scent. By now, he was convinced that she was sleeping with this Zach guy, and he was eager—determined—to find evidence of that, to prove what a slut she really was.

If they *are* there, he would simply do what he had to do. Whatever that was. The switchblade was in one pocket, pepper spray in the other.

And in his back pocket was a set of lock picks.

Frustrated by his failure to discover Zach's specific apartment number online, he had stopped by the building's main entrance the day before and scanned a posted list of residents. Zach's name was there, but with no corresponding apartment number, just a phone button to push. He'd waited patiently for someone to leave, someone who turned out to be an elderly woman with a black cat in her arms. In his most cordial, charming way, he had asked for her help. "I'm sorry," he'd said, "but I'm in a pickle."

"How's that?" she'd replied.

"I know my friend, Zach Anthony lives here, but I don't know his apartment number, and I'm supposed to send him a wedding invitation . . . and the wedding's only a week away. I don't want to call him and spoil the surprise. I thought you or someone else who lives here might know who he is and which apartment is his."

Surprisingly, she'd shown no signs of suspicion.

"He's a TV guy," Jessup continued. "You might have seen him in his station car, or carrying a TV camera. He's living with a young woman by the name of Gabby."

"Do they have a little dog?" she'd asked.

"I'm not sure. I'm from out of town and it's been awhile since I've seen him."

"I believe I know who you're talking about. They live on my floor … down at the end of the hall. In 303."

"Really? Wow, you've saved the day. I can't thank you enough."

"No problem. Perhaps you'd like me to give the invitation to him. Slip it under his door."

"No, no, I wouldn't put you to that trouble. And the invitation's in my car. Also, please, if you do happen to see him, don't say anything. I'd like it to be a surprise in the mail."

"That's fine," she'd said. "Are you the one getting married?"

"No. My brother. Zach's best friend."

"Well, have a good time," she'd said with a smile as she walked away, the black cat looking back at him over her shoulder.

Some kind of omen?

THE ELEVATOR WAS in the middle of the garage, a lighted sign and a camera above the door, to which he gave a smile and his middle finger. Once the elevator arrived, and after another glance around, he stepped in and pushed the button for the third floor.

Apartment 303. The end of the hall.

When the elevator doors opened, he found an old man and lady waiting, engaged in their own conversation. "Hello, there," he said, again with his winning grin. "Good morning. It's a fine day out there."

The old man looked surprised to actually be spoken to. "Well, good," he said. "We're heading out for our walk."

"Enjoy it," Jessup said, holding the elevator door open for them.

No one else was in the hallway, and he moved quickly to the door of 303. He had decided already that he wouldn't knock or ring the bell. He would take the chance and simply pick the lock and deal with whatever or whoever was on the other side.

With another furtive glance down the hall, he put on a pair of latex gloves, took out his lockpick and began to work.

It took him no more than two minutes.

When the lock snapped and he quietly pushed open the door, the first thing he heard was a low growl.

Once Knowles had escorted the two FBI agents out of the station, he returned to the conference room with Barclay in tow. "I thought we should brief George and then talk about what to do next. Why don't you do the honors, Gabby?"

She would have preferred that Knowles do it, but didn't want to argue, so she quickly began to recite the essence of their conversation with the two agents. She was interrupted once or twice by Knowles to clarify a point, but basically delivered about a ten-minute monologue. Barclay listened intently, and only when she'd finished did he venture a comment. "Pretty complicated story," he said, "but it sounds like there could be a kernel of truth."

"We thought so, too," Knowles said. "But there are still a ton of questions."

"Like?"

"Like if he is still around here, then why?" Gabby said. "He obviously knows both we and the cops are on his case, even if he's still not aware the FBI is involved. So why doesn't he simply pack his bags and take all of his money and move on? He could just forget the dead guy in the house, since we still don't know who the hell he is, and simply head for wherever it is that doesn't have an extradition treaty with the US."

"Could be he never did get that fake passport," Zach offered.

"Or maybe he *has* taken off," Barclay ventured. "We certainly don't know that he hasn't."

Knowles shook his head. "Like I told the FBI guys, if that's true, then why are his thugs still around? The ones who are still alive, I mean. If they are his thugs."

"I'll tell you why," Zach ventured, "because, for some reason, he can't afford to leave. Think about it. If the Feds are right and he came here to start a new life, under the radar, maybe he's become so well established in the years he's been here that he can't afford to simply pull up stakes and leave. At least not in a hurry. He may need time to make the proper preparations."

"Jeez, Zach," Barclay said, admiringly. "Why the hell aren't you on the reporting staff?"

"Because I don't have a big enough ego. You know, photographers are to be seen, not heard."

"I forgot," Barclay said, grinning.

"Zach could be right," Knowles said. "We were told Overton would be in his late forties by now. And who knows? He could have been here for the past ten or twelve years. New identity. Maybe a new business. New life. Hell, he could have a wife and family for all we know. For all anybody knows."

Gabby cut in. "Let's pursue that. If you were him and came to town with a boatload of money and a new identity, what would you do? You'd probably lay low for a while, get to know the town and all, but later, if you were the kind of 'boy wonder' the Feds say you are, you'd probably get bored and want some new action ... and a way to put all of that stolen money to work."

"Keep going," Barclay said.

"You probably wouldn't want to work for someone else ... and risk having them do a thorough background check on you. So, continuing that thought, you'd start your own business, reporting to no one but yourself. I don't know what kind of personal information the state demands of entrepreneurs registering a new business, but I bet it's not much."

"I'll check," Knowles said.

"That's a nice theory," Barclay said, "and even sounds plausible. But where do we go from there? There have to be scores, if not hundreds, of new businesses begun every year … and … he could have done what you're suggesting maybe ten or twelve years ago. And we don't know anything more about him, except his approximate age."

"The Feds did give us pictures of him," Zach said.

"Which may bear no resemblance to him today," Knowles replied. "And what's more, if we're thinking about this, the Feds must be, too."

"Don't be so sure," Gabby replied. "Those two agents are as new to this as we are. And maybe they're not as smart."

"I wouldn't count on that," Zach said.

They sat quietly for a time before Barclay said, "Let's keep all of this to ourselves, for now. Think more about it. Figure out where to go from here."

"I've got some contacts at the Secretary of State's office," Knowles said. "Maybe they can help."

"And I've got to get back to Cindy Maxwell at the medical examiner's office to see if she got any response to John Doe's picture."

"Good," Barclay said. "But one more thing. Let's not forget this is *our* investigation. No way do we allow these FBI dudes to take it over. Getting into bed with them is one thing, giving them a kiss goodnight is another. Agreed?"

"Absolutely," Gabby replied.

"OK. We'll meet again tomorrow morning."

"Wait a minute," Zach said. "Aren't we forgetting something in all of this? What about Craig Jessup? What's new with that?"

"Sorry," Barclay said. "I forgot. I met with Philips and gave him a picture of Jessup. He says he's shown it at the precinct roll call in the Uptown area and asked the patrols to keep an eye out for him. And my friend J.J. is still in the area, watching. It's the best I can do for now."

As they left the meeting, Gabby pulled Zach aside. "Do you have some time? I think we should take those pictures of Overton and pay Clarence Pedersen another visit. See if he remembers him."

"Let's do it," he said.

ON THE WAY TO the nursing home, Gabby put in a call to Cindy Maxwell. To her surprise, she answered on the first ring. "We've had about eight calls," Maxwell told her, "but none of them was very helpful. A couple thought they might have seen him recently, one in the checkout line at the grocery store and another at a Twins game, standing in front of them buying a beer. That ruled them out, of course, unless they were seeing his ghost. There were others who thought he was younger or older, but none of them knew anything about a tattoo. As I say, no real leads."

"So what happens now?" Gabby asked.

"We're going to wait a few more days, then bury the poor bastard."

"I'm sorry," she said.

"So am I. I don't like to see anybody put away without a name or anybody there to say a fond farewell."

"I understand. We'll keep in touch. There have been some new developments that may eventually lead to something, maybe even the guy's name."

"I hope so."

"What about the Fridley guy? Have you heard anything?"

"No. As far as I know, he's still John Doe Number 2."

Taking a moment before entering the nursing home, they sat in the car and studied the FBI photos of Overton, photos now more than a decade old. One was a carefully-lighted portrait obviously shot in some photography studio, showing the hint of a smirk; another was a police booking photo, somber and defiant; still others were taken from various newspaper accounts of the Ponzi scheme—showing him in handcuffs getting out of a car, trying to hide his face.

Gabby, after she'd closely examined the pictures, decided the remarkable thing about the man was that there was nothing remarkable about him. There were no distinctive features, nothing that would catch your eye or prompt a second glance. He wasn't handsome or ugly. He was simply average.

He had a full head of hair, carefully combed, with eyebrows that were perhaps thicker than normal and deep-set eyes. He had a chin more square than round, lips more thin than thick, ears that were … ears.

She thought she could see him several times and still not remember him the next time. He was, in short, not memorable.

Zach seemed to agree. "Kinda looks like any guy you'd meet on the street, or standing at the bar. I thought he might look a little more sinister … or something. Devious, maybe. Know what I mean?"

"Reminds me a little of an old high school teacher in Portland," she said. "Mr. Truax. He was kind of a pervert."

"Think about this," he said. "Maybe he's so ordinary looking that he wouldn't need to get a nose job or whatever. Especially after this many years. Maybe he looks the same today as he did then. Just older."

"I wouldn't put my money on that," she replied.

They found Clarence in much the same position as they'd left him a couple of weeks before, slumped in a wheelchair in the main section of the nursing home, eyes downcast, oblivious to a game of bingo going on behind him. But as they approached, he looked up—and they thought they could see a small sign of recognition. "Hello, Clarence," Gabby said. "Remember us?"

"Of course," he replied. "You're the TV people. I may be a little deaf, but I'm not dumb. I thought you'd be back here sooner. You said you would."

Gabby didn't remember that, but said, "I know, I'm sorry. We've been really busy."

"Yeah, yeah," he replied. "That's what my daughter says, too. So I sit here alone with a bunch of old people who are even deafer than I am. And dumber. Mumbling to themselves, drooling. Don't ever let anyone put you in a place like this."

Zach gave her a look, as if to say, "See, what did I tell you? This is a hellhole."

They pulled up chairs next to his wheelchair. "I'm sorry to hear you're so unhappy," Gabby said. "Is there anything we can do?"

"Get me out of here. Back to my house."

"We can't do that," she said, "but maybe one day we can pick you up and take you back to the old neighborhood for a visit. Would your daughter think that's OK?"

"Who cares what she thinks?" he replied, bitterly. "She's the one who brought me here. And, yeah, I'd like that."

"The reason we're here today," Zach said, pulling his chair closer, "besides wanting to see you, is to show you a few pictures. Do you remember telling us about a man who lived in the house next door before it went vacant? That you never met him, but saw him a few times?"

"I guess so, yes."

Zach held the series of pictures of Overton in front of Clarence, first one, then the next. "This may have been that man. Do you recognize him at all?"

Clarence took the pictures from him and held them close to his face. "I left my specs in my room," he said, "but I can still see good enough."

They waited.

Finally, he said, "This could be him, I guess. About the same size, I'd say. About as tall and thin as this guy in the pictures. But the face seems different, can't tell you why. Just different."

"But it *might* be him?" Gabby pressed.

"Might, I suppose. But I wouldn't swear by it."

As they got up to leave, he asked, "So, do you know who the dead guy is yet? The one in the house?"

"Not yet," she said. "But we're still trying. And thanks again for your help."

"I don't want your thanks, but I would like that little trip you promised."

"You got it," Gabby said, and gave him a quick hug.

Twenty-Eight

When they walked down the hall to their apartment late that afternoon, the first thing Gabby and Zach saw was their door ajar, open about five inches. "What the hell?" Zach muttered, slipping his backpack off and reaching for the can of Mace. "Stay back," he ordered Gabby. "Like hell," she replied, stepping up next to him.

Ignoring her, he nudged her to one side of the door, and, holding the Mace in front of him, pushed the door fully open. At first glance, he saw Barclay the poodle, leashed to a leg of an armchair, staring at him, cowering. Around his neck was tied a bright red ribbon, one he had seen Gabby use to tie a ponytail.

"Call the manager," he said. "Then Philips. We've had a visitor."

"What is it?" she demanded, pushing next to him, seeing what he saw. "My God."

Then she was on her phone.

Gingerly, Zach stepped inside—the Mace at arms-length, searching all corners of the living room. He waited and listened for any sound, and when he heard none, he stooped to pet Barclay, scratching his ears, hearing the soft rumble. "I'll be right back and set you free, buddy. Be patient."

Moving on, he no longer made any effort to remain quiet. If the visitor was still there, he would know soon enough.

And deal with it.

By now, Gabby was right behind him. "The manager is on his way up," she said. "And I left a message for Philips." She knew immediately who had been there, but how Jessup had found the apartment and broken into it was another matter.

Then she spotted it. In the far corner of the room, hung on a lampshade, was a pair of her pink panties, with a note attached. She walked closer and leaned over, not touching the note, but reading, *"These always were my favorites."*

She felt a small shudder. Her lips went dry, a faint taste of vomit in her throat.

"What is it?" Zach asked, walking over. Then read the note. "Asshole."

They kept going, now close together, each holding their can of Mace. They stopped at each room, pushed doors open, and stepped inside. Nothing else seemed out of place until they reached her bedroom. *Trashed.* Drawers overturned. Clothes scattered. Her few keepsakes lay smashed. The only photograph of her family, Mom, Dad, and two sisters, lay torn into small pieces, its frame twisted, the glass splintered as though it had been crushed by the heel of a shoe. Her favorite doll, which she had carried with her since childhood, lay on the floor, beheaded. And on her dresser mirror, a red lipstick-scrawled message:

You Can Run But You Cannot Hide! Bitch!

Looking into the bathroom, they could see the medicine chest had been torn open, its contents thrown into the bathtub. And, sitting submerged in the toilet bowl, was the small statuette of an Emmy award for her reporting in San Jose.

They could only stand and stare. Zach put his arm around her and pulled her close. "Take it easy," he whispered, feeling the shivers pass through her body, knowing his words would be of little comfort. She knelt down and picked up the doll and tried to reattach the head, fighting her anger, catching a sob still in her throat. It was the first time since they'd been together that Zach had ever seen her so traumatized, so near tears. Then his own eyes began to well.

Minutes later, as he left her to free Barclay from his tether, the manager showed up at the door along with a security guard. "What's going on here?" he demanded.

"Look for yourself, but don't touch anything," Zach said. "We've been invaded."

The two men walked slowly through the apartment, stopping at each room, somberly greeting Gabby as she emerged from the bedroom. "Holy Christ," the manager said, looking at the damage. "When did this happen?"

"Some time today," she replied. "We don't know when."

"And how?"

"We thought you might know," she said with anger.

"I have no idea. We keep things pretty secure around here."

"Not secure enough it appears."

"Have you called the police?" he asked.

"I've left a message for a detective we know. We should hear from him soon."

"Any idea who might have done this?"

"Maybe. We'll talk to the detective about that."

Before more words were spoken they heard a woman's voice at the door, loud enough to carry from front to back. "My heavens," they heard her say. "Have you been robbed?" She was now inside the apartment. "I heard the manager. What's happened?"

When Gabby got there, she recognized her as a neighbor, a woman who carried her black cat around like a baby. Zach was telling her, "Someone broke in while we were at work. You didn't see or hear anything, did you?"

She had no black cat today.

"No, no, I've been gone most of the day. Bridge club, you

know. We meet every week. I just got back."

"Well, thanks," Zach said.

"It's too bad, just before the wedding and all."

"The wedding?"

"Yes, your best friend. His brother was here yesterday, asking after you. Wanted to send you an invitation and needed to know your apartment number."

Zach and Gabby exchanged a look. The question was answered.

"And you told him?" Zach said.

"Why, yes. Even offered to deliver it myself. But he said he wanted to mail it."

"What did he look like?" Gabby asked.

"Like a hippie, now that you ask. Shaved head, a ring in his lip. Like a lot of guys you see in Uptown." Then, suddenly, it dawned. "You don't think … ?"

"He probably had nothing to do with this," Zach reassured the woman. "It was likely just a coincidence."

"So is there a wedding?"

"I'm not sure. I haven't picked up the mail yet."

"Well, I'll tell you one thing. I'm going to get another deadbolt put on my door."

With that, she was gone.

WITHIN AN HOUR, Philips was at the apartment, heeding Gabby's urgent call, and a half hour later, Barclay was there, answering Zach's call. Once both had looked around, they all met in the living room. By then Zach had taken video of all of the damage, moving from room to room, his camera missing nothing.

"Hell of a mess," Philips said. "I'm just glad you weren't here when he arrived."

"I wish I had been," Zach said. "Maybe we could have put an end to all of this."

"Careful what you wish for," Barclay said.

"Even though we know who did this," Philips said, "I've got a forensic team coming to lift any useable prints. In case we eventually need them in court."

"My guess is you won't find any," Gabby said. "Craig's too savvy to leave any behind."

"Maybe so, but the manager's also getting us the video from the security cameras at the front entrance and in the garage. They're supposedly both working, so we should have some kind of image."

"And you've got the neighbor lady's description," Zach said.

"By now," Gabby said, "I'll bet he's wearing a wig and sporting a mustache, with a ring hanging from his nose. Trust me, he's not about to be caught."

"All the more reason," Barclay said, "that I'd like you two to pack up some things and head downtown to the Hilton for the night. On me. Sleep in. Come in late or take the day off. You don't want to stay here and get in the way of the finger-print guys. The manager can lock up when they're done and I'll get you some help in cleaning the place tomorrow."

"OK," Zach said.

"Separate rooms, OK?" Gabby added, with a smile.

"Of course," Barclay replied, also with a smile.

As they were about to leave, Barclay the poodle crawled from Zach's lap across the couch and into the lap of Barclay the boss. "So is this is the dog that got kicked around?" he asked. "Tiny little thing." Scratching his ears. "What's his name?"

Before Gabby could say "You don't want to know," Zach said, "We haven't decided yet."

Best to let a nameless dog lie.

As it turned out, Barclay held to his promise and arranged for separate but adjoining rooms at the Hilton. After din-ner at one of the downstairs restaurants, they returned to the rooms. "Are you going to be OK?" Zach asked. "If I can sleep, sure," she replied. "We'll just have to see."

They had spent the time at dinner largely quiet, each absorbed by what had just happened, each still in a sort of daze. Gabby's anger had dissipated, but her anguish was clearly written across her face. She had made no attempt to apply makeup or comb her hair, and Zach could not remember her looking more distraught. "If you need me, just knock," he said. "Or better yet, I'll leave the door between us open."

"Thanks," she said. "I should be OK."

Once in her room, afraid her mother might have been trying to reach her, she put in a call to her. "I wondered if I'd ever hear from you," her mother said. "Your sisters were getting worried and so was I."

It was true. It had been days since she'd spoken to either her mother or sisters. There had never seemed to be time. "I know, I'm sorry. I've been terribly busy on a story, almost night and day."

"What kind of story?"

"It's complicated," she replied, but quickly tried to explain the Ponzi story in as little detail as possible. She made no mention of Craig Jessup or tonight's scare, or the fact that she was temporarily housed in a hotel.

"It sounds like a story your father would have loved to cover."

"I've thought of that ... and of him ... often. In fact, I can sometimes hear him whispering in my ear. Encouraging me."

"Really?"

"Really."

"He'd love that," her mother said. "I can't tell you how much I miss him."

"Me, too. Every day."

After telling her more about the events at home, her mother surprised her with, "I'm thinking of flying out there for a few days. Just a short visit."

"That would be great," Gabby said, "but this is the wrong

time, Mom. I wouldn't have much time to spend with you, and I still don't have my own place."

"You're *still* living with that boy?"

"He's not a boy, Mom. We're good friends. And I haven't had a chance to find anything for myself. Once I do, and once this story is over, I'll take a few days off and show you the wonders of Minnesota."

After more give-and-take, her mother reluctantly agreed, and they parted with Gabby's promise to stay closer in touch.

IT WAS TWO IN the morning and, again, sleep had not yet come. Despite the closed windows, she could hear faint sounds of the late-night downtown traffic and the occasional passersby talking in the hallway outside her door. She had showered, washed her hair, then read from the latest John Sandford paperback mystery until midnight in hopes it would help pass the time until sleep came. But instead it had only reminded her of the threats that were all too real, not works of fiction.

She knew it was silly to think sleep would arrive without a struggle, not with all of those images from the ravaged apartment floating around inside her. With her eyes trained on the darkened ceiling, she tried to form a picture of Jessup—wandering from room to room, touching and feeling for her as he went; finding the pair of panties, holding them to his nose, disappointed that they'd been washed, but with a self-satisfied smile as he wrote the note; rummaging through her closet, catching her scent, caressing the fabric of her clothes before scattering them; tearing the family photo into pieces, knowing, but never understanding, why neither her mother nor her sisters ever really liked him.

Again, as she had so often, she asked herself: *How could I—for months—have never known the real him? How could I have been so blinded, so smitten, that I never suspected what lay dormant?* Or, she thought, perhaps until that crucial moment when he lashed out at her, even he did not know the Hyde that lay hidden within him.

It was clear he had passed over some kind of psychological threshold that she would never fathom, that he had become more obsessed, more dangerous, with every passing day. The end, whenever and however it would come, was as unpredictable as it was frightening.

Finally, in frustration and with some hesitation, she got up and walked to the door of Zach's room. Knocking lightly, she opened the door. The light from the bathroom spilled into the room. He was lying on his back in his shorts, staring at the ceiling. Just as she had minutes before.

"You're awake?" she asked quietly.

"No. I always sleep with my eyes open."

"Smartass," she whispered, but smiled for the first time since she'd entered their apartment hours before. She walked to the side of the bed and sat on the edge of it. "May I ask a favor? Will you hold me? Like a friend? And that's all?"

He spread his arms. "Of course"

She laid next him on her side, her nightshirt tight around her hips, settling into his arm. His skin against her face had the freshness and scent of the soap she had just used on her own body. "You haven't slept at all?" she whispered, pressing her face against his chest.

"Not a wink. Your insomnia is contagious."

She laughed and raised up, looking down at him. "You know what? I'm not sure what I'd do without you."

She could see his smile. "What are friends for?" he said.

The last thing she remembered, sometime later, before sleep finally enclosed her, was the touch of his lips to her cheek.

Twenty-Nine

There are no secrets in a television newsroom. Or in any newsroom, for that matter. Not for long, anyway. A word here, a whisper there, a text message here, an e-mail there. Within an hour or two, at most, the story has been pieced together, usually with surprising accuracy.

Probably what you should expect from a bunch of nosy journalists.

So it came as no shock that by a little after nine in the morning, it was common knowledge in the Channel 7 newsroom that Zach's apartment had been crashed and trashed by a stalker out of Gabby's past, and that threatening messages had been left in his wake.

While many of the newsroom managers had known of Jessup for some time, most of the working grunts had not. Even Sarah Andrews had resisted spreading the information she had gained about Jessup, as had Ostby, after the knife attack. So the news, although still in rumor form, created a buzz big enough to quickly reach Barclay's office.

His assistant, Jeff Parkett, was in his doorway. "Is it true, what they're saying out there?"

"What's that?"

"That Zach's place got raided and ransacked."

Barclay could only grin. "I knew it wouldn't take long, but this sets some kind of record."

"It would have been nice for me to know," Parkett said.

"I'm sorry. I meant to call you last night, but it got too late. It was a pretty ugly scene," he said, describing the disarray in the apartment.

"How are they? Zach and Gabby?"

"Upset, of course. Zach looked better than Gabby, but both seemed to be in a kind of shock. I got 'em into the Hilton for the night and told them to come in when they felt like it. Or not at all. But we'll need to get a couple of people over to their place to help clean up."

"I'll take care of that," Parkett said. "But I think you should get out there and talk to the staff. Tell them what happened. Who this Jessup guy is, and why we all have to be on the alert. Who knows, if he got into that apartment and did what he did, he could sure as hell get into the station—and all of us should be aware of that."

"Good point. Get as many people together as you can in the next hour while I try to find Sam Ryan and let him know what's going on."

As it happened, Ryan was in his office and not traveling, and—for once—did not keep Barclay waiting. They had not met in person for some time. Ryan, true to his word, had left him alone to run the newsroom. In return, Barclay had tried to stay out of his way, keeping him informed of any developments via e-mail.

But this turn of events deserved a face-to-face meeting.

Once Ryan had heard Barclay out, he could only shake his head. "Are the two of them OK?"

"Shaken up, but OK."

"You know the bad feeling I've had about this," Ryan said, "from the first time you told me that this Jessup clown could be in town."

"All of us have," Barclay replied, "but I think we've done everything we could to keep them safe."

"I hope so," Ryan said. "As I told you then, I not only fear for them but for the reputation of the station if something dire were to happen."

"I understand, but we can only do so much." Then he repeated Parkett's fears about a possible station invasion. "We may want to think about adding even more security around here for a while."

"Done. What else?"

Barclay told him that while he would be talking to the news staff shortly, Ryan might consider speaking to the other department heads, to spread the word throughout the station.

"I'll do it this afternoon," he replied. "And please give my best wishes to Gabby and that young photographer."

"Zach," Barclay said.

"Of course."

"One more thing," Barclay said. "We're making progress on that other investigation we told you about. Not sure yet where it will end up, but it could be a pretty good story."

"That's great," Ryan said, "but your top priority should be finding this Jessup prick and getting the cops on his ass. Got that?"

"Got that," Barclay replied.

WHEN ZACH ROLLED OVER, he found the room bright with the morning light. Next to him was the imprint and warmth of Gabby's body, but no Gabby. He sat up, stretched, and slipped on the pair of pants he had thrown onto a chair the night before. After quickly brushing his teeth, he walked to the adjoining door and knocked lightly. "You there? You decent?"

"Sure. C'mon in."

She was sitting in a chair next to her bed, still in her nightshirt, her legs tucked beneath her. She looked rested and relaxed, a different person from the night before.

Her phone was in her hand.

Zach walked over and sat on the edge of the bed, next to her. "Who are you calling?"

"Philips. I want to go get Barclay back."

As a favor the night before, Philips had agreed to take the poodle home with him. He'd never had a dog and wanted to give it a try for one night, while they were at the hotel.

Zach glanced at his watch. It was a little before nine. "We should check in with the newsroom first," he said. "And get some breakfast."

"That's fine, but I bet the little guy is scared to death. We need to get him home."

"I'm sure he's doing great. Philips is probably spoiling him more than you do."

She unfolded her legs and got up, her back to the window, the sunlight making the nightshirt virtually transparent. Zach made no effort to turn his eyes away.

"You look like you got some sleep," he said.

"I did, finally. Thanks to you." Then, to his absolute surprise, she leaned over, put her fingers beneath his chin, tipped his head up, and kissed him fully on the lips, her tongue seeking and finding his.

"Don't look so shocked," she whispered. "You thought I was asleep, but I felt you kissing my cheek. You're not so innocent."

Before he could respond, she pulled him off the bed, "Now scoot. I'm going to take another shower. I'll meet you in the lobby in a half hour."

BY THE TIME BARCLAY got back from Ryan's office, many of the staff already had gathered around the raised assignment desk, waiting. Once he'd been told everyone who was available was there, he climbed up on the platform and raised his hand for quiet. When the hubbub settled, he said, "I want to make this as short as possible. We've all got our jobs to do, and I don't want to get in the way. But I do want to put the rumors aside and tell you what's going on ... because it could affect all of us."

He waited for the murmurs to fade. "For some time now, we've known that a stalker by the name of Craig Jessup is in the Cities. Jessup is a former boyfriend of Gabby Gooding. He assaulted and seriously injured her while both lived in San Jose. He was jailed on assault charges in California but skipped probation and has followed her here, threatening both her and Zach Anthony, whom Gabby is staying with temporarily. Late yesterday, while Gabby and Zach were at work, he broke into Zach's apartment and trashed it, leaving a threatening message behind for Gabby.

"The police have been notified, and they and others are searching for Jessup as we speak. Our concern is not only for Gabby and Zach, but for all of you ... for all of us ... in the off-chance that he may attempt to get into the station or approach one of you outside of the station. He has proven to be a dangerous man and one not to be meddled with. I will post his picture and description on the newsroom bulletin boards, but he often changes his appearance. Last seen, he had shaved his head, with a ring in his nose. It may be something else by now. Perhaps even a wig and a mustache."

Barclay had their rapt attention. Not a sound could be heard, aside from the muted squawking of the police radios from inside the dispatch booth.

He went on. "To this point, only a few of us in the newsroom have known about this, in hopes that Jessup would be caught and dealt with before he could do serious harm, and before he became the distraction that he has become. But his actions last night make this meeting essential. I would hope that you would pass on this message to those who are not here, but also give Gabby and Zach some space. I would also hope you would not talk about all of this beyond this room. That may be an impossible request, but I hope you would honor it. I would hate to see this in the newspapers.

"Finally, to complicate matters even further, Gabby and Zach and John Knowles are also involved in an investigation that carries its own threats ... an investigation that could prove to be ... and I emphasize *could* ... a terrific story for this station. Time will tell. And while I can't say anything more about it now, please understand that is why they have not been more involved in other newsroom projects.

"From the beginning, we have done everything possible to protect Zach and Gabby, and we will continue to do so until this nightmare is finally over."

Before he could step down, he was faced with a barrage of questions.

How are Gabby and Zach?

Where are they?

Did Gabby know this guy would follow her when she came here?

Will there be more security in the building?

What should we do if we spot him, or if he comes on to us?

What should we say if word gets out and we get a call from one of the papers or another TV station?

He did his best to answer the questions as fully and truthfully as he could, but after about fifteen minutes he'd had enough. "OK, folks, it's time to get back to work. We've got newscasts to get on the air, and that's not going to happen standing here. Keep your eyes and ears open and we'll do our best to keep you in the loop."

Thirty

Philips was waiting impatiently outside the apartment by the time Gabby and Zach arrived, sitting in his squad car with the babysat poodle by his side. "'Bout time," he said, as Gabby opened the door. "Much longer and I was afraid he might crap in the car."

She laughed as she took Barclay into her arms. "Hey, buddy," she said, scratching his ears, "did he treat you OK?"

"Ask me," Philips said, as he got out of the car. "He kept me up half the night, whining like a little baby. Missing you guys. I think I'd rather have a cat."

"Cats whine, too," she said. "And scratch. Trust me, I grew up with three of them."

"Then I'd better look more seriously for a wife."

"Careful. They can scratch and whine, too."

He gave her a look. "Maybe I'll just stay single."

While they talked, two guys got out of a Channel 7 van parked up the street. Zach knew them from the station maintenance staff: Darius Tompkins and Zeke Augustus. Both were carrying brooms, mops, and assorted cleaning supplies.

Zach quickly thanked them for coming, and after introducing them to Gabby and Philips, led all of them into the building and up to the apartment. Gabby, still holding the poodle, was last in line and hesitated at the door, gathering courage to see the mess all over again. Finally, she walked in. Everything was the same, except for the dust left from the police fingerprinting.

As he stood in the doorway of her bedroom, Darius gave a low whistle. "Wow," he said, "this dude made one hell of a mess." Then, looking back at Gabby, "But I'm sure glad you weren't here when he was."

"You got that right," she replied.

Before the cleanup could begin, she handed the dog to Zach and got down on her hands and knees to collect everything of value that was still in one piece, placing the various articles in a small suitcase. Then she gathered up her strewn pile of clothes and put them in a large plastic bag, to decide later which to throw away and which to keep, once they'd been cleaned.

The emotions that had drained her the night before were gone now. In the hours since, she'd been able to make peace with what had happened, viewing the scattered remnants of her life as if they belonged to someone else, a stranger whose clothes happened to be her size, a stranger whose small Emmy still lay sunken in the toilet.

She was looking at it as a reporter would. Sad, but nothing to do with her.

Finally, Zach took the two maintenance men aside to give them instructions while Gabby and Philips headed back to the living room. Only then did Gabby notice the small laptop computer that Philips was carrying.

"What's that for?" she asked.

"A little show-and-tell," he replied. "The video from the security cameras."

Phillips waited for Zach to return before he cued the video. As the images appeared, it was clear that Jessup had made no attempt to hide from the cameras or to destroy or disable them. In fact, he seemed to take pleasure in flaunting them, smiling, blowing a kiss, and, at one point, giving the camera a middle finger salute.

Gabby was mesmerized. It was the first time she had seen him in months...literally since the moments before the beating, the moments before she blacked out. In the days and weeks after, she had avoided any of his court appearances and had stayed away from any place she thought he might be. Or from any of the friends they'd had in common.

And the restraining order had kept him away from her. At least out of her sight.

So now, as she viewed the video, she was caught between anguish and laughter. Anguish at seeing him at all, laughter at how he looked. "My, God, he's a freak," she said, staring at his bald head and ring in his lip. "I'd have trouble recognizing him, and I lived with the guy."

Philips replayed the video twice. "We've made stills from the video and have distributed the pictures to all of the precincts in the city. But we can probably assume he's changed his appearance by now."

Zach said, "I've talked to the building manager and he's adding security in the garage, and I've got a locksmith coming to change to a better lock on the door."

"I don't think that will matter," she said, sinking into a chair. "He's made his point now. He's proved that he can get to us, and I doubt that he'll be back. He'll try something else. More imaginative. More daring. More dangerous. Just watch and see."

As they viewed the video, John Knowles was downtown in the Thirtieth floor office of Stuart Kingston, a vice president of the Wells Fargo banking empire and a friend of Knowles's from AA. They had met at the Hazelden treatment center many years before and had remained close ever since, attending the same twice-weekly meetings.

"Thanks for taking the time, Stuart. I know how busy you are."

"No problem. But I assume this is about business, not personal, or you'd have waited until after the meeting."

"True. I need to drain your brain about an investigation we're in the middle of, and I didn't want to do it there."

"OK."

"But I need your word that our conversation won't go any further than this office."

"You have it."

"Good. While I can't provide a lot of details, we have reason to believe a man wanted in an East Coast Ponzi scheme a number of years ago may now be living in Minnesota—with a new identity and possibly a new appearance." He went on to describe what they knew about Overton and the old Ponzi scheme, but did not reveal how they'd been able to connect him to Minnesota. "Our investigation got the attention of the FBI, and they're now working with us in a kind of uneasy alliance."

"Sounds fascinating," Kingston said, "but I don't see how I can help."

"Maybe not, but I thought I'd try," explaining briefly their theory that Overton—if he had come to Minnesota years before—may have used his Ponzi money to begin a new business here. "I figure a guy like you," Knowles said, "who knows everybody who's anybody in the business community, who's been around for a lot of years, might be able to help us track him down."

He handed Kingston the FBI photo of Overton. "This is how he looked back in 2002. Probably nothing like that now. But it may be worth having."

Kingston glanced at the picture, but then shook his head. "Let me get this straight. You want me to help you find a man with a new name, maybe a new face, with a ton of money to hide behind, who may or may not have come here years ago, and who may or may not still be living here with a new business."

"Nothing to it," Knowles replied, with a smile.

"If I didn't know you better, I'd think you'd fallen off the wagon."

"Let's hope not."

"Seriously..." Kingston started.

"Seriously," Knowles interrupted. "I know this is a big business community, but in some ways it's a small fraternity. You all belong to the same clubs and the same business groups. The Chamber. The Business Partnership. You eat at the same restaurants. You all have boats on Lake Minnetonka. You all play tennis or golf together. Your wives all know each other..."

"Wait a minute!" Kingston objected, with a laugh.

"I know I'm exaggerating and stereotyping," Knowles said, "but there is some truth to it." He paused. "If you would, I'd like you to give it some thought, ask around, discreetly, about anybody over the years who may have struck you or others as a bit strange. Who's never revealed much about himself, his background, or his family. Who may tend to be a loner, a bit secretive. Someone who may have been able to start a business without getting much...if any...financial help from you banker types. Know what I mean?"

"I know what you mean, and I'll do as you say, but you're really asking the impossible. I know a lot of people in business, but certainly not everyone. Not by a long shot. And we're only one bank..."

Knowles interrupted again. "If he is in business, it could be in the medical or pharmaceutical field. That's his background. He may have learned his lesson with Diabetrics and is running a legitimate enterprise now. That's only a guess, but it might be a place to start. The Feds would love to get their hands on him, and we'd love to get the story."

Kingston glanced at his watch. "I've got to get to a meeting," he said, "and I want to think about this. As you suggest, I'll ask around. But I'm certainly making no promises."

Getting up, Knowles said, "I understand. And I appreciate it. Let me know if you think of anything ... or anyone else ... I should be talking to."

"Will do," Kingston said, but without a lot of conviction.

WHEN SHE RETURNED to the newsroom from the apartment, Gabby went in search of Linda Wilkins, the intern who earlier had helped try to track down the mysterious tattoo on John Doe's ankle. An impossible search, as it turned out.

She found her in the station lunchroom. After apologizing for failing to keep her earlier promise of a cup of coffee and a conversation, Gabby asked if she was available and willing to give her a hand.

"Sure," she replied, "I've been looking for something to do."

Gabby said, "You've probably heard by now that we're looking for a guy named Craig Jessup who's been stalking me and tore up Zach's apartment yesterday."

"Yes. I was at Mr. Barclay's meeting. I'm so sorry."

"Thanks, but no need to be."

"So how can I help?"

"We'd like to find out where this Jessup is staying. The California authorities think he may have a motorcycle, which could mean that he's staying at a hotel or motel in the suburbs where parking the thing might be easier than downtown. We also know at one point he got on a bus in Uptown that was heading for Bloomington, although he got off after a few stops. But that's all we know."

Linda caught on quickly. "So you'd like me to start checking hotels and motels, beginning in Bloomington."

"You got it. There have to be a lot of them so it won't be easy. Pretty tedious, actually. And he may not even be staying in a motel or hotel. He could be camping somewhere."

"So?"

"So if he *is* staying at a hotel or motel, he may have had to use a credit card to check in. Which could mean he had to use his real name. We can only hope. We have no idea how much money he has, or how long he plans to stay."

Linda took a moment. "It would probably be smart," she said, "to start with the cheaper, less well-known places. If I didn't want to be found, that's what I'd do."

"Good thinking."

"May I ask a question?"

"Of course."

"Why hasn't this been done before?"

Gabby could only shrug. "Because there hasn't been time, I guess. We've been doing other things. But after the attack on Zach's apartment, the stakes got a lot higher."

"I'll start right away."

"Good. And if you need more help, I'll try to get it for you."

As Linda left the lunchroom, Knowles and Zach arrived, pulling up chairs across from Gabby. Knowles quickly described his visit with his "old AA friend," who's in the banking business. "I tried to get hold of you first," he said, "in case you wanted to come along. But you were still at the apartment … and I also thought this friend might be more comfortable if it was just me who showed up."

Gabby was impressed. "That was a terrific idea, John. How did he react? What did he say?"

"Frankly, that I was out of my mind," he said, repeating what Kingston had told him. "He wasn't encouraging, to say the least."

"But he's going to think about it?" Zach said.

"Yes, he agreed to do that. And to talk to some others, discreetly. We'll have to wait and see. I also have a couple other friends I trust who work for Medtronic and Boston Scientific, here in town. I hope to get together with them as soon as I can."

Before they got up to leave, Gabby reported on what Linda the intern had agreed to do, but then asked, "What else should *we* be doing?"

No one had a ready answer.

Thirty-One

The car with a small RE/MAX logo on the side door pulled up beneath an overhanging willow in the driveway of a large Prairie-style home in the wealthy Minneapolis suburb of Orono. Before the driver could get out, he saw a slightly built, gray-haired man walking quickly down the driveway. He'd clearly been watching for him.

"Glad you could make it," the man said as the real estate agent got out of the car and took his outstretched hand. "I'm Harlan Hawkins."

The agent, Jeremy Higgins, had only spoken to Hawkins by phone, but had done a computer search in advance of this meeting and found that Hawkins was the owner and CEO of Hawkins Investments, a boutique financial firm that apparently specialized in medical and technology stocks. Little other information was available. The firm had no website, which Higgins found unusual but not unheard of for a small, privately held company.

So he'd been curious to actually meet the man.

Higgins introduced himself and gave Hawkins his card. "I was glad to get your call," he said. "And I'm here to be of any help I can. But I'm curious as to how you found me."

"The business grapevine," Hawkins replied, vaguely.

"You've got a good reputation and a good sales record, from what I've been told."

"That's nice to hear," he replied, although he would have liked to know more. "So what about yourself? The only thing I know is that you're in the investment business."

"That's because I'm a private person and like to keep it that way. But I came from out West," he lied, "and settled here a number of years ago. Started my business, married late, and had a couple of kids. My firm is small, only a couple of employees, but we do OK for ourselves. That's about all you need to know for now. OK?"

As he spoke, Higgins tried to size up the man. About five feet ten or eleven inches, thin except for a slightly rounded tummy that his shirt could not entirely hide, a narrow face with tightly drawn skin that seemed to pull at his eyes and sharpen his cheek bones. Although not nearly as severe, it reminded Higgins of a man he'd once known who had survived a house fire and whose burned face had been reconstructed with skin grafts.

"I'll give you a tour of the house in a minute," Hawkins said. "But I thought we should talk about a few things first."

"Sure," Higgins said.

Hawkins led him to a small bench just off the driveway, below the willow. "What I'm about to say may seem a bit strange to you," he said once they were seated, "but I need your advance assurance of absolute discretion."

Higgins looked puzzled, but said, "OK, I guess."

Hawkins's eyes narrowed. "Here's why. My wife and two kids are up north at our cabin and know nothing of your visit here today. Or of my tentative plans to sell the house."

Higgins couldn't disguise his surprise. "*Really?* Why is that?"

"Because they love it here, and would be heartbroken if they knew I was contemplating a move. I have yet to break the news to them and wanted to get a sense of the value of the home . . . and its sales potential . . . before I do."

"How old are the kids?" Higgins asked.

"Four and seven. Both in private schools with lots of friends."

Young, Higgins thought, for a father who looked to be close to fifty. "So why are you thinking of selling?"

"Between us, I have a chance to move my business to Atlanta and merge with a much larger firm. It is a financial opportunity of a lifetime, and I don't want to let it pass."

"I would think your family would be excited about that," Higgins ventured.

Hawkins chuckled. "That's because you don't know my wife. Anita was born and raised here. Her whole family is here. All of her friends are here. The idea of moving to a new place, where she would know no one, would be anathema to her, no matter what our financial opportunity. She is a very strong, independent woman."

Higgins took a bold step forward. "So what if she refuses to move? Would I be wasting my time here?"

"That's not going to happen, but if it did, I would pay you handsomely for the time and effort you expend in giving me an appraisal on the house."

Higgins persisted. "Fine, but how long do you plan to keep this secret?"

"Yet to be determined. But since there is some urgency involved, I would like to get your report as soon as possible. And I will go from there."

"Whose name is on the title?" Higgins asked.

"Just mine. I bought the house before we were married and never bothered to add her name to the title documents."

"So you could sell without her knowledge or approval."

"I suppose I could, but, of course, I wouldn't."

Higgins sat back, again studying the man, unsure of what to think or whether to get involved. Certainly strange, that's for sure, and new in his experience. But as he looked up at the house, partially hidden by all of the trees, he could see what might be a million dollar sale or more—and the thought of that was hard to resist.

"But I have to emphasize," Hawkins said, "that you should speak to no one until our plans are finalized. Even to your colleagues. My wife knows many people in this community, and any word about my plans would likely get back to her. That would be unacceptable—until I have had the opportunity to speak to her myself."

Higgins got up. "OK, if you say so. You have my word. So let's take a look."

As they walked up the driveway, drawing closer, Higgins could see the house was everything he'd expected, and more. It was a like a giant tree house, sitting high atop the slope of the lawn, surrounded and sheltered by huge oaks, whose leafy branches draped over it like a green curtain, enveloping it, virtually hiding it from the road below. Floor-to-ceiling windows overlooked a cedar deck that wrapped around the house, a house which—at first glance—seemed the length of a football field.

Higgins, who had seen more than his share of awesome homes, could only look in wonder.

"As you can probably tell, it was designed by an architect who was a disciple of Frank Lloyd Wright," Hawkins said.

"I can see that," Higgins replied, still wondering why he'd never seen or heard of this place before. In all of his years of selling real estate in the area.

The interior was as impressive as the exterior. The large, open living room seemed—because of the large windows—to bring the outdoors indoors. All of the rooms were designed with that same purpose, spacious and open, full of light, built with a mixture of stone and wood, designed to make you feel part of the environment just beyond the walls.

Behind the house there was a small swimming pool and hot tub, and an array of playground equipment for the use of Hawkins's children.

As they wandered through the house, Higgins started to take a few notes and sketch the layout and approximate sizes of the rooms before he was told by Hawkins not to bother, that he had the original construction blueprints from 2003. "That will help," Higgins said, "but I have to tell you that it's going to take time to figure out an appropriate asking price. This is a very unusual house. I've never seen anything quite like it, and I'm not sure comparable recent sales figures would help. I'd like to be able to confer with my colleagues."

"That won't be possible," Hawkins said. "You'll have to do it by yourself."

"Then may I ask what you paid for it, and when?"

"$750,000 in 2005."

Higgins had thought it would be far more. "OK. That's a starting point. I'll get back to you with a report as soon as possible."

"The sooner the better. And," handing him a piece of paper, "please contact me only through this cell phone number."

As Higgins walked down the driveway to his car, he paused for yet another look at the house. Trying to escape an uneasy feeling that he was about to get involved in something a little too weird for his liking. But what the hell? A sale is a sale, a deal is a deal. Weird or not. At the same time, he was determined to find out more about this man who liked to keep secrets from his wife and kids.

THAT EVENING, TO THEIR surprise, Gabby and Zach were the guests of Barclay and his wife, Rachel, at their Lowertown condo. Rachel had long expressed the desire to meet the two of them, having heard so much about their exploits over the past several weeks and had seized her first chance to bring them here. At first, Barclay had resisted, afraid word of the invitation might get back to the newsroom and further alienate some of Gabby's detractors, who already were convinced she was getting preferential treatment. But in the end, Rachel had prevailed.

266 | RON HANDBERG

Gabby had also been wary, for some of the same reasons. But Zach had convinced her it would be a fun way to spend the evening, to ease some of the recent tension, and to allow them to get a glimpse of Barclay's private life. For as open as Barclay was in the newsroom, he was scrupulously guarded about his life outside of the station. And while many of the staff had met Rachel at newsroom social functions, none— until tonight—had been guests in their home.

After a quick tour of the condo, they settled down in the living room, Gabby and Zach on the sofa, with George and Rachel's cats by their sides or on their laps. Even Seuss, the skittish Siamese, allowed himself to be cuddled, much to Barclay's surprise. Gabby brushed aside Rachel's apologies for the feline intrusion, telling her of her own family's cats.

Once the get-acquainted conversation was over, Rachel said, "I was so sorry to hear what's been happening to you lately, and what happened at the apartment. It must have been terrifying to find it like that."

"It was," Gabby admitted, glancing at Zach, "but it wasn't so much the damage he caused as the very fact that he'd been there, touching my things, scribbling those notes. It made my skin crawl. It still does."

"George says everyone's doing their best to find this guy..."

"I know. And I appreciate that. And I can't tell you how badly I feel about bringing all of this about. If I'd stayed in San Jose, maybe things would have been different. Maybe they would have caught him by now. At least he wouldn't have followed me here, and caused all of the trouble that he has."

"That's nonsense," Barclay said. "Who knows what would have happened in San Jose? You're here. You're alive. And safe. And we'll find the guy, sooner or later. Before he can do any more harm or damage."

"I hope you're right," she said. "I just want it to be over."

As the evening wore on through dinner, the conversation ranged from Rachel's involvement in Barclay's investigation of the cold case murder of his old high school classmate to Zach's work on his screenplay to the current investigation of the missing Ponzi fugitive.

"It's frustrating," Gabby said. "We feel like we're getting closer to him, but we could be kidding ourselves. He could be long gone or never here to begin with. Nobody really knows for sure."

Zach cut in, "Maybe not for sure, but the evidence—such as it is—indicates that he *is* still around, invisible as he may be at the moment."

Rachel turned to Gabby, "George tells me that your father was a reporter, too."

"That's right," she said. "In Portland, for the *Oregonian* newspaper."

"Tell me about him."

"Wow," she replied, gathering her thoughts. "There's a lot to tell. You'll have to be patient and to understand that he wasn't just my father, but my idol. My hero." She paused. "He stood for everything that's right in journalism, and for everything that's right in being a husband to my mom and a dad to my sisters and me. Even though it's been a few years since he died, it's hard for me to talk about him … it's too raw … because it's still hard to believe that he's not around anymore."

Zach had heard some of this before, but it was all new to George and Rachel.

"He was a finalist for a Pulitzer three different times … and won virtually every other award the newspaper world has to offer, some of them several times over. He was proud of all of that, but that wasn't what drove him. He was out to get the bad guys, of whatever stripe, civil servants, white-collar frauds, anyone he found who was screwing over the public."

"My kind of guy," Barclay offered, admiration in his voice.

"From everything I've heard and seen, he *was* your kind of guy," she said. "And he tried to pass on to me the passion he felt about the business, as I know *you* try to do. When I was old enough, he asked me to help him with his investigations, trying to teach me some of the techniques and dogged persistence he had developed over the years. If I ever amount to anything as a reporter, it will be because of him. Because of what he taught me ... instilled in me, really."

Her eyes welled. "Then he was gone. In an instant. Dead on some sidewalk of a heart attack. I never had the chance to say goodbye, to tell him again what he had meant to me. To tell him I loved him one last time." She swiped at her eyes. "That's what makes me want to cry, every time I think or talk about him. That I didn't get to say those things to him."

Rachel took her hand.

"I'm sorry," Gabby said, a solitary tear now creeping down her cheek. "I should shut up."

Rachel gave her a moment. "So how is your mother doing?"

"Like me, I guess. But she has my sisters there for support, so that helps some. She wants to come out here for a visit, but I've asked her to wait until all of this is over."

"When she does come, I'd like to meet her."

"That would be nice. She'd like that, I'm sure."

LATER, IN THE CAR, on the way back to the apartment, Gabby took Zach's arm. "I hope I didn't embarrass you with that weepy stuff. I kind of made a fool of myself."

"No, you didn't make a fool of yourself, and no, you didn't embarrass me. I'm glad they got a chance to hear about your dad, to see what makes you tick."

She unbuckled her seat belt and leaned over to kiss him on the cheek.

He gave her a quick look. "What's that for?"

"For being you," she said.

Until now, they had not spoken of the night and morning in the hotel, avoiding the subject and its possible implications. But, she decided, no more. She rebuckled the belt and leaned back. "Will you hold me again tonight?" she asked.

Zach glanced over again, grinning. "With pleasure."

"Not like last time. Not as a friend."

He suddenly got serious. "What do you mean?"

"What do you think I mean?"

"You're sure?"

"Yes. I think it's time. Do you?"

"Are you kidding? It's all I've thought about since the first day we met."

"Really?"

"Really. But I didn't want to pressure you. To take advantage. To be a jerk."

"You had me fooled," she said. "Until the other night."

"I didn't think you were interested."

"You'll have to be patient. It's been a long time."

"I have all of the patience in the world," he replied. "You'll see. But I gotta tell you, I can hardly wait."

Then he laughed and hit the accelerator.

Thirty-Two

Barclay had just put aside his book and turned off the bed-side lamp when the ringtone on his cell sounded. Rachel groaned and turned over as he grudgingly searched for the phone in the dark. "Yeah," was all he could manage once he'd found it.

The display on the phone said 1:15.

"Who?" he asked, struggling to escape the covers and sit up.

"Pam Struthers, from the *Star Tribune*," was the reply.

The name was not familiar. "Hey, Pam, it's late."

"I know. I'm sorry. But my boss said I had to call to get a comment."

"About what?"

But he already knew. It was the call he'd suspected he would get but had prayed that he wouldn't.

The newsroom or the cops had sprung a leak.

"We have two sources," she said, "who tell us one of your reporters, a Gabrielle Gooding, is the subject of a stalker who's followed her here from California and who's apparently dangerous. We'd like you to confirm that along with any more details and your comment."

He carried the phone out of the bedroom and into the living room, stumbling over a footstool in the process. "Isn't this past your deadline?" he said, rubbing a sore toe.

"For the paper, yes, but not our website. We're planning to go with the story as we have it, but, as I say, we'd like to confirm what we know and get your comment."

"Gimme a minute. I'm not really awake yet." Playing for time to think.

"I don't have a lot of time. They're looking over my shoulder."

He knew that was probably a lie, but he gave her credit for pushing him. He would do the same. "So what have you got?"

"Not a lot, but enough to go with."

"Tell me," he said.

"This reporter, Gabrielle Gooding, recently moved here from San Jose, and apparently was followed by a guy who had assaulted her back there and later skipped out on his probation. That the station has known for some time that he was here and stalking her, but got the police involved when he invaded the apartment this Gabrielle … "

"Gabby," Barclay said.

"OK. The apartment she shared with a station photographer, one Zach Anthony. Doing some damage and leaving threatening notes. How am I doing?"

"Pretty good," he said.

"Also, that you've tightened security at the station and have warned other employees to be aware of the situation."

"OK."

"We don't have much more, because of the late hour. The Minneapolis cops have confirmed they're looking for him, but haven't yet found him or charged him. So we're not using his name. They won't tell us much more. Not yet, anyway."

"I don't have much to add," he said, "but for the record, you can take this down. Quote, 'Channel 7 management is doing everything in its power to protect our employees and to assist police in their efforts to apprehend this stalker and to see that he faces charges both here and in California.' Unquote."

"That's not much," she said.

"That's all you're going to get. And you're lucky to get that at this time of night. Goodnight, Pam."

He hung up before she could argue.

Rachel was at the bedroom door. "What was that about?"

He told her.

She turned on a light and came to sit next to him.

"Gabby will go crazy," he said. "She didn't want anybody to know, and now the whole world will know. It'll be everywhere. Even we're going to have to report it."

"Are you going to call her?"

"First thing in the morning. Let her sleep. She'll know soon enough."

"And so will he. Jessup, I mean."

"Probably."

"He'll panic and may go crazy, too," she said. "You have to get Gabby somewhere safe until all of this is over."

He scoffed. "Are you kidding? She'll never leave. Not in the middle of this other investigation. You heard her. She'll just ask herself what her dad would do . . . and, from what she says, he would never back off."

"Then you'll have to persuade her."

"Not likely. I'll just try to keep her calm."

THE SUN HAD JUST SPREAD its first rays on the bedroom window as Gabby and Zach lay intertwined in a jumble of sheets, her pajama bottoms clinging to her foot by one toe, shed within a moment of climbing into bed the night before. One of the sun's rays caught her half-opened eyes and brought her upright, unsure for a fraction of a second where she was and why she lay naked. Then she knew, feeling the warmth of Zach's body pressing against her back. He was still sleeping, his breathing deep, with what she took to be a look of contentment on his face.

She quietly slid out of the bed and slipped on a robe, still not quite believing what had happened only hours before. Despite the urgency both of them had felt, their love-making had been slow and—to her—amazing... and surprising because it felt so right. Few words had been spoken, murmurs really, as they'd gently explored each other's bodies. Touching, then moving on, breathing more labored, their bodies responding with a quickened pace. Then, unbelievably, it happened for both of them, together.

For Gabby, who made no claim of expertise, it had been unlike anything she had felt before. More loving, more caring, more sharing. Zach was, in bed, as he was in every other way: a gentle human being. And she couldn't have been more grateful.

As she headed for the bathroom to shower, her cell phone sounded from the kitchen, where she'd hurriedly left it the night before.

"Gabby?"

"Yes."

"Barclay here," he said, sounding official. "You awake?"

"Just."

"Listen up. I have some troubling news."

Her body went limp. "What?"

"The *Star Trib* website has posted a story on Jessup stalking you."

He could hear the sharp intake of breath.

"Someone in the newsroom or the cop shop must have leaked it. They called me late last night for a comment."

She sat down on a kitchen chair, trembling. "Will it be in the newspaper itself?"

"Probably not until tomorrow. The *Pioneer Press* may also have it by then."

"So everybody will know. And Jessup will know that everybody knows."

"Sooner than later, I'd guess, and his name and picture will probably be out there too, once they charge him."

"How about the other TV stations?"

"Probably, but I haven't heard from any of them yet."

"Sam Ryan?"

"I haven't talked to him, either."

"He'll be livid," she said. "Try to send me back to Portland."

At that moment, Zach appeared with a towel wrapped around his midsection. "What's going on?"

She held the phone aside and repeated what Barclay had told her.

"Fuck," was all he could find to say.

Back on the phone, she asked, "What do you want me to do?"

"Stay away from the station for now…"

"No," she shot back. "I'm not going to hide. We've got work to do, and we're not going to do it sitting here. We'll be in as soon as we can."

There was a pause at the other end. "OK," he finally said. "But don't talk to anybody. Let us handle the fallout."

FOUR HOURS LATER, working alone, Linda Wilkins, the intern, was making her nineteenth call to various hotels and motels in Bloomington and the surrounding suburbs.

It was all in search of Craig Jessup.

She'd been at it for two days without a hit and was about to quit, until—on that nineteenth call—she struck it rich.

Sort of.

The gold mine was the Empress, a small motel in suburban Richfield.

"Well, yes," a clerk named Lorraine said, "we had a guest by the name of Craig Jessup."

"Had?" Linda said, a little desperation in her voice.

"Yes, I'm sorry. He checked out a couple of hours ago."

The gold had turned to scrap iron.

"Tell me more, please."

"I can't tell you much more. Paid his bill, got on his motor-cycle and took off. Said he was heading out east. Nice young man, I must say. I'm so sorry you missed him."

"So am I. I wonder if you could tell me what he looks like these days?"

If Lorraine thought the question was odd, she didn't show it. "Funny you should ask. I thought he looked like he was wearing a toup, a rug, you know, which I took to mean he may have lost his hair to cancer or something. Of course I didn't say anything, but I felt bad for him."

"A mustache?"

"Yes, actually. But not too bushy."

Linda could think of only one more question. "Did you happen to get the license plate number on his motorcycle?"

"No, no, but I can tell you it was a big, black Harley. Looked brand new to me."

GABBY HAD SPENT the morning huddled in her cubicle, answering no phone calls and avoiding extended conversations with those who stopped by to wish her the best and to apologize for the unknown jerks who had leaked the news.

That's where Linda found her, staring into space. She reluctantly reported on what she had found, apologizing that she'd missed Jessup by only a matter of hours. "If I had made one more call last night," she said, "I might have caught him. But I was exhausted by then."

"Are you kidding?" Gabby said. "I can't believe you found him at all. Chalk one up for yourself. You could be a hell of a reporter."

Together, they immediately headed to Barclay's office with the news, which—of course—was the last thing he wanted to hear. "He must have seen the *Star Trib* website," he said, "and decided to get the hell out of Dodge while he could."

"Don't count on it," Gabby replied. "I'm betting he won't give it up, not after all of this. He's on a mission. In fact, he'll probably love the publicity."

"So what do we do now?" Barclay asked, more of himself than them.

"I'll give Philips a call," Gabby said. "He may want to stop by the motel."

"And I can keep checking other motels," Linda added. "Maybe he's landed somewhere else."

"I wouldn't bother with that," Barclay said. "By tomorrow morning his picture will probably be in the papers and he won't want to risk being recognized."

"Maybe I can check with the campgrounds and parks. Look for a big, black Harley."

He laughed and waved a dismissive hand. "Do you know how many big, black Harleys there are? But, sure, if you want to, go ahead."

Gabby said, "What about Sam Ryan? Have you talked to him?"

"Can't you see my blistered ears? I'm surprised you didn't hear him down here. He was not happy. Says we and the cops should have had Jessup by now, mixing his thoughts in with a few choice expletives. Some of which not even I have heard."

"I'll go talk to him," Gabby offered. "Try to settle him down."

"Don't. This is between me and him. Wherever that may lead."

Thirty-Three

Jim Higgins, the real estate agent, had abided by his pledge and had talked to none of his friends or colleagues about the Hawkins house. He did make one small exception, asking his wife, Janis—without mentioning the house or the potential sale—whether she knew of an Anita Hawkins and anything about her.

"Some," she said, "but not much. Why?"

"Just wondering. One of my golf buddies asked about her ... said she was pretty well known in the Orono area, and I thought you might have run into her."

"Which buddy?"

"Dan Stout," he lied again. "You don't know him. Not really a buddy, I guess, but part of our last foursome."

Wife Janis ran a small quilt shop in Excelsior, not that far from Orono, and drew a wide range of customers from the surrounding Lake Minnetonka area. "What does this buddy want with her?" she asked.

He shrugged. "I don't know. I just said I'd check with you."

"I've never met her, but the word is she comes from a wealthy family, an only child who inherited a bundle when her dad, who was one of the early investors in Microsoft, passed away seven or eight years ago. She's a mover and shaker in the Orono area, sits on a lot of civic-type committees. And is active in her kids' private schools."

"What about her husband?"

"I'm told he runs some kind of private investment firm that he set up after they got married to manage all of their money. Because he's supposedly rich, too."

"That's helpful," he said. "I'll pass it on."

"Fine, but keep me out of it."

"Of course."

Lying to or hiding things from his wife was not something Higgins liked to do or normally did, except for a small, rainy-day stash of cash that he kept tucked away in a separate bank account. So he was pleased she seemed ready to let the matter drop without more questions and without more lies on his part.

In checking county records, he had learned that Hawkins apparently bought the house directly from the seller not that long before the beginning of the Great Recession for 750 big ones, as Hawkins had told him, apparently in cash—because there was no record of a mortgage holder. If Higgins had to guess, the house had probably been on the brink of foreclosure, forcing the seller to move fast and to sell it at a bargain price.

His discreet efforts to discover more about Hawkins' investment business proved fruitless. He did learn that the firm's office was in a big Edina business complex, but because the firm was privately-held, there were no financial or employment records readily available. Which made sense now that his wife had told him he might be managing only the family portfolios, not the assets of other clients. If that was the case, he might not have to register with the SEC or state regulatory agencies.

Forget it, he finally told himself. *Who cares what he does or why all of the secrecy from his family. Get on with it. Figure out a price that's fair and will sell quickly. Pocket the commission and move on, letting the chips of Hawkins' marriage fall where they may.*

He just didn't want to be around to pick up the chips.

As HIGGINS SAT RUMINATING, Knowles's friend, Stuart Kingston, the Wells Fargo banker, was having lunch at the Minneapolis Club, a members-only downtown club that catered to the mostly white, mostly male elite of the business and political communities. Kingston sat at a round table in the center of the dining area, unofficially reserved as a revolving meeting place for friends and associates to lunch most every day.

The Club was the kind of place where—not eons ago—women were asked to arrive through a back door and courtesy neckties were provided to men who wanted to eat in the dining room, but who didn't wear ties or had forgotten them at home.

Between the portions of meticulously prepared morsels, the men at the round table traded talk about the stuff that absorbed them: the market, the Federal Reserve, the devilish Democrats, the SEC, and other big government intrusions in their businesses. Most were convinced the country was hellbent for destruction unless some right-thinking Republicans got back in power in St. Paul and Washington.

Kingston was more amused by the conversation than comfortable with it, but he enjoyed the give-and-take, and knew the round-table relationships were crucial to his business success.

The conversations were not without idle gossip, ranging from who was taking what job, who was divorcing whom, who the Feds were picking on now, and on and on.

At one point, in a pause in the conversation, Kingston decided to take a flyer, without a clue as to what he was doing... remembering only what John Knowles had told him. "I've got a friend," he told the group, "who's looking for a small, probably private firm to do some investing with. Despite my best sales job, he thinks our bank is too big and cumbersome for him, that he wouldn't get the kind of personal attention that he wants. Says that even I'm too busy for him."

"Some friend," the fellow next to him said.

"I know. But what can I say? He's especially interested in the medical and pharmaceutical companies. Not the Medtronics of the world, but the new start-ups, the ones breaking new ground. Any ideas?"

"There's J.G. Cummins," one of the men said.

"How about Howard Renk's firm?" said another.

Kingston jotted down the names, one by one. Maybe a half dozen in all.

Finally, Daniel Ruff, a local broker, said, "I do some trades in those areas for a small firm that works out of our building in Edina, Hawkins Investments, run by a guy named Harlan Hawkins."

"Did you say *Harlan* Hawkins?" Kingston asked.

"Yeah, why?"

"The name's familiar, that's all. What can you tell me about him?"

"Not much, really. Has a small office. Only a couple of employees. Somebody told me he's mainly involved in managing family money … so … now that I think about it, he may not be looking for new clients. But I can put you in touch with him, if you'd like."

"No, no, that's fine. And thanks. I'll get all of these names to my friend. He can make the contacts."

As he walked out of the Club, Kingston couldn't quite get it out of his head. *Harlan Overton, Harlan Hawkins. How common is the name Harlan?* he wondered. He didn't happen to know anyone with that first name, but what did that mean? *That could apply to a lot of names*, he thought.

The bigger question: if Harlan Overton wanted to hide, wouldn't he change *both* his first and last names? As Kingston thought about it, he supposed it could be more comfortable, more natural, especially early on, to retain your first name to avoid clumsy mistakes. The disadvantage, of course, is that it could make the search for you easier. *Unless* the searchers would mistakenly assume that you would have changed both your first and last names.

This is ridiculous, he told himself. *Confusing. Grasping at the thinnest of straws.*

But, he decided, he would at least give his friend Knowles a call. If nothing else, to prove he'd been trying to help. He could only hope he wouldn't laugh at him.

A FEW BLOCKS AWAY in the newsroom, Gabby glanced at the number of the incoming call. Not recognizing it, and, ever cautious, she was tempted to hang up when she heard a woman's voice. "Ms. Gooding?"

"Yes."

"This is Angela Metlove."

She did not immediately recall either the name or the voice. "Who?"

"Angela Metlove. We met a few weeks ago … across the street from the empty house."

"Right," Gabby replied, suddenly remembering the chubby woman gardener who'd told her about the lawn service truck.

"You asked me to call if I saw anything happening at the house."

"Of course. Thank you for remembering."

"This might not be important," the woman said, "but they've started delivering mail to the house."

Gabby was stunned. "Really? When?"

"Some time ago, I'm guessing. But we've been out of town for a couple of weeks, and I didn't see the person come and pick it up until today."

"The person?"

"Yes. A young guy. Heavyset, with kind of a scruffy beard. He was driving an old beater of a Dodge, missing a rear fender."

Gabby said nothing for a moment, absorbing what she'd been told.

"I even tried to talk to him," Angela continued. "You know, playing reporter like you. But he brushed me off, told me to mind my own...the f-word ... business. He was kind of scary, actually."

"I'm sorry," Gabby said. "But that was very brave of you."

"But I did get his license number," she said, pride in her voice. "262HGD."

Gabby wrote it down. "I can't thank you enough. This could be really helpful. But I'll take it from here, and, please, if he does show up again, don't confront him again."

"I won't, but he may not be back soon. He was carrying quite a bundle. Like it may have been piling up in that mailbox they have by the front door. Made me think he only comes once in a while."

PHILIPS WAS OUT OF the office when Gabby tried to reach him, and when she finally did, she quickly discovered he was not as excited about Angela's discovery as she was. "I can trace the plate number," he said, "and find out who owns the car, but that won't necessarily tell us who the driver was. And even if they're one in the same, I'm not sure we could question the guy."

"Why's that?" she asked.

"Because he picked up the mail wouldn't necessarily give us the right to stop him or bring him in. Not if he has permission to get the mail."

"But it's part of a criminal investigation," she argued. "He could tell you who hired him."

"Maybe, maybe not. And, hell, he may not even know. Remember the lawn care guy? He got hired by phone and never met or saw whoever paid him."

Gabby leaned back in her chair. "There must be a way," she finally said.

"I'll talk to my boss, or somebody over at the County Attorney's office, but I wouldn't get my hopes up."

She persisted. "Can you give *me* the name? That wouldn't violate his rights."

"Yes, it would," he replied. "It's illegal, and I could get in a heap of trouble."

"Think about it, please," she said. "We need to talk to this kid and we can't sit outside that house for days or weeks, waiting for him to show up again."

"I hear you … and I'll do what I can. Or maybe your guy, Knowles, can figure out a way. He must have contacts over at the state license bureau."

"I'll ask," she said, but there was not a lot of hope in her voice.

KNOWLES WAS AT HIS desk, head bowed, thumbing through an old Minneapolis White Pages, when Gabby knocked lightly.

"Hey, Gabby, C'mon in."

"What am I interrupting?" she asked.

"A wild goose chase, I think."

"In the telephone book? Do they even print those any more?"

He looked up and grinned. "I'm not sure, but I still have plenty of old ones."

Then he quickly repeated what Stuart Kingston had told him on the phone. *Harlan Overton, Harlan Hawkins.*

She couldn't help but smile, too. "That seems like a stretch, I'd say."

Knowles clasped his hands behind his head and leaned back. "I agree. I've tried to find out what I could on the Hawkins investment firm, but there's little information available without specifically requesting it from the company itself. Which both my friend and I found a little strange."

Gabby shrugged. "I wouldn't know about that."

"What my friend also found strange is the name Harlan itself."

"How so?"

"Strange in that it's not all that common. Like, do you happen to know anyone by that name?"

She didn't have to think long. "No, nobody. Sounds like a name from my dad's generation."

"That's my generation, too," Knowles said. "And I don't know any Harlans, either."

She leaned over the desk. "So what are you doing?"

"Since I couldn't find much about his firm, I decided to try and figure out where he lives, and how he lives. I know it seems like the longest of long shots, but since we don't have anything else right now, I decided to search the internet and these old residential phone books for the whole metro area, looking at all of the listings with the last name of Hawkins. There were about thirty of them in Minneapolis, about half that number in St. Paul, including suburbs. None listed a first name of Harlan."

"He could easily have an unlisted number," she said, "or no home phone at all. Just a cell."

"True. But then I checked all of the Smiths, Johnsons, and Olsons listed and found that nobody with those last names— and there were scores—claimed anyone with a first name of Harlan."

"So?"

"So … it supports our belief that Harlan is a pretty un-common name … and that it's curious to find a fellow with an uncommon name like Harlan dealing in the same kind of business we theorize Harlan Overton might be in … if he is still here. Investments, maybe in medical and pharmaceutical companies."

"So you're trusting your instincts … and your friend's … to put your nose in the phone books."

He laughed. "Silly, huh?"

She picked up the phone book. "Maybe. But there's one other possibility. If Hawkins has a home phone, it could be in his wife's name. Do you know what that is?"

"No. But I did notice a number of the phones were listed to women. Far fewer than men, but some."

"So why don't you check those out? Call a few of them and ask for Harlan. What can it hurt?"

"OK," he said. Then, as an afterthought, "Hey, I'm sorry. I didn't even ask what brought you here to begin with."

She quickly repeated the essence of her conversations with both Angela and Philips, not hiding her frustration. "We need to find and talk to this kid who picked up the mail," she said, "but Philips says it could be tricky. Legally, anyway."

"I'm no lawyer," Knowles said, "but he's probably right. And even if we did find him, he'd be under no obligation to talk to us."

"So what do we do?"

"I'll talk to our friends at the FBI. They may be more eager to find a way than Philips." He paused. "And if that doesn't work, there may be other avenues ... "

"Legal avenues?"

He smiled. "Have you heard about 'don't ask, don't tell'?"

"I won't ask," she said. "But don't get yourself in trouble."

"Not to worry. Give me some time to figure something out."

Thirty-Four

Jessup had been on his bike for what seemed like hours, driving the back roads in the outlying, mostly rural, counties, with no particular destination in mind, stopping occasionally at a wayside park or restaurant to try and figure out what to do next.

As Barclay had suspected, he'd checked the *Star Tribune* website the first thing that morning, as he did every morning, and discovered the stalking story. While he was not named in the story, he suspected—like Barclay—that more stories would follow, that his name as well as his picture would eventually be in the papers and on the Internet, not only to be seen and read in Minnesota, but, considering the San Jose connection, possibly in California, as well.

What's more, the publicity might well lead to a more intense search for him by the local cops.

The noose was tightening.

But those were not his only problems. He was almost out of money. The motel bill had taken all but his last few hundred dollars, and he had no ready access to more.

Unless.

He pulled into the parking lot of a small strip mall in Northfield, a college town fifty miles or so south of the Twin

Cities. While sitting astride the Harley, he took out his cell and placed a call to a familiar number in San Jose.

His father answered on the third ring.

"Dad, this is Craig."

"Who?"

"Craig. Your son."

There was a long pause as Jessup pictured his father struggling to sort through a jumble of thoughts and elusive memories. The dementia may have gotten worse.

"Dad, are you there?"

"Yes, yes, I'm here."

"It's Craig, Dad. I'm calling from Minnesota."

"Minnesota? Why are you there?"

"I'll explain later, Dad ... "

"The police were here." His mind suddenly cleared, like the fog lifting, letting the sunlight in. "Looking for you."

"Forget that, Dad. It's all a misunderstanding."

"They said you were in trouble again. That they were going to arrest you again. Is that true, Craig? Tell me it's not."

"It's not ... "

"Sweet Jesus, what would your poor mother think? God bless her soul. Her son arrested again ... "

"Dad, please, I need your help. I need some money."

"Money? For what?"

"To get me out of that trouble you talked about."

"I have no money."

"Yes, you do. You have lots of money. You just need to put some in an envelope and send it to me. You can do that, Dad. I know you can."

"The police said you were after the same girl you beat up. Stalking her, they said."

"Dad, please. I'll explain everything when I get home. But I need the money to get there."

"Your poor mother ... "

Then the line went dead.

Jessup could only stare at the phone, muttering, "Damn you, old man. Die."

There was only one other possibility. He tapped in another number, also in San Jose, and waited for Joel Andresen to pick up. Joel was his best friend, college roommate, the only person who had stuck with him through the whole ordeal of his plea deal and the mental trauma that followed. They had even taken a blood oath on one drunken night, pledging friendship forever, no matter what.

Or so he thought.

"Hello." He did not recognize Jessup's new cell number.

"Hey, buddy. Craig here."

The conversation was shorter than his father's. "Don't ever call again, Craig. Never. Get some help. Turn yourself in."

So much for his BFF.

For the first time since he set foot in Minnesota, Jessup felt at a total loss. He'd been here for weeks, wandering the streets of Minneapolis, living in a dump of a motel, eating fast-food shit, squeezing every dollar like it was his last, and in all of that time, never catching even the briefest glimpse of his prey, except on the television screen.

But he had never lost hope. Never doubted that he would succeed, whatever the obstacles, whatever the frustrations.

Until now.

He figured he had two choices: to use the last of his money to get back home and face whatever music there was to face. Probably more jail time for skipping out. To say nothing of no job, no prospect of one, no friends, and an alienated father who—in his muddled mind—might now try to disown him.

He thought it unlikely that Minnesota authorities would spend the time or effort to bring him back from California to face whatever charges they might decide were warranted here. After all, how could they charge him with stalking when he'd never even seen the supposed victim?

Or, he could stay here, find some way to get enough

money to live on until he could accomplish the mission that had so far eluded him. He remained confident that he could do that, propelled by visions of that final confrontation. He needed to see her face, to see and feel her fear, to hear her admit she had so badly damaged him, to confess her sins and beg for forgiveness.

That was his dream. That was his decision. He would tough it out, squeeze the few remaining dollars even tighter or find more money somehow. There was no turning back, no retreat, until he had finished what he had come here to do.

Thirty-Five

For Harlan Hawkins, it was an ordinary day until two seemingly inconsequential things happened that first gave him pause, then put him on edge.

And, finally, left him terrified.

The first came midday when he shared an elevator in his Edina office complex with a stock broker, Daniel Ruff, whom he knew only slightly and whose office was two floors above his.

"I think you may owe me one," Ruff told him.

"How's that?" Hawkins asked.

"I may have got you a client," Ruff said, repeating his Minneapolis Club conversation with Stuart Kingston. "I suggested you were the kind of small firm his friend might be looking for."

"Really? That was good of you, although I'm not really looking for new clients. But who is this friend?"

"I didn't get his name, but Stuart said he might be contacting you. So," he laughed, "if he does, and you decide to take him on, you might think about a little commission for me."

"Of course," he said with a smile, "but I wouldn't get my hopes up."

Hawkins could not explain—even to himself—why that

encounter had left him unsettled, but it had. Especially that bit about the friend's interest in pharmaceuticals and medical start-ups. Seemed fishy, somehow, especially under the current circumstances. So once they'd parted and he got back to his office, he did a quick computer check on Stuart Kingston. He found nothing unusual. He was just another Wells Fargo banker, one soldier in their financial army, from what he could tell.

Despite his misgivings, he gave it no further thought until he got home that evening and was sitting on the deck, enjoying a warm breeze and a cold gin and tonic. His wife came to join him with her own G&T, and after filling him in on what she and the kids had done all day, told him, "I got kind of a strange call today."

He took a sip of his drink, suddenly alert, but feigning little interest. "Really? What kind of call?"

"It was a man, asking for you. I didn't recognize the number on the caller ID, so I asked who was calling."

Hawkins put the drink aside and leaned in, his eyes never leaving hers.

"He didn't give me his name, but said he was an old friend of yours from out East. I said there must be some mistake, since you came from out West. He apologized and said he must have the wrong Harlan Hawkins. Then he hung up without ever giving me his name."

"That is strange," he said, "since I'm not listed in any phone book. I wonder how he settled on our number?"

"I wondered the same thing, but maybe he took a shot and called all of the Hawkins in the book hoping to find you. Or the Harlan Hawkins he was actually looking for."

"Did you happen to save his number, the one he was calling from, on the Caller ID?"

"I did. It's on the kitchen counter by the phone."

He got up to get another drink and to give himself time to think. As he walked away, he said, "I think we should get an unlisted number or cancel the landline altogether. Just use our cells."

She pulled back sharply. "We can't do that! Think of all my friends and the groups I belong to. We'd have to give all of them the new numbers. I want to save my cell for the kids and for a few very close friends."

"But it might save the crank calls like the one you just got," he countered.

"It doesn't happen that often. And I don't want to go through the hassle of changing it. So let's not talk about it anymore."

"OK, have it your way."

When he reached the kitchen, he took the note with the phone number from the counter and retreated down the hall to the bathroom, closing the door behind him. He took out his cell and punched in the number . . . waited for three rings . . . and then heard a recorded voice on the other end:

"This is John Knowles, Channel 7 News. Leave a message, and I'll get back to you."

It was as though he'd been hit with a stun gun. His body shook, his arm went limp, and the phone dropped to the floor with a clatter. It was like an epileptic seizure. He slumped onto the toilet seat, clasping his arms around his body to control the tremors.

From outside the door, "Harlan, are you OK? What was that noise?"

He took a deep breath. "I'm fine, Anita. My phone just fell out of my pocket."

"You're sure?"

"I'm sure. I'll be out in a minute."

But he knew it would take more than a minute to get composed, to stop the shaking.

Settle down! Think!

Why would that television station be asking for him? The same station that had nosed around the old house, that got the police involved and broadcast the sketch of poor Harvey? Had they connected the ownership of the house to him? But how? Was there a leak somewhere? But where? Only one person who was still alive knows who he was and where he was. And Hawkins had ultimate trust in him.

"Harlan?" His wife, again. "Are you OK? I'm worried about you."

"Anita, please! I'm sitting on the pot. I've got the runs."

"Oh, I'm sorry. I didn't know."

He realized now, far too late, that he should have sold the old house months ago. But there had been no way to do so with the body still in the basement, the removal of which they'd put off for fear of being spotted by the nosy old man next door or by one of the other neighbors. So he had—mistakenly—simply decided to leave things as they were until the right opportunity arose, reassured by the passage of time, and by the belief that even if the body was somehow discovered, it would be deemed a suicide, and that there would be no way to trace the ownership of the house to him.

Because no one, he believed, knew that Zimtronics and he were one and the same.

All of that would have worked, he now believed, had it not been for the persistent suspicions of the Channel 7 reporters and their eventual linkup with the cops. If he had simply left well enough alone and allowed the routine investigation to run its course, without trying to intimidate the reporters and further raise their suspicions, it might have remained a simple unsolved mystery.

The apparent suicide of an unidentified man. Ho-hum. Move on.

But that, unfortunately, is not how it is. He blamed himself. Mistakes and misjudgments were made. And the strange phone call only heightened his belief that unseen things were at work beyond his view or control, and that the danger of discovery was no longer as unthinkable as it had been a dozen years before when he'd fled New York and disappeared into thin air.

For now, however, his only alternative was to remain calm. And vigilant. And to prepare for another possible walk into nowhere.

The sale of his house would be a first step. Others would have to follow.

WHEN GABBY AND ZACH got to the newsroom the next morning, they again found John Knowles waiting for them, reporting on his phone call to the Hawkins house. "I did find him. He lives out in Orono."

"Good," Gabby said. "For whatever that's worth."

"Probably nothing, because when I told the woman who answered that I was a friend from out East, she said I must have the wrong Harlan Hawkins because her husband is from out West. No reason for her to lie. So he may not be our guy."

"You may be right," she said, pausing. "But let's think about it for a minute. If the rest of the world doesn't know where he is or who he is, maybe his own wife doesn't know who he really is, either."

He smiled. "Now who's reaching?" Then, "Or, maybe she does know who he really is and was misleading me to protect his secret."

"That could be, too. But I've given more thought to what you said yesterday... about how unusual it is to find a guy with a relatively uncommon name like Harlan who's also in the kind of business he's in. And who's almost impossible to find anything out about. The more I thought about it, the more sense it made to me."

Zach turned to Knowles. "What's his wife's name?"

"Anita. At least that's what was listed."

"So why don't we try to find out more about *her*?" Zach said. "Maybe we can get a better line on him by going through her."

"Good idea," Gabby said. "I'll try Google later, along with LinkedIn and Facebook and anything else I can think of."

At that moment her phone buzzed and she picked up. "Yes?"

The voice at the other end was low, almost guttural. "Write this name and address down. Quick."

"Who is this?"

"Never mind. Just take this down. The name is Barry Seester. 2231 McAdams Avenue South. He drives an old Dodge. Got it?"

"No. Give it to me again."

He repeated the name and address. Then hung up.

"What was that about?" Knowles asked.

"I think we just found out who the mystery mailman is and where he lives."

Knowles feigned shock. "Really?

She laughed. "You had nothing to do with it, right?

"Of course not. I told you, it's illegal to search those license records."

"Right. And I just won the lottery," she said.

PHILIPS WAS SITTING in his unmarked squad car in the middle of the block on McAdams when Gabby and Zach pulled up behind him. Three houses down, sitting in front of a small rambler, was the old Dodge with the missing rear fender.

Philips got out of the squad to meet them as they walked up. "So, tell me," he asked, "how did you manage to find him?"

"Anonymous call," Gabby said. "And that's the truth."

"One of Knowles's friends, I'd bet."

"He denies it, but we'll probably never know."

"Well, I saw Mr. Seester get here a few minutes ago," he told them. "So I know he's inside."

"Good," she said, starting to move away. "Let's go talk to him."

Philips held her back. "Hang tight for a minute. I gotta

tell you, this whole deal makes me uncomfortable. If we don't play it right, I could get my ass in a sling."

"Why? All we're going to do is ask him a couple of questions."

"Because we have no legal right to ask him those questions."

"So? If he refuses, he refuses," she said. "No harm done. But let's at least see what he has to say."

"OK," he said with reluctance still in his voice, "we'll give it a try. But I'm not going to push him. I don't want him filing a harassment complaint downtown."

Zach hung back as they approached the house and mounted the front steps. Gabby rang the doorbell and heard the chimes sound inside. The door opened almost immediately.

"Yeah?" said the face on the other side of the screen door.

Philips showed his badge. "Are you Barry Seester?"

"Yeah." He showed surprise and maybe a touch of something else. Fear? "What's this about?"

"I'm Detective John Philips. I'd like to ask you a couple of questions."

Seester moved a step or two backwards. "About what?"

Philips ignored the question. "Would you mind stepping outside?"

"Not until you tell me what the hell this is about."

"OK, I'll make it quick. We're investigating a suspicious death in a house in northeast Minneapolis. You were seen picking up mail from that particular house, and we'd like to know who asked you to do that."

Seester looked about as Angela Metlove had described him: young, heavyset, with an unkempt beard and a shaggy head of hair. She forgot to mention the sneer.

"I don't know anything about any suspicious death," he said, showing more anger than fear now.

"I didn't say you did," Philips replied, calmly. "We just want to know who asked you to pick up the mail and what you did with it after you picked it up."

Seester started to close the door. "Look, I've been around.

I'm no slouch. I know my rights. I don't have to answer your questions."

"True," Philips said. "Until I get a court order. I hoped we could avoid that."

At that moment, an older woman appeared at Seester's shoulder. "Barry, what's going on?"

"Nothing, Mom. It's nothing."

"I'm a police officer, ma'am. We're just asking your son a few questions."

"About what?" she demanded.

"I'll let him tell you that after he answers us."

"I'm not answering anything."

She grabbed his arm. "Barry. Talk to the officer."

He opened the screen door and stepped outside, leaving his mother inside, his back to her. "Look. I'm telling you, I don't know what this is about. A girl I know who works at a coffee shop about three blocks from here asked me if I'd like to earn an easy hundred bucks. She said some guy she didn't know was having coffee and said he was looking for somebody with a car who could pick up mail from a house once every week or so for a hundred bucks a trip. He gave her a phone number and asked her if she found somebody to have him call. She gave me the number and I called."

"Then what?" Philips asked.

"He gave me the address and sent me the hundred bucks, in cash. That's all I know. Sure as hell nothing about any suspicious death, for God's sake."

"When was this?"

"A couple of weeks ago. I only made the one pickup."

"Have you heard from him since?"

"No."

"Where did you drop off the mail?" Gabby asked.

Seester gave her a sharp look, as if seeing her for the first time. "And who the hell are you?"

"I know who she is," the mother said from inside the door.

"She's a reporter. I saw her reporting on that police thing out in Fridley. Channel 7, I think."

"You gotta be shittin' me," Seester said. "Is this going to be on the news?"

"No, no," Philips said. "She's just along for the ride. But answer the question."

"He told me to leave it in the back seat of my car at the Southdale Shopping Center parking lot at ten o'clock on Saturday morning and to go shopping. When I came back, it was gone. And there was an envelope with another hundred bucks on the seat."

"How did he know which car was yours?"

He glanced at the car at the curb. "I described it. It's hard to miss."

"Didn't all of that seem strange to you?" Gabby asked.

"Sure. But it was easy money. And I wasn't committing any crime."

"Do you still have his phone number?" Philips asked.

He paused. "No. I was waiting for him to call me again."

Philips said, "I need to know the name of the coffee shop and the name of the girl who gave you the number."

"It's a Dunn Brothers, and the girl's name is Kathy. But I'm not sure she's still there. I haven't seen her for a while."

Philips gave him his card. "If you do hear from this guy again, you call me, OK?"

"He will," his mother said. "I'll see to it."

As they walked away from the house, Gabby said, "Ten to one he's lying about not knowing the phone number, and twenty to one he'll be on the phone to the guy as soon as his mother turns her back."

"Why do you say that?" Zach asked.

"Because he's a smartass, and second, I don't think he likes cops and the idea of getting hassled. His whole screw-you attitude. And he probably thinks there's more easy money to be had if he lets the guy know about our little visit."

Philips shrugged. "You may be right, but there's not much we can do about it."

"Maybe not us," she said, "but I think we should let the Feds know what we've been doing. They may want to stop by and check the mailbox themselves."

"They've got no more right to do that than we do," Philips said.

"No, but from what I've heard, all they have to do is utter the word 'terrorist' and they can do almost anything they want. After all, who knows what Overton is doing with all of his money? ISIS is getting theirs from somewhere."

Philips laughed. "You are a piece of work."

When they reached their cars, Gabby said, "I think we should stop by the coffee shop and see if this Kathy is still around."

"You go ahead," Philips said. "I've got to head back downtown."

As it turned out, the trip to the coffee shop was a bust. Kathy was there working but had only the vaguest of memories of the man who had given her the phone number, which she, in turn, had given to Seester. "He was like any guy, I guess, middle-aged, thin, gray-haired, I think. I just took the phone number and didn't think any more about it ... or about him. And I haven't seen him since. Sorry."

"That's OK," Gabby said, giving her one of her cards. "But if he does happen to stop in again, would you give me a call?"

"Sure. Should I have *him* call you?"

"By all means, no. I'd rather that he didn't know we're looking for him."

"Is he some kind of badass?"

"We don't know. We'd just like to find him and talk to him."

By then, Kathy's attention had turned to another customer, and the conversation was over.

Thirty-six

Gabby and Zach were no more than inside the door of the apartment when her ringtone sounded. She glanced at the phone and mouthed, "My mother," to Zach.

He headed for the kitchen while she settled onto the sofa, allowing Barclay to climb into her lap. "Hey, Mom."

The words from the other end were sharp, almost hysterical. *"Why didn't you tell me?"*

Gabby was taken aback. She hadn't heard that frenetic a wail in her mother's voice since the day she'd called to report her dad's death. "Tell you what? What are you talking about?"

It was as if she hadn't heard. "Peggy called me from San Jose. She said she tried to call you but doesn't have your new number. She told me you're in the news there. That you're being stalked by that same awful Craig Jessup. She wanted to know if I'd heard from you."

Peggy Lester was one of Gabby's few friends at the San Jose TV station, whom her mother had come to know during one of her visits with Gabby in San Jose.

"Is that true?" her mother demanded, her words a steady stream. "That he's there? In Minnesota? How long have you known?"

What Gabby had feared might happen clearly had happened. Because she was known to San Jose television viewers, the Minnesota stalking stories had inevitably found their way to California and onto the local newscasts and websites. She should have prepared for it, but it was clearly too late now. She took a deep breath. "Mom, please, relax."

"Relax? How can I relax? After what he did to you!"

"I should have told you, but believe me, Mom, everything is under control. He *is* here looking for me, but I'm being protected ... and the police are searching for him at this very moment. There is no reason for you to worry."

Zach returned from the kitchen, concern written on his face. She waved him away. "We've known he was here for some time," she continued, "but we're dealing with it. I didn't tell you because I didn't want you to get upset. Like you are right now."

"What do you mean, you're 'dealing' with it?"

"Just what I said. I'm never alone. Never unprotected. I'm safe. And he'll be found before he can do anything more to me."

Her mother was unappeased. If anything, she was even angrier. "I don't believe you, Gabby, and when I'm done talking to you, I'm going to call Sam Ryan. I'm going to get you out of there!"

"No, you're not!" she replied, hotly. "I'm sorry I've kept this from you, Mom, but you have to calm down. I'm a grown woman now. I can take care of myself and I will not have you interfering in my life. No matter how concerned you are."

There was a long pause, then soft sobs revealing the impact of the first truly angry words Gabby had spoken to her mother since her teenage years.

"Mom?"

Another moment passed. "Yes?"

"I don't mean to hurt you, but you have to understand. If I leave here, Craig will follow me to wherever I go next. He has to be dealt with, somehow. He's obsessed and has to be stopped. And the chances of that happening are better here than in Portland or anywhere else. You have to trust me. I do

302 | RON HANDBERG

know what I'm doing. I didn't ask for this, but it is what it is ... and I have to deal with it. I can't keep running."

The silence that followed spoke louder than her mother's angry words.

"Mom?"

"I lost your father. I could not bear losing you."

"I know. And you won't. I promise. Girl Scout's honor."

She heard a soft chuckle. "You weren't in Girl Scouts."

"I know, but a promise is a promise. Girl Scouts or not."

"Will you call me every day?"

"I will. Every day. Scout's honor."

As she put the phone aside, Zach slid in next to her on the couch, his arm around her. "You OK?"

"Yeah. I guess so. I just feel bad. She doesn't need this kind of worry."

"Your sisters are there. Maybe they can calm her down."

"Don't count on it. One or both of them will probably be on the phone next."

Zach thought for a moment. "Maybe you should fly out there. Spend a couple of days with them. It would give you a break and provide some reassurance for them."

Gabby sat up straight, sending Barclay scurrying off her lap. "No way. I'm not going anywhere until this is over, one way or another. And I'm not leaving you, even for a few days. We started this together, and we'll finish it together."

Zach put his arm back around her. "OK, OK."

ACROSS TOWN AT an Applebee's restaurant several miles from his home, Harlan Hawkins was sitting at the bar staring into his gin-and-tonic, when a middle-aged man with graying sideburns took the stool next to him. "Been here long?" the man asked.

"Long enough," Hawkins replied, lifting his eyes, looking at the man's reflection in a mirror across the bar.

"Sorry. Got caught in traffic on 394. It's a bitch at rush hour."

Hawkins turned to him. "We've got problems."

"That's why I'm here," he said, signaling the bartender. "Brandy Manhattan, up."

The man was Leonard Jenkins, in his early fifties, a half-head taller than Hawkins, trim, nattily-clad in gray suit that matched his sideburns, with a blue button-down shirt and a paisley tie, looking, for all the world, like an eminently successful businessman.

He would also kill without a second thought.

He waited for his Manhattan, then said, "So what's up?"

"We may have to move on."

His drink was halfway to his lips. "What?"

Hawkins glanced in both directions, then leaned into him and quietly reported on the recent strange events, including the phone call from Knowles at Channel 7. "Something is going on. Something weird. I'm not sure what, but I've got a gut feeling that they're closing in on me. That they've somehow linked me with the house and the body. And perhaps with my past. I don't see how that can be, but why would that television station be looking for a Harlan Hawkins from out East?"

"Wait a minute," Jenkins protested.

"No, *you* wait a minute. I'm not blaming you. It's all on me. But too many things have gone wrong. We should have sold that house long ago ... we should never have left the body there ... we should never have sicced Harry on that Channel 7 photographer. We should have left well enough alone. But we didn't. We got scared. And careless."

"That's great hindsight," Jenkins said. "But we did what we thought we had to do at the time. What's done is done. And how could they connect you to the house? Nobody knows about Zimtronics and us. And who cares if they're asking about Harlan Hawkins? If they were asking about Harlan Overton, then it'd be time to worry."

Jenkins had been with Hawkins/Overton since the day he fled New York. He had been a silent partner in Zimtronics, a trusted associate who had shared in the riches from the Dia-betrics Ponzi scheme, but who—unlike Overton—had never been suspected for his role in the scam. He had followed Overton to Minnesota, went to work for a local brokerage firm, and had since served as Overton's advisor and the pro-tector of his secret identity.

But in a way, he was Overton's captive as well as his pro-tector. Overton had proof of Jenkins's complicity in the Ponzi scheme and had made it clear that if he was ever taken down, Jenkins would go down with him.

So, for better or worse, they were stuck with each other.

"I still think you're overreacting," Jenkins said.

"Maybe so, but I'm not about to risk fifteen to twenty years behind bars. No way."

"You can't just pick up and leave," Jenkins argued. "You've got a business, a house, a wife and kids."

"They're expendable."

"What? You can't be serious!"

"Deadly. I'm already getting an appraisal on the house, just in case I need a quick sale. And I can close the doors of the firm overnight and take my share of the assets. Anita has more money than she'll ever need and more than enough to attract a new husband."

"Jesus! Don't you love the woman?"

Hawkins shrugged. "Love? Hell, I don't know. I'm fond of her, but she has her own life. Her own friends. Her own ambi-tions. I've never really been part of that. She's good company, but ... "

"And the kids?"

"That's tougher. They'll miss me, I guess. But we aren't really that close, either. I hardly see them. They're either in school or with their nanny. And, hey, I'd rather have them visit me some day in the Bahamas or wherever than in some fucking prison."

"With all due respect, I think you've slipped off the deep end. Does Anita know anything about this?"

"Of course not. And won't, until I'm long gone. Then she may discover who the hell I really am ... or was. But it'll be a little late."

"This is unbelievable!"

"Relax. It'll work out. But we can't wait forever. It'll be easier for you. You're single. But we'll have to figure out a new identity for me. That'll be a hassle, but it's doable. We've done it before, and we can do it again."

Jenkins finished his Manhattan in one swig. "When are you talking about doing all of this? You've got to give me time to think. To plan. Hell, I've built my life here ... my business. Because I'm single doesn't mean I can just pull up stakes one day and leave the next. I'd do anything for you. You know that. But, God, you've got to give me a break on this."

"I hear you, but we have to be prepared. You can stay behind for a while and join me later, if you want. But I'll need you in the future just as I've needed you in the past."

"You didn't answer my question," Jenkins said. "When?"

"If and when I sense the risk is increasing. I won't be rash, but I won't be caught."

At that moment, both heard the muted sound of Jenkins's cell phone in his pocket. He took it out and listened, asking several quick questions. Finally, "OK, yes. Thanks. I'll get back to you."

He put the phone back in his pocket. "I sold you short. You may be on to something."

"What?" Hawkins asked.

"That was the kid who picked up the mail from the house. He had a visit this morning from a cop, a Lieutenant Philips, and a reporter from Channel 7."

Hawkins's head fell, almost hitting the bar.

"They wanted to know who paid him to get the mail and who picked it up. He said some neighbor across the street saw him do it and must have called either the cops or the reporter."

Hawkins stared at him. "What'd I tell you!"

"He says he played as dumb as he could. He had to tell them where he got my number and where he left his car with the mail. But he didn't give them the number and he wonders if that's worth anything more from me."

"I knew it," Hawkins blurted. "This isn't over. My gut was right. We may have to pack our bags sooner than later."

With that, he wiped his drink glass clean with a napkin, as he always did, and headed for the door, Jenkins trailing behind him.

ZACH WAS IN BED, but Gabby was still up, at her computer—using all of the search engines available to find whatever she could about Anita Hawkins. She would not be disappointed. Anita was everywhere she looked, and might be—Gabby finally decided—one of the most hooked-up ladies in the state.

The list was endless: A member of the Minnesota Orchestra Board, a Trustee of her kids' private schools, a member of the Executive Committee of the League of Women Voters, and the vice chair of the county Republican Women. And more, including memberships in a local Right to Life chapter and a Save the Lakes committee.

From what she could tell, Anita had more than 9,400 Facebook friends, along with hundreds of LinkedIn connections.

Impressive as all of that was, there was relatively little personal information about her. Age forty-four, a graduate of Hopkins High School and, with "distinction," the University of Minnesota, majoring in sociology. Married to Harlan Hawkins in 2006, mother of two children, Samuel, age 7, and Gretchen, age 4. A resident of Orono, and a past member of the City Council.

There was no record of her ever having a job, at least in her post-college life.

By the time Gabby turned off the computer, her head ached and her eyes burned. Could a woman apparently this smart, and this connected, be married to a man she didn't really know? For that many years? An ultimate con man and longtime fugitive? Would she simply have accepted whatever he had told her about his past? Without suspicions? Without checking?

Hard to believe, but not impossible, she guessed. After all, hadn't she herself fallen in love with a man about whom she had known so little? Who had neglected to tell her of his earlier marriage until she had learned about it from others, who had carefully disguised the violent side of his personality until she'd discovered it the hard way?

Gabby sat back and closed her eyes, trying to put herself in Anita's place a dozen or so years before: in her mid-thirties, unmarried, childless, beginning to feel a little desperate, meeting a man a few years her senior, also unmarried, who's apparently well-to-do, with a big house in Orono. He seems taken with her and, like her, would like to settle down. Maybe have kids. He tells her he's from out West, moved around a lot, with parents who died years before, no siblings or other close relatives. Came to Minnesota with a nice inheritance and eager to begin a new life and a new business.

Maybe he was a little vague on details, but not enough to raise her suspicions. He was a practiced liar, and by the time he met Anita, he'd developed a history that would pass all but the most determined inquiry. And she, for better or worse, was not about to delve more deeply into his past. She had met the man she would marry.

It was a nice theory, Gabby decided, not implausible. But, even if her imaginings were true, it would do little good to approach her—since she would know no more about the real Harlan Hawkins or his past than they did. making her as much of a victim as all of the others he had conned.

Unless, of course, she did know the truth.

Thirty-Seven

Desperate men do desperate things.

Craig Jessup was a desperate man.

By now, he had exactly sixty-two dollars and thirteen cents left in his pocket. He had spent everything else in his small stash on a blaze orange jacket and pants, a black ski mask, and a small starter pistol at the Cabela's sporting goods store in Owatonna, south of the Twin Cities.

Those duds were now tucked in his saddlebags as he rested on his bike in a secluded, wooded area outside the small, sleepy town of Nestoga, which was actually more of a crossroads than a town. It had no stoplight or even a stop sign, with more houses abandoned than lived-in.

He had passed through it several times over the past few days, slowly, throttle down, never at the same time of day, always wearing his helmet and chaps. Not once had he seen anyone on what passed for the main street. There were a couple of cars and one pickup, parallel parked, and one or two dogs, but no people.

And never a sign of a police or sheriff's car.

This was a small farming community, and with the planting season, almost everybody, he suspected, was working in the fields.

There was a small grocery store, Jessie's, at one end of the town, next to Billy's bar and cafe, with a two-pump Esso gas station at the other end. Between them, in the middle of the block, was the Hanover State Bank, a narrow, brick building that looked as if it had been there since the early 1900s, surviving, apparently, because of the loyalty of local farm families whose ancestors had begun banking there the day it opened.

On one side of it was the crumbling façade of what once was a movie theater, The Gypsy; on the other, the broken windows of Ollie's Shoes, with a faded, tattered Red Wing Shoes poster still hanging inside.

On one of his trips through town, he had paused long enough in front of the bank to see that its hours were eight to five, Monday through Friday, nine to noon on Saturday.

It was now 7:30 on a Thursday, and his latest adventure was about to begin.

Jessup got off his bike, pulled the blaze orange jacket and pants out of the saddlebags and slipped them on, stuffing the ski mask into one of the pockets. In another pocket were his switchblade and the small starter pistol.

It wasn't as though he hadn't thought about what he was about to do. He had thought of little else. But in the end, he'd decided he had no choice. With his name and picture in the papers and on the web, he couldn't risk trying to get a job. And a desperate decision to gamble some of his few remaining dollars on the slots at the Mystic Lake Casino had proved foolish and fruitless.

So here he was, with sixty-two dollars and change, ready to begin a life of real crime from which there would be no hasty retreat. His life had come full circle, from the deputy mayor of a large California city to a wanted stalker, and now, to a would-be federal felon.

The thought of it filled him with fear … and, for perhaps the first time in his life, a sense of self-loathing. Which he quickly dismissed.

But despite his fear, he also felt a surge of excitement—as if he was about to climb a sheer cliff with no rope or to swim in waters infested with sharks.

Clad in his blaze orange, he pulled up in front of the bank at precisely 8:03, scanned the deserted main street but, again, saw no one. Only one car was within view, parked in front of Billy's bar. Probably the owner's, he guessed.

As he got off the bike, he paused for a moment to give himself one final chance to reconsider. Too late. Too bad.

Then he walked through the front door of the bank and pulled the ski mask over his face, leaving only his eyes and nose visible and trying to ignore the churning in his stomach and the pounding in his chest.

The only person inside was an older woman, whose gray hair was pulled back into a bun, who was standing behind the teller's cage, head down, absorbed, thumbing through a stack of papers.

Somebody's grandma.

He stood not more than a foot from her before she finally looked up, her smile turning instantly into a portrait of fear. Eyes wide behind her granny glasses, mouth agape, lips trembling.

He put the starter pistol on the counter and quietly repeated a line he'd heard in the movies: "No alarm, no dye-pack, no tracker. Just the money. You won't be hurt."

She grasped the counter with both hands, and, for an instant, he thought she would collapse in a heap.

"Relax," he said. "Give me all of the money in all of the drawers, and I'll be gone, and you'll be safe."

He handed her a satchel he had carried in with him. "But you'll have to move quickly," he said, his voice calm, controlled. "Before anyone else happens by."

She did as she was told, moving from one teller position to another, her eyes never leaving his, blindly scooping up the bills and stuffing them into the bag.

When it was back in his hands, he said, "Now, I want you to sit down on that chair behind the counter and wait for thirty minutes. Do not use the phone. Do not sound an alarm. Or I will be back another day, looking for you. Do you understand?"

She nodded and sat on the chair, her hands clasped tightly in an effort to stop the shaking.

"Thank you for your cooperation," he said as he turned and headed for the door. "And have a nice day."

In the days before, Jessup had carefully scouted the web of back-country roads that spread out from Nestoga, picking one that was the most remote and which passed the fewest farms. On one of those roads, at a safe distance out of town, he stopped to strip off the blaze orange clothing and then discarded them, along with the ski mask, in a stand of trees well off the road.

Then it was off to the campground where he was staying—a full forty miles away, the satchel of cash tied securely to his handlebars.

He could hardly wait to count it all.

THIRTY-FIVE MINUTES LATER, three squad cars from the Rice County sheriff's office were parked outside the Hanover State Bank, and an hour later, an unmarked car from the Minneapolis office of the FBI was there, as well. The teller, Gladys Entwine, still shaken, had by now moved from the chair to the office of the bank president, one Charles Gidding.

Despite the gentle questioning by the deputies and the FBI agents, Gladys was able to tell them little more than the bank security cameras showed: a six-foot-or-so man clad in a blaze orange outfit and ski mask, who showed a small gun, and who was unfailingly polite as she gave him all of the cash in the drawers.

The total take was still being calculated, but Gladys thought it would be in the low thousands.

She did say that after he left, she heard the roar of a motorcycle starting, and as she carefully rose from her chair, caught a glimpse of him driving away in what she thought was a black bike.

A statewide alert had long since been issued for a black motorcycle with an orange-clad rider, but no one had much hope that it would yield results. Too many black bikes, too many six-foot men, none likely any longer in orange. What's more, neither the deputies nor the Feds could remember the last bank bandit who'd fled on a motorcycle.

Outside the closed door of the bank, a small crowd of the curious had gathered, but none of them was able to provide the authorities with any additional information. They just wanted to make sure their money was safe.

Thirty-Eight

When Gabby and Zach got to the station that morning, they were summoned to the conference room where the two FBI agents, Dimitri and Upchurch, waited, chatting with John Knowles. They had called Knowles the night before, asking to meet to "catch up" on any developments. As it turned out, however, they came with little new information of their own and were there largely to learn what, if anything, Gabby and company had come up with since their last meeting.

"So what *have* you been doing?" Gabby asked.

"Only this," Dimitri said, "We've been trying to get a better handle on the ownership history of the house where the first body was found, without triggering any alarms."

"What do you mean, 'alarms'?" she asked.

"As we told you before, we don't want Overton or anyone else connected with Zimtronics to know that the FBI is aware of the house or its ownership. Or that we've been snooping around."

"And?" Her question hung in the air.

Upchurch took over. "This much we know. The house was bought in the summer of 2002, in cash, from an older couple. The husband is deceased, the wife in a nursing home, near death. The purchase agreement was signed on behalf of

314 | RON HANDBERG

Zimtronics by someone whose signature is illegible. And the real estate agent who handled the transaction has no precise memory of who that someone was this many years later."

Dimitri said, "The payments of house taxes and other bills are automatically withdrawn from a Zimtronics account at a US Bank. But, again, the signatures on the bank documents are not readable. And the phone number listed on the document never existed."

"Damn," Knowles muttered.

"All correspondence from the bank, the state and county, and the utilities apparently was being sent to that commercial mailbox until it was shut down after the body was found."

Gabby asked, "Did John tell you that the mail is now being delivered to the house? At least it was."

"Yes," Dimitri said. "And while I hate to admit it, you're way ahead of us on this. We'll try to find out who authorized the delivery. Without raising alarms."

Gabby got up and leaned against the table. "What I still don't understand is why Overton used Zimtronics to buy the house in the first place. Why didn't he just put it in his new name, whatever that is?"

Upchurch said, "The only thing we can figure is that he didn't want to reveal any personal information about himself in buying the house, regardless of how safe he thought his new identity was or how little risk there may have been. He simply wanted to hide behind a corporate name, figuring the less known about him, the better."

"Anything else?" Zach asked.

"No, sorry," Dimitri said. "It's all we've had time to do."

"So what about you guys?" Upchurch asked. "What have you been up to?"

As they were about to respond, there was a rap on the conference room door, and Barclay walked in. "Sorry to interrupt, but this may be of interest to all of you."

"What?" Gabby said.

"It just came over the AP a few minutes ago. A bank robbery in the little town of Nestoga, in Rice County. A lone bandit hit the bank just after eight this morning and took off on a black motorcycle, maybe a Harley. About six feet tall, wearing a ski mask and dressed in blaze orange. No sign of him since."

It took an instant, but then Gabby's eyes widened. "You think?"

"Who knows?" Barclay said. "Could just be a strange coincidence."

"Maybe so, but ... "

"What's going on?" Dimitri cut in, his glance shifting from one to the other.

"Long story," Gabby said, but then—as concisely as possible—recited the saga of Craig Jessup and the current hunt for him. "We know he was riding a black Harley and could be getting desperate by now."

"You have any idea of where he is?"

"No. We're not even sure he's still here, but there are warrants out for him, both here and in California, and the local cops are watching out for him."

"Describe him."

"Six feet," Gabby said, "maybe 180 pounds. Good-looking, blond, with a receding hairline. But he's changed his appearance several times already, so it's hard to know what he may look like now."

Upchurch walked out of the room with his phone, returning minutes later. "Our people are still at the bank," he said, "but they don't have much more information. Guy was in and out in a couple of minutes, showed a gun, and scared an old lady teller half to death. I gave them what you just told us, but so far there haven't been any sightings of him or his bike. They've issued an APB, but that's about it."

Barclay spoke up. "We should be careful here. This could have nothing to do with Jessup. We don't want you guys looking for the wrong man. Or Jessup facing a bunch of gun-toting cops who mistakenly think he just pulled off a bank job."

"Let us worry about that," Upchurch replied. "This will give our buddies at the bank a start."

"Meantime," Dimitri said, "tell us what you've been doing on the Overton mystery."

Gabby smiled. "Gotta promise not to laugh, but we think we've found your man."

"Really?" with a grin. "Should we arrest him now or later?"

"You may want to wait . . . since we don't really have any proof."

There was silence around the table.

Finally, Knowles took a deep breath and started from the beginning: the discovery by his banker friend of a Harlan Hawkins, who was in the investment business, specializing in medical and pharmaceutical stocks; who shared a similar and relatively uncommon first name with Overton; whose background was something of a mystery; and who seemed intent on guarding his privacy.

"When I talked to his wife and said I was a friend from out East, she said her husband was from out West, which I thought indicated we had the wrong guy. But Gabby believes it might mean that even his wife doesn't really know who her husband is."

"We promised not to laugh," Dimitri said, "but can we at least chuckle?"

"Go ahead," Gabby said, with a slight scowl. "I know it sounds out of left field, but we think we may be on to something."

Upchurch didn't try to hide his skepticism. "Really? Then tell us more."

"We've been able to find virtually nothing about him or his past, searching in all of the predictable places," she said. "Plenty about his wife, who's extremely active in civic and community affairs, but he is an empty vessel. We do know he's in his late forties or early fifties, which could fit Overton, and that he got married in 2006, a few years after Overton may have arrived in Minnesota. They have two young kids, live in Orono, and are said to have plenty of money."

"If he's in the investment business," Dimitri said, "he must have provided personal and professional information about himself to the SEC or state authorities. All of that has to be on file somewhere."

"That's what we thought, too," Knowles said. "But my friend indicates that he may just be dealing with family money, his and his wife's, which he thinks doesn't require those kinds of disclosures. But you would know more about that than we do."

"That all seems like a mighty stretch," Dimitri said, "but we'll do a little checking of our own. Is there anything else?"

"Not really," Gabby said. "But please keep us in the loop."

As THEY ALL GOT UP to leave, Craig Jessup sat huddled in his tent, carefully counting the dollars he plucked from the satchel. A stack of twenties in one corner, fifties in another, and a pile of all the other bills, excluding a few hundreds between his crossed legs. He had not yet finished, but already the total was over $1,700. There would be more than $2,000, he guessed, by the time he was done.

Enough to last him until his task was completed. And, perhaps, enough seed money to begin a new life.

Except for two RVs and a pop-up camper parked some distance across the way, the campground was all but deserted. His Harley was next to the tent, covered with a small tarp he had also bought at Cabela's. He felt safe for now, still amazed at how easy it had been. In and out of the bank in less than three minutes, encountering no one in town or on the back roads he had chosen for his getaway.

Still, he knew there would be a widespread search for him, made easier because of the bike and more intense because the

Feds would be involved. But he took comfort in the time and distance he had put between himself and the bank, and by the fact that there were scores of black motorcycles on the road, especially at this time of year, driven by guys in chaps and helmets just like his.

He did feel bad for the old lady in the bank, scaring her as he did. He wished it could have been someone younger, who'd likely get over the shock more quickly than the grandma. But, he decided, you deal with what you're dealt and don't look back.

His own grandmothers were a distant memory. Both had lived in other parts of the country and both had died, like his mother, when he was still in his early teens. He had grown into adulthood living with a father who never could shake the grief of his wife's early death—never, not for a day—leaving his son, for all intents and purposes, parentless.

And now, in the wake of what he had just done, his father's trembling words on the telephone came back to haunt him. *"Your poor mother..."*

When the final bill was counted, the total was $2,340.

Thirty-Nine

If Harlan Hawkins was later to look for someone to blame, it would have been unfair to direct all of his anger at his Realtor, Jeremy Higgins. After all, Higgins had simply left the Hawkins house file open on the desk while he went down the hall to take a piss. The real blame should fall on his assistant, a young woman by the name of Nancy Carlson, who happened to glance at the file while straightening up his desk, not aware she was seeing something she shouldn't see, or that the something she shouldn't see shouldn't leave the office.

So she couldn't really be blamed either, when, a day or two later, she mentioned the potential house sale to her mother, Alice, who—a day after that, at the close of a morning meeting of the county Republicans—happened to be chatting with her friend, Anita Hawkins. "I was sorry to hear that you're thinking of selling your home," she said. "It's such a lovely place and seems so right for you and the family."

Anita, caught up in the conversations of others around her, was not sure of what she had heard. "I'm sorry," she said, turning sharply, "but what did you just say?"

"I hope you're not thinking of moving out of town," Alice persisted. "Your leaving would be such a loss to the community."

Anita stepped back, confusion on her face and in her whispered voice. "I have no idea what you're talking about," she said. "Where in the world did you hear that we're considering a move?"

Alice suddenly knew that she had stepped across some kind of unseen line and tried to retreat and fib, for the sake of her daughter if nothing else. "Uh, somebody must have said something at the grocery store; I can't remember who. Or maybe it was at the coffee shop. If it's not true, I apologize. I'm not the kind who spreads rumors, and I certainly wouldn't have said anything to anyone else before talking to you."

"I hope not," Anita replied, "because it's certainly not true. And I would hate to see a rumor like that spread. I just can't think of who might have started it ... and why."

"Well, I'm very relieved," Alice said. "Because—as I said—it would be a great loss to all of us who know and work with you. I just can't see how you have time to do all that you do."

At that moment, before more could be said, another woman tapped Anita on the shoulder, diverting her attention, giving Alice time to quietly escape. She could hardly wait to get outside and to give her daughter a call. Or, on second thought, maybe not. Who knew? Without realizing it, she may have just opened Pandora's box.

After a brief conversation with the other woman, Anita turned to search the room for Alice, hoping to learn more about the mysterious rumors. But by then she was gone, leaving behind all kinds of questions. If Alice had heard those rumors, she thought, others must have heard them as well. Why hadn't someone else said something to her? Again, who could have started them, and why? She could hardly wait to talk to Harlan that evening. Maybe he had heard the same rumors and had simply dismissed them, not wanting to trouble her.

It wasn't until she was on the way home that she suddenly stopped the car and pulled to the side of the road, remembering only then, with a start, that Alice Carlson's daughter, Nancy, worked for some real estate agent, though she couldn't remember who. But it wouldn't take her long to find out and to get to the bottom of all this.

AN HOUR LATER, Gabby and Zach were pulling into the Crystal Lake cemetery in north Minneapolis. What had been a sunny morning had turned cloudy and blustery with a fine mist in the air, the droplets clinging to the oak leaves overhanging the entrance to the cemetery. Not long before, Gabby had received a rushed call from Cindy Maxwell, the assistant M.E., telling her that John Doe was about to be buried . . . that every effort to identify him, including the wide circulation of his doctored photo, had failed, leaving them with no choice but to finally put him to rest, nameless, in a donated plot.

For now, there would be no grave marker, no flowers except for a small bouquet of daisies Gabby had stopped to buy, and no mourners, only onlookers. Just three others besides Maxwell were there, huddled in the mist next to an unadorned casket soon to be lowered into the soggy ground: Detective Philips, who, like Gabby, had been called at the last minute; Henry Scowly, a short, squat employee of the nearby funeral home that had volunteered to handle the burial; and the Reverend Austin Downey, a stately pro bono minister the cemetery had asked to preside at the service.

None of them, of course, ever knew, or would ever know, the man whose remains lay inside the coffin.

As Gabby and Zach left the car and approached the grave, Maxwell came to meet them, apologizing for the late notice. "I wasn't sure you'd want to come," she said, "but I finally decided I should give you a call."

"I'm glad you did," Gabby said.

As they walked, Maxwell went on, "I wanted more time to ID him, but my boss finally lost his patience and ordered me to make these arrangements. Believe it or not, this is only the fifth John or Jane Doe I've put in the ground in all of my years of doing this job. I kept hoping that somebody would come forward, but," looking away, wiping the mist from her eyes, "nobody did. And nobody deserves to die an anonymous death like this guy, and to be buried with only strangers looking on."

"Anonymous, hell," Zach said. "At least one person knows who he is: the guy who put a bullet in his head."

"And," Gabby said, "even if someone else did know him, they probably wouldn't want to get involved, once they'd learned how he died."

"Maybe so, but I haven't given up all hope," the M.E. said. "I know the FBI is in touch with Interpol and some of their other contacts overseas."

At the graveside, they greeted Philips and were quickly introduced to the funeral director and minister. "We should get started," Maxwell said, glancing up. "The weather's getting worse."

She was right. The mist had turned to a drizzle with distant flashes of lightning to the west followed by low rumbles of thunder.

Gabby flipped the hood of her rain jacket over her head and leaned forward to put the small bouquet atop the casket, then stepped back, allowing the minister to move closer, a small Bible in his hands. "Could we please bow our heads for a moment in prayer," he said, as they all stood silently, staring down at the mound of dirt next to the grave, the heavier rain now carving small valleys in the soil. "We are here to wish God's speed and God's blessing to a man about whom we know so little, but who—like all of us—was a child of God, and who almost certainly was loved in his lifetime, not only by God, but by the mother and father who brought him into this world and must have cherished him."

Unnoticed, Zach had moved to the rear, unobtrusively recording the service with a small, handheld camera, the video to be used, they'd decided, only if the larger Ponzi story was ever to be told on the air.

"He died an untimely, horrible death," the minister went on, "the victim of an evil act, but we can be assured that God was by his side in that final moment, opening the gates to heaven as he took leave of this earth. May he rest in everlasting peace in the cradle of God's love."

As she stood there, head bowed, Gabby felt awkward and a little contrite, knowing that God had never been a part of her life. Growing up, her family had seldom gone to church, for reasons never really discussed and which she had never clearly understood. Or questioned. Maybe it was because Sunday was one of the few days her dad had, yes, *religiously* refused to work, reserving that day to be with the family, no matter what. But in the days and weeks after his sudden, heartbreaking death, Gabby was left to wonder whether their family's long-standing indifference to God, their lack of expressed faith or belief, had, in the end, made some kind of fateful difference. A thought that resurfaced now as she stood by the grave of this lost, nameless soul.

Hunkering under the funeral director's umbrella, the minister went on to pray for whoever was responsible for this man's death, then hurriedly recited three Bible verses, ending with the twenty-third Psalm, "Surely goodness and mercy shall follow me all of the days of my life. And I will dwell in the house of the Lord forever. Amen."

As they wandered away from the grave, Gabby briefed Philips on what the Feds had discovered about the ownership of the house and of Jessup's possible involvement in the Nestoga bank robbery.

"No kidding," Philips said. "If he did do the bank, it puts him in a whole new category of crime. Did he use a gun?"

"I think so, yes," Gabby replied.

"Did he hurt anyone?"

"No, not physically, anyway."

"Still, he could face some real hard time. If it is him, and if they catch up with him, it could be the answer to your problems. He'll be going away for years."

"Don't count on them catching him," she said. "As we've already discovered."

"Well, *we* certainly haven't forgotten about him, but there haven't been any new sightings in the city. And I've been ordered to move on to some of my other cases."

"Because?"

"Because I haven't been of much help to you lately. And because the Feds now seem to be taking over."

"No one's 'taking over,'" she said, with heat. "It's still our investigation, and I hope we can keep in touch."

"Of course," he said as he headed for his car. "Call me anytime."

BY THE TIME Harlan's Lexus pulled into the driveway later that day, the skies had cleared and Anita Hawkins was at her deck, waiting impatiently, sipping on her second gin-and-tonic. The children were in the backyard play area with their nanny, Julie, who'd been instructed to keep them occupied until they were summoned for dinner.

Since that morning's Republican meeting, Anita had made a number of calls, eventually learning that Alice Carlson's daughter did indeed work at the local RE/MAX office. Which could explain the rumors. But despite her gnawing curiosity, she had decided to make no further inquiries until she spoke to her husband...who now joined her on the deck.

"Hey," he said, shedding his suit coat. "How's your day been?"

"Disconcerting," she replied.

"Really?" He replied with a strange look. "Why's that?"

"Pour yourself a drink and I'll explain."

"OK," he replied, moving toward the kitchen. "Where are the kids?"

"Out back with Julie."

A few minutes passed before he was back, glass in hand, wearing an expression she could not quite read. A mixture of curiosity and concern. Maybe something more.

He sat down across from her. "So what's going on?"

Watching him carefully, she said, "I heard the strangest rumor today..."

He said quickly, "A rumor? What rumor?"

"That our house is up for sale... that we may be moving."

His jaw dropped. "*What?*"

His response was of pure total shock. His secret was out. *But how?* And what did Anita know? Glancing at her, he was relieved to see that his reaction seemed to convince her that he was as surprised by the news as she had been.

Recovering, he said, "Where the hell did that come from?"

"That's what I want to know," she replied, "and I may have a clue," explaining the RE/MAX connection. "I don't want to blame Alice's daughter without knowing, but I can't think of who else might have started such talk."

Hawkins remained quiet for a moment, thinking, assessing the possible damage. Finally he said, "I think you're right. Let's not rush to judgment. You know how rumors can start. It could have been anyone. It might be best to just forget it for now... unless we hear of the same rumor from others."

"No, no," she said. "I think you should at least speak to someone at RE/MAX. Find out what, if anything, they know. Maybe someone came to them asking about our house, and whether it's available. That could start a rumor like this."

"OK. I'll find out who runs the place and talk with him. Or her. But I don't want to make a mountain out of this molehill. I've got better things to do. And so do you."

"Not necessarily," she said. "I need to get to the bottom of it. I can't have misinformation like this spread around if I'm serious about the legislative endorsement."

He sat up straight. "Legislative endorsement? What are you talking about?"

"It's still hush-hush, but a week ago, the party's executive committee came to me and asked if I'd be interested in possibly running for Jennifer's seat in the State House. A couple of us were discussing the possibility this morning when Alice approached me with this rumor."

Jennifer Answab was a three-term House member from their GOP-dominated legislative district, who had earlier announced her plans to retire.

"And you're actually considering it?" he asked.

"Sure. Why not?"

"Without consulting me?"

"Of course I would, but it's still early, and I didn't want to bother you. Anything could happen. But I don't want a rumor like this getting in the way if I do decide to run."

As he sat looking at her, he thought: *Forget about those rumors, dear. They'd do nothing to your campaign compared to the news of a disappearing husband, who also happens to be a federal fugitive.*

Then he smiled.

Forty

In the three days since the bank robbery, Jessup had ventured no more than fifty yards from his tent, then mainly to use the campground's toilets and shower. He had met and talked to no one, avoided eye contact whenever possible, and resisted the temptation to travel to any of the nearby small towns for groceries and beer, choosing to exist on the small stockpile of supplies he had accumulated before the robbery.

He built small fires in a stone fireplace near his tent to heat his soup and assorted other canned delicacies, to perk his coffee, and to fry his bacon and eggs. The meals weren't particularly healthy, minus any fresh fruits or vegetables, but they weren't that different from the stingy diet he'd become accustomed to since leaving California.

Now, of course, he could afford anything he wanted but was not free to go get it. At least not yet.

Not wanting to take chances that first day, after counting the stolen cash, he'd waited until dark and the campground was quiet before he pulled up the tent stakes, tipped the tent, and quietly dug a two-foot-deep hole where it stood—scattering the dirt onto a grassy area and depositing the satchel full of the bills into the hole. Then he put the tent back up and covered the hole beneath the tent flooring with his sleeping bag.

The campground was not Wi-Fi friendly, which made his computer useless, but his iPhone kept him in contact with the outside world. He used the *Star Tribune* and *Pioneer Press* websites to follow the first-day stories of the robbery and search, stories which would fade in the days that followed.

In the first hours after the robbery, he'd seen one, perhaps two, State Patrol helicopters flying an apparent grid pattern that he guessed was in a wide radius of the bank. Since then, there'd been no signs of any squad cars or further helicopter flights... so, for the moment, he figured, the greatest risk of discovery had passed.

His self-imposed isolation had given him plenty of time to think, yet he still was without a concrete plan for what would happen next. He wanted to stay put for at least another day or two, to allow the cops and the Feds to hopefully exhaust any further efforts to locate him. But beyond that, what? And when?

His mission certainly had not changed. He *would* find a way to get to Gabby and finish what he had set out to do. But the specifics of how he would accomplish that mission were still to be decided.

For now, he mostly stayed inside his tent, safe from the flies and mosquitoes and out of the sight of other campers. But he could not avoid those trips to the toilet, or to charge his phone, or to take other short excursions for exercise and to stretch his legs. It was on one of those trips to the shower that he happened to notice an attractive young woman who had left her car, a small Fiat, in the parking lot and was wandering the campground, as if looking for someone or for an appropriate camping site. But, tellingly, she was clad in anything but camping attire, more like she had just come from the office or school—tailored slacks, a long-sleeved blouse and low-heeled shoes.

If she glanced in his direction, he didn't see it... and, for the moment, didn't think much more about it... or her.

But he was wrong. She *had* seen him, fleetingly, out of the corner of her eye. But she'd kept right on walking, looking straight ahead, catching her breath, trying to stabilize the image that had come and gone so quickly. *Could it have been him? After all this time?* Think! About the right height, a shaved head and blond beard, with a blue towel wrapped around his neck. *Had she finally found her man?*

It wasn't chance that had brought Linda the intern to this particular campground. After all, she had visited sixteen others, public and private, in the past ten days—all on her own time, all since she'd just missed finding Jessup at the Richfield motel, and all since she'd suggested the campground search idea in her last meeting with Gabby and Barclay, an idea that Barclay thought had little chance of success, but to which he had given his reluctant approval, *"But, sure, if you want to, go ahead."*

So, using her time between University classes and on the weekends, relying on a list she'd obtained online, she began her quest at several campgrounds close to the metropolitan area, but finding nothing at those, had expanded the search into the outlying counties. The task was tiresome and time-consuming, especially at the larger, more crowded campgrounds that were often full on the weekends. She would drive through the grounds when she could, or walk when she had to, always looking for a black Harley and a blond, six-foot-tall dude.

No surprise that over time she had spotted a number of Harleys, some of them black, and a lot of younger guys, none of whom seemed connected to the Harleys or bore a close resemblance to the elusive Craig Jessup. Despite the frustrations, she had continued to press on, stopping by at least one new campground every day, finding only disappointment, knowing each time that he could have moved on by then or have simply been out of sight when she happened by. So it was little wonder she had slowly come to the conclusion that he might, indeed, be a human needle in the haystack.

Until now.

No particular lead had brought her to this small campground, except that once she'd learned Jessup might have been involved in the Nestoga bank robbery, she'd decided to move her search even farther south—closer to the scene of the robbery where campgrounds were fewer and farther between. This was the fourth one she had visited in the days since the robbery, with three more to go before she might have to admit failure and return home for good.

Until now.

As she moved down the gravel path, she risked a quick look back, but by then he had disappeared into a cement-block building that she thought might house restrooms and showers, as she'd seen at other campgrounds.

Keep walking, she told herself. *And keep calm.*

After stepping out of the shower and drying off, Jessup glanced out the slanted window louvers and saw that the young woman was now farther down the path and had stopped at the pop-up camper to chat with a woman sitting outside on a lawn chair. As he watched, he saw the older woman point in the direction of his tent, then shake her head and shrug her shoulders—as if to say, "I have no idea."

Jessup wasn't sure what it was about this young woman that gave him pause, but for the first time since he'd come here he felt a pang in the pit of his stomach. But why? There had been other women at the campground he had seen and who had seen him without causing him concern. Maybe it was that this one seemed so out of place, dressed as she was, or that she was here alone in this out-of-the-way spot, without apparent purpose, wandering around, stopping to talk to strangers. And, finally, remembering what he took to be her searching look in the direction of his tent and her questions that the lawn-chair lady clearly could not answer.

About him?

In the twenty-five minutes it took Linda to complete her circle of the campground, she had stopped to speak to two other campers, who knew no more about the man she had glimpsed than the first lady. She had also tried, unsuccessfully, to reach Gabby by phone, leaving both a voice and text message: "I think I may have found Jessup at a campground in Faribault County, not that far from Northfield, but I'm not sure. Call me back when you can, please. I can't be here much longer." She was also tempted to call 9-1-1, but again hesitated, until she could be more certain.

In those same twenty-five minutes, Jessup had slipped back into his clothes, trotted from the shower to his tent, and then moved on to the woman's Fiat, parked in the nearby lot. He took a quick look inside, seeing a briefcase and a stack of books in the back seat, an open map and an empty Dairy Queen cup and crumpled napkins in the front seat.

And, as he walked around the car, he saw stuck to the back window two decals: one from the University of Minnesota, with Goldy the Gopher's toothy grin, the other from ... *Channel 7 News.*

Now, he was back by his tent, fiddling with the flap, as Linda walked down the path opposite him, heading for her car, clearly—and deliberately—paying him no heed.

"Hey," he said, moving to intercept her. "Are you looking for someone? Can I be of any help?"

She stopped momentarily, but then moved quickly away. "No, thanks," over her shoulder. "I was just checking out campsites."

"Really?" he said, catching up with her. "You're sure about that?"

"Of course," she said, stopping to face him, defiantly, but with heart beating. "Why would you ask that? And who are you, anyway?" Turning, "I have to get going."

"That might be difficult," he said. "I just noticed you have a flat tire."

"What!"

"See. The left front. Flatter than a pancake. Looks like it might have been punctured."

She frantically dug into her purse for her phone, but before she could touch it, it was in *his* hands. "Wouldn't do that," he said, checking it quickly for recent calls made, then dropping it and crunching it with his heel, heaving it into the woods. "Wouldn't scream or yell, either," he said, flashing his switchblade.

She could only stare at him, eyes wide, mouth open, the scream caught before it ever reached her throat. Not that it would have helped. She could see no one who looked to be within the sound of her voice.

"And I'd like your car keys, too. Quick!" When she hesitated, he grabbed the purse, searched for the keys, and threw them in the same direction as the phone.

Then he took her firmly by the elbow and began to lead her back toward his tent. She tried to pull away but he only tightened his grip. "Sorry," he said as they walked, "but please don't resist. It won't help. By the way, what's your name?"

"None of your fucking business."

"Whew. Nasty." He stopped and took her billfold out of her purse, checking the driver's license. "Linda Wilkins. Nice name, I like it."

"What do you want with me?"

"I saw the sticker on the back window. I assume you work for Channel 7. And that you may have been here looking for me."

"You're full of shit. The car belongs to my boyfriend ... and I have no idea what you're talking about, or who you are."

"Name's Craig Jessup. I'm a friend of Gabby Gooding."

"I don't know anybody by that name."

"Then why did you just call her on your phone?"

She had no reply.

"Here's the deal, Linda-the-news-lady. We're going to tear

down the tent, pack it and some other things up, and take a ride on my bike, which is under the tarp. And I'll tell you this now ... so listen up. If you don't give me any trouble, and if you do as I say, you will not be hurt. That's a promise. I will drop you off in the countryside somewhere, within an hour or two's walk of help, and be on my way ..."

"You're crazy," she said.

"No, not crazy. Determined. I have little to lose, do you understand? And please don't try to run. I'd just have to catch you and tie you up or something."

She glared at him, but didn't move.

"Now give me a hand with this tent."

Close up, she thought, he looked nothing like the dangerous sociopath who'd been described to her and others. Certainly not crazy. His voice was gentle, nonthreatening. His grip on her elbow, while firm, could have been tighter, more painful.

He seemed to sense what she was thinking. "Look, I'm not a bad guy. All I've wanted to do since I got here is to talk to Gabby. But I can't get near her ... "

"Because you beat the crap out of her ... "

"That was a mistake, I admit. A moment I deeply regret. But, trust me, she got her revenge. She's cost me everything: my job, my friends, my life, if you really want to know."

"Boohoo," Linda replied, gathering courage. "From what I hear, she's done nothing to you except try to get away. And what do you do? You follow her here, threaten her, stalk her, trash her place, scare the livin' hell out of her. All in the name of what? Love? Spare me."

"That's enough, news lady," he said. "I'm tired of talking to you. You'll never understand."

Within the next few minutes the tent was down and packed away with his other belongings and loaded on to the Harley. She saw him take the satchel out of the hole in the ground.

"What's that?" she asked.

"My immediate future," he replied, tying it on to his handlebars and starting the bike. "Now get on behind me, and no funny stuff."

True to his word, the last she saw of him was in a cloud of dust, racing away, leaving her standing alone on some god-forsaken graveled country road, squeezed between fields of newly planted corn and soybeans, the only sound that of some far-away tractor, plowing or planting new fields.

Not another word had been said between them, except for, "Get off," when he pulled to a stop, abruptly abandoning her, but leaving his license plate number firmly etched in her memory.

The next thing she saw, an hour or more later, was another cloud of dust, this one trailing behind an old Chevy pickup, heading down the road in her direction. She stepped to one side, facing the truck, and held out her hand. The pickup skidded to a halt, an old man with a scruffy hat and a grizzled beard behind the wheel.

She leaned into the open side window. "I need help," she said. "I need water. I need a phone."

"Get in, young lady," the old man said, "and I'll get you all three. Quick as a cat."

Then they were off... in yet another cloud of dust.

AFTER LUNCH, BARCLAY was back in his office when Linda was able to reach him, but it took him a moment to realize who was calling and to decipher her breathless words. "Calm down, Linda," he finally said. "You're where?"

"At a farm in LeSueur County," she said, and then, without waiting, told him as quickly but as completely as she could what had just transpired with Craig Jessup. "My God," he said, but then listened without interruption until she finally ended with, "I'm fine, I really am. He didn't hurt me, but he left me in the middle of nowhere. Where I'd probably still be if Jocko hadn't happened to drive by."

Barclay wasn't sure what to say. "So you're with this Jocko?"

"And his wife, Betty, yes. On their farm. They've been great."

"You've called the cops?"

"Of course. Jocko is friends with one of the sheriff's deputies. He got him on the phone and I told him what had happened, along with a description of Jessup and his bike license plate number. The deputy said he'd call the State Patrol and the FBI, who are supposed to meet me back at the campground."

"I'm amazed. And you're sure you're OK?"

"Yes, I'm sure. He put a scare into me and left a bruise on my arm. But he could have done a lot more, if he'd wanted to." Then, "But he also punctured one of my tires, destroyed my phone, and threw my car keys away."

"We'll take care of all of that," Barclay said. "But now tell me, just where the hell is this campground?"

She described the location.

"And how did you find it?"

"A long story," she said, but briefly told him of the extended campground search she had pursued without telling him or anyone else. "I just did it on my own and was about to give up until I finally spotted him today."

"I'll be there as soon as I can," he said. "And I'll try to bring Gabby and Zach with me."

"I didn't mean to cause you any trouble," she said. "I did try to reach Gabby earlier, before he caught on to me … "

"*Trouble?* You did a hell of a job, Linda. You're a brave, resourceful young woman, and I'm proud of you. And I mean that."

After he'd hung up, he thought, *If I'm still around, and if she's still around, I might just have found my next young reporter.*

When he couldn't find Gabby in her cubicle or Zach in the editing booth, Barclay stopped by the assignment desk. "They left about an hour ago," Harry Wilson told him. "With Knowles. Said they had a date with their FBI buddies and would be out of contact. That's all I know."

"OK," Barclay said, "but when they check in, have them call or text me. Linda, our young intern, found Jessup at some campground, but he's on the loose again. I'm on the way to meet her at the campground now."

The last thing he heard as he hurried away was Wilson's, "How the hell...?"

Forty-One

Gabby, Zach, and Knowles were squeezing into the back seat of an unmarked FBI car in the parking lot of a sports bar in suburban Hopkins. They'd been summoned there by agents Dimitri and Upchurch, who were in the front seat—watching the bar's front entrance.

"Glad you could make it on short notice," Dimitri said as the three huddled in the back. "We told you we'd keep in touch and thought you might like to see your mysterious Harlan Hawkins in person."

Gabby was amazed that the FBI was actually living up to its promise to cooperate, to keep them in the loop. To invite them here, like this, she knew was unusual, if not unheard of. But she also knew that Dimitri and Upchurch would not be here had she had not shared their long-shot suspicions about Hawkins. They or their bosses must now have felt some ethical obligation toward them.

"He's inside the bar?" she said.

"Yeah. He got here about forty-five minutes ago."

"You've had him under surveillance?"

"Yes," Dimitri said. "Since we talked to you in the office."

"No kidding?" Knowles said. "And that's legal?"

"We wouldn't be here if it wasn't," Upchurch replied testily.

"Then you must know something we don't know," Gabby said.

"Not really, but we thought your theory was interesting enough to pursue. We figured there wasn't much to lose except a few wasted days."

Zach said, "So you've seen him now and have pictures of him. Does he look like this guy, Overton?"

"Certainly not exactly like the old pictures of him," Upchurch said. "But there is a resemblance according to our guy in New York who covered the old case and who's seen our surveillance footage. Height, stature, bearing, that kind of thing. No slam dunk, but enough to keep us interested."

"So what are we doing now?" Gabby asked.

Dimitri turned his seat. "We've got one of our guys inside, sitting at the bar, watching."

"And?" Knowles's question hung in the air.

"For the first half hour, Hawkins was by himself, sipping on a bottle of beer," Upchurch said. "And then another guy joined him, and they're now in deep conversation."

Gabby asked, "What other guy?"

"We don't know yet. We're running his plates as we speak."

JEREMY HIGGINS, THE RE/MAX agent, was in the midst of apologizing to Hawkins for the leak on the possible house sale. "My assistant, Nancy, is really sorry she screwed up, but I can't fire the young woman for doing something she didn't know was wrong at the time. I told her she has to be more discreet in the future, but I didn't want to make too big a deal out of it or she'd think something really *was* odd. You understand?"

"I understand that *you* screwed up, not her," Hawkins said, not hiding his anger. "I swore you to secrecy, yet you allowed the cat to get out of the bag. And now Anita's asking questions."

Higgins spread his hands. "So what can I do?"

"You can get me a goddamned appraisal, that's what. And soon!"

Higgins sat back, feeling again—as he had earlier at the house—a real sense of unease in dealing with this man. It was not only the virulence in his voice, but the piercing look in his eyes. There was something fearsome about him, not physically, and not exactly sinister, but unsettling at best. Not a man to be messed with.

"I've almost finished the analysis," he said, "and I can give you a preliminary estimate, if you'd like."

"Go."

"A million-three to a million-four, for a quick sale. Probably more if you could wait and let the word get around."

"Do you know of anyone who would pay that kind of money, quickly and quietly, and give Anita time to find something else?"

Higgins thought for a moment. "I might," feeling even more ill at ease.

"OK. So put your feelers out, but with absolute discretion. Understand?"

"I understand, but I'm still confused. Do you actually plan to sell the house and move without your wife's knowledge? Or approval?"

"You're asking personal questions, but, yes, without her immediate knowledge or approval. She can join me later if she chooses."

Higgins pressed on. "So is this a divorce we're talking about?"

"That's not really any of your business, is it?"

"Then I'm not sure about this, Mr. Hawkins. You may have the legal right to do what you're doing, and I may have the legal right to assist you. But isn't there some kind of ethical question here? Moral question? For me, at least?"

"I don't see why. I own the house, free and clear. Anita has no legal stake in it, and it is up to me, not you, to make things right for her and the children."

Higgins shrugged and got up to leave. "All right. I'll make the inquiries and get back to you as soon as possible. But I have to tell you, I'm not comfortable in doing it."

"You don't have to be. Just find me a buyer."

BY THE TIME HIGGINS emerged from the bar, his license plates had told those in the FBI car who he was.

"What's he talking to a Realtor for?" Gabby asked.

"A wild guess," Dimitri said, slyly. "Like maybe he plans to sell his house?"

"And plans to get out of town fast, like they say in the movies," Zach offered.

At they watched Higgins get into his car, Dimitri's cell sounded. He listened for a moment, then turned back to them. "Our guy inside said as soon as the other guy left, Hawkins got up and headed for the men's room carrying his beer bottle with him, discreetly wiping it off with his napkin as he went. And came back without it."

"Which means what?" Knowles said.

Upchurch replied, "Either that he's extremely fastidious or that he doesn't like to leave fingerprints behind."

At that moment Hawkins emerged from the bar and walked toward his Lexus, passing not that far from their own car, giving Gabby, Zach, and Knowles their first glimpse of the man. He was maybe five feet ten or eleven, slight of build, with thinning gray hair and facial features that had a stretched, leathery look—as if he'd had one too many Botox treatments. Not ugly by any means, but slightly strange.

Before getting into his car, he stopped for a moment and looked around, including a glance in their direction. Then he slipped behind the wheel and drove off.

"You think he saw us?" Gabby said, leaning back in the seat.

"Our car, maybe, but not us," Dimitri said. "Not with the darkened windows. But he did seem to be checking things out."

"So what do you think?" Knowles asked.

"I think we're going to keep watching him," Upchurch said.

Zach asked, "That's all?"

"We may want to chat with his Realtor friend, but we can't do much more for now. Not until we have probable cause to question him." Then, "But I will say this. I think your instincts, as improbable as they may have seemed at the time, may be on target."

Gabby's dad was once again on her shoulder, whispering, *"See, Gabs."*

HAWKINS WAS NO MORE than five minutes from the bar before he was on his phone talking to his Ponzi partner and protector, Leonard Jenkins, recapping his conversation with his Realtor. "He's going to try to find me a buyer as quick as he can, but I may not be able to wait even that long."

"Why? What are you talking about?" Jenkins said.

"First of all, I don't really trust the guy. Not only did he allow those rumors to get to Anita, but he also has some ethical concerns over my plans and clearly doesn't approve of them."

"Can you blame him? Knowing that you're ready to up and leave your wife and kids? Jesus, Harlan ... "

"I know, but it wasn't only that. There were a couple of other strange things. You know how paranoid I can get ... "

"Do I ever."

"Well, the bar wasn't that crowded and there was this guy, kinda well dressed, sitting at the bar. By himself, apparently waiting for nobody. Just sitting there, sippin' some kind of soft drink, supposedly watching SportsCenter on the TV above the bar."

"So?"

"You know how many FBI guys I saw when I was arrested and booked in New York? When I was in and out of court?

Dozens, probably. You've seen enough of them, yourself. They've got a certain look about them, and this guy in the bar had that kind of look. Only he tried hard not to. It could be my imagination ... but I'm telling you, he just sat there. Using his phone once or twice, doing his best to ignore me."

"C'mon, you see FBI shadows everywhere."

"Hear me out. There was also a big black sedan parked on the other side of the lot. Maybe a Crown Vic. Dark windows ... "

"Antennas?"

"Not that I could see, no."

"Then forget it. Dark sedans are a dime a dozen, and I don't think you'll find an FBI squad without a cluster of antennas sticking out of the roof or trunk."

"You may be right, but I don't want to fiddle-fart around. I gotta trust my instincts and get the hell out of here as soon as I can."

"OK, OK," Jenkins said. "So what can I do?"

"Get me a new life. You know the drill. New name, new IDs, new Social Security number, new passport. You've done it before. Do it again."

"That'll take some time. And money. You know that."

"I don't have a lot of time. And don't worry about the money. Just get on it."

Forty-Two

As Linda expected, a State Patrol squad car and one from the sheriff's office were parked at the campground as she and Jocko drove up in his old pickup. Two officers were across the way, standing where Jessup's tent had once stood, talking to the pop-up-camper lady Linda had spoken to a few hours earlier.

"You're going to be OK?" Jocko asked as they got out of the truck. "Want me to stick around until your boss gets here?"

"No, please, I'll be fine."

Glancing over her shoulder, he said, "If you show me where he threw your phone and keys, maybe I can get the trunk open and fix that flat tire of yours before I go."

"Thanks, but I wouldn't do that. The cops may want to look for the keys themselves for possible fingerprints or whatever."

"You're probably right, but here," taking a map out of his back pocket, "in case they're wondering, this'll show them the exact spot where I picked you up. See that little x? May help them trace where the guy was headed. And if they have any questions, they can call me. My number's right there on the map."

"You've been wonderful, Jocko. I can't thank you enough."

Before he could get back into the pickup, Linda stopped him and gave him a hug and a quick kiss on the cheek. "Thank your wife, too," she said. "And I'll be back in touch." With that, he smiled, touched his cheek where the kiss had landed, tipped his weather-beaten old hat, and was off.

As he pulled away, the two officers approached and quickly introduced themselves: Sergeant Todd Richardson, the state trooper, and Deputy Eric Warner, both buttoned up in their starched and pressed uniforms with their Smokey Bear hats.

"You're Linda Wilkins, right?" Richardson said.

"That's right."

"And you called the sheriff's office."

"Right again. I told them what happened and gave them a description of Jessup and his bike's license plate number."

"We appreciate that. Everybody in the state is looking for him."

"Good," she said. "I hope you get him soon."

"And you're OK?" Richardson asked.

"Pretty much, except for this," showing him her bruised elbow and then pointing. "My car keys and busted iPhone are out there in the weeds somewhere, where he threw them."

"He punctured your tire, too?"

"Yeah. Probably with the switchblade he showed me."

The deputy, Warner, asked, "And you're sure this guy is Jessup?"

"Of course. He even admitted who he was. And you must know that there are warrants out for him both in Minneapolis and California and that he's also a suspect in the Nestoga bank robbery."

"We do know," Richardson said. "The FBI is on the way now to talk to you. But in the meantime, tell us what happened." They led her to a picnic table about twenty feet away. She took a seat and leaned back, starting at the beginning of her search and ending with today's encounter and all that followed.

"So how do you think he knew you were looking for him?" Warner asked.

"I'm not sure, but I know he saw the Channel 7 decal on the back window of my car. Which was stupid of me to have there. That, and I guess I don't I look much like a camper."

"Well, you're a brave and lucky young lady," Richardson said. "I'll give you that."

"I know."

"And now he's facing a kidnapping charge to go along with everything else."

"I guess so, but he doesn't seem to care."

WITH HIS ALMOST TWO-HOUR head start, Jessup had made it safely across the border into Wisconsin where he thought it might take longer for local law enforcement to get word of his campground escapade, allowing him more time to figure out his next move.

With his satchel of bank loot, he checked into a small, dingy motel, Maynards, on the outskirts of River Falls, a small college town about thirty-five miles from the Twin Cities, which he hoped was still large enough and populated with enough young people to give him cover. But even with that, he knew his time was limited, that within hours, no more than a day or two, the search for him would cross the border—just as he had.

Once he'd checked in and paid cash in advance for three days, he asked the motel clerk (her name tag said Colleen) if there was someplace nearby where he could rent a car. "There's an Avis up the road in Hudson," she said, "but here in town you might try the Ford dealer. I hear he rents cars sometimes. I can give you directions."

"Good," he said. "I'll try that. And if it works out, would it be OK if I left my bike here while I'm gone for a day or two? I could park it alongside the motel, out of the way, covered with a tarp. I'd leave my keys with you for, you know, insurance."

She looked puzzled and hesitant. "Sure, I guess so. But why do you need a car when you have the bike?"

"I've got a job interview across the river in Hastings, and I need to, you know, dress up and look good. Make a good impression. And that's not easy riding up on a Harley."

She laughed. "I suppose that's right."

"And I'm also going to need some new clothes," he said.

"That's easy. There are several clothing stores on the main street. Just follow the highway into town. You can't miss 'em."

He glanced at her left hand. No ring. "I appreciate the help," he said, putting on the charm, "and maybe … if I do land that new job, you might let me take you out for a drink to celebrate."

She blushed. "That'd be nice, but you'd have to talk to my boyfriend first. He might not approve."

"Yeah, well, you win some, you lose some," he replied, with a smile.

BY THE TIME BARCLAY finally found his way to the campground, the FBI and the State Patrol troopers had come and gone. They'd left a sheriff's deputy to search for Linda's phone and keys, and—after he'd found them—to fix her flat tire.

But now he was gone as well, leaving her sitting alone on the bench when Barclay walked up. She looked exhausted, barely glancing up as he sat down next to her. "Hey," he said, handing her a bottle of water and a pastry he had bought on his way there. "I thought you might be a little thirsty and hungry by now."

"Thanks," she said, taking the bottle and nearly draining it. It seemed to revive her.

"You want to talk?" he asked.

"Not really. I'm kind of talked out."

"OK. We can save that for tomorrow. Or whenever. I just want to make sure you're OK."

"I will be. I just need a little time. I've told the cops and the FBI everything."

"Good. I'll drive you home in your car and have someone come and get mine later."

"You don't need to do that," she said. "I got here, I can get home."

"You're sure?"

"Yes, but thanks for the offer. And thanks for coming all of this way, for nothing, I guess. That was good of you. And I need to apologize. I shouldn't have done what I did without telling you, keeping in touch. You're the boss. I'm an intern. It was kind of stupid."

"You *did* tell me. Way back when. I just didn't think you'd do it and never thought to ask again."

As she took a bite of the pastry, she said, "One other thing. Maybe I shouldn't say this, but Jessup didn't strike me as the devil he's said to be. As I told you on the phone, he could have hurt me far worse than he did. I think he's a very troubled guy, who I have no doubt is a great danger to Gabby, but he may be a greater danger to himself. With the stalking, the bank robbery and this, he could go to prison for the rest of his life. But as I told the cops, he doesn't seem to care. He just wants to find Gabby … and do whatever … "

"That's what makes him a sociopath," Barclay said. "He can be a charmer one minute, a potential killer the next. Have no sympathy for him, please. I truly believe Gabby would be dead or severely injured by now if we'd given him half a chance. And the fact that he's still on the loose, with absolutely nothing to lose, scares the living hell out of me."

"You're right, I know," she said. "But, it is funny, even after that short time with him, I can see how Gabby might have been fooled by him in the beginning. Before he turned violent."

Barclay smiled. "Maybe understanding how that could happen will help you sometime in the future."

As they split and went their separate ways. Barclay got a call from Gabby, who was on her way back to the station with Zach and Knowles, and who had just retrieved his messages and the earlier one from Linda. As soon as he began to tell her what had happened at the campground, she put her phone on speaker. "Keep going," she said, "we're all listening now."

It took him more than ten minutes to tell the story, and when he finally finished, he said, "I just left Linda a few minutes ago. She's on her way home now."

Gabby couldn't believe what she'd heard. "And she's OK?"

"Exhausted and still a little scared, I think, but, basically, OK. It 's been a pretty full day for her—facing off with Jessup and everything that followed. I was surprised she was still awake and alert when I got to her."

Knowles said, "Did you hire her on the spot?"

Barclay laughed. "I thought we should probably wait until she finishes college. But I suspect she could have a future with us, if she wants it."

"I can hardly wait to see and talk to her," Gabby said.

"You may have to wait. I told her to take a few days off. And I want to get together with her parents, too. I suspect they won't be too happy about all of this."

Zach cut in. "So what happened with Jessup?"

"Nobody knows," Barclay said. "The cops have his description and plate number, and there's a statewide alert out for him, but as far as I know, he's still at large. He told Linda that all he's wanted to do is talk to you, Gabby, but that he can't get near you. Blames you for costing him his job and his friends … his life, basically. He's crazy, Gabby."

"And he knows the world is closing in on him," she said.

"That's true. Which means we have to man the barricades, even more than we have. There's no telling what he might try. Or when. As he told Linda, he has little to lose."

Zach, who was sitting next to Gabby in the front seat, could see a small shiver ripple across her shoulders.

Forty-Three

Jerry Higgins was at his desk, back to the door, staring out the office window, pondering his situation, when there was a rap at the door. Nancy, his assistant, was standing there, a flustered look on her face. "You've got visitors," she said, glancing over her shoulder.

"Yeah? Who?" Irritation in his voice.

"The FBI," she said, with another look behind her.

He spun in his chair. "You're kidding?"

She shook her head. "No. They showed me their credentials."

He got up, straightened his tie, and pushed the papers that were on his desk into a drawer, feeling a sudden tightening in his chest. "OK, show 'em in, I guess."

She stepped back and motioned to the two men in the reception area.

They walked into the office, their billfolds still open, revealing their IDs. "Thanks for seeing us," one of them said. "I'm Special Agent Roger Dimitri and this is my partner, Nathan Upchurch. Do you have a few minutes?"

"Do I have a choice?" Higgins said, with half a laugh. "I've never met FBI guys before."

"We're harmless," Upchurch said, with a chuckle. "We just want to talk. Mind if we have a seat?"

350 | RON HANDBERG

"Of course not," he said, trying to maintain his cool. "Be my guests."

For a moment, there was an awkward silence. Then, Higgins said, "Can I get you anything? Coffee? Water?"

"No, thanks," Dimitri replied. "We're fine."

"Then maybe I should shut the door."

"I'll get it," Upchurch said, moving to the door and then back to his seat.

"So what can I possibly do for the FBI?" Higgins asked, although he knew without really knowing.

"We'd like to talk to you about one of your clients," Dimitri said. "Harlan Hawkins."

"Really?" He asked, as though he was surprised. "What about him?"

Upchurch continued. "That's what we'd like to know. What about him?"

Higgins got up and went to stand by the window. "You've obviously caught me by surprise, and I'm not sure what's appropriate here, whether I have any obligation or right to discuss one of my clients with the FBI. Or anyone else, for that matter."

"You're not a doctor, lawyer. or a priest, Mr. Higgins," Dimitri said. "There's nothing to prevent you from talking to us and telling us what you're doing for him."

"But why should I?" Higgins asked.

"Because," Upchurch said, "you're a good citizen and because he's a person of interest to us. That's all we can really tell you."

"Maybe I should call my attorney."

"Feel free," Dimitri replied, "but I suspect he'll tell you what we're telling you ... that you have an obligation to answer our questions."

Higgins sat back in his chair, feeling a sudden chill. "OK then, if you say so. What do you want to know?"

"Everything," Upchurch said.

Higgins took a deep breath. "Well, I don't have much to tell you. I just don't know that much about him. He's a very private man. And I haven't made much of an effort to learn more than he's been willing to tell me."

"Why is that?"

"Because he's made it clear he wants it that way."

"Go on."

Higgins could see they weren't going away, so, despite his misgivings, he began with his first contact with Hawkins and ended with his demand of the day before that he find a buyer … and quickly. "I told him I felt very uncomfortable with what he was asking, but he's been very insistent."

"He plans to leave his wife and kids?" Dimitri said. "Just like that?"

"I know. It's unbelievable. But that's what he says."

"Have you found a buyer for him?"

"No, not yet. But I have a couple of leads. He has a very saleable home, and the price I've suggested is very reasonable."

Dimitri got out of his chair. "Do you mind leaving us alone for a few minutes?"

"Of course not," he said, and headed for the door, closing it behind him.

Nancy was waiting at the reception desk, her eyes wide. "What in the world is going on?"

"Don't ask."

"Are you in some kind of trouble?"

"No, no. Relax. They just have some questions."

"About what?"

"I can't say. So let's leave it at that."

Ten minutes later, the door reopened and he went back in.

"We've found a buyer for the Hawkins house," Dimitri told him once they were all seated again.

"What? Who?"

"The Federal Government. We're always looking for bargains."

"You're not serious," Higgins said.

"Oh, yes we are. Within a couple of days, we'll provide you with a buyer. An upstanding citizen with impeccable finances and a background that will withstand the most meticulous scrutiny."

"An FBI plant," Higgins ventured.

"Correct. He will insist on seeing the house and meeting Hawkins personally before closing on the transaction. You will be responsible for seeing that happens."

"You can't ask me to do that," Higgins said.

"Why not?" Upchurch said, leaning in.

"Because it would violate a trust ... and ... "

"And?"

"I should have said this before ... because ... I think Mr. Hawkins could be dangerous."

Dimitri, looking surprised: "What makes you say that?"

"His demeanor, I guess. It may be my imagination, but I sense something threatening about him. I can't really describe it, but he gives me the willies."

"You would have no reason to worry," Upchurch told him. "We'd see to that."

"Do I have a choice in this?"

"Of course, but if you agree, you would be doing your government a great service."

"Before I do, you have to tell me what he's done to gain the FBI's interest? I think I deserve to know that."

Dimitri and Upchurch exchanged glances. Finally, Upchurch said, "We're not sure, but there is a strong possibility that he is a federal fugitive who has been on the run for a number of years. We need your help to determine the truth."

"My God," Higgins muttered.

"So will we have your cooperation?" Dimitri asked.

"You have to give me some time to think. To talk to my wife. Maybe my attorney."

"Not your attorney, please," Upchurch said. "What we've

told you is extremely confidential, and any leak could jeopardize our investigation. You have to give us your word on that."

Higgins said nothing, staring into space. Finally he said, "OK. Give me a call in the morning."

Both men got up. "One more thing," Dimitri said. "We'll need the phone number you use to contact Hawkins."

Higgins looked at his cell, wrote down a number, and gave it to them.

"We'll wait to hear from you," Upchurch said, "but we hope you don't disappoint us … and your country."

With that, they were gone, leaving Higgins staring out the window, now with the knowledge that he had just experienced a life-changing event.

AN HOUR LATER, the two agents were in the Channel 7 conference room with Gabby, Zach, and Knowles, reporting on their meeting with Higgins. "He's going to let us know in the morning," Upchurch said, "but I think he may cooperate. If not, we may have to exert a little more pressure. He's clearly afraid of getting involved, but he's also afraid of Hawkins himself."

"No kidding," Gabby said.

"He said he feels threatened by the guy," Dimitri said. "Which is one of the reasons he's felt compelled to continue dealing with him. That plus the promise of a nice commission on a million-dollar house."

"So what do you hope to accomplish with the plant?" Knowles asked.

"To get a closeup look at the guy, for one thing," Upchurch said. "See if he might reveal something about himself that we don't already know. Maybe find a way to lift a set of prints, on one of the documents or whatever. We'll play it by ear, as they say."

"The FBI already has somebody like this in-house?" Zach asked.

354 | RON HANDBERG

Dimitri replied, "We're working on it. Our IT guys are creating a deep profile on the net, making up a mythical man whose background should survive the closest scrutiny by Hawkins or anyone else."

"We also have at least one of Hawkins's phone numbers," Upchurch said. "And we're hoping we develop enough credible suspicions to persuade a judge into letting us do a wiretap. We'll have to see."

"One other bit of news," Dimitri told them. "Interpol finally got back to us on the dead guy in the house."

"With an ID?" Gabby said, hopefully.

"No, we're not that lucky. But they did tell us that the tattoo on the guy's ankle is probably the symbol of a Russian soccer team, based in St. Petersburg."

"He's Russian?" Knowles said.

"Apparently. Interpol's trying to find out more, but the Russians aren't exactly a font of information. Whoever he is, he must have gotten into the country illegally sometime in the past, because—as you know—his fingerprints and DNA don't show up in any of our records."

Gabby said, "I have another question."

"Go ahead," Upchurch replied.

"You told us at our first meeting that three of Hawkins' co-conspirators in the Ponzi scheme got five to seven years in prison, right?"

"Right."

"Which would mean they'd be back out on the street by now. And probably have been for several years."

Upchurch again: "So?"

"What do we know about them? Where they are? What they're doing?"

"We'd have to ask our guys in New York. But why?"

"Just this. For weeks now, we've all been trying to figure out why Hawkins or one of his cronies would have killed the guy in the basement, if they did. Why would he be a threat to them? Then I started thinking … what if one or more of those co-conspirators emerged from prison more than a little pissed off that Hawkins, or Overton, got away scot-free with millions of dollars, leaving him, or them, broke, with nothing but prison shirts on his or their backs?"

There was silence around the table.

"What if, and I mean *if*, they somehow did a better job than the FBI in discovering where Hawkins had disappeared to? Who knows how, but maybe they did. And maybe they sent one of their goons, i.e., the guy in the basement, some member of the Russian Mafia, to try and collect some of Hawkins's ill-gotten gains? Some payback. And what if Hawkins found the goon before the goon found Hawkins?"

"As we learn once again, you've got quite an imagination," Dimitri said, but with a touch of admiration in his voice.

"I'm sure there are other explanations," she said. "Maybe he was one of Hawkins's own goons, like the guy in Fridley, who got on the wrong side of him, who somehow became a threat. But I don't think we can forget the other possibility, unlikely as it may be."

"We'll talk to New York and find out what became of those other three," Upchurch said. "And get back to you."

As they started to get up to leave, Knowles said, "I have one other question. "Do your bosses downtown know how closely you're working with us on this?"

Dimitri replied, "Of course. We wouldn't be here if they didn't. They're not exactly comfortable with the situation, nor are we, but they also know we wouldn't be where we are in this investigation without your leads. So they've told us to keep you with us every step of the way. And that's a promise."

Forty-Four

Gabby and Zach were back at the apartment that night when she got a call from Detective John Philips, whom she had not seen or talked to since the John Doe funeral. "I've got good news and bad news," he told her once they'd exchanged greetings. "The good news first, OK?"

"Good," she replied.

"We found out where Jessup is . . . or was."

"Yes!" she cried out. "Where?"

"In River Falls, across the river in Wisconsin."

Gabby knew it was a college town, but not much more. "Is he still there?"

"I don't know. That's the bad news. I only know that he's rented a car and could be anywhere, I suppose."

She sank back into her chair. "Crap. But how did you find him?"

"Remember the motel he stayed at in Richfield? The one your intern discovered? Well, I stopped by there later and got a copy of the credit card he used to register. And we've had it on the watch list, if you will, ever since. We got a call a few hours ago from Visa, telling us the card was used to rent a car from a Ford dealer in River Falls. It's the first time he's used the card since that motel."

"Have you told the FBI guys?"

"Of course. I just got off the phone with one of them, Dimitri. He told me the two agents who were at the campground with Linda will be heading to River Falls now. They've got jurisdiction across state lines, which I don't have."

"Did Dimitri tell you the story of Linda and Jessup at the campground?"

"Yes, briefly. And I'm glad she's OK. She sounds like a young Gabby."

"Only smarter with a lot more courage."

"Don't sell yourself short," Philips replied.

"So if he's got a rental, you must know what he's driving."

"A used Ford Fusion with Wisconsin plates. But if he's as smart as we think he is, and as worried, he may have changed the plates by now ..."

"What do you mean?"

"Simple. All you need is a screwdriver. Find a car in some crowded parking lot and trade plates. You can do it in about three minutes ... and it may take the owner of the other car days before he notices what's happened."

Gabby said, "So you think he might be gone by now."

"Probably, but we may learn more from the FBI guys later tonight or in the morning."

"That's great work, John."

"Don't thank me, thank your intern. She's the one who found the motel ... and led me to the credit card."

"I will thank her," Gabby said, "First chance I get."

Just as she put down the phone, Zach emerged from the bathroom, fresh from a shower, with a towel wrapped around his waist. After hearing what Philips had just told her, he thought for a moment, then said, "We should call Barclay right away. Let him know what's happening."

"OK, but what can he do?" she said.

"Maybe nothing, but he should know what we know."

Gabby settled back on the couch. "Is this ever going to end?" she asked, more to herself than Zach.

"Soon, I think. He must know he can't stay on the run forever. And hopefully we'll be ready for him whenever he does decide to end it."

BARCLAY HAD JUST finished dinner when he got the call from Gabby. "Philips says the FBI is in River Falls now, and may know more later tonight or tomorrow."

"Good," he replied. "I think we should meet in the morning, and decide what to do next. I've got a couple of ideas."

"Like?"

"Like I'll tell you in the morning. Meantime, you should try to get some rest."

"Thanks. I'll try."

BY THIS TIME, the two FBI agents had met with the owner of the Ford dealership who learned—much to his chagrin—that his rental car was now in the hands of a fugitive who had robbed a bank, among other things. "I had no idea," he told the agents. "He seemed like a very nice young man who said he was going to use the car on a job interview. And that he'd have it back the next day."

"I wouldn't count on that," one of the agents told him. "You might want to give your insurance company a call."

They also visited three other motels in River Falls before finding the right one. But here, too, Colleen, the clerk, could provide little helpful information, except that his motorcycle was parked next to the motel. A search of his room also proved fruitless. It was as though he had never set foot in the place.

The clothing stores downtown that Colleen said he might have visited were now closed for the night and would be checked the next day. But the agents doubted they would provide anything very useful. Nor would Colleen's updated description of Jessup help much, since it was little different from the one Linda had given them at the campground.

So, once they'd confiscated his motorcycle, using the keys Jessup had left at the motel, they headed back for the Twin Cities, no wiser now than before on the whereabouts of their elusive prey.

When Gabby, Zach and Knowles walked into Barclay's office the next morning, she could not remember him looking more serious, more somber. "Grab some chairs," he said, and then introduced a man sitting beside him. "This is John Jacobs, or J.J., as we call him. You've not met him before, but he's the former St. Paul cop I told you about, the one I enlisted to keep an eye out for Jessup in your neighborhood."

"I'm the guy who found him, then lost him," J.J. said as he unfolded himself from his chair and shook hands with each of them. "Nice to meet you all," with a drawl, "although I kind of feel like I already know you. From a distance, I mean."

From Barclay's earlier description, Gabby knew J.J. was close to eighty, but she never would have guessed it by looking at him. Tall, slender, and muscled, with no facial wrinkles and without an ounce of fat that she could see.

Barclay went on. "After your call last night, Gabby, I called J.J. and asked him to be here this morning. In my gut, I think we've reached a critical point with Jessup. I know I've said that before, but with this latest move, abandoning his bike and grabbing a car, I think he's become even more desperate ... that he's either going to take off and hightail it back to California or he's going to finally make good on his threats. And my gut tells me he's going to do the latter, not the former."

Zach interrupted. "I agree. I told Gabby the same thing last night."

Back to Barclay. "Best case, we can hope the FBI or the local cops get him before he does anything, but I'm not ready to count on that. He's too smart, too slippery. So I think we have to be even more prepared for whatever might be coming."

"I don't disagree, but what more can we do?" Gabby asked.

"That's why J.J. is here. After I got the hell beat out of me in that old cold case you all know about, J.J. stepped in and became my bodyguard, if you will. He was with me every minute, day and night, making sure I stayed safe." Looking at Gabby and Zach, he said, "I plan to have him do the same for you two."

Zach came out of his chair. "With all due respect to Mr. Jacobs, no fucking way!"

"Sit down, Zach!" Barclay snapped. "And listen. This is not your decision. As your employer, I am ultimately responsible for your well-being on the job. I didn't ask for this and neither did you. But I'm not going to look back after you've been bushwhacked by this weirdo and know that I could have done something more.

"J.J is an experienced cop. He's been in more dangerous situations than you have hairs on your head. He's licensed to carry a gun and knows how to use it. He's not going to be in your way, he's not going to interfere with your jobs, but he's going to do his best to keep you safe and sound. And I trust him."

Zach sat back, still simmering, as Gabby asked, calmly, "So how will this work?"

"We still have to figure out the details, but I've set aside a desk for J.J. next to the assignment desk and will give him some busywork to do while he's there. When you leave, he'll go with you, riding in the back seat of the car."

"Jesus Christ," Zach muttered.

"And while I hate to ask this, Zach, I will anyway. We'd like to impose on you and temporarily move a cot into your living room, set up some room dividers, and create a small bedroom for J.J. He assures me he doesn't snore and will absolutely respect your privacy. And," with a smile, "not eat you out of house and home."

Zach started to protest again, but Gabby poked him in the

arm. "Lighten up. He'll be one more person to cuddle your damn dog."

"He's more your dog than mine, anyway, but OK. I still think you're going way overboard, but forget about setting up the bedroom in the living room. We can move the cot into Gabby's room, and I'll sleep there. J.J. can take my room. It'll be a hell of a lot easier, if it's OK with Gabby."

"Fine with me," she replied with a small grin she hoped no one else would notice, knowing the cot would likely never be used.

"Good," Barclay said. "How about you, J.J.?"

"Whatever. Let's just hope the arrangement doesn't last too long."

Before they got up to leave, Knowles briefed Barclay on what the FBI's Dimitri and Upchurch had told them about their meeting with the Realtor, Higgins. "They think he's going to arrange a meeting between an FBI 'buyer' and Hawkins … and that they also hope to get permission for a wiretap. Sounds like they're getting close."

"That's great," Barclay said. "But let's not forget that our first concern is Jessup."

Forty-Five

Once Realtor Higgins had agreed to the FBI plan, it took two days for Dimitri and Upchurch to arrange for a phantom buyer for Hawkins's house—another FBI agent from the Omaha office whose personal and financial credentials were carefully crafted and tailored to withstand the most scrupulous of background checks by Hawkins.

During those two days, Higgins had received three calls from Hawkins, demanding to know what progress had been made in finding a buyer. Higgins had put him off, telling him he had a couple of solid leads and hoped to have a firm offer within a day or two and that he'd get back to him as soon as possible.

All of those calls had been monitored by the FBI, which had managed to get permission for the wiretap from a somewhat reluctant but friendly federal judge, who was finally persuaded by the Fed's belief that Hawkins was not only a long-sought-after white-collar criminal, but also a potential murderer.

With one exception, those calls to Higgins were the only ones made from Hawkins's cell phone. All other calls were either from his home or from his office, none of which raised any suspicions. The exception was to a man the FBI was able to identify as Leonard Jenkins, who worked for one of the larger downtown brokerage firms. The conversation was brief but guarded, which—when Dimitri later heard it—gave him pause.

Hawkins: *I'm moving ahead with my plans as quickly as possible. I expect something may develop in the next few days.*

Jenkins: *What do you mean?*

Hawkins: *Just what we've talked about.*

Jenkins: *You're sure?*

Hawkins: *Yes. Have you done what I asked?*

Jenkins, hesitating: *Yes, but it's taking more time than I thought.*

Hawkins: *I don't have more time. Get it done.*

Dimitri's background check on Jenkins proved interesting. While he had no criminal record and no apparent connection with either Diabetrics or Zimtronics, it did show that he had worked in New York as a broker during the same years Hawkins was there, and that he had moved to Minnesota at approximately the same time as Hawkins.

On first glance, there was no evidence that they'd known one another in New York. But there was also no evidence that they hadn't. And it had to be more than a coincidence that they had come to the state at the same time and were now apparently more than mere acquaintances. Dimitri decided to check further with his colleagues in New York and to do a more thorough check on Jenkins's time in Minnesota.

The truth was, Jenkins had been scrambling. The craftsmen he had used in New York a dozen or more years before to create Hawkins's false identity were now out of business, which left him frantically searching for someone who could be trusted and who could do the job quickly. Finally, a former associate in New York, one Tony Poplin, told him there was an ex-con now living in suburban Minneapolis, who'd recently been released from the federal prison in Sandstone, Minnesota, after serving three years on a counterfeiting conviction.

Poplin told Jenkins, "He's a first-class forger and has all the equipment he needs to create the documents you want. Just get him the new information, you know, new name, pictures, Social Security numbers, and all the rest, and he'll make you everything you need. Driver's license, passport, whatever. It may take him a few days, but he'll do topnotch work."

""What's this guy's name?" Jenkins asked. "And if he's so good, how'd he get caught?"

"His name's Chicki Mestaso, and he got caught because his bimbo of a wife tried passing one of his phony hundreds at a neighborhood bakery, which probably hadn't seen a hundred dollar bill all year. The cops were there before she could get out the front door."

"So?"

"So he served his time and has since replenished all of his equipment, printers, scanners, and all of the new sophisticated shit. He'll do the job for you."

"And he can be trusted?"

"Once I tell him what you can do to people, it'll scare the hell out of him, and he'll toe the mark."

"How do I get in touch with him?"

"I'll have him get back to you."

"Your check will be in the mail."

"Thanks. I'll watch for it."

As THE FBI was doing its work, Gabby, Zach, and J.J. were settling into their new routine, and—to their surprise—it was working out remarkably well, both at the apartment and in the office. J.J.'s presence in the newsroom certainly did not go unnoticed, his mission there remaining a secret for all of two seconds. Everyone was aware that Gabby's stalker was still on the loose and word of his campground confrontation with Linda Wilkins was now also common knowledge.

Many in the newsroom remembered J.J. from the time he'd been there to protect Barclay, and they accepted the fact that he was now there to provide a similar service for Gabby and Zach. For all of them, really, since some still believed that Jessup might be crazy enough to invade the station in search of Gabby.

So, while they realized the sign on the station's doors said "NO GUNS ALLOWED," they were relieved to know that at least one gun *was* allowed, sitting in J.J.'s holster.

At the apartment, Barclay the poodle quickly had become J.J.'s best buddy, all but ignoring Zach and Gabby in favor of J.J.'s lap and bed. J.J. had never had a dog and was surprised—and delighted—that Barclay had so quickly befriended him. In all ways, J.J. kept to his pledge to respect the privacy of his hosts, trying as much as possible to be where they weren't in the hours they were at the apartment. He went to bed early and got up early, sharing meals and conversation when asked and when appropriate, but also keeping to himself as much as he could, giving them the alone time they deserved. He had a job to do, but was determined to do it as inconspicuously as possible.

The reality was they spent very little time at the apartment. He was amazed at the hours the two of them worked, doing what he wasn't exactly sure, except that they were involved in some kind of an investigation that he wasn't privy to. As for himself, he was mostly bored with the work Barclay had given him to do, updating newsroom files and such. But he was less bored than he would have been at home alone and was grateful to be doing something useful, in some ways, just like the old days.

HER VOICE, ON the phone, was more pleasant than Jessup remembered it. "Maynards Family Motel, your home away from home, Colleen speaking."

"Hey, Colleen, this is Craig Jessup. How's it going?"

There was a long pause … a pause that told him everything he needed to know.

Finally, "I can't speak to you," she said.

"Really? Why's that?"

"The FBI was here. Day before yesterday. They said you robbed a bank and kidnapped a woman."

"Don't believe everything you hear, Colleen."

"They took your bike, know you rented a car."

For someone who wasn't supposed to talk to him, she was saying a lot. But it was now clear that they had traced his credit card to the Ford dealer.

"That's too bad. I liked that bike."

"I have to hang up now."

"So you can call them?"

"Yes. They told me to if you called."

"That's fine, Colleen. Just tell them I'm in Montana, OK?"

While he hoped to be in Montana or beyond within a couple of days, he was right now on the top floor of the Mall of America parking ramp. He had been moving from floor to floor much of the day, stopping occasionally to venture inside to use the bathroom or to get a quick bite to eat. He felt relatively safe here—since thousands of people jammed the mall and its parking ramps every day, the crowds all but swallowing up any one individual. As Detective Philips had predicted, he had switched his license plates twice and was now actually living in another campground, this one near Shakopee in the southwest corner of the metro area, convinced that whoever was looking for him wouldn't think he'd risk staying at yet another campground. Time would tell, of course.

GABBY WAS AT HER computer, searching for information on soccer teams based in St. Petersburg, Russia, when she heard a smattering of applause ripple across the newsroom. Standing up, she could see Barclay leading Linda Wilkins across the way, stopping frequently to allow others to greet her or shake her hand.

Gabby quickly moved in that direction, intercepting them before they reached his office. When Linda saw her, she broke into a smile, and shyly accepted Gabby's hug. "You are a hero," Gabby said, stepping back, holding her shoulders at arms length. "I can't tell you how proud I am of you."

"Don't be, please," Linda replied, clearly embarrassed by the attention. "I was stupid to get myself into that situation. I should have known better."

"Bullcrap," Gabby said. "You did what good reporters are supposed to do. I'm just so glad you're OK."

"I know. I was lucky."

Barclay said, "C'mon into the office and give Gabby a briefing. She's been like a fidgety kid waiting to see you. And while you two talk, I'm going to try and find Mr. Ryan and tell him what's been happening."

He left them alone and, with Gabby's encouragement, Linda calmly retold her story from the beginning, concentrating on the brief time spent in Jessup's custody. Only then did she show some emotion. "I have to admit, I was scared to death, but I also have to tell you what I told Mr. Barclay, that despite what I knew about him, I could see what you might have seen in him when you first met. For as dangerous as I knew he was, there was a certain charm or gentleness about him. It's hard to describe, but deep down, I never really believed he would harm me. Mr. Barclay says that's what makes him a sociopath, and I guess that's true. But, still..."

"George is right," Gabby said, "and to prove it, I may sometime tell you my whole story. He can be two entirely different people, and it sounds like you saw a little of both. I'm just glad you came out of it OK, physically, at least. Are you all right otherwise?"

"Now I am, yes. My folks were angry, but they're better now, too."

"Good," Gabby said. "And I hope you're getting paid for all of the work you did."

Her face brightened. "Mr. Barclay made me count all of the hours I spent visiting the various campsites and the time I spent with Jessup and after. And he's paying me at the same rate as he pays you and the other reporters."

"You deserve no less," Gabby said.

"And he also told me to be sure to talk to him as I get near graduation."

"Just watch," Gabby laughed. "Before long, he'll be asking you to call him George."

Forty-Six

Despite his objections, Hawkins agreed to be at the house when Realtor Higgins brought his mock buying prospect to inspect it. "Why do I have to be there?" he had argued earlier. "Show it to him yourself. You know what I want."

"He wants to meet the owner," Higgins had said. "You can't blame him for that. You know the house, I don't. He doesn't want to deal with me."

So it was, finally, that Hawkins arranged a time for the showing when his wife and two kids were visiting Anita's mother across town.

"This better be good," he'd told Higgins. "I'm in no mood to fuck around."

The prospect was Shane Alexander, a.k.a. FBI agent Brian Johnson, who, upon meeting Hawkins, explained he was in the process of moving with his family from suburban Washington to the Twin Cities to take a new job with General Mills. Conservatively-clad in a gray suit, striped tie, and a button-down blue shirt with cuff-links, he appeared to be every bit the successful lawyer he pretended to be.

Hawkins thought he already knew all about him. Once Higgins had given him Alexander's name, he had done as thorough a check as possible with the Internet tools at hand, finding only the FBI-designed mythical biography: Forty-three years old, married to Marsha for fourteen years, with two kids, a girl and a boy, seven and eleven respectively. A Yale law graduate, an attorney with the Federal Trade Commission in DC for twelve years, in private practice in Baltimore before that. Plus a long list of other personal and professional details.

As they walked through the house, Hawkins asked, "So what are you going to do at General Mills?"

"Help them fight the cereal wars," Alexander replied. "Keep their competitors honest in their advertising, their nutrition claims, that kind of thing. I have some experience in trademark and patent litigation. Basically, I'll be there to help their legal team in any way I can."

"So when do you start?"

"In a month or so. But at this point, only the head of the legal department knows I'm coming. I'm replacing somebody on staff, so they're keeping my hiring hush-hush for now."

"You wouldn't mind if I called him, would you?" Hawkins asked. "You know, just to check on things?"

"Not at all. Just so it goes no further than him. I'll give you his name and number before I leave."

Dimitri and Upchurch had expected this question and had already prevailed upon the actual head of the General Mills legal department to cooperate if called upon, as a public service. They'd also made sure that Alexander was listed on the FTC roster in DC in case inquiries were made there. They knew there were possible loopholes in the plans, but their IT colleagues had done as much as they could to create Alexander's false identity in the two days they'd been given. Now, they could only hope for the best.

"This is a beautiful home," Alexander said as they moved from room to room. "Unusual style. Impeccable condition. My wife and kids will love it, I know. I hear it's in a terrific school district."

"That's true," Hawkins said, "although our children are in private schools."

"Really? Why's that?"

"It's what my wife preferred," he replied.

"So tell me about yourself," Alexander said. "Mr. Higgins has told me very little."

"Because there's very little to tell that you would need to know. I run a private investment firm managing our family assets. I'm selling the house because I have another business opportunity in Atlanta."

"Mr. Higgins did tell me that the house title is in your name alone. Is that right?"

"Yes. You'll only need my signature on a purchase agreement."

"I'd want my wife to see it before I sign anything, of course."

"Higgins will have to arrange that, but if possible, I'd like to have a tentative agreement with you before you leave today. There is another potential buyer Higgins is not aware of, who has approached me privately, but I would prefer to do business with you and not deny Higgins his fair commission."

Higgins stood off to one side, his mouth agape.

"How would that work?" Alexander asked.

"You're the lawyer. But I've drafted an agreement outlining what I believe is the agreed-upon sale price of $1.3 million, which would be valid unless your wife, upon her inspection, specifically rejects the agreement. The final purchase agreement would be signed, perhaps by my attorney acting on my behalf, and the money transferred to my specified account on the occasion of her acceptance. It also provides for a three-month closing date to allow my wife and children time to relocate."

"They're not coming with you?"

"That's a private matter that has no bearing on the agreement. As I told you, I have clear title."

Alexander was amazed. As an FBI agent, he was also an attorney, and had never heard of such a proposition. But his only interest was in leaving with a piece of paper with Hawkins's fingerprints on it.

"Could I see the agreement?" he said.

"Of course," Hawkins replied, handing the document to him.

Alexander studied it carefully, discreetly holding the paper by its edges. "This is very unusual," he finally said, "but as long as my wife has the final say, I see no problem in signing it. I love the house and I know she will, as well. I'd hate to see it go to someone else."

"Good. I've made three copies, one for each of us, and one for Higgins's files. I'll sign all three and give them to you for your signature. Higgins can initial all three as a witness."

With that, he took out a pen and began signing, handing the pen to Alexander for his signatures and then to Higgins for his initials. As instructed, Higgins used his own pen while Alexander surreptitiously tucked away the pen he'd been given.

If the ever-cautious Hawkins harbored any suspicion, he didn't show it. He even forgot to ask for the promised name of Alexander's would-be boss at General Mills. Instead, he looked relieved that the transaction had been completed and that he was one more step closer to a new life.

Outside, as they walked to Higgins's car, Alexander said, "Your country owes you its thanks."

"And a commission of about seventy-five grand," Higgins said.

Alexander laughed. "This sale will never go through. The agreement is bogus from the get-go. And, who knows? You might have another chance some day. If Hawkins is who we think he is, he'll be behind bars, not signing anything. And even if he is the rightful owner of the place, I think it will be successfully argued that he used Ponzi money to buy the house in the first place ... and that that money will go back to some of the people he screwed over.

"The only losers in all of this are his wife and kids. But I'm told they're pretty well-off in their own right."

"Don't tell that to the kids," Higgins said. "They're losing a father."

"I know, and that's sad. But they were bound to find out, sooner or later. Maybe it's better that they know now."

Higgins opened the car door. "Well, I'm glad I'm done with it. He still scares the hell out of me."

DIMITRI'S RESEARCH ON Leonard Jenkins had provided nothing surprising or more suspicious about the man: single, a model employee at his brokerage firm who lived in one of the plush high-rise condos in downtown Minneapolis. Still, Dimitri could not dismiss the strange call that Hawkins had made to Jenkins in the wiretap: Question: *Have you done what I've asked?* Answer: *Yes, but it's taking more time than I thought.* Response: *I don't have more time. Get it done.*

Although there clearly was not enough evidence to ask for yet another wiretap on *his* phones, but knowing there was little time to waste, Dimitri was able to persuade his boss—who was already under pressure from Washington to increase the FBI pursuit of white-collar criminals—to assign two teams to trail Jenkins for a couple of days.

It was a long shot, Dimitri knew, but one that he thought could be worth the effort.

Bingo!

It was on the second day of that surveillance, while Higgins and Alexander were inspecting Hawkins's home, that the team followed Jenkins to a modest house in suburban Brooklyn Center, a small home but with an oversized garage. Quickly checking, the leader of the surveillance team was able to learn the home belonged to one Edward "Chicki" Mestaso, a convicted counterfeiter released six months earlier from the Sandstone Federal Prison.

Parked down the street in a van with a Stanley's Plumbing logo on its side, the team was able to record Jenkins's entry and exit from the home, a package under his arm when he entered, no package under his arm when he left.

Calling for instructions, Dimitri ordered the team in the van to stay and maintain surveillance of the house while the second team, in an old Ford Escape, was to continue trailing Jenkins. "I'll be there as quick as I can," he told the team in the van, and to the other team, "Be careful; I just learned that Jenkins has a conceal-and-carry permit for a .45 automatic."

His next call was to Gabby. "You might want to bring your cameras out to Brooklyn Center," he said, giving her the address of the home. "We could be making an arrest that will be of interest to you. Come in a private car, not your station car, and park behind a van on the street, and do nothing until you get a signal from me. Understood?"

"Yes," Gabby said.

"One more thing. You can shoot your video of the suspect as we lead him past you, but you cannot interview him. Not this one or the others that follow."

"OK, but can you tell me more?"

"Not now. Later. And tell no one else, or you might screw things up."

"Gotcha," she replied.

It took Dimitri almost two hours to get there, in part because he had to await a search warrant from the same judge who had approved the wiretap, a judge who was now fully-informed on the progress of the case. When he did arrive, he and two other agents from the van, with backup from a Brooklyn Center squad car, quickly approached the house, covering both the front and back.

In the meantime, Gabby, Zach, and J.J., in Zach's old Nissan, were parked down the street, camera ready when summoned.

While Dimitri stood to one side of the front door, his gun hanging loosely by his side, another of the agents rapped loudly and pushed the doorbell button at the same time. Then he stepped aside. Within a minute, the door opened a crack. Dimitri said, "FBI. We have a search warrant. Open the door and show us your hands."

The door swung open, and Chicki Mestaso stood barefooted and bare-chested, pants drooping, an astonished look on his face, but with his hands held high. "What the fuck?"

"Move aside," Dimitri ordered as he pushed his way in, followed by the other agent. A woman with scrambled hair and a half-open robe stood to one side, clutching a young child by the shoulders. While the other agent escorted the woman and child into another room, Dimitri cuffed Chicki and sat him down. "You never learn, do you?" he said.

Chicki was traumatized. "I don't know what you're talking about."

"About the package that was delivered a couple of hours ago by somebody named Leonard Jenkins. Sound familiar?"

The other agent returned with the package in hand. "What d'ya know? Sitting on the kitchen table. And we didn't even have to search."

"I haven't even looked inside it," Chicki protested. "I don't know what this is all about."

"We'll soon find out, won't we?" Dimitri said, slitting open the package with his gloved hand and pulling out the contents, studying them. "Seems like a lot of information about somebody named Charles Whitehead. But with pictures of somebody we know as Harlan Hawkins."

"I don't know either of them," Chicki said.

"Really? Well, let's check that garage of yours. See what we can find that might help solve the puzzle."

Chicki's head sank into his chest. Then, "OK. I'll tell you what I know. But I haven't done anything yet. Haven't broken any goddamned laws. You can't arrest somebody for thinking about doing something, but not doing it."

"Oh, yes, Chicki, we can. Just watch and see."

At a signal from Dimitri, Gabby and Zach jumped out of the Nissan and walked quickly up the street, camera rolling, arriving just as Chicki emerged from the house, hands cuffed in front of him, with Dimitri holding one of his arms and another agent trailing behind. The traditional perp walk. J.J. stayed behind, watching from a distance.

On seeing the camera, Chicki screamed, "Is that TV? What are they doing here?"

"You're a star, Chicki," Dimitri said. "Wave and give 'em a big smile."

"Screw you and your mother, too," he shouted, turning his head away from the camera as he was led to the FBI car and placed in the back seat, profanely protesting all the way. While Zach continued to shoot, Dimitri pulled Gabby aside, quickly explaining who Chicki was. "We got him before he could get started on the documents and will be moving all of his equipment out of the garage as soon as we can."

Gabby said, "Can we stay to get that on video?"

"Sure. The truck should be here soon, and I'll let one of the agents know you're going to stick around."

"So are you going after Hawkins now?"

"Not yet. We have what we hope may be his fingerprints and will have him under surveillance, but we've got some other things to do first."

"Like what?"

"Like toast one of his colleagues. The one who made the arrangements with Chicki. But that will take a little time. And another search warrant."

"Can we be there when that goes down?" she asked.

"If possible, yes, but that could be a little trickier. I'm not sure where we'll make the bust. I'll try to keep in touch."

As Gabby glanced back at the car, all she could see was the back of Chicki's middle finger.

Forty-seven

Leonard Jenkins first suspected something was amiss when he tried to contact Chicki a day after he'd dropped off the package and got only his voice mail. Not once, but three times in the next three hours. The FBI agent stationed at the house was aware of the messages, having monitored the calls, and on the fourth one, instructed Chicki's wife to answer, with a script in hand. "I'm sorry, he's not here," she told Jenkins. "He was called out of town, up to Hibbing."

Jenkins was incredulous. "Hibbing? That's halfway to Canada."

"I know," she said, hesitating. "But his brother had a motorcycle accident. He's in the hospital in very serious condition."

"You've got to be kidding me. I told him to call me if anything came up. When will he be back?"

The woman looked at the agent and he mouthed "Soon."

"He should be back soon, maybe tomorrow," she said.

Jenkins persisted. "Do you know, did he start work on the package I dropped off?"

The agent shook his head.

"No, I don't know. He doesn't tell me about his business ... not since, you know ... "

"OK. Have him call me as soon as you talk to him. My name is Jenkins. He has my number. It's very important, OK?"

"OK," she replied, and looked at the agent.

He gave her a thumbs up, and then made his own call to Dimitri, reporting on the conversation. "I think he's getting itchy. Sounds a little panicky."

"OK," Dimitri replied. "We may have to move sooner than we thought. But we're still waiting on the search warrant."

"What do you want me to do?" the agent asked.

"Keep babysitting. In case he calls again."

While Dimitri was dealing with Jenkins, his partner, Upchurch, was on the phone to the New York FBI office talking to the only agent who had been there at the time of the Ponzi arrests some fourteen years before. The agent's name was Theodore "Ted" O'Brien, whom Upchurch had never met, and who—it turns out—was literally weeks away from retirement. Upchurch had briefed him in one of his earlier calls, but had not spoken to him in a couple of weeks.

"So you really think you've found Overton?" O'Brien said. "Until you called, I'd almost forgotten about the asshole."

"He goes by the name of Hawkins now," Upchurch told him. "And we're trying to finalize the ID as we speak."

"Good for you. I was one of those assigned to watch him when the prick skipped out on his bail. Cost me a promotion. I'd like to be there when you bring him in … and give him a kick in the balls. For old times' sake."

Upchurch laughed. "We'll see what we can do, but at the moment, I'd like to ask you about Overton's three other Ponzi buddies who went to prison while he went into the wind."

"What about them?"

"Do you know where they are now? What they're doing?"

"Not offhand, no," O'Brien said. "It's been too many years. But wait, I do know one of them, can't remember which, died in prison. But the other two … "

"Could you check on them for me?" Upchurch asked.

"Sure, but why?"

Upchurch quickly explained Gabby's theory without naming her, that one or more of them might have arranged to send a Russian Mafioso to find Hawkins and retrieve some of the Ponzi money, but that the Russian ended up dead in a basement for more than a year. "So we'd like to know if any of the Ponzi guys have Russian connections and could have arranged for sending the guy to Minnesota. We still don't know who he is, except that he may have played for a soccer team in St. Petersburg."

"Sounds farfetched to me," O'Brien said, "but I'll check them out and also talk to our mob specialists ... and get back to you."

"That's all I can ask," Upchurch said.

HAWKINS WAS AT HOME when he got a call from Jenkins sounding one shade short of frantic. "Something's strange," Jenkins said, breathing heavily, as if he'd just finished a hundred-yard dash.

Hawkins retreated to the deck, beyond the hearing of Anita, who was in the kitchen with the children. "Calm down. Take a breath. What are you talking about?"

Jenkins quickly explained his trip to Chicki's and his subsequent efforts to reach him. "I left all of the stuff with him yesterday, but now he's supposedly up north, tending to his brother, who was in some kind of motorcycle accident."

"So?"

"So he was supposed to call me if anything came up. I told him the job was urgent ... that I couldn't take any delays."

"And?"

"I don't know. Could be my imagination, but his wife sounded a little strange on the phone. Hesitant, maybe scared. The whole thing spooks me."

"And you talk about me seeing shadows," Hawkins said.

"I know, but I just don't like the feel of it. He should have called me."

"Do you trust this guy?"

"Shit, I don't know. He comes highly recommended, but I don't know that much about him … except that he's an ex-con and good at his job."

"I think you should relax. If he doesn't call by tomorrow, get back to me then. OK?"

"OK, but if I were you, I'd keep my eyes open."

Despite his calm and professed lack of concern, Hawkins already had taken steps to prepare for a speedy departure, if necessary. He'd sold all of his stocks and bonds and was prepared—at a moment's notice—to transfer all his assets to an offshore bank in the Bahamas. The only things missing were the new identity documents, which he deemed crucial to a successful escape and new life, and which he was determined to wait for.

At least as long as possible.

As he put the phone down, Anita walked onto the deck. "Who was that?" she asked.

He paused for a moment, trying to think ahead. "An old friend of mine from Sacramento," he lied. "Alan Fisher. Says he's got a terrific investment idea and wants me to fly out as soon as I can."

"Really?" she said. "What kind of investment idea?"

"Real estate. A new senior-housing complex that's in development. Wants me to get into it with him on the ground floor, so to speak."

Anita asked, "You'd be risking your money, not mine, right?"

"Of course. But I think it may be worth a look. And Alan says there's no time to waste. So I think I'll pack my suitcase just in case I decide to go."

"OK," she said, "but don't forget the kids' concert a week from today."

"No problem," he replied.

GABBY WAS AT HER desk when Dimitri's call came through. "Are you and Zach available?" he asked.

"Sure, I think so," she replied, glancing toward the editing booth where Zach was working on the video that he'd shot of Chicki's arrest. "Why?"

"Because we'd like to stop by in about a half an hour and have you follow us. We think we're about to make another arrest that you may want to get on camera."

"What arrest?"

"We'll tell you when we get there. But it's all connected with Mr. Hawkins."

Gabby tensed up. "Hawkins himself?"

"Not yet, but soon, we think. We now know that the fingerprints on the phony house sale documents belong to him, and we've also recorded some telling conversations between him and the guy we're about to arrest."

"Good," she said, "We'll be in our car outside the station's front entrance, waiting."

IN HER EXCITEMENT over the unfolding drama, Gabby had all but forgotten Craig Jessup. But he had not forgotten her. Not by a long shot.

For days now, he'd been carefully biding his time and feeling more secure by the day. Clad in the new, nondescript clothes he had bought in River Falls, he felt about as safe as possible under the circumstances. With that added courage, he had been parking the stolen rental back at the Mall of America and taking the light-rail into the city, dividing his time between downtown near the TV station and Uptown near the apartment.

He certainly knew he was taking chances, no doubt about that, but he also knew he would have no hope of dealing with Gabby and her boyfriend while camping in Shakopee. He had to get close and stay close, if there ever was to be an opportunity for him.

He was buoyed by the fact that he had actually *seen* Gabby for the first time the day before. He'd been sitting outside the Hilton Hotel across from the station, head lowered, sipping on a Caribou coffee, when she and two men, one of them the old guy who had followed him in Uptown, and another who must be Zach, left the rear door of the station and walked catty-corner across the street to a parking ramp. He followed at a safe distance and watched the ramp exit as—a few minutes later—they pulled out in an older Nissan. It had all happened too quickly for any kind of action, and without wheels, he was helpless to follow.

But he had learned two important things: that they drove an old Nissan and, apparently, they now had a bodyguard.

Forty-Eight

Gabby watched in the rearview mirror as the black SUV pulled up behind them and Dimitri emerged, leaving another agent inside, partially obscured by the tinted windows. After taking a quick look around, he opened their rear door and slid into the back seat next to J.J., gave him a quick greeting, and said, "Are you all set?"

Gabby turned in her seat. "I guess so. Once you tell us what's going on."

"If all goes well," he said, "we're about to arrest the man we told you about but didn't name at Chicki Mestaso's place ... the guy who tried to arrange the false IDs for Hawkins. His name is Leonard Jenkins, whom we now believe to be a longtime accomplice of Hawkins, maybe dating back to his days in New York and maybe a partner in the Ponzi scheme that we never knew about."

"Hot damn," Zach said.

"Where is he?" Gabby asked.

"On the twelfth floor of the IDS Center. He's a stock broker for the Slotgen investment firm. A very successful broker, from what we've been told. And clean, as far as we know. But Hawkins must have some kind of a hold on him, because he's clearly in bed with him and apparently does whatever he asks."

"Like killing a guy and leaving him in a basement?" Zach said. "Or blowing another guy's head off in a Fridley house?"

Dimitri smiled. "We'll have to ask him, won't we? But we think we have enough now, based on his phone conversations with Hawkins and his dealings with Chicki, to get an indictment. And who knows? Once he's in cuffs and staring at some prison time, he might even be willing to talk to us."

"So what happens now?" Gabby asked.

"Upchurch and two or three other agents are at the IDS now, waiting for my word to go. Unfortunately, we can't let you and your camera up there as we make the arrest itself. It's private property, and we could get into all kinds of trouble. But once we know where we're going to take him, either to the Federal Building or the Hennepin County jail, I'll let you know in plenty of time for you to be there and get him doing the perp walk. And you'll have it by yourself, just like we promised at the beginning."

"That's great," she said.

"But there's a caveat," he said. "You can't use the video until this whole case comes together. Same goes for the Chicki arrest, until we have Hawkins in custody and the charges are made public."

"What about Hawkins?"

"We have him under surveillance and have a GPS device attached to his car—so we'll know where he is when we decide to move. But first things first. We want to get Jenkins under wraps now."

With that, he got out of their car and tapped a number on his phone as he walked back to the SUV.

JENKINS WAS AT HIS desk, his office door ajar when he heard muffled voices in the outer office. Among the garbled phrases only one came through loud and clear: "FBI."

Panicked, disbelieving, he got up and rushed to the door, closed it and hit the lock button.

Then came a loud rapping on the door and a rattling of the knob. "Mr. Jenkins, this is the FBI. We have a search warrant and a warrant for your arrest. Please open the door, Mr. Jenkins."

"In a minute, in a minute," he shouted. "I'm coming."

Suddenly sweating, he reached for his phone and—in a desperate last act of loyalty—punched in a quick text to Hawkins. "Get out. FBI." Then he erased the text.

Upchurch and the other agents had cleared the surrounding offices of startled workers and stood to either side of Jenkins's door, guns drawn. "Mr. Jenkins, open the door!" Upchurch shouted. "We don't want to break it down."

From inside: "I'm coming, dammit."

From outside: "Are you armed, Mr. Jenkins?"

From inside: "No, I mean I have a permit, but my gun's in my briefcase."

From outside: "Leave it there. Last warning. Open the door and extend your arms where we can see them."

Jenkins knew he had little choice. So, slowly he moved to the door, unlocked it, and opened it far enough to extend his arms, as ordered. "What is this about?" he demanded. "This is an outrage!"

Before he could move, handcuffs were slapped on his extended wrists. "Now come out slowly," Upchurch said.

Jenkins did as he was told, seeing the agents for the first time. "I can't believe this," he exclaimed. "Let me see your warrants."

Upchurch held out the warrants. "You can read them in the car."

Then, from another of the agents, "Where is your weapon, Mr. Jenkins?"

"I told you, in my briefcase. It's legal. I have a conceal-and-carry permit."

The agent moved past him and into the office, returning with the .45 automatic in a sealed plastic bag. He stopped next to him, and said slyly, "For your sake, I hope you didn't use this for blowing somebody's head off."

"That's ridiculous," Jenkins snapped. "You're crazy, and you'll pay for this."

By now, a small crowd of Jenkins' coworkers had returned to gather in the hallway, shock written across all of their faces. He shouted at them, "This is all a big mistake. Don't worry, I should be back in the office tomorrow."

"I wouldn't count on that," Upchurch told him as they led him away.

HAWKINS WAS ON THE phone, making final arrangements with his banker for the transfer of funds to the offshore account and didn't bother to check his cell phone for another half hour after that conversation ended. When he finally did see Jenkins's cryptic message, he felt blood rush to his head, paralyzing him, nearly causing him to topple over in his chair. *Think!* he told himself. *Don't panic, but move, and quickly.*

Obviously, they had got to Jenkins. But how? And how much time did he have before they came after him? Not long, he guessed.

Pulling himself together, he walked into the outer office and told his two young employees, Dwight and Clarice, "Something of an emergency has come up, and we're going to have to close up shop. So take the rest of the day off and check with me tomorrow before you come in."

Clearly concerned, Clarice asked. "Is it serious? Is there anything we can do?"

"No, no, but thank you. I'm sure everything will be all right."

As they got up to leave, he returned to his office, shut the door and made a hurried call to Delta Airlines, confirming a flight to Denver two hours later, the earliest available that also gave him time to get to the airport. Then, he texted Anita, "Have to leave now for Sacramento. Sorry. Will call you later. Give my love to the children."

Next he stuffed all of his crucial documents and enough cash to last him into an oversized briefcase, gave one last look at his office, and closed the door behind him.

Forever.

OUTSIDE THE FEDERAL Building in downtown Minneapolis, as Gabby and Dimitri watched, Zach's camera followed Jenkins as he was escorted from the FBI car to a side door. Flanked on either side by Upchurch and another agent, Jenkins tried to cover his face as Zach backpedaled ahead of them, shooting. As they reached the door, Jenkins finally turned to face the camera. "If you use one second of that," he snarled, "I'm going to sue your ass, trust me!"

Then he was through the door and out of sight.

Minutes later, Upchurch emerged, phone in hand, talking to the agent posted outside of Hawkins's office complex. "He's on the move," the agent told him. "Just got in his car, carrying a big briefcase."

"Heading where?" Upchurch said.

"Too early to tell, but he's not wasting any time."

"Keep on him," Upchurch said, and then placed a hurried call to the FBI office, connecting with the agent on duty. "Check the airline bookings for a Harlan Hawkins. Try Delta first. Then the others. Quick as you can."

Dimitri was also on the phone to a cooperating Orono cop stationed in an unmarked squad car down the street from Hawkins's house. "He may be heading your way," Dimitri said. "Do not stop him; do not arrest him. Do nothing until our agent arrives unless his wife and children try to leave. Then hold them there."

Upchurch said, "Jenkins must have gotten word to Hawkins before he surrendered. Our mistake."

"So what happens now?" Gabby asked.

"We wait until we see where he's heading. We should know soon."

388 | RON HANDBERG

Soon turned out to be about four minutes, when a call from the agent trailing Hawkins informed everyone that he was heading east on 494 toward the airport. Six minutes later, a call from the FBI office confimed that Hawkins was booked on a 1:45 Delta flight to Denver.

Upchurch glanced at his watch. "We've got an hour and ten minutes, unless he changes to another flight. Airport security has been instructed not to do anything until they hear from me."

Dimitri made two more quick calls, the first to the trailing agent, briefing him on what they'd just learned. "Follow him into the terminal and let airport security know what could happen in the next hour or so." The second call was to the Special Agent in Charge (SAC) of the Minneapolis office, requesting permission to make the arrest in a public place like the airport. "As far as we know, he's not armed," Dimitri said, "but there's always the chance that he is."

The SAC, a woman named Andrea McMillan, who had followed the case every step of the way, asked why they couldn't detain him before he got into the terminal.

"We only have one agent on him," Dimitri said, "and no time to get backup there. I don't want to put our guy in that situation."

"OK. But don't make any move until he's cleared security and we know he's not armed. And make sure you clear the immediate area before you move in for the arrest."

"Gotcha," Dimitri said.

Then, "What about our TV friends?" she asked.

"We plan to take them with us. Just like we promised from the get-go."

There was a long pause. "All right. But you know it could be my ass when Washington hears about it."

"If we get this guy, it shouldn't be a problem. And a promise is a promise."

As HE DROVE, Hawkins had tried to see if he was being followed, but that proved to be impossible on the crowded freeway. So he'd tried to relax, and by the time he parked his Lexus in the airport ramp, he took no special notice of the blue Fusion that followed two other cars into the ramp and parked several spaces away.

In the twenty-five minutes since he'd left the office, he had received and ignored three texts and three phone messages from his wife, her words growing increasingly shrill and angry with each message. "Where are you? I've tried the office. No one's there. What the hell is going on? Please call me, now!"

As he walked into the terminal, he turned the phone off and shoved it into his briefcase, knowing it could be the last time in a long time that he would hear her voice. Maybe ever. Too bad, he thought, but she would be OK. Self-reliant and wealthy in her own right, she would learn to live without him. No doubt she'd be embarrassed and humiliated by his disappearance, but that too would probably pass with time. And probably without tears, for he still wasn't sure, after all these years, that she actually loved him. Respected him, yes, admired him, even. But they'd never been particularly close in any kind of loving, sustaining way.

The children, of course, were a different matter. He truly would miss them and the joy and satisfaction of watching them grow into adulthood. But perhaps they could reconnect some day, as he remembered telling Jenkins weeks before in the bar: "*I'd rather have them visit me in the Bahamas or wherever than in some fucking prison.*"

Once he'd picked up his boarding pass and passed through security without incident, he stopped to buy a *New York Times* and a copy of the *Economist* at the newsstand and moved on to Gate 15 on the Green Concourse. With a half hour to go before he could board the plane, he settled into one of the chairs, put in his ear buds, closed his eyes, and was lost in Gershwin's *Rhapsody in Blue*.

WITH UPCHURCH AND Dimitri leading the way and showing their credentials, Gabby and Zach passed through airport security without pause, meeting the agent who had followed Hawkins to the terminal on the other side of the screening area. His name was Bob Barnes. He nodded a greeting and pointed toward the Green Concourse. "I left him at the gate," he said, "with a couple of the airport cops to keep an eye on him."

"He hasn't spotted you?" Upchurch asked.

"Nah, he seems oblivious. Looks like he's dozing in his chair. If he's on the run, he could've fooled me."

They followed him down the concourse, the camera on Zach's shoulder, Gabby trailing behind, trying to keep her adrenaline in check.

"So what's the plan?" Barnes asked.

"Once we get there," Upchurch said, "let's ask the Delta people to start loading all of the zones except his. That should leave him fairly isolated."

"Good," Barnes said, moving ahead. "I'll alert them."

DESPITE THE CLOSED EYES and the music in his ears, Hawkins was not unaware of his surroundings. In fact, his eyes were half open more often than they were closed, his peripheral vision studying those seated nearby and catching the hustle and bustle of the passing crowds in the concourse. Everything seemed quite normal—except for the presence of two policemen sitting at a Starbucks table across from his gate, chatting and apparently paying no attention to anything or anyone but each other. Maybe they're on break, he thought, but he couldn't remember ever seeing airport cops acting like that.

So, to be sure, he picked up his briefcase and papers and started toward the men's room some distance down the concourse, watching to see what, if anything, they would do. But, after only a few steps, he heard the Delta agent announce that the boarding on Flight 2066 to Denver would begin immediately, starting with first class and priority passengers and then with those in Zone 3. He glanced at his boarding pass. Zone 4. Would he be next? Not wanting to take a chance of missing his call, he returned to his seat.

The cops seemed to pay him no heed. And he relaxed once more with Gershwin in his ear.

As he sat there, two more zones were called. His was the only one yet to be announced, which left him virtually by himself, stewing irritably.

Then two men took seats on opposite sides of him, each clasping one of his arms tightly. It happened so quickly he had no time to react.

"Mr. Overton," one of them said, "I am Special Agent Roger Dimitri of the FBI. You are under arrest. Please do not resist in any way."

Hawkins was speechless. "Overton?" he finally sputtered. "You must be mistaken. My name is Harlan Hawkins." He tried to pull his arm free. "Just check my identification."

"Nice try, Mr. Overton. But we know who you really are. And your long vacation from the law is over, I'm afraid."

As he said that, Upchurch reached across and put a cuff on each of his wrists.

"You can't do this! I have a business. A wife and children."

"We know," Dimitri said. "We know all about you. Past and present."

It was only then, as Hawkins twisted in his seat, that he saw Zach and Gabby ten feet away, their camera focused on him and what was happening. Zach, now wearing his Channel 7 cap, moved quickly to the front of him, capturing the handcuffs on his wrists and the stricken look on his face. Reacting as he had more than a decade before when he faced television cameras in New York, Hawkins tried to cover his face, crying out, "My God, my God."

By now, the two airport cops had moved over to them and a small crowd of onlookers had gathered around them.

"Let's go quietly, Mr. Overton," Dimitri said, pulling Hawkins to his feet. "No sense in causing more of a scene."

"I have to call my wife. My attorney."

"You'll have your chance to do both," Upchurch said. "But not here."

As they started down the concourse, with Zach recording every step, Hawkins pulled to a stop. Looking at Dimitri, he said, resigned, "How did you find me?"

"Ask them," Dimitri said, pointing at Zach and Gabby. "They did it. And, oh yeah, you should have changed your first name, too."

BACK IN BARCLAY'S OFFICE, with John Knowles and J.J., there was an excited exchange of high fives before they settled back to discuss what comes next. "I'm not sure," Gabby told them. "Once they get processed, I suppose they'll be formally charged and arraigned. That could take a day or two, I think, before a bail hearing is held. In the meantime, they'll remain in custody, and the other media are shut out for now."

"Fat chance of Hawkins getting bail," Zach said, with a laugh. "And that's probably true of Jenkins, too, until they figure out what role he played in all of this and until they do the ballistic testing on that .45 automatic of his."

"And with Chicki's previous record," Gabby said, "he's probably in for a long stay."

Barclay said, "So we'll be there when they do decide to make the charges public."

"Of course," Gabby said. "And we've been promised that we'll receive our due credit. I think the US Attorney from New York is even flying in for the announcement. And it's on that night that we can run the full story using all of the video we've collected, along with interviews with Dimitri and Upchurch."

"How about Hawkins's wife," Zach said.

"Who knows?" Gabby said. "If she's innocent in all of this,

she might be eager to talk for the sake of her own reputation. I'll certainly give it a try."

"So we have until the Fed announcement," Knowles said, "to put as much of the story together as we can."

Barclay got up and shook each of their hands. "I don't have to tell you guys that you've done a terrific job. I couldn't be more proud. Unfortunately, we're going to have to wait until the Feds make the announcement before the rest of the staff can know what you've accomplished."

"That's fine," Gabby said, "and now all we have to worry about is Craig Jessup."

"Trust me, I haven't forgotten," Barclay said.

Speak of the Devil and he doth appear.

Forty-Nine

Jessup was in the rental car parked down the street from Zach's apartment building, waiting for more than an hour before seeing the older Nissan pull into the garage, the big door closing behind it. He checked his watch: 7:08. That gave them fifteen minutes to get up to the apartment and settled, he thought, maybe have a beer. Maybe turn on the Twins-White Sox game. Whatever.

While he was in no particular hurry, he had finally decided that this would be the night. The wait was over. Come what may.

In the days since he'd dropped Linda off on the country road, he had managed to lengthen his beard, but had shaken off the hippie look and was now carefully attired in a button-down striped shirt and a neatly pressed pair of khakis, carrying a lightweight briefcase. He looked like a young, but cool, technology geek returning from the office.

He waited for another for twenty minutes before getting out of the car, allowing the sun to slip behind the buildings across the street, replacing the splashes of light with deepening shadows. He sauntered down the street and stopped in front of the main entrance of the apartment building where he had stood weeks before talking to the old lady with the black cat in her arms. After a quick look around, he went inside the entryway, picked up the phone, and pushed the button marked "Manager" with the name "David Taylor" in smaller letters beneath it. He heard three rings, then, "Yes, can I help you?"

"I'd like to speak to you about renting an apartment," Jessup said.

"No. You'll have to come back during business hours," the voice replied.

"I'm only in town for the day," Jessup said. "Could I at least get an application to fill out and send to you?"

There was a pause at the other end, Taylor debating. Stick with his beer and the Twins on TV and risk losing a renter, or take five minutes to walk down the damn hallway with the application? He decided to take the walk. "I'll be there in a minute," he said.

Jessup hung up and waited, his back to the door, the switchblade clutched in his right hand. Behind him, he heard the buzzer sound and the door swing open. "Here you go, buddy," said the voice from behind. Jessup swung around, smiling as the switchblade sprang open and was at the man's throat before he could utter another word.

He leaned into him. "Easy, now, Mr. Taylor. No shouts, no whistles, no nothing, OK? Just turn around slowly and walk ahead of me to the elevator. Like I'm an old friend who's come to visit. The knife will be at your back, just behind your heart. Make any abrupt move or shout and I'll cut through you like a piece of cheese."

Taylor, wearing a sweatshirt and a pair of jeans, twisted his head for a better look at Jessup, his breath almost bubbling with beer. "Who the hell are you?"

"At the moment, your worst enemy. But if you do as I say, we'll be best friends."

"You're the same guy who trashed Zach's apartment, aren't you?"

"How'd you guess?"

"Once a freak, always a freak."

Jessup grabbed Taylor's hair and pulled his head back, putting the knife to his throat. "Zip it," he hissed into his ear.

The hallway was still empty as they got to the elevator. "Here's the deal, Mr. Taylor. We're going to take the elevator to the third floor, walk to 303, and you're going to knock on the door. You're going to tell whoever answers that you've got a package from FedEx. And say it like you mean it. When they open the door, we'll simply invite ourselves in."

"What if they don't open the door?"

"Then you'll just say you'll leave the package outside the door. And we'll wait."

"What do you have against this woman, anyway?"

The elevator door opened. "*Against her?* Hell, I love her. I've just got to convince her of that."

The door closed and Jessup hit the button marked "three."

"Funny way to show it. Tearing up the place, writing that 'bitch' crap on the mirror. Now this."

Jessup flicked the knife open and closed. "Time to shut the hell up, and do what I told you."

The elevator door opened.

"Sure you don't want to think about this?" Taylor said, but felt the prick of the knife in his back as they came to the door, Taylor in front, Jessup off to the side, out of the view of the peephole. "Do it," Jessup whispered.

Taylor pressed the doorbell button and waited. "Yes?" came a voice from within, a man's voice.

"Dave Taylor. The manager. I've got a FedEx package they just dropped off for you."

"Thanks, Dave. Just leave it outside the door. I'll get it later."

"OK."

Jessup pulled him aside out of view, fingers to his lips, holding the collar of Taylor's sweatshirt.

ACCORDING TO HIS WATCH, exactly three minutes and twelve seconds had passed before Jessup heard the deadbolt lock turn and saw the door open a crack. In a split second, he slammed his shoulder into the door, heard a sharp cry from the other side, and pushed Taylor violently through the opening and into the room, the knife held high.

Zach was sprawled on the floor on his back, trying to scramble to his feet. Gabby was on the couch, holding Barclay, staring, startled, her face a mixture of panic and disbelief, a mirror of that horrible moment months before in San Jose when he'd launched his first blow to her midsection.

She tried to shout but had no voice, the scream lost somewhere inside her.

As Zach tried to push himself up, Jessup stepped hard on his ankle. "Stay there!" he ordered.

At that moment, the man Jessup knew only as the bodyguard rushed out of the back bedroom, a Glock pistol in his hand. Jessup, behind Taylor, who was shielding his body, shouted, "Drop it, old man."

J.J. hesitated.

"Do it! Or this man dies."

J.J. dropped the gun and slowly raised his hands.

Jessup pushed the door closed behind him and, catching his breath, ordered Zach to get up and on to the couch next to Gabby. To J.J., he said, "Move away from the gun, and sit on the floor, legs crossed."

Gabby finally found her voice. "Don't do this, Craig. Think!"

Still holding Taylor in front of him, Jessup moved to one side of the room, a satisfied smile playing on his lips. "That's all I've been doing, Gabby. For months now. Thinking. About you. About us. About what we had. About what we could still have, if you'd only listen. That's all I've wanted. A chance to talk, to get a new start. But you ran out of my life, leaving me with nothing. No hope, no future."

Zach started to get up. "You're a lunatic, you know that. A maniac. You belong in prison or a goddamned institution."

"Sit down and shut up," Jessup ordered. "If anyone dies in this room, it'll be you. You deserve it. You've been screwing her, haven't you? *Haven't you?* But I bet you're not half the man, I am. Is he, Gabby?"

Gabby said nothing, but put her arm around Zach and pulled him close.

"Isn't that sweet," Jessup said with a snarl.

Ignoring his warnings, Gabby put Barclay aside and stood up to face him. "What do you want, Craig?"

The snarl vanished and his eyes welled. "I want you, Gabby. I want to disappear with you, to have the honeymoon we never had. I want my *life* back, and you with it."

She moved a step closer. "It will never happen, Craig. It's way too late. It was too late the first time you hit me. It's over, Craig. No matter what happens here, you'll never have me. I'd rather lay dead on this floor than to feel your hands on my body or your breath in my face. You sicken me, do you understand that?"

A tear fell to his cheek. "You're upset. I understand that. I made a big mistake, I know that now. But it's *not* too late. You loved me once. You can do it again. Why do you think I've done what I've done? It was all for you. Can't you understand that?"

As they spoke, Zach caught Taylor's eye and held it, then gave a nod of his head. Taylor seemed to understand.

"We're going to go now, Gabby. So please come over here ... and when you do, I'll release Mr. Taylor. You don't want to see him hurt, do you?"

"You'll never get past the front door," Zach said.

"I'd better or you'll have to bury us both. Now get over here, Gabby."

Before Gabby could move, Zach gave another quick nod, and Taylor suddenly leaped aside, tumbling to the floor. In the same instant, Zach was off the couch and diving for Jessup's legs, catching him just above the knees, sending them both sprawling. But Jessup still clutched the knife in his hand.

Gabby screamed, and J.J. scrambled to his feet, reaching for his gun.

Jessup rolled and was back on his knees, the knife raised above Zach, ready to plunge, when the single shot rang out, the bullet catching Jessup just above the heart—the impact launching him backward, leaving his lifeless eyes staring at the ceiling.

It took five minutes after the 911 call for the first uniformed cops to appear, then, in order, Detective John Philips, Cindy Maxwell, the assistant medical examiner, who happened to be on call, and, an hour later, the FBI agents who had been tracking Jessup.

Interviews were held, statements and photographs were taken, and J.J.'s gun was confiscated.

For his part, J.J. knew he had had little choice. It was literally Zach's life or Jessup's. But he also knew it was a moment that would live with him for what remained of his life. For in all of his years as a police officer, he had never once fired his weapon at a person, let alone taken a life. And, he'd decided now, as he stood over the body, that he would never carry a gun again.

Through it all, Gabby sat stoically on the couch, holding Zach's hand, answering questions from Philips and the others, refusing to look at the still-uncovered body of her onetime lover. She made only one call—to George Barclay, relaying the facts to him as though she were reporting on any other death.

"Are you sure you're OK?" he'd asked.

"Yes," she'd replied simply.

"Can I believe you?"

"You told me once never to lie to you. I never will."

Maybe.

Because once everyone had left the apartment and the body was gone, she retreated to the bedroom, shut the door, and cried as she had never cried before.

Fifty

By the time Gabby and Zach got into the newsroom the next morning, word of the confrontation and death of Craig Jessup had spread far and wide, including the newspaper and TV websites and on the air on Channel 7's early morning news. But because the police had not yet released an official account of the incident, the stories were brief and lacking in detail, including the one written by Barclay:

> A California man being sought in the stalking of a Channel 7 reporter, who was also suspected in a bank robbery and the abduction of another woman, was shot and killed last night after he reportedly invaded the apartment where reporter Gabrielle Gooding was staying, threatening her and others in the apartment with a knife. The fatal shot reportedly was fired by a retired St. Paul police officer, John Jacobs, who had been hired by this television station to provide protection for Gooding and a station photographer, Zach Anthony, in whose apartment the shooting took place. No one else in the apartment was seriously injured, and neither Gooding nor Anthony has commented on the incident, requesting privacy.

The story went on to provide background on the stalking allegations, identifying Jessup, and also providing details of the FBI search for him in connection with the bank robbery and the Linda Wilkins abduction.

Not unexpectedly, both Gabby and Zach were besieged with requests for interviews, which both declined, even refusing to discuss it with the curious and sympathetic members of the staff. Gabby did call her mother to report on what had happened before she could hear the news elsewhere. "I told you everything would be all right," Gabby told her, "but I never thought it would end this way."

Her mother was aghast. "I knew something like this might happen. I told you so. You must have been scared out of your wits."

"I was, but everything's OK now. He won't be after me anymore."

"Well, I'm coming out there. No matter what you say. I'll arrange for the tickets tomorrow."

"That's fine, but please give it a couple more days. That Ponzi story I told you about will break soon and I'll need to be on it full time. So, please, wait till I call you."

Indeed. No sooner had she put down the phone than she received another call, this one from Agent Roger Dimitri. "We heard about your close call," he said. "I can't tell you how happy we are that you're OK."

"Thanks. I appreciate that."

"But that's not why I called. With what you've been through, this might be piling on, but we plan to announce the charges against Hawkins, Jenkins, and Chicki this afternoon, two o'clock at the Federal Building. And we'd like you, Zack, Knowles, and Barclay to be there for the news conference, to recognize your part in solving this case."

"Jeez, I don't know," Gabby said. "We'll certainly be there for the news conference, but I don't know about being recognized. I'll have to talk to George. We like to cover the news, not be part of it. And I've already had enough of that for one day."

Dimitri paused. "I understand, but our US Attorney, and the one from New York, along with my boss, insist that we acknowledge your part in all of this."

"I'll talk to George," she said. Then, "How are Hawkins and the others doing?"

"As well as you can do behind bars, I guess. Hawkins knows he's done for, but Jenkins and Chicki are still fighting and not talking. But if we get the ballistics report back from the lab in time, we may also be charging Jenkins with murder. We think the .45 slug we found in the Fridley house may be a match for the .45 he had in his briefcase."

"How about Hawkins's wife?"

"I'm told she visited him once. Loved to have been a fly on that jailhouse wall."

"Do you think she knew?"

"Not as far we can tell. Apparently he conned her like everybody else. And I feel bad for her and the kids."

Barclay shared her misgivings about attending the news conference and accepting the Fed's accolades, but he said that Sam Ryan insisted they go. "He told me, 'What the hell? You guys have earned the recognition and who knows, it might even help the ratings a smidge.'"

"OK," she said with a small smile.

"And just watch," Barclay said. "He'll want to come, too."

"What about him?" she asked.

"He's pleased as punch that Jessup got his due and that you and Zach are OK. He wanted to come down and talk to you, but I told him to wait. That you've got enough on your plate."

"Thanks. That would be the last thing I need."

THE BRIEFING ROOM in the Federal Building was packed with reporters and cameras, the media heeding the advance word

from the US Attorney, Cyrus Sinclair, that an important announcement would be forthcoming. Sitting on the podium
was a phalanx of federal and local officials, including the US
Attorney from New York, the FBI SAC, Andrea McMillan,
FBI agents Dimitri and Upchurch, and Detective John Philips.

Gabby, Zach, Knowles, and Barclay sat side by side in the
second row of chairs, the Channel 7 camera, in a row of others, manned by another photographer from the station.

When all of the camera equipment had been set up and
the hubbub in the room had quieted, Sinclair stood to address the crowd. "In a moment, we will pass out a news release
that will provide details of what we are about to announce.
But, first, I'd like to provide the highlights.

"Thirteen years ago, in 2002, in New York, federal officials
broke up a giant Ponzi scheme involving a bogus company
called Diabetrics and arrested four of the principals of the
company. Three pleaded guilty to a variety of federal charges
and went to prison. The fourth man, Harlan Overton, fled
while on bail, escaping with millions of dollars in stolen
money. He had not been seen since, despite extensive efforts
by the FBI and others to find him.

"On Tuesday, Overton, who now goes by the name of
Harlan Hawkins, and who has lived in the Twin Cities area
for most of those thirteen years, was arrested by the FBI at
the Minneapolis-St. Paul airport, and we believe he was trying
to flee once again. He is now in custody and will soon be returned to New York to face the charges he once eluded, along
with others involving his flight."

The cameras were rolling and reporters frantically scribbling notes.

"In addition," Sinclair said, "we have arrested one Leonard
Jenkins, who we believe was an accomplice of Overton's in the
Ponzi scheme, who also aided in his flight, and has provided
protection for him in Minnesota."

He went on to also outline the charges against Edward

"Chicki" Mestaso, and then concluded, "The people behind me all played a role in apprehending these men. Their names and the parts they played will be detailed in the news release.

"As you might suspect, it is difficult for law enforcement agencies like the FBI and the Minneapolis Police Department to give credit to *civilians* for their part in solving a complicated case like this. But I would be remiss in not thanking a group of journalists from Channel 7, whose early and unrelenting investigation of Hawkins provided the FBI with the essential leads it needed to crack this case and lead to these arrests. Their exhaustive search began with the apparent suicide of a man found in the basement of a northeast Minneapolis home weeks ago and led to where we are today." Pointing to Gabby and the others in the second row, he added, "They can tell their story in their own way in their own time, but for now, I would like to formally thank them for their role in bringing this long-sought-after federal fugitive to justice."

With that, the news releases were passed out outlining the specific charges against each of the men and providing more details of the investigation and the arrests. Questions flew from every side of the room, many of which were deflected because they might jeopardize the prosecution of the men.

Finally, one of the reporters rose to ask Barclay a question, "As a news organization, were you comfortable working so closely with the Feds?"

Barclay smiled. "Good question. And I *will* answer it. But not until after we report the story in full tonight at ten o'clock. I hope you'll tune in."

With that, the news conference broke up, and as they left, with questions swirling around them, Gabby once again felt her dad on her shoulder, whispering.

"Ain't the news business a blast, Gabs?"

Epilogue

In the few hours after the news conference, virtually the entire newsroom staff, from Barclay on down, was thrown into the task of preparing different versions of the Ponzi story for the late afternoon newscasts, culminating with the granddaddy of the stories for the all-important ten o'clock news.

As they did that, the station's promotion staff was using every on-air opportunity to promote the forthcoming exclusive report on the fall of a federal fugitive who had been hiding for years in plain sight in the plush suburb of Orono.

For Gabby, the hours were a blur, as she and Zach sat hunched over in the editing booth, she at the computer writing, he on the video board integrating her words with all of the video that had been shot in the days before, and including excerpts from the news conference itself. It was a patchwork quilt that somehow they had to make into an understandable and compelling story in those few, feverish hours.

Later, Gabby would admit she remembered very little of those hours, relying solely on her instincts and training and on Barclay's patient prodding, to finish what turned out to be a seven-minute story for the late news, a virtually unheard-of amount of time to devote to a single story in a thirty-five-minute newscast.

The video ended with the airport arrest of Hawkins, his stooped-over, hand-cuffed figure being led down the concourse, giving one final forlorn glance over his shoulder at the trailing camera.

When the video ended, Gabby delivered her final words, on-camera:

> *In a matter of days, unless he chooses to fight extradition, Hawkins will be returned to New York to face the old Ponzi charges. He could face up to twenty or more years in prison.*
>
> *His wife, Anita, has issued a short statement: "For all of these years, I had no idea of Harlan's true identity, and if these charges are true, our children and I are the greatest victims of his deceit. We can only ask that our privacy will be respected in this most difficult time."*
>
> *The two other suspects, Leonard Jenkins and Edward Mestaso, are still behind bars and will be until bail hearings can be held. The story will continue to unfold in the days ahead, and Channel 7 News will be there to cover every development."*

WHILE SITTING AT THE anchor desk, delivering the story, Gabby was unaware of a gathering crowd in the darkened studio beyond the cameras. The entire nighttime staff was there, along with many from the daytime shift who had returned to the station after drinks or dinner to witness the coup. Also there were Barclay and his wife, Sam Ryan, Agents Upchurch and Dimitri, and Detective John Philips.

And, of course, Zach Anthony, John Knowles, and J.J.

As she spoke that final line, and as the screen faded to a commercial, the lights on the studio came to life and the small audience burst into applause. Momentarily stunned by the sight of the crowd and the applause, she could only sit, fastened to the chair, dumbstruck until Zach finally came to her, took her hand, and led her off the set.

The applause continued until the final commercial was about to end and the studio lights dimmed, with a shout from the floor director, "Quiet in the studio!"

IN THE MIDST of the celebration that followed the news-cast, the remarkable irony of the last two days was not lost on Gabby—that no sooner had the nightmare of Craig Jessup ended than this almost-impossible dream had come true. And, as she stood in the midst of the crowd accepting congratulations, her thoughts were both of the wasted life of Jessup and, again, of the too-short life of her dad, who she could only wish had been here to see this.

IN THE DAYS that followed, several things of importance took place.
—Harlan Hawkins did waive extradition and was returned to New York while efforts got underway to find and recover what remained of his Ponzi loot.
—Hawkins's wife, Anita, and their children remained in seclusion, although a friend privately alerted Gabby that she might eventually be willing to talk.
—Ballistics proved that it was, indeed, a bullet from Leonard Jenkins's .45 automatic that killed the still-unidentified man in the Fridley house. Jenkins was charged with murder in Anoka County and was refused bail.
—John Jacobs, J.J., was held harmless in the death of Craig Jessup, the shooting determined to be "justifiable."
—The FBI in New York continued to investigate a possible connection between one or more of Hawkins's former Ponzi colleagues to the man who may have been sent to find Hawkins, and whose long-dead body in the basement started it all.
—Agents Dimitri and Upchurch received special commendations from the director of the FBI, himself.
—And Detective John Philips was promoted one grade and assigned to the department's white-collar crime unit.

Two nights later, as Gabby and Zach sat in the apartment, waiting to pick up her mother at the airport, Gabby took Barclay the poodle from between them and held him close. "So what happens to him?" she asked.

"What do you mean?"

"When I get my own place, are you going to let me borrow him now and then, keep him overnight, take him for walks?"

"Of course." Then a pause. "But are you really sure you want your own place?"

She gave him a sharp look. "What do you mean? I can't keep staying here. Now that things are over."

"Why not?"

She said, laughing, "Because my Mom would have a fit, for one thing. And she's going to be sitting right here in a couple of hours."

"Give me a minute," he said as he got up and walked toward the bedroom. "I have something to show you."

Moments later, he returned with a gift-wrapped box.

With a curious look, she put Barclay aside, took the box and unwrapped it, finding inside the fully restored doll that Jessup had beheaded and all but destroyed in his bedroom rampage. "Oh, my God," she said, holding up the doll, then pressing it against her. "You did this? She's beautiful."

"Look in her pocket," he said.

"What?"

"Look."

She gingerly opened the pocket of the doll's apron.

A diamond sparkled within.

She looked from it to him, her eyes as wide as he had ever seen them. "Are you kidding me?"

"Of course not."

Holding the ring up, she said, "I don't believe this. A ring? An engagement? Are you serious? We haven't even really talked about us. About the future."

"It's all I've been thinking about," he said, "and I've been hoping you have, too." Then, glancing at his watch and smiling, he continued, "And if you'll give me the chance, I'd like to make an honest woman out of you before your Mom gets here."

"You mean it? You're sure?"

"I've never been more sure. If you'll have me, a, poor, lonely photographer."

She laughed and leaned over and kissed him.

He took the ring from her. "I wish it could have been bigger," he said.

"Bigger? Zach, it's as big and beautiful and bright as the sun and the moon and all of the stars in the sky."

"Hey, what a lovely thing to say."

She laughed again. "If you really want to know, I've been practicing. And what did you expect? I am a writer, you know."

Then she held out her hand and slipped the ring on her finger.

Acknowledgments

All of my books were a long time in the writing, and *Dead Too Long* was no exception. As with those previous books, I have many people to thank for their support and insightful comments as I wound my way through the story. Foremost among them is my wife, Carol, always supportive, always encouraging, and always patient. But there are many others, including our son, Greg; my brother, Gordy; grandsons Nate and Sam Louwagie; their aunt and my friend, Pam Louwagie, a *Star Trib* reporter who is as talented and resourceful as Gabby but without her baggage; friends David Nimmer, Nancy Mate, Fred Webber, Quent and Bee Neufeld, Brian Bellmont, Phil Klees, and Sharon Nesbit, a wonderful writer who also provided crucial copyediting for this book. Special thanks to former Hennepin County medical examiner Garry Peterson and to current M.E. investigator Roberta Geiselhart, who first told me about DTLs, and to Kelley Lindquist and Irene Peterson, who helped with the Russian language translations. And, finally, to Kelly Keady and others at Forty Press, who agreed to launch the book and send it on its way into your treasured hands.

About the Author

Ron Handberg has spent his entire career in broadcast journalism, beginning as a writer/reporter at WCCO Radio in Minneapolis all the way to News Director and, finally, as VP/General Manager of the television station. Over those years, the station's news department became one of the most honored in the country, winning numerous national and international awards for its reporting and documentary production. This is Ron's sixth novel.

C

CPSIA information can be obtained
at www.ICGtesting.com
Printed in the USA
FFOW02n2346120816
26776FF